not
bad
people

not

bad

people

A Novel

BRANDY SCOTT

wm

WILLIAM MORROW
An Imprint of HarperCollinsPublishers

P.S.™ is a trademark of HarperCollins Publishers.

HarperCollins books may be purchased for educational, business, or sales promotional use. For information, please email the Special Markets Department at SPsales@harpercollins.com.

Originally published as *Not Bad People* in Australia in 2019 by HarperCollins Australia.

FIRST U.S. EDITION

Designed by Diahann Sturge

Title page and chapter opener art © LifestyleStudio / Shutterstock, Inc.

Library of Congress Cataloging-in-Publication Data

Names: Scott, Brandy, author.
Title: Not bad people : a novel / Brandy Scott.
Description: First edition. | New York, NY : William Morrow Paperbacks, 2019.
Identifiers: LCCN 2018058811 | ISBN 9780062854124 (paperback) | ISBN 0062854127 (trade paperback)
Subjects: | BISAC: FICTION / Suspense. | FICTION / Family Life. | GSAFD: Suspense fiction.
Classification: LCC PR9619.4.S355 N68 2019 | DDC 823/.92—dc23 LC record available at https://lccn.loc.gov/2018058811

ISBN 978-0-06-285412-4

19 20 21 22 23   10 9 8 7 6 5 4 3 2 1

For my mum and dad, for making me a reader

not
bad
people

Chapter 1

Aimee took a slurp of pinot noir and tried to decide who she didn't need in her life anymore. There wasn't really anyone. She loved her children, obviously; she and Nick had a great marriage, the best, even after a decade and a half. The cat was displaying worrying levels of incontinence, and the vet had started to make noises about ultrasounds and potential tumors, and don't worry, there's always chemo—for a *cat?*—all of which sounded hideously expensive, but the kids adored Oscar and besides, they could afford it. Sort of. She'd just hide the bills. She wasn't particularly fond of her mother-in-law, but the woman was nearly seventy and riding on one lung, so getting rid of her seemed like a waste of a wish. Or a resolution. Whatever.

A letting-go exercise, Melinda had said. Bring a bottle, and something you want to be free of.

"Something or someone?" Aimee asked her friend, who'd finished writing her own list ten minutes ago, naturally, and was rummaging under the sink for more wine.

"What?" asked Melinda. A head of ginger curls popped over the kitchen bench. "Are you still dithering?"

"I don't really have anything to let go of," said Aimee. "I like my life just as it is."

"Lucky you," said Lou, from the other side of the dining table. She sounded tired. Lou was always tired. "I've got too many to fit. I'm going to need another piece of paper."

Melinda gave a little snort as she opened up a new bottle. "It's supposed to be about self-improvement," she said. "Letting go of a bad habit, or a resentment. Something you don't want to carry into the new year." She flicked the screw top into the bin. "I so thought this would be your kind of thing."

Aimee doodled a small flower on Melinda's pale wooden tabletop, then quickly rubbed it off. "I like the idea," she said. "I'm just . . . blank. Give me another minute." She pushed her glass across. "And another drink."

The wine Melinda poured her came two-thirds of the way up the glass. Aimee reached for it guiltily. She'd have to get a taxi, send Nick to pick up the car in the morning. God, would she even be able to get one of Hensley's three cabs on New Year's Eve? Her husband was down at the river supervising the fireworks, a display Aimee herself had helped organize after an exceptionally wet December. "Don't you want to come see?" he'd asked. "After all your hard work?" Aimee didn't. She was happier being a long-distance observer.

The taxi company rang out without answering. Bugger. She should have booked one before she left home. Or they could have just done this at hers. Aimee would have preferred it if everyone had come over to her place, with her squishy sofas and multiple spare beds, furniture already battered so it didn't matter if someone spilled something, where they could all have gotten properly drunk and just crashed out. And then her friends would still be there in the morning, and she could have made pancakes and big pots of tea, and they could have hung out all day if they wanted. "Aimee, Aimee," Melinda had said when Aimee suggested it. "You do actually have to leave the house occasionally."

Maybe that's what she should wish for: a bigger life. Wider horizons. But Aimee had everything she needed right here in Hensley, much of it in this room. She smiled at her two oldest friends—cousin, technically, in the case of Melinda, although nearly everyone in this town was related to one another, if you went back far enough. The three of them had been a unit since primary school, despite the age gap: scrappy Lou, ambitious Melinda, romantic Aimee. Schemey, Dreamy, and Trouble, Melinda's dad had christened them. They weren't an obvious fit, but out here you became friends with the people whose houses were closest and whose parents could tolerate drinking with each other.

Aimee gazed fondly and slightly pissedly around the open-plan kitchen, at Melinda's pale skin and sinewy arms, the silk vest she'd said was Country Road but Aimee knew was designer. She smiled lovingly at the slight muffin top escaping Lou's faded jeggings, which Aimee and Melinda had privately agreed were Not a Good Idea, but what could you say? They'd grown even less similar over the years, but they had the strongest friendship of anyone she knew. Aimee felt a little emotional just thinking about it.

"Finished," said Lou, waving her little notecard triumphantly. Aimee reached into the middle of the table and pushed over a matching envelope. The stationery Melinda had supplied for their letting-go exercise was sorbet pink, its edges rimmed with gold, like something from a posh florist. Aimee wondered if she'd bought the cards specially. They looked very Melinda: expensive, exclusive, and just a bit much.

"So what did you put?" Aimee leaned over. There was so much *wrong* with Lou's life, bless her. Where would you even start?

"Yes," said Melinda, leaning in from the other side. "What did you put?"

"No," said Lou, covering her card. "Sorry. Private."

"I'll tell you mine," said Melinda.

"You don't have to." Aimee doodled another flower. "We can guess."

"Can we?" asked Lou. "I can't." She pushed her chair away from the table. "What on earth do you have to let go of, Mel? You don't have any shitty relationships or jobs you've outgrown. No ungrateful children. No bad habits. You don't even have a junk drawer."

"Yes, but this is Melinda, professional superwoman," said Aimee. "It'll be about adding things, won't it. *Achieving*. Building on her empire. It's only us mere mortals who have to cast off our imperfections." She caught Melinda's eye. "Oh, come on, you've got an awesome year ahead, Mel, admit it. Raising

a trillion dollars, expanding into America. Is world domina-
tion on the list?"

"Ten million," Melinda corrected, leaning back against her
kitchen bench—her award-winning kitchen bench, with its
double farmhouse sink and a vintage coffee grinder salvaged
from a country hospital and featured just last month in *House
& Garden*. Aimee coveted the sink, but wasn't sure about the
six-burner stove. She'd questioned Melinda when she had it
installed. Melinda didn't cook. Melinda said she also didn't
care. Aimee admired that about Melinda. Aimee cared too
much; everyone said so.

"Although it might be more," Melinda was saying now. She
smiled into her wineglass. "I don't want to boast, but it does
look as if we'll be significantly oversubscribed."

"Ah, you can boast to us." Aimee put her pen down and
picked up her glass. "We're only teasing. You know we're
super proud of you." She smiled a little blearily at Melinda,
the woman who'd taught her everything from how to insert a
tampon to how to parallel park. "To LoveLocked, Australia's
favorite success story."

Lou leaned over and clinked glasses with them both. "To
LoveLocked," she echoed. "And a fantastic new year."

MELINDA PUSHED THE French doors open and led her friends
onto the balcony. No matter how often she stood out here, the
view never got old, nor the private thrill that it was hers. The
whole of Hensley lay spread before them: river whispering in
a corner to the left; purple hills rising behind the town lights

to the right. On the outskirts, uniform rows of vines stood in shadow now, imposing order on the landscape. Hensley was small, but it was wealthy. Wine money mostly, and finance, from bankers who'd earned enough to enjoy the dubious privilege of stashing wives and children in a desirable country town and driving two hours into Melbourne a couple of times a week. Twats, the locals called them: Tuesday, Wednesday, and Thursday in the city, Friday to Monday in the country. Melinda knew the drill well, although she no longer had to do the drive if she didn't want to. These days, the meetings came to her.

"Let's get this done then," she said. "I've still got a party to look in on."

"And I want to see what kind of state Tansy arrives home in," said Lou. "I've told her twelve thirty, and if she gets in a minute later, I'll—well, I'll probably do nothing. Or at least, nothing that will have any effect."

"It's not getting any better?" Aimee pulled a sympathetic face and handed Lou her wine.

"Everything I say, everything I suggest, I just get called a hypocrite." Lou took a healthy gulp. "Drinking. Smoking. Eyebrow piercing. Driving across Victoria to a music festival with some guy who doesn't have a last name. She's even started—"

Melinda leaned down and fussed with a dwarf lime tree so Lou couldn't see her smile. Lou had been the first one of them to get drunk, to get stoned, to lose her virginity. The only one of them to lie about her age and get a dolphin tattooed on her arse. Aimee had been too much of a rule follower, Melinda too much of a goal setter. The others still teased her about her vision boards and ten-year plans.

"So I said, 'If you don't have enough time for hockey, you don't have enough time for pole dancing.'" Lou gave a little snort. "And it's not a bloody sport, I don't care what anyone says. Body confidence my arse. Thirteen grand a year for St. Ursula's and she wants to become a pole dancer—"

"Aimee." Melinda used her boardroom voice to cut across the chatter. "Shall we get started? Did you bring them?"

"In here." Aimee placed a large cardboard envelope on the table.

Melinda picked the folder up, examined it. "I thought they'd be in a box."

"There's not much to them," said Aimee. "Quite frankly, you're lucky I even found them. They were in the loft, behind the kids' old dressing-up box. Next to the remains of a dead rat Oscar probably killed six months ago. Now that was disgusting, a pile of bones and fur with the stomach—"

"Okay." Melinda just wanted this done now. She'd hoped the letting-go exercise would be meaningful, that the others would gain something from it, but the whole project had lacked the positive spirit she'd been aiming for. Lou was becoming irritable, as she always did when she drank too much, and Aimee wasn't taking it seriously at all. "So let's assemble them or whatever, and attach our cards. I want to let them off before the fireworks."

The sky lanterns were surprisingly delicate: thin rustling paper attached to a wire ring, a miniature hot air balloon with a strange, industrial smell. Melinda blew into hers experimentally; the tissue parachute filled, then deflated.

"Do we need to make a wish?" asked Aimee, as she tied her notecard to the narrow wire.

"No," said Melinda. "Just let your mind picture what you want to let go of. A really bold image, lots of colors, sounds. And then imagine all that bad stuff sailing off, into the sky, leaving you forever."

"Is that what they teach you on your leadership retreats?" asked Lou. "Because it sounds awfully like the rubbish Aimee shares on Facebook. You could save yourself a fortune."

"Lou!" said Aimee.

"If you want to do it, do it. If you don't—" Melinda shrugged. Lou could stay exactly where she was, how she was; Melinda didn't care. Except she did, of course. If she could change Lou's life for her, she would. Fill her card with wishes for her friend, rather than herself. She tried sometimes. Lending Lou motivational books and recommending podcasts, inviting her to come and hear speakers in the city. Lou always refused, politely but definitely.

"Hey," said Lou, smoothing out her lantern. "These have got your and Nick's initials on them."

Aimee shrugged. "Wedding madness," she said. "I even had our napkins monogrammed. We've still got stacks of those as well."

Aimee's wedding had been a lavish, yet tasteful affair. Melinda and Lou were bridesmaids, in strapless dull black satin. They'd lined up along the vines with four flower girls, two page boys, and a ring-bearing Labrador as Aimee and Nick recited their original blank-verse vows. The dinner after was less enjoyable. Melinda had fended off more than a dozen inquiries as to why she wasn't getting married and whether she was scaring them all off, ha ha ha, before she finally snapped and told an elderly aunt that she had herpes. The rumor had gotten back to the only eligible man at the reception, someone's cousin from Adelaide who'd been happily slow dancing with Melinda until his father tapped him on the shoulder and told him not to bloody go there, son. Melinda had spent the rest of the night propped against a trellis with a bottle of red.

"So what happens now?" she asked, emptying the last of a bottle from the same vineyard into a sticky glass.

"We push the wire loop through the waxy candle thing," said Aimee. "Then light it. That's the tricky bit. If you're not careful, the whole thing will go up. Nick's mother nearly lost an eyebrow."

The sky was darkening, its velvet morphing from dark blue into black. They lit the little paraffin squares and saw the lanterns swell in response.

"Come on," said Melinda, and they lined up along the edge of the balcony, three thirty-something women who'd been finishing each other's sentences and keeping each other's secrets for nearly three decades. You didn't get to choose your family, and these women were hers. More supportive than her real family, anyway. And just as infuriating sometimes.

"I do love you guys, you know," Lou said suddenly, into the silence.

"We know," said Aimee.

"I'm just a bit stressed out," said Lou. "Bloody Tansy is being impossible, and I can't seem to—"

"Shhh," said Melinda. "Let it go."

"Literally," said Aimee, wobbling her lantern.

Lou giggled. "I just want to explain why I'm being such a bitch."

"Don't worry," said Aimee. "We're used to it." She blew her friend a kiss. "And we love you too."

Melinda smiled. This was more like it. "Right then," she said. "All together. One, two, three."

THE LANTERNS ROSE slowly, drifting lazily on unseen currents. Lou was surprised. She'd expected them to shoot up and off like they had at the wedding. Or maybe she was misremembering that. Everything about Aimee's big day, Aimee's entire relationship, had seemed to happen so fast: one moment Nick was dating Melinda and the next he'd fallen for Aimee, knocked her up, proposed, married her, and knocked her up again, all before Aimee was twenty-three. Lou had expected Melinda to be upset, but Melinda had just shrugged and said they were better suited, and wasn't it great that Aimee had ended up with someone so stable.

Stable. Lou watched her little lantern waver, the light inside it flickering like a trapped firefly. What would it be like for life to feel stable, rather than a constant struggle? A never-ending battle against willful teenagers and rising expenses. But it would all soon be worth it: the tight budget, the extortionate education. Two more years, barring unforeseen disaster. Two years until Tansy was off to university, with a part-time job and a student loan covering her fees, and Lou would finally have her life back. Although she didn't plan for it to be stable, exactly. The first thing she was going to do when Tansy was settled was travel. Spain, Greece, France. Finally having the overseas adventures the others had experienced in their teens and twenties while Lou was pureeing carrots and scrubbing baby sick off rented carpets. Her own midlife gap year. Lou couldn't wait. Maybe she'd start a blog.

"They're not going anywhere," Aimee fretted.

"Shhh," said Melinda. "They are. Be patient."

Lou leaned over the balcony. To the left of them stretched the riverbank, where Tansy and the rest of the town's teenagers were no doubt drinking and snogging and smoking shit they shouldn't be. Beyond the river stood the vines that made the region so prosperous, six acres of which paid for Aimee's four-bedroom house and allowed her to stay at home writing poetry all day, living in her imagination, which, Melinda and Lou agreed, was lovely, but might not be the healthiest thing. They kept a close eye on her.

"See," said Melinda. "They just needed to get high enough."

The lanterns were flying now, three tiny night-lights bobbing in front of the river that gave the valley its Goldilocks climate: not too hot, not too cold, but just right to keep half the town in Range Rovers and the other half picking for pocket money during the season. Lou used to pick grapes. She'd stopped when Aimee married Nick, switched to strawberries and chestnuts. She didn't need her best friend handing her a check.

"So where's the party?" Lou asked.

"Meadowcroft," said Melinda. "I've got a driver coming."

Above the town, the first fireworks exploded to a muffled cheer. "Do you think you could drop me off?" said Aimee. "I really shouldn't be driving."

"Me neither," Lou admitted. "I don't need to give Tansy any more ammunition."

"I'll order another car," said Melinda, as a second round of fireworks went off, the sound echoing off the hills.

"You don't have to do that," said Lou.

"It's not a problem," said Melinda. "We've got an account." She pulled a phone out of her silky trousers and started to type.

Lou turned. "Could you ask them——"

"Hey!" Aimee said, pointing. "Look!"

There was a flare of light in the distance, a yellow dot that grew steadily brighter.

"One of the lanterns must have caught fire," said Aimee.

Lou squinted, trying to bring her pinot vision into focus. The glowing dot didn't look like a lantern on fire, but to be fair she was nearly a bottle down.

Melinda shrugged. "Don't worry, it's just paper. It'll burn out in a minute."

But it didn't. Instead, the small circle expanded as it rose steadily upward, then popped—that was the only word for it—into a cartoon ball of fire, yellow and orange and white.

Aimee turned to Melinda. "Quick, give me your phone."

"No," said Melinda, holding it out of reach.

Aimee stared at her. "But we have to call it in."

"No," Melinda said again. "You'll just cause a world of hassle."

"But what if it sets fire to something?"

"Aimee, it won't." Melinda's voice was firm. "There's nothing up there for it to set fire *to*."

Lou cupped her hands around her eyes. The little flame was floating above the ranges, like an angry star.

"The fire danger rating's been low for ages," Melinda said. "People are literally barbecuing in the streets. You don't need to worry."

The fireball was breaking up now, falling toward the earth in a shower of sparks. It was too far away to see where, exactly; too far and too dark. Lou tried to figure out the right thing to do.

A third round of fireworks exploded, then a fourth. "Look, everyone's staring at the sky; someone else will spot it," said Melinda. A fifth explosion, and a golden constellation fizzed above the river. Then in the distance, the familiar wail of an emergency vehicle, followed by the whoop of a police siren. "See? Sorted. And it's gone out anyway."

Lou gazed over to where the glowing ball had been. Like a magic trick, the small blaze had disappeared. Thank God for that. Lou didn't like trouble; she'd seen enough for one lifetime. "Let's go inside," she said.

Chapter 2

Pete lay in a cradle of twisted metal, pain racing from one limb to another. His shoulder looked wrong somehow, and his arm had split open, like a sausage; he could see white fat and bone beneath the blood, but never mind that, he needed to get out of the plane before the whole thing exploded. He felt for his seat buckle with the other hand and found fingers, warm and sticky. Lincoln. Pete's brain came rushing back to life as he remembered that he wasn't alone, Lincoln was with him, the whole flight had been Lincoln's idea and therefore Lincoln would be trapped as well, in the Cessna, with the world bursting into fire all around them. The flashes came from both above and below—some from the engine, gently burning, others from the night sky, as though the heavens were sending up distress signals on their behalf.

"Lincoln," he whispered, for some reason unable to shout. "Lincoln!" There was no answer. Pete reached painfully toward his son and snapped him free, then tried to maneuver Lincoln's gangly teenage limbs up and out of the sparkling hole that was now the windscreen. The ground tilted dizzily toward him as the little plane swung with their weight.

He tugged at his son, as hard as he dared, careful to support the neck, worried that something was broken, that he'd do more harm than good, but more worried about an explosion, with the flames, the fuel. The fuselage was blistering hot as he finally dragged them both up and over and then thumping onto the ground, Pete cushioning the blow as Lincoln landed on top of him. There was a quick series of pops and he felt his ribs go, his whole torso ignite with pain, but he ignored it as he dragged them both backward, agonizingly slow against the packed earth—where had they even landed? A farm?—toward what he had no idea, but away from the smell of fuel.

Three feet, six feet. Pete pulled them across the ground, like swimming the backstroke almost, pushing with his hips, his feet, one arm, whispering to his son, "Come on, Lincoln, hang in there, mate, take it easy." Nine feet, twelve feet—a major achievement given the fact each breath was like a knife—but not far enough. There was a deafening explosion, close enough to singe the ends of his hair, but instead of the world going red, it all went black.

Chapter 3

"Did you have a good time?" Aimee tried to keep her voice casual, to sound almost uninterested in her son's answer as she watched him dump his cereal bowl in the sink and tried to read his body language.

"It was all right. S'pose."

"Just all right?" Aimee peered at his eyes to figure out if he was hungover or simply tired. Or worse, had been smoking something. Lou had horrified her in the car home last night with stories of what Tansy and her friends were taking—pills of all sorts, crushing up other children's ADHD medication and *snorting* it, Lou had admitted.

"It was fine." Her son shrugged as he sprayed water into the sink, rinsing off his bowl as well as the surrounding work-bench and floor.

"Byron—"

"S'all right. I've got it." He grabbed a tea towel and made a few ineffectual swipes at the bench, sending a stream of water flooding toward the bank of ancient kitchen appliances lined up under the window. The edge of the towel caught a pot of basil; it toppled into the sink. "Ah shit."

Don't tell him off, Aimee, you'll only make him uncomfortable. Byron had grown nearly two inches in the few months since his birthday, and acquired a pair of hands that seemed far too big for him. They were man's hands, Aimee observed, as she took the tea towel from him and mopped up the deluge, righted the plant. Grown-up hands. They seemed all wrong on her fifteen-year-old boy, the boy who now towered over her, liked to pat her on the head. The boy who seemed to have a grown-up social life as well, with friends she didn't know and activities she wasn't privy to. Grown-up activities, possibly. And how did she feel about that?

She tried once more. "So who was there?"

Byron gave a sigh. "People, Mum," he said. "There were people there."

"I'm only asking."

"It was just another boring night in Hensley. Same people, same conversation. Just with added fireworks." He sighed again. "We live in fucking Riverdale, Mum. You've known everyone I hang out with since I was four years old."

"Don't swear at your mother." Nick's voice, from the doorway, was mild, but Byron stopped slouching immediately, pulling his shoulders back and gaining another inch Aimee wasn't aware he possessed.

"Sorry." Byron grabbed his backpack, shoving a small box from his pocket—cigarettes? *condoms?*—into its murky depths and zipping the bag up before Aimee could get a proper look.

He smiled at her, sudden sunshine from behind indifferent clouds. "Hey, can I take the car? Just to go down to Murt's? Please?"

The car. Damn. "Absolutely not, Byron, you don't have your license." He started to protest, and Aimee held up a hand. "You know the score. Anyway, I left it at Melinda's."

"Bugger." The clouds—and the slouch—returned.

"Byron."

"Bugger isn't a swear word."

"Just don't, all right, mate?" Nick ruffled his son's hair as they passed each other in the doorway. "And be back for dinner."

"'K."

And he was gone, leaving Aimee no wiser or calmer about the previous evening's activities.

"You need to talk to him," Aimee told Nick as he collapsed into the nearest sofa, six feet three inches of sweat-stained T-shirt and faded rugby shorts. She could see the circles around his ankles where his boots had rubbed the hair away, the line of farmer's tan across his biceps as he reached for a pillow.

"Byron? He's okay. He's just at that stage where speaking to us is exhausting, and unnecessary."

"No, you need to *talk* to him." Aimee gave her husband a meaningful look.

"What, about sex?" Nick laughed. "I think he knows how it all happens. We had that chat years ago."

"Yes, but it's different now." Aimee perched on the edge of

a faded armchair, a hand-me-down from a relative that had been absorbed so thoroughly into their own family history she couldn't even remember the original donor.

"What, because he's gay?"

"Nick!" Aimee shot a look at the door.

"Aims, he told us, remember?"

"Yes, but—" Aimee felt like someone's ancient maiden aunt. "We can still be *sensitive*."

Nick started inching off his socks. "I don't think he wants us to be sensitive," he said. "I think he wants us to act like it's normal. Which it is."

"I'm not saying—" Aimee closed her eyes. He knew what she meant, dammit. Why did he have to make it difficult? "He's only fifteen. I'd be concerned whoever he was having sex with."

"Who's having sex?" Shelley wandered into the kitchen, followed by their overweight Labrador, Lucinda.

"No one," said Aimee.

"Your mother thinks your brother is," said Nick.

"Nick!" said Aimee.

"He's not," said Shelley.

"There you go then," said Nick.

"He watches a lot of porn, but he hasn't actually done anything yet," said Shelley. "Says there's no one around here to do it with."

"Shelley!" said Aimee.

"I'm going to give this dog a bit of a run around," said Nick. He smiled at them both, his easy good-guy smile. "See, Aims.

No need to get your knickers in a twist." And he was out the door, Lucinda trotting uncertainly behind him.

Aimee straightened her ancient bathrobe, twisted her hair into a dark knot on top of her head. She had the Donnelly curls, like Melinda, only Aimee's were more likely to be a frizzy mass than Melinda's serumed cascade. Aimee had also managed to inherit the Donnelly arse and hips, still more an L than an M, while Melinda's bottom half would barely dent an S. Wouldn't dare. She claimed it was Pilates, but Aimee secretly believed that Melinda's body was scared of disobeying her, like everyone else.

She smoothed down the sofa, pissing off the cat. Oscar hissed at her, ears back. "Oh bugger off," said Aimee. "You're lucky to even be in here."

His recent bowel issues meant Oscar was supposed to be confined to the laundry, but the children—and the cat— had protested noisily. Aimee brushed at a smear of dirt Nick had left behind, checking that's all it was. She could see her husband out the window, lobbing a ball for Lucinda, uncon- cerned. Maybe he was right. Maybe there was nothing to worry about. Byron was growing up; she had to learn to give him space. Aimee moved into the kitchen and made herself a comforting cup of tea. And it wasn't like he could get preg- nant, or was even in the market to get anyone else pregnant. She should leave it alone. Not question, not pry. Respect his privacy. Aimee sat down at the kitchen table next to Shelley. A dignified silence, that was the thing.

"So how do you know Byron's not sleeping with anyone?" she asked her daughter.

Shelley gave her a look. "Really, Mum?"

Aimee sighed. "Well, you can't throw something like that into the conversation and just leave it *hanging*."

"So ask Byron." Shelley crunched into a piece of toast.

"I can't have that kind of conversation with him." Aimee smiled winningly, reached over to stroke a smooth forearm. "Not like I could with you."

"Stop smarming, Mum."

"But I could. You're my daughter. We have a special bond."

"There's nothing for us to have a conversation about. I'm not having sex with anyone either."

"Well, of course you're not." Shelley was only thirteen, and an easy thirteen at that. Still happily wearing clothes her mother bought her, not a sniff of boyfriends or underage activities. Aimee thought of Lou's constant battles with Tansy and said a silent prayer of thanks.

"I could be. Other people are."

"Oh God, don't joke. You're my good child. You're the one I rely on to keep me sane." Aimee tried not to guess which of Shelley's friends were already at it. "But Byron—I'm concerned. That's all."

"Would you be concerned if he was straight?"

"Of course."

"Liar."

"Shelley!" Aimee set her mug down on the table, hard.

"Don't you dare try and make out I'm some kind of . . . bigot. That's not fair."

"Then leave him alone."

"I've been nothing but supportive. You know that. I bought him all those books when he first came out."

Shelley rolled her eyes.

"And he knows both your father and I are absolutely fine with whatever he does."

"You just want to know what it is he's doing."

"Yes." Aimee tucked her hands into the comforting pockets of her terry-cloth robe. "As I will with you, when it's your turn."

Shelley stood and walked her plate over to the sink. Rinsed it off, with soap, then dried it and placed it carefully back in the cupboard. "He told me, okay?" she said finally. "If it makes you feel better. He was having a moan about his skin. Said he'd probably still be a virgin when he goes to uni at this rate. But don't you dare say anything or he'll kill me."

"I won't," Aimee promised. "And—the porn? I assume that's all online." They had an unlimited data plan; maybe it was best to change that. If only so he got some homework done.

Shelley sighed. "You okay now?"

"I am." She was. "Thank you, darling." Aimee reached over to give her daughter a grateful hug.

Shelley pulled a face. "You've got tea in your mustache," she said, sidestepping her mother and heading for the door.

Aimee wiped her top lip on the sleeve of her bathrobe. There you go. Nothing to worry about. Fingers crossed both her children would remain safely bored and virginal until they went off to university. Aimee got up humming from the kitchen table and made her way to the bench. She'd have a piece of toast herself, maybe even an egg. Scrambled, why not? She cracked two fresh eggs from Shelley's hens into a bowl and pulled the local paper toward her while she whisked. There was a large picture of an accident on the front page, twisted metal and first responders. Awful. Thank goodness none of them had tried to drive last night.

Aimee shook out the newspaper so she could read the accompanying story below the fold. She got three paragraphs in before she dropped the whisk. The mixing bowl tipped off the bench, egg splattering all over the tiles, but Aimee barely noticed.

"Oh my God," she whispered, eyes glued to the paper as though the words might rearrange themselves if she stared hard enough. "Please, no. Oh my God."

Lou SAT STIFFLY upright on her parents' green velour sofa— her sofa now, she reminded herself—and wondered where her daughter was. As no doubt her parents had spent many an evening wondering about Lou. The irony wasn't lost on her. Although she hadn't been half as bad as Tansy. Yes, she'd yelled and sworn and slammed doors and all the usual teenage stuff, but she'd never stayed out all night. Or stolen from them. Lou shook her head at the half-empty liquor cabinet. Tansy and her friends hadn't even bothered to pull its stupid wooden roller door back down. Just left it gaping, all the good stuff gone, and quite a lot of the rubbish as well. Blue Bols. Who even drank Blue Bols? There'd been a bottle of champagne as well that she was saving for her birthday. What was the point? Lou asked herself. What was the point of buying anything nice when it just ended up getting lost or ruined or stolen? Well, things were going to change. The situation couldn't continue. It had gone on for long enough.

The back door creaked open, then was gently shut by someone trying not to make a sound. Lou let the footsteps tiptoe halfway down the hall before calling out.

"In here," she said. "Now."

Tansy looked tired and slightly sheepish. She was wearing a crumpled red dress Lou didn't recognize, and a pair of tarty open-toed boots they'd fought over before.

"Really, Tans?" she said, jerking her head toward the liquor cabinet.

Tansy went for defiant. "We'll replace it," she said. "We couldn't get anything in town. They were checking IDs."

"You couldn't get anything because you're not supposed to be drinking," said Lou. "You're not old enough."

"You always say you'd rather have us here where you know what we're doing," Tansy countered.

"When I'm here," said Lou. "And I don't know what you've been doing, because you haven't been home. And because you turned your phone off. So I've been sat here, on this bloody sofa, worried out of my bloody mind, for the past nine hours. You're lucky I didn't call the police."

"I didn't turn my phone off," said Tansy. "It ran out of battery."

"BECAUSE YOU WERE OUT ALL BLOODY NIGHT."

"All right, all right," said Tansy, backing toward the door. "Calm down. I stayed at Zarah's. It's not a big deal."

"IT IS A BIG DEAL." Lou took a deep breath and tried not to turn into her mother. "It is a big deal," she said again. "You can't do this. You're sixteen years old. You will come home and sleep in your own bed, and you will be home when you're told, and you will not take my stuff, and you will bloody well behave yourself."

"Or?"

"Or you'll board." Lou had already thought this through. "And not at St. Ursula's either." She'd recently moved Tansy to the private day school in the hope it would keep her on the straight and narrow: clearly not. "I'll send you to Sacred Heart. They can sort you out."

"But that's in the middle of nowhere."

"I know," said Lou. "Great, eh?"

The look on Tansy's face was close to hatred. "Bitch," she said.

Lou stared at her daughter, scowling in the doorway of Lou's own childhood home. She had the same dirty blond hair as Lou—although Lou's had a bit of help, these days—the same top-heavy figure. The same habit of standing with her toes inward. This was like having an argument with herself. There was something especially hideous about having this fight in the same room where, for weeks, she'd argued about her own future—and Tansy's—with her parents. Surrounded by the same stupid Lladró figurines, under the same ugly brass light

fittings. Lou and Tansy had moved in nine months ago, after
her parents' death. She didn't have the money to redecorate,
or even the energy to move the awful china somewhere out of
sight——the thought of touching her parents' things still made
her feel slightly odd——but the moment she did she'd rip the
whole bloody lot out. She didn't need any reminders. And yet,
she was about to do to Tansy what they'd done to her.

No. This was different, Lou reassured herself. Completely
different.

"Sit down," she said.

Tansy, surprisingly, sat.

"You're going," said Lou.

"Going where," said Tansy.

"Sacred Heart," said Lou. "I've had it."

"You can't," said Tansy.

"I can," said Lou. "Nothing's going to change otherwise.
We're just going to keep yelling at each other and it's only going to get worse. You need discipline, and I don't seem to be
able to give it to you."

A mobile phone began to ring. "Don't you dare answer
that," said Lou.

"It's not mine," said Tansy. "Mine doesn't have any battery,
remember?"

Lou rummaged inside her handbag and shut off the call.

"You can't send me to boarding school," said Tansy. Her
face was white——hangover or fear?——with two high pinpricks
of sweaty pink flush. "We can't afford it," she said belliger-
ently, an almost perfect echo of Lou.

Lou sighed. "We can," she said. "I've been saving hard, for university, but at this rate, you won't bloody make it to uni."

"You didn't go to uni."

"That's got *nothing* to do with it. My circumstances were slightly different, and you know it."

"Don't blame me because you didn't get to go to university."

For the love of God. "I'm not blaming you. For Christ's sake, Tansy, I'm trying to do what's best for you. I'm trying to make sure you don't end up like me, stuck in this bloody town for the rest of your life because of a few stupid mistakes you made when you were too young to know any better."

"Are you calling me a mistake?"

"No!" said Lou. "And you know I'm not, so stop trying to put words in my mouth." Her mobile started up again. She turned it over: Aimee. Not now, Aimee. Lou switched off the phone. "I just want something different for you," she said, wriggling down off the sofa and shuffling awkwardly across the carpet on her knees till she was crouched beside her daughter. "More opportunities. Decent qualifications." Lou bent her head until they were making eye contact. "I don't want you to end up like me," she said again. "Trust me, Tans, you want to do better than this. You *can* do better than this."

Tansy looked very pale, and very young. "It's too late," she said.

"No, it's not." Lou gripped the small hands in front of her. Child's hands still, the nails bitten down to the quick. "You've got loads of potential and you've still got two years of high school to go. You can turn this around, I know you can. That's why Sacred Heart is such a good idea. You'll be away from any distractions, somewhere you can start fresh and get your head down."

Tansy was crying now. "But I can't."

"Yes you can. Of course you can."

"No I can't." The voice was almost a whisper. "Mum, I'm so sorry, but I think I'm pregnant."

MELINDA GROPED FOR her mobile in the dark. London was eleven hours behind, New York sixteen: she'd stopped turning it off to sleep months ago. Once they went public she'd delegate answering random middle-of-the-night questions about production lines and sales targets to one of her managers, but for now, she was too afraid of anything going wrong. "You get one shot," her IPO advisor Clint had said. "Don't fuck it up."

Except it wasn't an international center of finance calling, it was Aimee. And it wasn't the middle of the night, it was ten A.M. How had that happened? Her type-A body clock rarely let her sleep past five. Melinda smiled to herself. Well. She'd had a good night. A *very* good night.

"Helloooo," she whispered, wondering if Aimee could hear it in her voice.

"It wasn't paper."

"Eh?" Melinda rolled over toward the edge of the bed.

"It wasn't paper. On fire. I mean, it was, but I think the explosion was a plane."

Melinda closed her eyes at the panic in Aimee's voice, the words tripping over each other. It was a tone she hadn't heard in years, but she still recognized it. And knew enough to dampen its embers down straightaway. "Aims," she said lightly, "what on earth are you talking about?"

"The *fire*." Aimee sounded scared. "Last night. When we let off the—you know."

"The lanterns?"

"Shhhh."

"Okay, okay." Melinda sat up. "What about—them?"

"I think we might have caused an accident."

"Oh, Aims." Melinda pulled the duvet up over her breasts. "Of course we didn't."

"But we might have."

Melinda sighed. "And how do you figure that?"

"Because." Aimee was whispering as well. "It was around the same time, and in the same area, sort of. And the newspaper says that the engine *exploded*."

Melinda edged regretfully out of her Westin Heavenly bed, purchased after a particularly memorable weekend at the hotel chain's Melbourne property. The relationship had come to nothing, but the bed was still one of her best investments. She slipped on a Japanese robe and padded out onto the balcony. God, it was bright.

"All right," she said, dragging a deck chair into the shade. "Tell me exactly what the paper says."

Aimee began, falteringly, to read. Melinda stopped her after the second paragraph.

"Aimee, Aimee." Melinda glanced down into her robe. There were bruises on her left breast, finger and mouth marks.

She shivered, remembering. "They flew into a hill. End of story."

"But how do you know?"

"Well, there's no way those lanterns could have traveled as far as the ranges, for starters. They're just tissue and wire. They don't have engines."

Aimee was silent.

"And they've got very limited fuel. They just burn out."

"But—"

"But nothing." Melinda got back to her feet. "Trust me on this one, okay? You're hungover, and reading things into this. This has got nothing to do with you. With us. It says they went into a hill. In the ranges. In the dark. There's no mystery."

"You're sure?"

Melinda examined herself in the glass door. Some of last night's mascara had transferred onto her upper lids; she carefully wiped it off. "I'd bet the company on it."

"O-kay."

"Believe me. Our little lanterns won't have made it over the river." Melinda stretched. "Look, I've got to go." She paused, smiling. "I've got someone here."

"No way. Really? Who?"

Melinda stepped back inside, enjoying the mystery. "Just someone," she said. "I'll call you later." She hung up before Aimee could ask anything more.

"Everything all right?" He was awake now, propped up in bed, a rare male presence in her ultrafeminine bedroom. The chest hair and thick arms looked out of place amid her broderie anglaise pillowcases, the satin throw cushions that had been well and truly thrown. Melinda kicked one aside as she made her way across the room.

"Absolutely." She climbed back in beside him, unsure of how close to get now that they were both sober. He was older than she'd realized, and slightly chunkier, but still good looking. Salt-and-pepper hair, morning-after stubble. A couple of unfortunate tattoos, but it wasn't as if she was perfect. He stretched out an arm and she rolled into it, letting her breasts brush against his side.

"Good," he said, staring down at her nipples. They hardened from the attention, and he grinned. "Really good." He pushed her robe back and stroked a rough hand across her breasts. Melinda made an appropriate noise as he bent his head down. God. How long had it been? A good nine months of pointless waxing and exfoliating, but it just showed, it paid to keep it up. Act as if, her books said. Melinda sucked her stomach in as his hand drifted lower.

"Did you turn your phone off?" he asked, one thumb moving in slow circles, not quite in the right place, but close enough.

"Mmmm," lied Melinda, tilting her hips. Yes. There.

"Good," he said again, grinning at her. Clearly a man of few words. "Your friends call far too early."

"It's not really that early," she murmured, enjoying the growing intensity as his fingers moved faster. Fantastic. She wouldn't even have to fake this one.

The fingers stilled. "What time is it?"

Melinda pressed herself against the hand, willing it to continue. "Ten?" she said. "Quarter past maybe."

"Fuck." The fingers withdrew. "Sorry, Mel. I've got to go."

"Oh." And just when things were getting interesting. "Really?"

She got a quick half hug, then he was up and pulling on his jocks. "I promised I'd take the kids over to the lake," he said, searching under cushions. "At eleven. Bugger."

"Right." She tugged her robe back on, tied the sash tight to give herself a waist. He was wearing a shirt now, his underwear bulging beneath it, and just one sock. She pointed to the other under the chest of drawers, but didn't get up.

"But this was great," he said. "I'm really glad we did this."

"Sure."

He paused, midtrouser. "I've got your number, right?"

Melinda shrugged.

"Hey," he said. "Don't be like that. I need to be on time for these things." He shoved a wallet in his pocket. "I'll make it up to you. Take you out for dinner. In the city. Somewhere swanky."

"Okay."

"Anywhere you want. You name it. My treat."

Melinda forced herself to look excited at the idea of a meal she could easily pay for herself, at a restaurant where the maître d' would already know her name, and she'd have to ring first and tell him not to use it, not to make a fuss of her, so her companion didn't feel less important. "Give me two minutes to pull some clothes on and I'll drop you off," she said.

"You don't need to do that," he said, lacing up a pair of slightly scuffed dress shoes. "I'll get a taxi."

"You sure?" A quick nod. "Well then, I'll walk you out. Give the neighbors a bit of a thrill."

"Ahhh, maybe not." He paused, his bulk blocking the doorway. "Probably not a good idea for me to be seen with someone else at this stage, while it's all still going through the lawyers. It'll just upset her."

"Right."

He bent down and kissed her, hard, gave her breast a quick squeeze. "But I'll be back," he said, as he let himself out. "That's a promise."

Melinda leaned against the hard wood of the door, the sexy feelings from just a few minutes ago evaporating in the A/C. This was the problem with dating in your late thirties. They came with baggage. Cargo, sometimes. Ex-wives, kids, custody battles. Lawsuits. And you couldn't rule them out on that basis, or else there would be literally no one, only weirdos who had never married. Like her. What she needed, she reminded herself as she scooped up the local paper, was to be open-minded. Melinda had spent four hundred dollars on a half-day course about how Mr. Right is Overrated, where a stiletto-shod twenty-something wearing too much bronzer had tried to convince six businesswomen twice her age that lowering their standards wasn't necessarily a bad thing. It increased the catchment area. Stop worrying about the little things, she'd advised, such as whether a man had hair, dress sense, a job. You need to think older, she'd insisted, waving a hand smug with diamonds. You're all working. A retiree might be useful! And then, when the women had risen up in revolt, bronzer-girl had snarkily pointed out that they weren't going to be dating people in their own age group anyway, because all the forty-year-old men were dating thirty-year-olds and the thirty-year-old men were dating twenty-year-olds, so they might as well get used to it.

Melinda popped a capsule in the coffee machine. Dave had hair. And teeth. He was on the right side of fifty. The sex had been fun, not weird or gross in any way. She knocked back the espresso like a vodka shot. He'd paid for drinks, and the taxi home. He wanted to see her again. He'd said so, twice. The fact that he was considerate of his soon-to-be ex-wife and kids was a good thing, surely. Admirable even. You wouldn't want to date a jerk. Melinda smiled. And he'd been good with his hands. Very good. The caffeine hit her stomach with a reawakening jitter, and she decided to head back to bed and finish herself off. This was a good start to the new year. Only eleven hours in, and she already had a lover. Melinda shoved the newspaper in the bin and went to find her vibrator.

THERE WAS DÉJÀ VU, and then there was life openly mocking you as karma bit you on the arse. Lou didn't believe in God, but she could imagine Him laughing as she paid for the pregnancy test, could imagine her parents beside Him, tutting smugly, full of I-told-you-so's as she drove an almost catatonic Tansy back home. Could picture them all rolling hysterically around whatever heavenly judgment cloud they sat on as Lou led her daughter into the same avocado-and-peach bathroom she'd used for her own test seventeen years ago. *Your chickens will come home to roost one day*, her mother loved to tell her. *Mark my words.* Lou turned away as Tansy pulled her knickers down, tried not to look shocked at the lack of pubic hair. There was a pathetic tinkle as Tansy forced herself to urinate.

They sat, waiting, for the test to decide their fate, Lou on the floor, Tansy on the toilet, making the world's worst small talk.

"So how many periods have you missed?"

"Two."

"Have you been sick?"

"Sort of."

"Oh, Tans."

"I know. I *know*."

There was no need for the test, obviously. But still they sat, hoping, just in case it proved them wrong.

When it didn't Tansy said nothing, just crumpled forward and buried her face in her hands, knickers still around her ankles. Lou leaned her head back against the cold bathroom tiles. Images of cobbled European streets and foreign balconies flitted through her mind. Paella. Sangria. The Eiffel Tower. Not for her, once again. She sighed and got to her feet. It was only a couple of yards from one end of the bathroom to the other, but it was far enough for Lou to kiss good-bye to one future and reluctantly acknowledge another. She knelt down and placed her hand on Tansy's quivering back. "It's going to be okay," she whispered. "Don't worry. It's all going to be okay."

IF SHE SHIFTED all the wineglasses to the unit on the far wall, she'd have more room in the pantry for her baking stuff. But then where would they keep the good china? Aimee stood in the middle of her kitchen, every surface covered by three generations of mismatched crockery, and tried to focus on the task at hand. Maybe at the bottom of the wall unit, to anchor the glassware, keep everything steady.

"If we had a cellar door," Nick said, from somewhere behind her, "you wouldn't have to keep all this crap in here." His answer to everything: create a dedicated space where customers could leisurely taste and buy wine. Customers whose happiness and well-being Aimee would ultimately be responsible for.

"If we had a cellar door," she countered, without turning around, "we'd just have more crap."

A banging door signaled his escape to the calmer surrounds of the vineyard. Aimee dragged a stepladder into the pantry and began to pull linen from the top shelves. White. Cream. Ecru. The napkins opened themselves out as they fell, parachuting slowly to the ground where they lay like shrouds over the stacks of cups and saucers.

"Mum, what are you doing?"

Aimee put one tentative foot on a middle shelf so she could reach the place mats at the back. "Can you hold the ladder, darling?"

Shelley stepped carefully through the obstacle course of china, frowning.

"Thanks, love." Aimee leaned forward and grabbed an

armful of her mother-in-law's embroidered runners and place settings. She'd kept it all in case it came back into fashion, but the trend for everything retro didn't seem to include Monica's god-awful cross-stitch. "Watch out!" she called, as she dumped the entire lot over the side.

"Mum, we sorted all this out last month," said Shelley.

"I know."

"So why are you doing it again?"

"Just keeping busy." Aimee pushed a pile of fabric off another shelf. A damask tablecloth caught a cluster of antique vases, one of which tipped over with an ominous crack.

Shelley stared at her mother. "Are you all right?"

Aimee didn't answer, just wiped the shelf clean.

"You know that was a Wembley swan you just broke, don't you?"

"I know."

Shelley frowned. "Do you want a cup of tea or something?"

No, she didn't. She wanted to keep moving, to keep doing, not stop and sit and *think*. "I'm fine," she said. "Absolutely fine."

"Okay, okay," said Shelley. "I'll leave you to it then." She paused at the door. "Can you give me a ride to Emma's later?"

No, thought Aimee, heart stilling. She couldn't. Shouldn't. She needed to stay right here, resist the urge to venture out and see things for herself. Just count forks and wipe out drawers, keep her brain busy. She'd been taking care of her head long enough to know the drill. "I can't, love," she said, grateful for an excuse. "I left the car at Melinda's."

"We could bike over and get it."

Her daughter's face was hopeful, and Aimee felt selfish.

"Please," asked Shelley.

Then again, maybe it would be good for her to get out in the fresh air. Because that was another weapon in her self-care arsenal: exercise. Get the blood circulating, put the focus on the body, not the head. And she didn't need to go anywhere near the crash site, could stick to the back roads. Come straight home afterward, no diversions.

"All right," she said. "Let me sort this lot out and I'll get changed."

Aimee pulled on a pair of leggings—still too tight. "You need to lay off the cheesecake," she told her reflection. But quietly, in case Shelley was nearby. She didn't want to be responsible for her daughter developing a bad body image.

She wrestled her hair into a ponytail, shoved her car keys down the side of her sports bra. I'll just open the kids' windows, she thought, ducking into Shelley's room. Tidy as ever, bed made, even in the school holidays. Byron's was usually a different story: dirty dishes, half-drunk chocolate milk, abandoned sandwiches thick with appreciative ants. Aimee steeled herself. But there was only Byron, typing away in the messaging box of his favorite world-building game. He shut the screen down as she walked in.

"Sorry, love," she said. "I thought you were out."

"Got bored."

"Really? It's such a nice day out there. Shelley and I are going for a bike ride. Why don't you come?"

He looked at her as though she'd suggested cleaning his room for fun.

"Or you could go skateboarding, or down to the river. Why don't you call some of your friends, see what they're up to."

"They're busy."

"There must be someone you can hang out with."

He shrugged, but with a brief flash of angst among the acne. There was a fresh crop on his chin, the spots red and embarrassed for themselves. God, hormones were a bitch. Aimee reached out, her own worries forgotten. "Let me put some arnica on that. It'll calm it right down."

Byron twisted away. "Get off."

He was so awkward, bless him. Like she'd been. But it must be so much harder for him, with all this new territory to navigate. *A virgin till university.* Not that there was anything wrong with that. Aimee sat down on the edge of her son's bed.

"You know, love," she said gently, "I didn't have a proper boyfriend till I was nearly twenty, and that was your dad. He was the first guy to ever ask me out."

Byron flushed. Aimee felt herself blushing too, but she took a deep breath and kept going. It was important that he felt okay about himself, especially now.

"I had terrible skin, worse than yours, and my hair was horrendous. A total frizzball. None of the guys wanted to speak to me, let alone go out with me."

Byron slumped in his chair. "Mum—"

"I'm saying I understand, that's all. And that you don't have anything to worry about. This is all completely normal. Your

skin'll clear up. You'll meet someone. And it's probably better to wait." God, how should she put this? Directly, all the
websites said. No euphemisms. They'll appreciate how open
you are. "And gay sex is just as emotionally involved as straight
sex. You don't want to rush out and do it with just anyone.
It'll be better if you're really ready, and with someone you
care about."

"Mum. *Please*."

"I know some of your friends are probably doing it. But
there's no shame in not being experienced. I didn't sleep with
anyone till I got together with your father. And you're still so
young. You need to—"

"MUM. STOP TALKING. PLEASE, JUST STOP TALKING."

"Okay, okay." Aimee got to her feet, inched backward out
of the room. "But you know you can always talk to me if—"

The door was shut before she could finish her sentence. Ah
well. At least she'd shown she understood. And she'd talked
about sex like it was a normal everyday thing, which it was.
So hopefully he'd take fewer risks if it didn't feel taboo. Aimee
mentally congratulated herself on her courage. *See, Nick, he did
need another chat, and obviously I was the only one brave enough to
have it.*

There was a slow hand clap on the landing behind her.

"Oh, Mum," said Shelley, sounding disappointed. "You are
such a dick."

Chapter 4

Pete lay listening to the gentle breathing of machines and the soft lies of medical staff. "It's all right, Pete," they kept telling him. "It's going to be all right."

The sight loss was temporary, or at least as far as the doctors could tell. A psychological response to the accident. Nothing permanent. Just give it time. Same with the ribs and the facial fractures. His shoulder had separated, something Pete didn't know could even happen, but his injuries were mild, considering. The catheter? "Just to help you out, mate. Till you're back on your feet."

What they wouldn't tell him was what was going on with Lincoln. "Intensive care," they said, "but don't worry, we're looking after him. You just rest up and take it easy." Platitudes. No real detail. And it wasn't like he could read their expressions. But he could hear the whispers just beyond the swinging door, the soft sobs of his sister, clutching his good hand as though she had nothing else to hold on to. He tried to press her for information but she just cried harder, said she didn't know any more than what the doctors told him. He could hear the lie in her hesitation, but it wasn't fair on the woman.

"I want to see Cameron," he said. His elder son didn't bother to bullshit anyone, wasn't worried about feelings and sensitivities; he'd tell him the truth. Pete kicked the end of the bed out of frustration. "Where's Cam? Someone get Cam."

Chapter 5

Light streamed through the stable windows, setting Melinda's jewelry displays alight. Gold plating gleamed and silver shone, the lockets winking at the audience in the early morning sun.

Melinda was also on fire. Still buzzing from the weekend's unexpected sex, she stood in front of her jewelry, glowing just as brightly. This was her strength: talking about her product, explaining how it changed the lives not just of the women who bought it but also of those who sold it. "You don't bullshit," Clint said, explaining why she had to be such a poster child for LoveLocked. "You're passionate, but not creepy. They trust you. It sounds like you really love this stuff."

That was because she did really love this stuff. Melinda stared unblinking at her audience; they gazed back with the rapt attention of particularly devout churchgoers. She'd agreed to all the publicity, posing in her shoe closet for fashion magazines and gossiping with interviewers, but she'd fought him on the location for this season's launch.

"If this is going to be about me, then investors need to see where I come from," she'd insisted. "Let's show them who I am." She'd worried that people wouldn't make the trip out, that Hensley would be too far, even with the promise of Aimee's latest vintage and courtesy drivers. But they had. Nearly forty journalists and bloggers and fund managers were squeezed among the barrels in Aimee's old stables, standing-room only in the back. One reporter had even flown in from Sydney. Result.

Melinda motioned to Clint to show she was ready. She heard the hollow static of her microphone being switched on and felt her heart speed up in response. Showtime. "Thank you all so much for coming," she said, crinkling her eyes to show she meant it. "I don't need to tell you this is a very important season for LoveLocked, possibly the most important launch we've had since we started. If you guys don't like it, I'm screwed."

They laughed on cue, and Melinda grinned.

"Look, you all know we're going public this year. It's no secret. But I have other news as well." She wrapped her arms around herself, hugging her "approachable" silk wrap dress. Clint had outlawed the tailored suits. "LoveLocked is going global," she said, a warm glow of pride in her chest. "We're taking this collection to the U.S. and Europe, setting up a whole new business overseas. How exciting is that? I'm so proud to join the growing line of companies showing the world that Aussie fashion is more than just Uggs."

Another laugh, louder than the dated joke deserved. Getting them tipsy had been the right idea. Aimee had deliberately held back on the canapés.

"So this season's collection is extra special, because it's going to introduce us to the world. And also because—well, it's pretty special." She had them now, she could relax. "Look, I'm not going to stand here and give you a sales pitch. You know the designs will be awesome, because they always are. You know the key pieces will sell out, because they always do. I'm not going to bore you with product descriptions when you've got good wine to drink."

Melinda picked up her own glass, took a decent mouthful. "Very good wine." She waved the glass at the tables behind her. "But there are some additions I think you'll like. We're bringing in more sizes to our range of baby lockets. Introducing a new line of engravable key pendants. And we're making a few changes to the financial model as well, to give our curators more earning potential." Clint's changes, not hers. She didn't love them, but he said investors would want to see evidence of increasing revenue streams. "The design team is here if you want to meet them. Clint's able to talk about the public offering. Jacinta has USBs with high-res images of everything. Other than that, have a good look round and feel free to grab me with any questions. I'll be here all morning." Melinda raised her glass in the air. "And make sure you don't leave without grabbing a few bottles of the excellent Verratti pinot noir. On us, obviously. You can use it to placate your editors for staying out so long."

They laughed again, shifting impatiently in their chairs, those who had them. "Off you go then," Melinda said. "Try stuff on, grab a sample pack. Knock yourselves out." She smiled particularly widely at the hedge fund managers near the stable doors. "And thank you, not just for coming out today, but for all the support you've given LoveLocked over the years. We couldn't do this without you."

AIMEE WATCHED MELINDA say farewell to the last of her guests, squeezing an arm here, leaning forward to kiss a cheek there. She was so *good* at this, dammit. Like she was good at everything. There was a time when Aimee had thought she'd have a big, successful career as well, when university supervisors had talked about potential and prizes, maybe even a Fulbright. Although Aimee had ended up taking a different path.

"Can you grab their empty glasses?" she whispered to one of the servers. "But nicely."

She didn't regret it, the life she'd created for herself. It was full of love and family and security. Today was a little out of her comfort zone to be honest—Aimee didn't usually speak to buyers or visitors. That was the deal when they'd taken over the vineyard, back office only. Nick understood. But Melinda had asked, said today was important. So Aimee stood with her husband, pressing wine on people, trying to focus on their questions. "It's good for us as well," Nick had told her, and it was. Several journalists had taken brochures, scribbled notes about their latest awards. One was even coming back to do a proper interview.

Aimee gave Melinda a thumbs-up as she finally pulled the old stable doors closed. It had been a great day for them all.

"Fuck, I'm glad that's over," said Melinda, collapsing dramatically into a chair, but her eyes said otherwise. Her pale skin was glowing, her well-behaved ginger curls tumbling over the shoulders of a very un-Melinda-like floral dress.

"So your dad couldn't make it then?" Aimee said casually, finally pouring herself a glass now that she was off duty. A big glass.

"He's working," said Melinda. "Couldn't get away."

Aimee raised an eyebrow but didn't press it. She focused on Melinda's dress instead, which was far too nice to have come from the local shops. Yellow and red tulips crawled over her hips and breasts, up toward her flushed neck. Hang on. Was that a *hickey*?

"Ah." Aimee grinned, pouring Melinda a glass as well. "I forgot to even ask. Who was the bloke?"

"Bloke?" asked Lou, waving away the rest of the bottle. "No thanks. Driving."

"Bloke," confirmed Melinda, pulling a plate of savories across the table and away from the white-shirted teenager insistent on taking them from her. "Not finished," she told him. "Go away."

"Patrick, you can leave. We'll clear up." Aimee looked around the stables, surprisingly clean for the hubbub of twenty minutes ago. "You guys can all go if you want. Thanks for helping out."

She didn't have to tell them twice. Her teenage serving squad was out the door as fast as she could hand them their under-the-table cash. The only one who hovered was an unusually subdued Tansy, looking uncertainly toward her mum.

"You can wait in the car," Lou told her. "I'll just be a minute."

"Don't go," said Melinda. "Stay here, celebrate with me."

"Can't," said Lou. "I need to take Tansy into Fenton."

"Put her on the bus."

Lou shook her head. "So, come on then," she said. "Who's this bloke?"

Melinda smiled, shy almost, looking more like a teenager herself than the thirty-something owner of a successful company. She raised a hand automatically to the base of her neck. So it *was* a hickey. Aimee pulled up a chair.

"I've met someone," Melinda said, ultracasual, but Aimee knew better.

"Who?" she demanded. "Tell us."

"A guy called Dave." Melinda took a particularly lascivious bite of her salmon tart. "Dave Tolford," she reported, licking a pastry crumb from her lips.

"Nice?" Lou reached over, grabbed her own tart.

"Very."

"Hot?"

"Oh yes."

"So what does he do?"

"He's in real estate," said Melinda. "Commercial. Lives in Meadowcroft."

"Local, but not too local," said Lou. "Sounds good. How did you meet him?"

"Dave Tolford?" asked Aimee. *Hang on.* "I thought he was married."

"Separated." Melinda pulled the salmon out of a second tart with her teeth, smiling as though she'd caught it herself. "And getting divorced."

Aimee frowned. "Are you sure?"

Melinda paused. "Y-es. Why?"

Oh shit. "Just—"

Melinda stopped smiling. "Just what."

"Nick," called Aimee. "Nick!" He wandered in the back door. "Umm. Craig's friend, Dave Tolford. Is he still married?"

"The property guy?" asked Nick. He rested his hands on Aimee's shoulders, gave the top of her head a quick peck. "Yeah. I saw him and his wife at the races just the other week. They seemed pretty solid."

"Are you sure?" asked Lou.

"Pretty sure," said Nick. "They have some wicked fights, from what I've heard, but I think she just likes the drama." He shook his head at Lou. "Stay away from him, Lou. That man's not on the market, and even if he was, the wife would kill you."

"It's not me," said Lou.

"Ahh." Nick looked at Melinda with genuine sympathy. "Bugger. Sorry, Mel."

"Sorry, Mel," echoed Aimee.

"Don't worry about it," Melinda said grimly, tipping the dregs of an empty bottle into her glass. "Plenty more salmon in the tart."

Aimee put her hand over Melinda's. "Let's open another one of those."

Melinda shook her off. "It doesn't matter," she said. "It

was only one night, very drunk." She picked up her handbag, pushed her feet back into her heels. "But I don't really feel like celebrating anymore, if you don't mind. Think I'll head off."

"Me too," said Lou. "Tansy's waiting."

"Don't go," said Aimee. She grabbed a bottle from the display rack, one of their best vintages, but too bad. "Stay for one more," she begged, looking from one friend to the other. "Please?"

"Nah." Melinda was rooting around for her car keys. "I need to get this stuff home."

"But . . ." Aimee checked that Nick had gone, that the door to the house was closed. "I need to talk to you guys about something."

Melinda paused, but didn't put her keys away. "What?"

Aimee pulled the crumpled article out of her pocket. She'd debated bringing it up at all, but she needed to discuss this properly. Just for closure. That's what she'd told herself when she'd picked the newspaper out of the recycling. Stuffed it back in. Took it out again. All she needed was a bit of reassurance so she could nip this *wondering* in the bud and get a decent night's sleep. "I think we need to talk about this," she said, passing the clipping over to Lou.

"Is that the story you read me on the phone?" asked Melinda, craning her head.

"No!" said Aimee. "It's a new story. An update."

"Aims." Melinda set her handbag down on the table. "We went over this. It's not something you need to worry about."

"But I'm worried that it is. I'm worried that I should worry."

Lou looked up. "Why am I reading this?"

"Because Aimee thinks we brought down a plane with her two-dollar Kmart lanterns."

"Really?" Lou turned the paper over for more clues.

"I think we might have had *something* to do with it." Aimee gripped the stem of her glass. "Maybe. I think we should discuss the possibility, at least."

"There's no need." Melinda looked faintly pissed off now. "I told you. It's got nothing to do with us."

"But the crash was closer than we thought." Aimee fought to keep her voice low. Rational. "Closer than it even says there in the paper. It wasn't really up in the ranges at all; it's more near Maddocks Clearing."

Melinda stared at her. "Please tell me you haven't been out there."

"I was driving Shelley over to a friend's house." Aimee could hear herself gabbling now. "It was on the way. I didn't stop."

Melinda walked over to Aimee and wrapped her arms around her. Melinda smelled like wine and perfume and expensive oils. She smelled reassuring. "Sweetheart, listen to me. We didn't have anything to do with the accident. It's physically impossible. Those lanterns are floating in the river somewhere, if they even made it that far. Okay?"

Aimee nodded into Melinda's neck. "Okay."

"It's just stress, coming out sideways. I know you guys are worried about money at the moment. Your brain is latching on to something. Don't let it."

Aimee looked over at Lou, who was messaging on her phone.

Lou nodded. "What she said."

"Promise me you'll let it go. No reading the paper, no googling. Put it out of your mind." Melinda gave Aimee a squeeze. "It wasn't us," she whispered. "This is all in your head."

Aimee felt the relief flow through her, better than any vintage. "I promise," she said. And meant it. "Thank you."

HENSLEY'S MAIN STREET was the Australia that foreigners dreamed about. The town's main artery was lined on both sides with cafes and family-owned fruit shops, proper pubs and friendly butchers. The local council had decided decades ago that it wouldn't bloody pander to weekend visitors from the city. It had seen what had happened to Kimerlee and Fenton, even Meadowcroft, as a result of chasing the tourist dollar. Main streets full of fancy kitchen gear and artisan cheese shops, and nowhere a man could get a decent drink. Gentrification had ruined half the towns in the valley, was the considered opinion of the Hensley Council: membership—seven; members who weren't related to the mayor—zero. So the council had effectively banned tourism. Since 1993, every application to open a tourism-related business had been turned down on a trifling technicality. Those who tried to take complaints about the policy higher found themselves very unpopular in the sort of country town where popularity was everything.

As a result of Hensley's refusal to gussy itself up, the town had remained an anachronism, a genuine untouched piece of Australiana—and catnip to wealthy tourists looking to stay somewhere "real." They flocked in for weekends and public holidays, exclaiming over the unspoiled authenticity of the place as they crowded the footpaths, congratulating themselves on their ability to blend in with the locals as they stood in the middle of the street taking photos of tin awnings and faded shop signs, stopping traffic and causing more than one minor accident.

Melinda dodged a confusion of Japanese pensioners walking exquisitely slowly toward the rotunda as she ferried a carton of jewelry to the back of her building. Originally the town's commercial hotel, it had been shut down three years ago in a fit of pique and trumped-up fire safety concerns after one too many rowdy backpacker parties. Melinda had pounced. Promising Mayor Rex and the rest of the council that she would never, ever let a tourist cross the doorstep, she'd let out the lower floor to small businesses—a mattress company, an Italian bakery, an accountancy firm—and converted the upper floor into a giant apartment for herself, complete with wraparound balcony and the best view in town. The commercial rent was slowly paying off her renovations as well as the mortgage, and Melinda had added the building to LoveLocked's balance sheet on account of the fact that she stored inventory there, a move that her Kiwi accountant tenant described as being "pretty legal." It wasn't quite the single-girl-in-the-city unit she'd planned to buy. And it certainly wasn't the stylish-but-warm family home she'd always assumed she'd end up in. But on a summer night with a G&T and her girlfriends and enough mosquito repellent, it was good enough.

"Excuse me." Melinda shuffled the carton of charm brace-
lets from one arm to the other. It was too hot for this; the
tops of her thighs were sticking together. "Coming through.
Excuse me."

Elderly Japanese nodded politely and moved slowly. Too
slowly. Sometimes, Melinda could see the council's point. She
dumped the box on top of the others and headed back to the
Range Rover for another load.

This was the problem with being single. You had to do
everything, absolutely everything, yourself. She opened the
trunk and sat in it, momentarily overcome by heat and pissed-
off-ness. Every bill, every decision, every heavy box, every
spider, was yours to pay or make or carry or kill. And she could
do it. Of course she could do it. It was just that sometimes, she
didn't want to.

Melinda had no idea how she'd ended up on her own. She'd
had boyfriends in her teens, twenties, thirties. Fewer in her
thirties, to be fair, but she'd been busy. Boys and men had
loved her, or at least had said they did. One had proposed.
Two had—briefly—moved in.

But now the periods of being single were growing longer,
and the periods of seeing people were growing shorter, and
becoming less enjoyable. A new pressure had arrived with her
late thirties, as potential partners grilled each other in what
felt more like job interviews than first dates. Was the person
scooping taramasalata across the table sane, solvent, addicted,
damaged goods, marriage material, or desperately trying to
have children before their ovaries stopped delivering? And

there was less casual sex these days, less let's-just-try-this-and-see, because the women didn't have time to try it and see, and the men didn't trust them. Single men viewed women in her age group with a suspicion usually reserved for financial advisors, scared they'd lull them into a false sense of security with reassuring chat about wanting to keep things casual, and then trap them into babies they couldn't afford and marriages they didn't want. Which was hysterical, when you thought about it. "I haven't decided if I want you around for the weekend, let alone the rest of my life," Melinda had informed one would-be boyfriend who accused her of "rushing things" when she suggested going halves on a friend's birthday present. Get over yourself.

But that was the other thing that had changed: the balance of power. It wasn't politically correct to say it, but her value was definitely declining with age. Melinda had the status that the business gave her, but the right sort of man didn't seem to care about that. Only the sort who hoped she'd take care of his debts. Her ex-boyfriends all seemed to go on to marry kindergarten teachers and receptionists and yoga instructors. Younger, easier women. Women with fewer opinions, women who didn't make enough of their own money to be threatening, or enough of their own potential to be competition. What do you even have to talk about? Melinda wondered of the men who married these women, women who had no interest in politics or current affairs or what was happening to the economy. Don't you get bored? I'd get fucking bored.

She lugged another box down the street and dumped it on

the curb before the tape on the bottom could give out. There was a hideous irony in the fact that guys she wouldn't have even spoken to ten years ago now considered themselves out of her league. And it wasn't as if they were improving with age. As single women like Melinda got older, they started looking better: a bit of Botox, more money to spend on haircuts and highlights, more expensive clothes. The men didn't make an effort; they didn't bloody have to. Being single and heterosexual seemed to be enough.

Melinda slammed the trunk shut and kicked the final box along the footpath. And when you did finally meet someone nice and interesting and gainfully employed, they were married. Melinda didn't believe in the phrase "it's not fair," was always the first person to say that life wasn't meant to be fair, that no one had promised fairness. But really? Really? Surely she deserved a break.

"Fuck," she muttered, as the box tipped over and velvet cases spilled onto the street. "Fucking *fuck*."

"Do you want a hand with that, Mel?"

Nick leaned out of the window of his battered pickup, son next to him in the front seat, dog in the back. Melinda straightened herself up.

"I'm fine," she called back. "I can handle it."

"I didn't ask if you *needed* a hand," he said, climbing down into the road. "I asked if you wanted one."

The concern in his voice made her eyes wet. "Please."

"Where are the rest?"

"Round the back."

Nick stuck his head through the car window. "Byron," he said, "get out here and give Mel a hand."

He didn't need to be told twice—good kid, that one—just put his phone down and clambered out, knees and elbows in all directions. He and Nick had the boxes upstairs and in her storeroom in a matter of minutes, ignoring her instructions to just leave them on the landing.

"It's a bloody mess in here," called Nick. "Want us to sort it out?"

Melinda shook her head. It was bad enough that someone else's husband was coming to her rescue. As usual. *Oh, for fuck's sake, Mel. Just be grateful it's done.*

"Thanks, Nick," she said, as they both waited for Byron to finish in the bathroom.

"No worries." He perched on the edge of her linen sofa, looking healthy and reliable and almost as handsome as he had when they were dating. Nick's face was weathered, but in a way that added character. He looked like what he was—a decent guy. A little thought flickered through Melinda's head: *lucky Aimee.* Followed by another: *foolish Melinda.* She walked quickly into the kitchen.

"Tea?" she called, from the safety of the sink. "Beer?"

"Nah," he replied, as the toilet flushed. "We'd best get back. Aimee's putting a roast on. I promised I'd rustle her up some veg."

"Right then." She busied herself at the sink, relieved but slightly disappointed. "Thanks for helping."

"Just shout if you need to take that stuff anywhere. Byron

can cart it around for you. He's not got anything better to do this summer."

"That'd be great."

Nick rubbed the fob of his keys against the door frame. "I'm sorry about Dave," he said finally.

Melinda flushed. "It's okay." *Just go now.*

"Nah, it's not. He shouldn't have done that."

Melinda shrugged.

"You want to come to ours for dinner? There'll be loads."

"I'd rather be by myself, actually. Thanks all the same."

"Righto." Downstairs, they heard the front door slam, then Byron talking to the dog. Nick stared at her, cleared his throat. "Mel—"

"I really don't want any sympathy right now. Honestly, it will just make me feel worse."

"I wasn't going to give you any." She could see him searching for something reassuring to say. "Just . . . you're looking good, Mel. Really good. Just wanted to say that."

She snorted.

"Catch you later." She heard the latch turn, and then he too was gone.

Melinda opened the refrigerator and assessed her options. Hummus. Smoked salmon. Rice crackers. The modern single woman's equivalent of a supermarket takeout meal for one. She shoved it all on a bread board, added a handful of cherry tomatoes, and made her way onto the balcony, returning for a half bottle of white. Fuck the emails. She was taking the rest of the day off.

Beneath her, Hensley moved happily into midafternoon, friends calling to one another as they headed to the pub for a cold one, tourists soaking up the sun on the town's wooden benches, legs stretched into the footpath with little regard for pedestrians. Melinda made herself comfortable in a deck chair and watched other people's lives play out below. The mother snatching at a toddler about to walk into the road. The teenage couple wrapped around each other outside Larry's Meats, tattoos blurring as they snogged and groped. Larry's wife, Sandra, with her frosted updo, shooing them away.

A spectator. That's what she'd become. Someone who watched from the sidelines as other people got on with life, getting married and setting up a home and raising children and growing old and grumpy together. Melinda wasn't sure she wanted all that, but it would be nice to have the option. To feel like you were part of the Game of Life, with its winding but sure pathway from the chapel to the grave. Not someone who got invited to be an extra in other people's lives: to sit at their dinner tables, make small talk with their in-laws, come round for Christmas if you're free. She was always free.

Melinda didn't believe in wallowing—she gave Lou stern lectures about the dangers of negative thinking, of becoming stuck in a self-defeating cycle—but sometimes it was strangely pleasurable. She licked hummus off a spoon and felt sorry for herself, alone on a balcony big enough for a football team of friends and family. Tomorrow, she'd pick herself up and get back to business. The business of being Melinda. But today, she was just going to sit here feeling like shit.

And so she did, as the sun started to lose its power and the tourists headed indoors. Sat and ate and drank and watched and felt like shit, ignoring the vibration of her phone, the Meadowcroft number flashing up on its screen once, twice, followed by a message that she deleted, unread. She might be lonely, but she wasn't one of those women. The kind of woman who slept—knowingly at least—with other women's husbands, who waited for them to leave their spouses, or didn't even bother to pretend they would. At least she could take pride in that.

Chapter 6

"Hey, Lincoln." Pete felt nervously for a shoulder, not wanting to disturb any tubes or machines that might lie between them. "Lincoln, it's me, Dad."

"It's okay, you can hold his hand." The nurse took Pete's good arm, guided it toward his son. "There you go."

Pete leaned over to where he imagined Lincoln's head must be. "Check us out, eh?" he said, for want of anything more intelligent. "Bloody great mess we've made of this one." He gave the fakest of laughs. "What would your mum say?"

"That's it." The nurse's voice behind him was reassuring. "Just speak normally. He can hear you."

"How do you know?" It came out harsher than Pete intended.

"His eyelids are twitching." The nurse was unruffled. "Which is a great sign. His brain's just having a bit of a rest, that's all. There's no real damage. He'll wake up when he's ready. You'll see." She paused at the faux pas, then pressed ahead. "You've both been pretty lucky, by the sound of it."

Pete gave a snort.

"Seriously. I've seen people in worse shape after a night out."

It was probably true. He tried to return the joke. "I suppose we're like the blind leading the . . . Never mind."

A warm hand rested lightly on his shoulder. "Just talk to him. It will help."

Pete nodded and searched for a subject that wasn't his son lying in intensive care. "So Cam's coming back for a bit," he said finally. "That's great, eh? Be good to see him again. He called last night from Vanuatu, said he's over there working. Not quite sure what he's up to, but . . ." Pete paused. "Good to see him making an honest go of it anyway." The hand in his was clammy, despite the cool, dry room. "He's an odd one, Cam. Not like you. Straight as a fence you are, just like your mum." He squeezed the hand. "She'd be proud of you, you know. Really proud." Bloody hell. What was this rubbish he was coming out with? Pete swiped his eyes against his good arm.

"That's it, keep going." The voice was in the corner of the room now, still encouraging.

"I sound like something from a bad episode of *Neighbours*."

The nurse chuckled. "It's hard not to, in here." There was a liquid sound, like tea or water pouring. "Just tell him what you've been doing."

Which bit? The endless staring into the dark, the panicking that Lincoln would never wake up? The nightmares in which Julia screamed at him for nearly killing their son?

"So my face looks like a horror movie apparently, all smashed bones and bruising. Shame it's not Halloween, I wouldn't need a costume. The arm's a bit bung, but it'll come right. I'm in a wheelchair for the moment, just for a few days, although I can't see where I'm going anyway, so . . ." Pete faltered. Surely the point of this was to be cheerful?

"Keep going."

"Anyway, they might be sticking us in the same room to-morrow." *Can't see why not*, the doctor had said, when Pete asked. *Probably good for you both*. "Fingers crossed. We can keep each other company. Tell jokes. Cause trouble for the nurses."

"Oi!"

"It's all going to be okay, Lincoln." He hoped so, anyway. "We'll be back to normal in no time." As normal as they'd ever been without Julia.

There were footsteps in the doorway, then a low cough.

"Doctor?" Pete turned toward the noise.

"Police, actually." The voice was apologetic. "But I can wait outside. Come back later, if that's easier."

"No, no." Pete gave Lincoln's hand another gentle squeeze. "You're fine. They're moving me in with him anyway. We'll be sick of each other by the end of the week." He pushed his wheelchair carefully back from the bed. "But I've already given a statement."

"I know, sir." The policeman sounded young, younger than him anyway. "But we need to go over it one more time. Make sure we haven't missed anything."

Chapter 7

"We're not going to see very much at this stage," the ultrasound technician warned, as she rubbed the gleaming aqua gel across Tansy's ridiculously flat stomach. "But we should get a heartbeat, at least. And it will help us determine when baby's due."

Lou flinched, both at the twee use of the word, and at the word itself being used anywhere near her daughter, with her protruding hip bones and white cotton underwear. Today's pair had strawberries printed on them. Lou nodded at the technician. "Great," she said.

Tansy watched the probe rolling over her stomach with polite disinterest. "It's cold, Mum," she said.

"I know," said Lou. Although she'd only had one ultrasound with Tansy, when her parents were trying to convince her to change her mind. She'd told them at fourteen weeks, when she couldn't hide the situation any longer; her waistline had disappeared, and even with the convenient dress-over-jeans trend, she was starting to look pregnant rather than just fat.

She'd also figured it was too late for them to do anything about it. She was wrong.

"We've still got a bit of time to take care of it," her mother had said grimly, too righteous to use the word *abortion*, but not to suggest that her daughter have one.

Lou had dug her heels in, surprising her parents, her friends, even herself. She wasn't getting rid of the baby, or giving it away. She was keeping it and they could all go to hell. Her mother had begged, her father had threatened, but Lou was determined. Why had she wanted the baby so badly? She couldn't even remember now. A mix of hormones and defiance probably—the automatic position that anything her parents suggested had to be wrong. Not that she regretted Tansy, obviously, but the freedom and opportunities she'd given up? Lou would never tell a soul, but she wasn't completely sure she'd make the same decision again.

"There we go." The technician swiveled the monitor so they could get a better view. In the middle of the speckled screen sat a small, empty circle. The technician made crosshairs with her mouse, zoomed in. The circle appeared to pulse slightly, although it was hard to tell. Tansy and Lou stared at each other.

"Great," Lou said again.

"Great," said Tansy.

"That's the yolk sac," the technician chattered, determinedly upbeat. "I know it looks like there's nothing in it, but there is, I promise. And we can see that it's in the right place, so that's one less thing to worry about. I think"—she drew the crosshairs again, measuring—"you're probably around seven weeks. That sound about right?"

Tansy turned away from the monitor. "Can I get dressed now?"

The technician nodded, handing her a clutch of paper towels. "Someone will be in in a moment to take some blood, just to check everything's as it should be." She smiled conspiratorially at Lou. "Shall we head back to reception, give Tansy here some privacy?"

The reception area was decorated with tasteful inoculation reminders and framed photographs of smiling babies with parents who wanted them. Lou shook her head as the receptionist tried to force multiple brochures on her. "I have done this before, you know," Lou said dryly.

"Of course," said the receptionist, still gathering. "But the guidelines change. You want to make sure you're up to date with the latest recommendations."

Lou hadn't followed any recommendations. She'd been out of the house before six months and fending for herself, living on toast and tomato soup and cartons of long-life orange juice. Telling herself that women had had babies for centuries without fancy vitamins and tests, that Tansy would be just fine. And she was—huge and healthy and screaming her face off before she'd even left Lou's body.

"We can do it all on Medicare, right?" she asked.

The receptionist glanced down at Lou's nice shoes, her good dress, worn in honor of Melinda's launch. "You're not going private?"

"We can't," she said flatly. "Besides, isn't Australia supposed to have some of the best health care in the world? Lucky country and all that?"

The woman looked taken aback. "Of course. I just assumed, since you were here——"

"This was easiest," said Lou. "Quickest." And a good three towns away. "But we don't have insurance."

The receptionist nodded. "Well then. St. Margaret's in Hensley is said to be excellent."

It was; Lou had given birth there herself. She'd experienced none of the judgment she'd received from her parents, even though she knew several of the nurses went to the same church. There'd been nothing but love——a big private room with a river-facing window, a doctor who kept her in longer than necessary so she could get used to the feeding and the crying and the sheer mind-bending fact of having a baby. Lou had felt properly cared for for the first time in years.

"Mum, can we go now?" Tansy stood in the corridor, still in her waitress uniform.

"We have to speak to the doctor," said Lou. "She'll want to see that everything's okay."

Tansy twisted in her patent kitten heels. "Can't I wait in the car?"

As though it wasn't even her baby. Lou and the receptionist exchanged a look.

"No, Tans," Lou said gently. "You need to be here for this."

AIMEE TUGGED DOWN the sun visor to avoid being blinded as she crossed the river. The sun was low, right at her eye line as her four-wheel drive bumped its way over the wooden single-lane bridge. Harrys Bridge, it was known as, although no one was entirely sure who Harry was anymore, or ever had been. Locals hated the bridge, which killed both tires and speed. Tourists loved it. Aimee also loved it, although she pretended not to.

She turned the radio up as she drove along River Road, hills rising on one side, water meandering past on the other. She'd written poems about this road, a secret ode to Harrys Bridge even, buried deep in her hard drive away from the mocking eyes of her children. Some of her poems she entered in competitions. Some of them had won prizes, one a Governor's Award. She'd published a book the year before, launched at the town hall and stocked in Sam the newsagent's. More than two hundred copies had been sold. Aimee strongly suspected Nick had bought at least half of them.

Still, it was success, of a sort. Nothing like Melinda's success of course, her name in the business pages and her face on TV whenever there was a documentary about female entrepreneurship. Melinda was undoubtedly Hensley's shining star, its most famous citizen. She got asked to draw the meat raffle at the local show, was a regular speaker at school prize givings. And yet for the life of her, Aimee didn't understand why Melinda had come back.

Hensley was the type of place where you either belonged, or you didn't. You were either local, born and raised, or you were forever a blow-in, even if you'd lived there for thirty years. Lou was local. Born in the small hospital, like her daughter, now working for the local council. She had the drawling accent, the bad highlights, the lot. People still referred to her as "Lou Henderson, Ken's daughter," even after everything that had happened. Aimee knew Lou dreamed of leaving, spoke of nothing else once she had a drink in her, but she also knew that Lou would never get around to it, Tansy or no Tansy. Lou wasn't the leaving type.

Aimee had wanted to be local since she was eight years old, when her parents had moved them out from Melbourne, ostensibly to be closer to her mother's sister, but really so her father could carry on his affair with his office manager in relative peace. Yet even with a big house and a decent-size plot, her family was still considered city, her commuting father never invited over for a beer, her mother asked to pay for groceries, rather than being invited to start an account. Aimee's mother had liked being different, with her casual mentions of David Jones and Pelligrini's, thought it made her better than the other women somehow. She couldn't see that it just meant she got left out.

Aimee stopped at the Duffys' house and slid a loaf tin into their mailbox. Gave a toot before she drove off to let Helen know she'd returned it. From her very first day in Hensley, Aimee had been determined to fit in. She spent her birthday money on moleskins and R.M.Williams boots, and all her time with the farm kids, the ones whose families had their names on pews and foundation stones. She wanted to feel part of something. To have roots. Nick, apart from being Melinda's boyfriend, had been perfect in that respect. Aimee would have fallen in love with him anyway, but the fact that he was old Hensley, his great-great-grandfather one of the town's first settlers, just made her love him all the more.

She took a right at the vicarage, its sandstone glowing in the setting sun. Aimee had known, even at eight, that she'd never leave Hensley. Lou had wanted to leave from roughly the same age. It was the one thing they'd always disagreed on. But Melinda—Melinda had escaped, as they'd all predicted. And then she'd come back.

Aimee pulled up outside the Nealsons' place and picked out half a dozen plums from their roadside stand. She stuffed five dollars in the tin, more than the sign asked for, but it had been a tough year and she knew the Nealsons had remortgaged. As she and Nick might have to. Aimee dropped in another two dollars for luck and headed home.

Melinda had never explained why she'd come back to the town she'd so patently outgrown. Or rather she'd explained, but not sufficiently. *I want to get back to basics*, she'd told Aimee when she pitched up and rented a cottage on the edge of town, despite the fact that there was nothing basic about Melinda. *I want to give back*, she'd said when she bought the hotel, plowing hundreds of thousands of dollars into it, despite the fact that altruism and Melinda had never been on first-name terms. *I missed it*, she'd said simply when Aimee found her standing on the edge of a family barbecue, everyone ignoring her, even the kids.

Because Hensley could be cruel. It didn't forgive a slight, and Melinda's leaving to make something of herself and then returning, flush with cash, to buy half the town, hadn't won her any friends. Hensley liked to roll her out and show her off, but it didn't love her. People moaned about the loss of the bar in the old hotel, despite the fact they had three other pubs to drink in. Shopkeepers insisted on calling her by her full name; people whispered about how long she'd stay "this time." She didn't get included in community gossip—she was gossip.

And there was nothing *here* for Melinda. Aimee wavered at the T-junction, trying to decide: left or right. Even as a teenager, Melinda had been shinier than the rest of them, brighter, more ambitious. Not traits that got you far in Hensley. Hensley was for the stoic, the steady, the slightly old-fashioned. It was also for families. People in Hensley tended to marry young and forget to divorce. Aimee worried about Melinda's romantic prospects. Hensley was not a hotbed of single older men.

A car behind her honked; Aimee bit her lip and swung to the right. Drove a few hundred yards and made a U-turn. No. She drove back through the junction, then U-turned again. Felt her pulse settle as she headed toward the hills.

Of course, it was hard to tell if Melinda even wanted to get married. She'd had loads of chances, over the years. Lots of relationships she could have taken further and didn't. And she was gorgeous, Melinda, by far the best looking of the three of them. Lou was cute: blond and short and curvy with big boobs, although she was starting to look older than she was. Stress, probably. Her crow's-feet were deep and she was beginning to get cleavage wrinkles, not helped by the hours they'd spent in their teens lying in Melinda's backyard, basting themselves with baby oil and rotating like rotisserie chickens. Aimee looked younger than Lou, or at least she hoped so, quickly glancing in the rearview mirror to check. And more natural, keeping well away from the local hairdressers and discreetly popping down to the city to get her gray touched up. No chunky Hensley highlights for her. But she wasn't stunning like Melinda, whose teenage ginger freckliness had turned into proper Nicole Kidman beauty in her twenties.

Aimee drove on, trying to focus on the scenery, the papery gum trees and dappled shade, rather than where she was going. Well, not going exactly, more passing. Because she wouldn't stop. She hadn't, not once all day yesterday. Slowed down maybe, as she drove by on her way to drop off a teenager or a case of wine. But nothing unusual, nothing an ordinary person wouldn't do.

No, Aimee wasn't sure that Melinda even wanted a family. She'd never really seemed that interested. Not like Aimee, who the others joked would have stolen a baby if she hadn't had her own. Not like Lou, who'd love to do it all properly, you could tell, but put Tansy ahead of any new relationship. Melinda always seemed like she had more important things to be getting on with.

Maddocks Clearing appeared on her left, and Aimee slowed down so she could see who was there. Just so she knew. The same police car, which hadn't moved in twenty-four hours. A dirty cream-and-brown truck she'd also seen before. And a little red hatchback, which looked familiar, as did the well-dressed woman standing next to it. Aimee dropped to a crawl and recognized one of the journalists from Melinda's launch.

The woman waved and Aimee pulled over, guiltily relieved. Because it was a perfectly normal thing to do, wasn't it? Stop to say hello?

"Everything all right?" Aimee asked. It was the journalist Melinda had been particularly excited about, the one who'd flown in from Sydney. "What are you doing all the way out here?"

"I'm doing a story on the plane crash," the woman said, passing her a business card through the car window. Stacey Manning, from one of the big papers. "Two birds with one stone and all that. Can we have a quick chat?"

Aimee got out of her car, feeling exposed. She should have kept driving, headed straight home after all. She leaned against the comforting warmth of the car door. "Are the nationals really interested in this?" she asked. "It's only a small accident."

"Yeah, but it's a good story," Stacey said. "A dad and his son, New Year's Eve, a town in shock. Raises a lot of questions about how these planes are maintained, what kind of training these pilots get. And the boy's in intensive care, apparently. So it could be an even bigger story."

"Right," said Aimee, feeling faint.

"I'm normally business and finance, but with cutbacks and everything, the editor said to take a look while I'm down here, so I'm going round talking to people," Stacey chattered on.

"And what are they telling you?" Aimee forced herself to look normal.

"Well, they don't know much," said Stacey. "About what caused the accident, I mean. But they obviously think something did, or else those guys wouldn't be out there." She pointed to the orange-vested officers crouched in the tall grass. "So that's interesting."

Aimee looked out into the clearing, at the blackened aircraft and the men buzzing around it like high-vis flies. In the center stood an older man, his hat tipped back on his head as he gave them directions. "Is that Arthur MacKenzie?" she asked.

"Yeah, he's in charge," said Stacey. "At least till the air transport guys get here. So, can you give me a couple of quotes?"

"Sorry?"

"For my story. Reaction from locals, impact on the community. Do you know the pilot and his son?"

Peter Kasprowicz had sat on a couple of committees with her, years ago. Aimee'd sent a card after his wife passed away, but she couldn't remember the last time they'd had a conversation. "Not really," she said. "Knew of them."

"I understand he's a widower?"

Aimee nodded. "Julia died four or five years ago. Cancer. Used to sing in the church choir, taught Sunday school. She was really lovely."

"So how's the community reacting?" Stacey had her phone out. "Can I video you?"

"Video?"

"For the website." Stacey pulled a face. "Sorry, we have to."

Normal. Aimee nodded, looked into the little lens. "Um,

everyone's really upset, obviously. It's a tight community out here, we take care of our own. And Pete's well known, he's deputy principal of the local secondary school. So everyone'll be very concerned about him and Lincoln." *The boy's name was Lincoln, right?* "But they'll be looked after. I'm sure there's already more food in their fridge than they'll ever get through." She gave a stupid, nervous laugh that surprised them both. "And we'll find out who caused this. I mean, if someone caused this. There's no suggestion anyone did, of course. Because it might be—look." Aimee reached out and lowered Stacey's phone. "I haven't seen them in years. They moved over to Meadowcroft, the kids went to school over there. I don't really have much to say."

"No worries," said Stacey. "That was fine." She dropped her phone in her bag, turned toward her car. "I have to get back, dump this thing at the airport. But I appreciate your time."

"Stacey." One of the search team turned his head as she called; Aimee walked quickly over to the little red car and lowered her voice as she crouched beside it. "Could you maybe not use that last part? It wasn't really what I meant to say."

"Sure." Stacey shrugged as she buckled up.

"And the boy?" Aimee tried to sound casual. "You said he was in intensive care."

"Not just intensive care." Stacey was searching for the airport in her GPS. "He's in a coma. Head injuries. Doctor wouldn't go on the record, which is often a sign that they're not sure he'll make it. In my experience, anyway."

LOU SAT ON the back step and lit her first cigarette in more than a decade. The action seemed alien, the snapping of the lighter clumsy, but the smoke filling her mouth and leaking down her throat wasn't foreign at all. It was gloriously familiar, bringing with it the same old sense of ease. The feeling, for just a moment, that everything was going to be okay.

Lou relaxed against the cobwebby brick and breathed out a stream of artificial relief. There was no danger of Tansy catching her, because Tansy had reverted to her old self as soon as they'd gotten home. The childish uncertainty, the fear that had seen Tansy grasp her hand while waiting for the doctor, had vanished the moment they were back in the house. She'd pulled on a miniskirt and those awful open-toed boots and announced that she was going into town.

"It's the *holidays*," Tansy had whined when Lou suggested that she might want to stay in. We could just hang out, Lou had said. Make popcorn, play a board game or something. Tansy had looked at her with barely veiled contempt. "It's not like my whole life has to stop," she'd muttered as she'd flounced off to call whoever and complain about her unreasonable mother. Lou had given in in the end. What was the point? The worst had already happened.

She took another drag, aware that she could hardly afford to take up smoking again. Followed it with a slug of Cointreau, one of the few spirits magically left in the liquor cabinet. Tansy had no idea. Because her life *would* stop, just as Lou's had, her options shrinking, starting with her geographic reach—how far she could realistically get with a pram and a six-pound baby bag and no car or money for a bus or train to anywhere better—followed by her educational prospects, her career options, her future partners.

Lou rolled the glass between her hands. She thought of all the crappy minimum-wage jobs she'd slogged at, trying to juggle a few hours a week with a toddler, the credit cards she'd taken to plug the gap. Her current job had at least pulled them out of debt, allowed her to send Tansy to a better school, even finally save a bit of money for their future— ha!—but it was hardly her dream position. Lou had to take what she could get.

She'd wanted more for Tansy. And, selfishly, for herself. Lou had wondered, just briefly, on the drive back from Fenton, if she could somehow leave Tansy to get on with it, as her parents had with her. But she knew there was no way; Tansy was nearly two years younger than she'd been, and Lou wasn't her parents.

Yet for the first time, she could understand what her parents must have felt. Just a little. The frustration, that years of educational trip organizing and homework supervising had all been for nothing. The helplessness, as they saw their daughter engulfed by something she was in no way ready for. And the anger. They'd certainly been angry, raging, that Lou hadn't listened to their pious, oblique lectures on "saving herself." Lou had been much more open with Tansy, and therefore she was angry too, angry that her otherwise streetwise child didn't have the sense to use a bloody condom.

And maybe she shared a faint glimmer of hope with them

as well, despite herself. There was still a chance that Tansy wouldn't want the baby. She'd been so freaked out by the doctor's questions, so disinterested in the scan. Lou had held back from asking. One thing at a time. But there was plenty of time. Seven weeks. That was nothing.

Lou's neighbor appeared in the garden opposite and gave her a wave. "Forgot it was out here!" Angelique called, as she gathered up washing so dry the tea towels could have stood on their own. Lou was used to staring at her neighbor's laundry; in this part of town, that was your view. Clotheslines, trampolines, rusty bicycles. Hensley was wealthy, but not everyone in Hensley was wealthy. Not everyone had Melinda's 180-degree balcony and river sunsets. Some just got a cold concrete step and a neighbor's faded Jockeys.

Lou lit up a second cigarette—last one, she told herself—and poured another slosh of Cointreau. She allowed herself a moment of guilty fantasy that Tansy would decide against going through with the pregnancy, that they could both carry on as planned, Tansy away to school and uni, Lou finally out of this town, traveling and having her own adventures. This whole situation could simply disappear. It didn't need to ruin everyone's lives, again.

But she wouldn't push. Wouldn't even suggest it. She'd give Tansy the time and space to make her own decisions. Lou hadn't even asked who the father was, just turned the radio on as soon as they got in the car, drove back from the clinic in a silence they both seemed to appreciate. No, she'd leave Tansy alone. Because while she might understand her parents' position—a little, only a little—she was not who they were, and she'd never do to Tansy what they'd ended up doing to her.

"LIGHTS ON OR off?" asked Nick, as he climbed in beside her.

"On," said Aimee. "But let's be quick. Just ten minutes, then sleep."

"Right you are," he said, rearranging the pillows behind them. "Tell me when you've had enough."

Aimee scooted under the duvet, nestling herself against his warm skin. This was the best part of her day, when the house was tidy, the kids were in bed, and she and Nick could lie next to each other and quietly read. An article about running a profitable cellar door for him—as if Aimee would ever allow hundreds of strangers to roam around her property—and something life-affirming for her. Aimee's Oprah books, Nick called them, her bedside stack imploring her to Face the Fear and Do It Anyway.

It was also the only time they got to talk, really talk, about what was going on. With the vineyard, the kids. Their catching-up time. Their putting-right time. Aimee understood why men were more comfortable speaking side by side; it took the judgment out of things. Made you more honest. And yet Aimee had avoided all conversation about the accident since New Year's Eve. She hadn't told him about the letting-go ceremony at all.

To be fair, on New Year's Eve itself, they'd both been quite pissed. Nick hadn't wanted to read or talk, just reached for her with whiskey breath and a hard-on, and she'd been more than happy to be distracted from the bright flash in the sky. Afterward they'd both fallen straight asleep, Nick snoring so heavily she'd had to move into the spare room.

But this was the third night she'd lain next to him since they'd let the lanterns off, and Aimee was still debating whether to say anything. To tell him she was worried about what they'd done. It wasn't like them to hide anything from each other. Aimee and Nick had an open-bathroom-door sort of marriage. The man had massaged vitamin E into her perineum, for goodness' sake. She'd once licked a stuck contact lens off his eyeball. Aimee folded the corner over on her Deepak Chopra and placed it in her lap.

"Good day?" he asked, not even looking up from his issue of *Wine Business Monthly.*

"Mmmm," she said. "It was okay."

If she told him, he'd talk it through with her, she knew. But was that fair? Nick had enough on his plate at the moment. A heavy November frost had hit the lower-lying areas of the vineyard, wiping out the chardonnay crop and tens of thousands of dollars. The last thing he needed was to worry about what was going on in Aimee's head. And he would worry, she knew.

"Just okay?"

When there wasn't any reason to. She wasn't getting obsessed or anything. She was just a little concerned. But Nick wouldn't see it like that. He'd start watching her, treading carefully, wondering out loud if she might like to go and talk to someone.

"Yeah."

Which she didn't fancy at all. So there was no point in bringing anything up.

"This morning went well, I thought," said Nick.

And if Aimee was honest, she was embarrassed to admit to her fire-volunteer husband that she'd watched the lantern burn, and not done anything about it.

"Feel a bit sorry for Melinda," he added.

"Me too."

He turned a page in his magazine. "I saw her in town, gave her a hand with her boxes. She seemed a bit flat."

Something niggled, something unconnected with the accident. "Hey, did you tell Mel we were having money issues?"

He shrugged. "Dunno. Might have."

Because Aimee hadn't. "When?"

"Not sure." He turned another page. "Why?"

"No reason." And there wasn't, not really. Nick had chosen Aimee, clearly and completely. "I want to be with someone who wants the same things I do," he'd said, on their first proper date. "Mel and I were moving in different directions, and I didn't want to go in hers." Aimee hadn't pushed it. Nick and Melinda were on friendly enough terms, Nick's parents were delighted, and no one seemed to blame her for dating him so soon after he'd broken up with her oldest friend. And Aimee did want exactly what he did: a family, in the town they both loved, settled and steady and safe.

"You're not bothered, are you?"

Which was almost exactly what Aimee had asked Melinda,

when Nick first suggested the two of them grab a drink. She'd phoned Melinda at the London pub she was working in, shouted down the phone to be heard over the customers. "Couldn't care less," Melinda had said, and Aimee knew it was true. Melinda was off having adventures, roaming around Europe, not worrying about what was going on in little old Hensley. "He's better suited to you than me," Melinda said, and Aimee knew that was true as well. Nick hadn't even freaked out when she'd gotten pregnant so quickly. Just drove her back to his parents' house and got a diamond ring out of his sock drawer. "Bought it the first week we were together," he'd said, getting down on one knee in the middle of his bedroom. "Whadya reckon? Could you handle living here for a bit until we're sorted?" They'd never left.

Aimee leaned over and kissed her husband. "Not bothered at all," she said. "Just wondering how she knew."

Nick put his magazine down. "What did you get up to anyway, after the launch? I came back here to sort your spuds out, and you were gone."

If he pressed her, she'd tell him. "I went over to Maddocks Clearing."

"Where Pete Kasprowicz's plane came down?"

"Yes." If he asked, then that was a sign. To confide. To come clean.

But "poor bastard" was all he said. Nick rolled over toward the light. "You had enough now? Can I turn this off?"

"Sure," she said. "I'm done."

Chapter 8

Cameron leaned forward in his economy-class seat, a jockey on a horse, willing the plane to go faster. He rested his forehead against the seat in front, the shuffling of its occupant banging the edge of the tray table gently into his skull.

"You okay, love?"

"Fine."

"You don't look okay," the elderly woman next to him insisted. Someone's grandma, all talcum powder and muted florals, her wedding rings buried in the spotted flesh of her fingers. "Are you a nervous flyer?"

He shook his head, mentally willing her to shut up.

"I find a small whiskey helps, myself," she confided. "I could ask the stewardess, if you like."

Cameron gritted his teeth against her concern. "Bugger off," he whispered.

"Has something happened? Do you want to talk about it?"

He didn't. He went back to letting his forehead judder against the molded plastic. *Come on, come on.* He'd been too late last time. Not his fault. But he had to be there now. The speaker came on, the captain warning about turbulence, and Cameron undid his seat belt. Better to distract himself with the bumps of the plane than think about what might be waiting for him on the ground. *I'll be a better brother*, Cameron promised. *A proper brother. Stick around. Take you with me. Whatever you want. Just fucking hold on, Lincoln. Just hold the fuck on.*

"Do you want a mint? I've got some—oh goodness. Here, have a tissue. There you go. No shame in crying, that's what I always told my boys. Let it all out, love, you'll feel better after, I promise. That's it. Good lad."

Chapter 9

It was Lou's birthday picnic. Melinda and Aimee's idea, a big celebration down by the river, just friends, family, and a few thousand of her closest neighbors. Because it was also the first day of the Hensley Town Festival, an event conceived in the very bowels of hell. Nine long days of go-kart races and fundraisers, baking competitions and art exhibitions, tea parties and vineyard tours and self-congratulatory speeches and picnic lunches. Like this one. Lou had always felt it the ultimate irony to be born in the same week as the town she couldn't wait to be shot of. And now she was thirty-five and Hensley was one hundred and sixty, and both of them were still bloody here.

Lou stood at the top of the main street, watching the activity down by the river, and rearranged her face into a smile. Because she had to be cheerful at events like this lest the others think she'd stopped making an effort. She caught them watching sometimes, checking for signs that she hadn't given up. Which was laughable. The thing about raising a child on your own was that you didn't get to give up. You might not always wear the cleanest clothes, or wash your hair, or greet your friends with enthusiasm and good humor, but you didn't get to stop. You didn't ever, ever get to stop.

"Louise," called a high-pitched voice. Sharna from the post office. The town's unofficial crier, she waved as she maneuvered two small grandsons and her husband down toward the river. "Happy birthday! I understand the girls have organized quite the celebration for you! Aren't you lucky?"

Lou gave her an ironic thumbs-up. "So lucky!"

And grateful. That was the other thing with being a single mum—you had to be so grateful, all the bloody time, for everything anyone did for you, no matter how unwelcome. The invitations to seminars on how to fix your life. The set-up dates with deadbeat single dads who'd never paid for a diaper. The "thoughtful" gifts. Last year, Melinda and Aimee had bought her a massage voucher that cost as much as her monthly power bill. *Pamper yourself!* She'd gone, but the whole time she'd lain there, having her chakras opened with hot stones, Lou had just thought, *What a waste.*

She could see Melinda below, spreading out a blanket smack bang in front of the rotunda. Perfect for watching the band, yet far enough away from the crowds and the speakers. But of course Melinda would secure the prime spot. Nothing less would be acceptable. There were wicker picnic baskets dotted artfully around, a silver wine bucket next to her, filled with ice and what looked like sun cream and fancy sprays. Aimee's contribution, no doubt. Nice to have the time to mess about with things like that. Lou had spent the morning doing the council accounts, gone in at five so she could have her birthday afternoon off.

No. Stop it. She shook her head, literally shook it, to try and force the nasty thoughts out. *Enough.* These were the women who'd rallied around her when no one else wanted to know, who'd driven hundreds of miles back from uni every month to check that she was okay, who'd left groceries on her doorstep and then denied it so she could save a bit of face. God, what was wrong with her? Since Tansy's announcement, Lou had been hit by a wave of self-pity and resentment she hadn't experienced since her first months of motherhood. And she didn't like it.

Melinda was looking for her now, hands on hips, scanning the crowd. Lou took a few steps onto the grass, but instead of plunging into the mass of excited parents and children, she swerved, ducking behind a row of fast food stalls. The smell wasn't the best—oily and hot, the popcorn already rancid—but at least it was private. Lou pulled a box of cigarettes—the third she'd bought since the doctor's appointment—out of her handbag, and lit up.

One puff, two, head swiveling to make sure she couldn't be seen. This was like being back in high school. Lou perched awkwardly on an upturned plastic crate, trying not to crush her new dress. She needed to sort out her attitude, like she was always telling Tansy. Aimee and Melinda organizing a party for her was lovely. It was just that the last thing Lou felt like doing was celebrating. There was nothing to celebrate, from where she was sitting.

Lou took a final drag. But she would, for her friends. Eat and drink and laugh and pretend nothing was wrong. Accept her spa voucher or pointless sequined clutch with fake enthusiasm, and try to ignore the fact that her life at thirty-five was no different than it had been at thirty-four or thirty-three, or thirty-two. Or how it would be at thirty-six. She still had nowhere to carry a sequined clutch.

Lou rubbed her cigarette along the stubbly grass. She fished a roll of mints and an old body spray out of her handbag and sanitized herself, reapplied her lipstick. At least she looked nice. She took a moment to rearrange the crepe cocktail frock she'd picked up in the Country Road sale: still $160, way more than she'd normally spend, but it made her look curvy rather than dumpy and showed off her cleavage. Lou had felt almost attractive in the changing room, with its flattering lights and magic slimming mirror. She caught the teenage boy manning the hot dog stand staring as she hoicked up her breasts and gave him a wink. He went bright red and dropped a sausage, fumbled trying to retrieve it and dropped the tongs. Lou laughed out loud. *Still got it.* By the time she stepped back into the crowd she was genuinely smiling. *Right then. Let the bloody celebrations begin.*

EVERYBODY WANTED SOMETHING. Melinda kept a taut smile on her face, as tight as the gazebo strings she was adjusting, as a steady stream of Hensleyites stopped by her patch and tried to interest her in their business ideas, their expansion plans, their unwanted kittens.

"A cat?" she asked, hammering in the strings with her little mallet. "What would I want with a cat?"

"Mum thought it might be good for you," reported a horribly honest child. "Since you're all on your own. Said you probably needed the company."

Melinda was still fuming when Lou came trotting down the hill in something far too low cut. "Do I look like a crazy cat woman to you?" she asked Lou, kissing her. She stopped, sniffed. "Have you been smoking?"

"Tansy." Lou pulled a bottle of something nasty looking out of her handbag and sprayed it around, covering them both in cheap vanilla. "This looks amazing," she said, taking in the gazebo, the pastel picnic rugs, the chilled bottles of champagne. She fingered the gingham bunting. "Aimee do this?"

"No!" said Melinda. "I did. I can be domestic as well, actually."

"Oh shit, sorry," said Lou. "But of course you did. It's color coordinated, and it's ready on time." She looked around their little campsite. "Where is Aimee, anyway?"

"Still at the house, icing your cake," said Melinda. "Where's Tans?"

"Helping her, apparently." Lou grabbed a piece of mango from a bowl of chopped fruit. "Wonders will never cease." She shook her head, gave a bright smile. "This does look fantastic," she said. "Thank you so much."

"It does, doesn't it?" Melinda squeezed Lou into a side hug. "Happy birthday, my lovely. Wait till you see what we've got you for a present."

The embankment was filling up now, passersby staring enviously at their floaty tent and all its goodies. "Is it too early for a drink?" asked Lou.

"Never," said Melinda. "Actually—I'm really glad you're here first." She popped the cork on a bottle of Moët. "Oh, why not," she said, when Lou raised an eyebrow. "It's your birthday. Let's go crazy." She dropped a strawberry into Lou's glass and filled it. "To you," she said, clinking.

"To us," said Lou. "Still speaking, after thirty years."

"Miracle, isn't it?" Melinda pulled Lou down onto one of the blankets. "Speaking of us. And speaking of speaking, can you do me a favor and have a word with Aimee?"

"A word?"

Melinda lowered her voice. "About this plane accident."

"Oh God." Lou had clearly forgotten. "Pete Kasprowicz and his son. That was awful."

"I know, I know," said Melinda, not wanting to get into details of the awfulness. "But I'm worried about how Aimee is taking it."

"Taking it?"

Was Lou living on another planet? "Her obsession with it. And," Melinda glanced over her shoulder, "this whole crazy idea that our letting-go exercise might have had something to do with it."

"Right." Lou swirled her champagne, brow creasing. "Do you think there's any chance it did? That we did?"

"Not at all." Melinda was emphatic. "You know we didn't. It was miles away."

"Yes."

"There were fireworks everywhere. It was dark. They flew straight into a hill. And I don't mean to be rude, but Peter Kasprowicz is only an amateur pilot."

"Right."

Melinda topped up Lou's glass. She needed to shut the situation down before it became one. Because when Aimee got obsessed about something, she started reassurance seeking, and Melinda did not need Aimee asking everyone in town if they thought she and her friends had caused a plane accident. She shuddered internally at what Clint's reaction would be. "Reputation is everything at this stage," he'd said. "I don't want anyone to even catch you littering."

"Look," said Melinda. "You know what Aimee's like when she gets one of these ideas stuck in her head, decides she's responsible for something. She stops being able to see straight. Her thoughts loop. It's *painful* for her."

Lou nodded.

"I don't want to see her go through that again."

"Especially since she's not on her medication anymore."

"She's not?" Shit. "Well, let's make sure she doesn't have to go back on it."

Lou took a swig of her champagne. "I worry about her

sometimes," she said. "Sitting in that big old house all day, scribbling in her notebooks."

"Exactly."

"All that time in her own head. It can't be good for her."

"She needs a proper job. Or to be more involved in the vineyard. *Something*."

Lou nodded, as Melinda knew she would. It wasn't the first time they'd had this conversation.

"You know my theory," said Melinda. "Nature abhors a vacuum. If you're not working, you have time to come up with all sorts of crazy. Look at the gossipy school mums you have to deal with."

Lou pulled a face.

"So, are you with me?" Melinda looked Lou straight in the eye, her closing-the-deal look. "Actually, maybe don't have a word, but if she mentions the accident, can you just not engage? Remember what the therapist woman said last time. No enabling, no reassuring. If she brings it up, we shut the subject right down."

"Okay." Lou took another swig of champagne. "That sounds sensible."

"I'm only thinking of Aimee," said Melinda. "I don't want to see her go downhill again." She took a decent swallow of her own drink. "And I'll be honest," she said, as the bubbles hit her bloodstream, "I don't really fancy people in town having another reason to talk about me. I imagine you don't either."

Lou stared off toward the river. "No," she said, sounding sad. "I'd rather they didn't."

Maybe that was a little near the bone. Lou had been the talk of Hensley for months when she'd gotten pregnant. Who was the father, would she keep the baby? While Melinda skipped happily back to university, Aimee following, visiting whenever they were home with stuffed toys and little outfits, but whispering their relief to each other on the way back to Melbourne afterward. Thank goodness it wasn't them.

Melinda shuffled around so she was sitting next to Lou, looking at the crowds gathered below them on the riverbank, unpacking tarpaulins and picnics, but nothing as nice as theirs. She put an arm around her friend. "I'm sorry," she said.

"For what?"

"For not being more tactful," said Melinda. "And for not telling you enough what an awesome job you're doing raising Tansy."

Lou gave a hiccupy snort-laugh.

"You are," said Melinda. "A fantastic job. You should be proud of yourself. I know you think she's out of control sometimes, but I don't think she's that different from how we were." She thought of Lou's secret teenage tattoo, of Aimee's ill-advised Goth stage. "She's beautiful and energetic and clever and she'll sort herself out. Honestly, this is just a phase. Tansy's going to be fine."

Lou shuddered a little, and Melinda squeezed tighter. "Oh Lou-Lou," she said. "Don't get teary. See, this is what happens when you drink before lunch. And you know what the cure is?" Lou shook her head. "More champagne. Here. Pass me your glass."

AIMEE SAT HAPPILY under the gazebo enjoying the band, the darkening sky, the twinkling fairy lights. And the champagne. She was especially enjoying the champagne. She'd arrived to find Lou and Melinda already half-drunk and felt obliged to catch up. Which she had, easily. Melinda kept producing bottle after bottle, like some kind of Moët magician, making one of Aimee's favorite occasions even more special.

Aimee adored the Hensley Town Festival, always had. At events like this she could feel the whole town wrapped around her, like a warm blanket. She waved at Sam the newsagent and his wife, at the Surthis and their new baby. She loved the sense of community, the sharing of scones from Tupperware containers. She volunteered for everything during festival week, or at least all the safe activities, things like cake judging and flower arranging, where only feelings were likely to be hurt. Back-room roles. Although this year she'd somehow agreed to write a poem for the town's anniversary and recite it, in front of everyone, at the annual concert. The mayor was giving her top billing. Actually, Aimee wasn't looking forward to that particular event so much. That particular event might necessitate a Valium.

But right now, it was time for cake. Aimee was particularly proud of the cake. Three layers of chocolate espresso torte, made with almond flour so it was extra dense, heavy cream between the layers. She and the girls had spent all morning trying to replicate a marbled mirror icing that Shelley had seen on YouTube, scraping it off three times before they got it right.

She gave a nod, and Shelley and Tansy pulled the cake out of the cooler. "Tah dah!" they said, wobbling slightly. Clearly the adults weren't the only ones enjoying the champagne.

"No way," said Lou. "Did you two make this? This is amazing."

"Well, Mum helped," said Shelley.

Lou nodded. "Good to see she's earning her keep."

"Set it up on one of the tables," Aimee directed. "*Carefully.* Byron, give them a hand." She rummaged in her bag, pulled out the special candles she'd bought earlier. "Bugger. Has anyone got a lighter?"

No one did. Aimee sent the kids off to ask around.

"Honestly, that is one hell of a cake," said Lou, inspecting it. She laid a gentle finger on the mirror icing, glassy and perfect. "It seems a shame to stick candles in it."

"But we have to," said Aimee. "You need to make a wish."

"Didn't we already do that for New Year's?" said Lou.

The mention of their letting-go ceremony struck Aimee's chest like a tiny arrow, but it didn't penetrate. Didn't set her heart racing. Good. She was secretly proud that she hadn't brought up the accident all day, despite the morning paper reporting that there was going to be a formal inquiry. She'd practiced her deep breathing and kept her thoughts to herself. The champagne was helping with that too, making everything feel lighter. Maybe she should develop a drinking problem. She gave a little giggle.

"Aimee?" said Lou.

"Nothing." Aimee smiled. "So what did you wish for? When we . . . you know."

"To get out of here, of course," said Lou. "What do you think?" She looked at Aimee. "What did you wish for?"

Aimee was conscious of Nick beside her, ready with the cake knife, of Byron hovering awkwardly at the edge of the gazebo, of Shelley eagerly holding out a box of matches. "Nothing important." She put her arm around her daughter. "Good girl." Hang on. Why were there only two teenagers? "Where's Tansy?" she asked.

"She met some people, down by the stage." Shelley looked uncomfortable. "She said she'd be back later."

"Well, that's just bloody rude," said Nick. "I'm going to go find her."

Lou looked embarrassed; Aimee shot him a warning look.

"No," said Nick. "It's your birthday, she should be here. Shelley, you call her and tell her to come back."

Lou shook her head. "Don't bother," she said. "We were lucky to keep her this long. Let's just get on with it."

"Right then," said Aimee extra brightly. "Who's going to be brave and stick these candles in for me?"

Shelley stepped forward, taking the bright yellow 3 and 5 from Aimee's hand, and screwing their plastic bases into the cake. The icing cracked as the glaze gave, tiny fissures running in all directions.

"Oh no," said Lou.

"Doesn't matter," said Nick, handing her the knife. "You're going to have to cut into it anyway."

Lou moved so she was behind the cake, positioned the knife above the shiny icing.

"Wait!" cried Shelley, shaking the matches. She held the wavering flame carefully to one candle, then the other, and Aimee tried not to think of their lanterns. "You need to make a wish," she said, forcing the image out of her head.

"Wish," they all called. "Wish, wish!"

Lou gave them a half smile and bent her head forward. Melinda held her hair back, as though they were sixteen again and someone was going to vomit.

"Well?" asked Nick. "Was it your usual, or does being thirty-five warrant a whole new wish?"

"Don't be silly," said Aimee. She winked at Melinda and motioned for her to get ready. Melinda turned slightly so Aimee could see the blue and green package behind her back. "We know what Lou's wish is," said Aimee. "To see the world." She grinned, bubbling with the delicious anticipation of what was coming next. "Well, maybe this will help."

Melinda set the fat little parcel on the table in front of Lou. They'd wrapped it in maps, layers and layers of them, torn from an old picture book of Byron's: Italy, Spain, Japan. Aimee had deliberately not used the Australian pages.

"Open it!" the children called.

Aimee got ready with the camera, the proper Nikon, not just the one on her phone. She couldn't wait to see Lou's face when she unwrapped this year's present. This was even better than the vintage Betsey Johnson clutch. Aimee and Melinda had truly outdone themselves.

Lou took her time, turning the parcel over, feeling the hard little sides of it. She's guessed, thought Aimee, but no, Lou looked completely taken aback when she finally peeled off the last layer of paper and took out the passport.

"What—" Lou's face was white. "But how?"

"We applied for you!" Aimee was fizzing, like the champagne. "Melinda's idea. Tansy found us your birth certificate and your driver's license photo, and we filled in all the forms. Melinda had to pretend to be you, and Sharna at the post office had to pretend not to know she was really Melinda, but let's not dwell on that bit too much—"

"No, let's not," said Melinda.

"But we knew you wouldn't mind. And—here you go!"

Lou looked shell-shocked.

"Hey." Nick leaned over the table, tapped a white envelope sticking out of the passport. "I think the girls have another surprise for you."

It was a travel voucher, for five hundred dollars.

"Just to get you on your way," said Melinda.

"You can use it with any airline," said Aimee.

Lou put her face in her hands and burst into tears.

MELINDA HAD TAKEN over, and for that Lou was grateful. She hustled the three of them into a taxi, threw her car keys at Nick and instructed him and the kids to pack everything up.

"To the old commercial hotel," she told the driver, while Lou sat between her friends and cried. Cried in a way she'd never cried before, not when she'd realized she was pregnant, not when her parents had disowned her, not when she'd found herself filling out application forms for child support rather than university. She cried so hard her breathing couldn't keep up, as though a dam had burst and sixteen years of disappointment was finally gushing free. The others hugged her nervously; Lou was a little freaked out herself. She knew she was pissed off, but not that she was this *miserable*. By the time they reached Melinda's she'd run out of tears and was hiccupping like a colicky baby.

"Right," said Melinda, when they were all inside and she had the kettle on. "What on earth is going on?"

"Tansy's pregnant."

It was a relief to finally say it. Lou felt a perverse pleasure in the shock on Aimee's and Melinda's faces. See. This *was* earth shattering. This really was the end of the world.

"Fuck," breathed Aimee, who never swore.

"Bloody hell," agreed Melinda. "Oh, Lou. I'm so . . . sorry?" She put the fancy tin of tea bags she was holding back down on the bench. "God, I don't even know what the appropriate response is."

"I don't think there is one," said Lou. Hallmark didn't make "Congratulations on your Pregnant Teenager" cards.

"What does she want to do?" said Aimee.

"Who's the father?" said Melinda.

"Does she want to have the baby?" asked Aimee. "Keep it?"

"I don't know," said Lou, slumping against the bench. She could feel the damp of the sink seeping into the back of her new dress, already irreparably crumpled by the taxi ride. "I don't really know anything," she admitted. "We haven't really talked about it."

"Why the hell not?" said Melinda.

"I didn't want to push her."

"Well, you clearly have to." Melinda picked up the tea bags again, made a big bustle out of sorting out mugs. "You have to make her tell you."

Lou crossed her arms. "I'm not going to make her do anything."

"But you need to know who the father is, at least," said Melinda. "What the circumstances are. She's still only sixteen, isn't she? So this could be a case of . . . well." She pulled a carton of milk out of the fridge, poured it straight in their tea without sniffing it. In Melinda's house, the milk was always fresh. "I mean, she could have been coerced. Taken advantage of. Especially if he's older."

Lou shook her head. "I don't think Tansy needs anyone to take advantage of her," she said grimly. "God, that sounds awful, but you know what I mean. Anything she's gotten herself into, she's gotten herself into." Gotten them both into. Lou tried not to think about the stiff little passport in her handbag, its virgin pages that would stay that way. "She's always been . . . I couldn't . . ." Lou stopped. Tansy was just Tansy. That was the problem.

"Now, Lou," said Melinda, passing her a mug, "this is not your fault."

Lou frowned. "I didn't think it was."

"Well, just with all the statistics." Melinda had switched to her slightly patronizing voice, the one she used with the slower sales associates who didn't quite get it. Lou had been one of Melinda's "curators" when Tansy was young. The fact she'd managed to handle having Melinda as a boss for nearly a year without becoming violent was a minor miracle.

"Statistics?" asked Lou quietly. "What are you suggesting?"

"You know, teenage mothers creating more teenage mothers. The cycle."

"I *created* this?" Lou's hands tightened around her tea. "We're part of a *cycle*?"

"Sugar?" Aimee moved between the two of them. "Biscuits? Have you got any biscuits, Mel? I really fancy something sweet."

Melinda flushed, her neck blotching a deep pink as though someone had thrown hot tea at her. "It's just more likely, that's all. Kids with Tansy's upbringing. To repeat what they know. It's really common. What I mean is, you can't blame yourself."

Lou placed her mug back on the bench. "I don't," she said slowly. "But it sounds like you think I should."

"No!" said Melinda. "Of course not. I'm just saying I see how you could, if . . . Oh, never mind. This is coming out wrong."

"Yes," said Lou. "It is."

"Lou?" Aimee pulled the French doors to the living room shut behind her as she stepped outside. "Sweetheart? Can I join you?"

Lou shrugged. Aimee decided to take that as a yes. She stepped around Melinda's artfully distressed deck chairs and terra-cotta pots of basil as she made her way across the balcony. Lou looked almost luminous in the streetlights, leaning over the wooden railing in her floaty dress.

"Can I have a puff of that?" Aimee asked, holding out her hand.

Lou snorted. "You don't smoke."

"Neither do you."

"Well, desperate times and all that." Lou still didn't turn her head.

Aimee shuffled over so they were standing side by side. Below them, families flooded back into the main street from the river, laughing and calling to one another, clearly having a much better evening than Aimee and her friends. "You know she doesn't mean it," she said.

Lou said nothing.

"She doesn't understand. Because she doesn't have her own." Aimee took a drag of the cigarette Lou passed her and tried not to think about the last time they were on this balcony together. "Ugh. Nope, still foul." She handed it back with a shallow cough.

"It was a shitty thing to say."

Aimee nodded, trying to swallow away the burnt tobacco taste. "It was."

"Do you think it's my fault?"

"Of course not. Don't be daft." Aimee searched for the right words, words that would make things better rather than worse. "And neither does she. It's just . . . you know what she's like. She sees life as a series of challenges, to excel at, and motherhood doesn't work like that, obviously."

"The reason I'm not pushing Tansy on this isn't because I'm a lousy mother. The reason I'm not pushing her is because I don't want to be *my* mother. I don't want history to completely bloody repeat itself."

"I know." God, the hours she spent interpreting Melinda's comments for those who required a little more humanity in their interactions. "I get it, I really do. But Melinda's black and white, you know that. Something is either right or wrong, and if it's wrong, how do we fix it. She doesn't really deal in flexibility." Aimee sank into a deck chair. She didn't feel drunk anymore, but the champagne had definitely loosened her tongue. "I sometimes think it's just as well she didn't have her own," she said. "I don't think she'd have been very . . . cuddly."

Lou stubbed her cigarette halfheartedly on the railing and threw it over the side. Little sparks escaped it as it fell. "No," she agreed. "She's far too wrapped up in her own life for children. Too self-absorbed. All those courses. All that travel. You can't do that if you've got kids."

Aimee willed herself to stay in the chair, not to get up and check to see where the smoldering cigarette had landed. "But I don't think she ever really wanted them either," she said, speaking more to distract herself than continue the conversation. "I mean, you wouldn't exactly describe her as maternal."

"Well, she can stop telling me what to do with mine then."

"She can't help it," said Aimee. "She likes to manage things." She forced herself to lean back into the generous cushions. The cigarette would go out, and there was only concrete beneath them anyway. "Maybe the world is just divided into two types of people: parents, and those who've never experienced the madness."

"Parents, and people who were never meant to be." Lou sounded bitter. "At least you understand. I mean, this could be you and Shelley."

"Well, let's be honest, it would never be Shelley," said Aimee. "I don't have to worry about anything with her, thank goodness."

"Lucky you."

"But I worry about Byron all the time," Aimee said quickly. "And then I worry that worrying makes me horrible and old-fashioned and prejudiced."

"It doesn't," said Lou. "It makes you his mum."

"I'm scared I'm getting it wrong."

"You're not," Lou said loyally.

Aimee sighed. "Nick always seems to say the right thing. But me? If I ask too many questions, I worry I'm prying. If I don't ask, I worry I'm being neglectful. That he might think I'm not taking an interest *because* he's gay, you know?" Aimee bit her lip. This was the stuff that kept her awake at night. "I like to think I'd be freaked out by Byron growing up regard-less, but what if this isn't a normal mother-type freak-out? What if I'm not as open-minded as I think?"

"I think you're overthinking it."

"Well, there's a first."

Lou laughed out loud.

"Maybe there is no perfect balance," said Aimee. "Care too much, they end up in therapy. Don't care enough, they end up in therapy."

"Or pregnant," said Lou.

Aimee shook her head. "Now that's where Melinda *is* right," she said. "This is so not your fault. You've done everything you could for Tansy." And Aimee was going to give that girl a piece of her mind later, for running off on her mum's birthday. Especially now. "Children are going to make their own mistakes regardless," she continued. "All we can do is pick up the pieces, and hope there aren't too many of them." She reached over and took Lou's hand. "But Tansy's pregnancy doesn't need to take over the rest of your life. You do know that, don't you?"

"She's sixteen."

"So you help her out for a couple of years. But not forever. Not if you don't want to."

Lou closed her eyes. "I just felt like I was almost done with the hard stuff, you know?"

"You are almost done," said Aimee. "This is a delay. Not a cancelation." She gave Lou's hand a squeeze. "You'll still use that passport, I promise."

Lou shrugged.

"Lou, listen to me. You don't have to raise this child for Tansy. God, she won't even want you to. At the beginning, yes, of course. She'll need you. But eventually"—Aimee pictured Tansy's stubborn little chin, the same as Lou's—"she'll put you in a taxi to the airport herself."

"I guess." Lou wandered over to the edge of the balcony, pulling herself up onto the railing in a move that made Aimee's stomach drop. "I didn't wish to travel though," she admitted.

"Sorry?"

"Tonight. Blowing out the candles. Nick was right." Lou was fiddling with her lighter again. "I wished she wouldn't have the baby."

"Ah," said Aimee. *Crikey.* "Then you really do need to have a chat with her, sooner rather than later, don't you?"

JUST AS WELL she never had children. Not particularly maternal. Too self-absorbed. Melinda sat on the end of her bed and replayed the nastiest of the insults in her head. What else had Lou and Aimee said? *Not exactly cuddly.* Melinda wrapped her thin arms around herself, clutching her tiny biceps, the muscles she trained four times a week to define. Because yes, she did go to the gym, just as she went to conferences and personal development courses and away on work trips, because you had to fill your life with *something.* It wasn't selfish, it was practical. She could hardly sit at home twiddling her thumbs, waiting for the husband-and-baby fairy to turn up.

She could see the two of them silhouetted through her gauze drapes, heads close together, completely unaware of their voices floating through the open door to Melinda's bedroom. Was that really what they thought of her? Was this how they talked about her when she wasn't around? Melinda stared miserably at her highly impractical, non-child-friendly cream silk rug. It must be. They'd been so casual, so matter-of-fact. Oh yeah, Melinda, not mother material. Presumably they didn't think she was wife or girlfriend material either. Melinda pressed her lips together. It was one thing for *her* to worry about her lack of meaningful relationships, but another thing entirely for everyone else to think she wasn't capable of having them. And it must be everyone, she realized. Because people had stopped asking when she was going to settle down, had stopped teasing her about whether she could hear the clock ticking. Her father hassled her brother, Matthew, about grandchildren, but not Melinda. Worse, he never really had.

Melinda stumbled into her bathroom and ran herself a glass of water. A new packet of birth control pills sat next to her toothbrush; she'd been taking them for her skin since she was thirteen. Handy, she'd thought, not to have to worry about pimples and accidents, to know exactly when you were due. When she'd realized you could skip a cycle, she'd decided to stay on the pill for the rest of her life. "Aren't you worried," one of her university housemates had asked—a girl who went on to become a biochemist, no less—"that it will permanently mess with your hormones?" Melinda had ignored her, in love with the convenience of periods-on-demand, but what if her housemate had been right? What if the reason she had no real maternal instinct was that she'd been medicating it away? Worse, what if other people could smell it? The pill mimicked the first month of pregnancy, didn't it, which meant she might not be giving off some vital ovulation pheromone. Maybe all men got from her was Clarins and Chanel, and not the *eau de fertile* they were sniffing around for.

Melinda leaned her forehead against the icy cold of the bathroom mirror. She stared down in her black silk vest at her small, stretch-mark-free breasts and tiny pink nipples. *Like a teenager's*, Dave-the-married had marveled. *You've got the body of an eighteen-year-old.* But he'd still returned to the generously curved mother of his three children. Melinda had googled her, found a Facebook page full of homemade birthday cakes and fancy-dress costumes. Like a candidate for mother of the bloody year.

"This is not helping," she hissed at her reflection. "This is *negative thinking*." There was a dull ache behind her forehead; her hangover was kicking in. Melinda opened the medicine cabinet and fished out a box of aspirin, knocking her birth control pills into the sink. They stared mockingly up at her in the moonlight, round and cute and peach and pointless. "Fuck off," Melinda told them, picking up the little plastic strip and flicking it into the bin.

"Melinda?" A male shadow hovered in her bedroom doorway. "Are you in there?"

Nick. "Hang on," she called, tidying her hair with her fingers. "Won't be a minute." She gave her teeth the world's quickest brush, silently spitting, before stepping back into the bedroom.

He was inspecting the fifty-five-inch television she'd had installed above the dresser. Curved screen, surround sound. "This'll keep you company at night," the delivery guy had joked. Melinda had given him a scathing online review.

"I came back to drop off the cake," Nick said, tearing himself away from the TV. "Make sure everything was all right." He looked slightly ridiculous with a Tupperware container tucked under his arm like a football. "What are you doing hanging out here in the dark?" he asked. "And where are the others?"

Melinda quietly pulled the balcony door closed. "Headache," she said. "Too much champagne." She forced herself to smile. "Lou and Aimee are outside having a chat," she continued. "About Tansy. Mum stuff. You know."

"Ah." Nick shuffled uncomfortably as his gaze bounced around her bedroom, from her open underwear drawer to the unmade bed. "Bet you're glad you don't have to deal with all that."

For fuck's sake, had the whole world written her off? She stared icily at Nick. "Actually, I'm still thinking I might."

"You?" Nick gave a half laugh. "You always said you didn't want any."

"Well, maybe I've changed my mind."

"Really."

"Yes, really," said Melinda. "I've realized I might have been wrong." She pictured Aimee giggling over her lack of maternal instinct and felt a sudden kick of nasty in her blood. "About a lot of things."

Nick stared at her, inscrutable in the shadows. "Shame you didn't figure that out earlier."

Melinda could take that either of two ways; she chose the safer option. "I'm planning to adopt, actually," she said, the idea coming out of absolutely nowhere. "So age won't matter."

"Right," said Nick, stone-faced. "Well, good for you."

It could have been eighteen years ago; the conversation had the same cold deliberateness of their old arguments. Small, pointed sentences, dropped with the precision of heat-seeking missiles. "Thank you," Melinda said, turning her back on Nick and their shared past, and heading for the safety of the well-lit living room. "I'm very excited about it."

"Excited about what?" Aimee and Lou were cuddled up on the sofa like teenage BFFs, a tub of melting ice cream between them. "Oooh, is that the cake?" continued Aimee. There was a smudge of double chocolate near her elbow on Melinda's off-white upholstery. "Thank goodness. Daytime drinking always makes me hungry." She wriggled excitedly, further griming the ice cream into the couch. "Cut us a slice, will you, Nick? A big fat one, lots of icing."

Nick opened a drawer in the middle of the kitchen island and pulled out a stack of plates. "Aren't you going to tell them?" he asked.

Outplayed. Melinda shot him a look. "I'm thinking about adopting," she said.

"What, a baby?" asked Aimee.

"No, a fucking puppy," said Melinda. "Yes, a baby. Or a child. Whatever's possible." Silence. "Well, you needn't look so surprised."

Lou didn't look surprised. She looked horrified. "But you—"

"Have been thinking about it for a while, actually," said Melinda. "Ever since I visited the orphanage in Vietnam." Another solo holiday. Two weeks on her own, taking cooking lessons and village tours, anything to keep herself occupied. "I just think it's time."

Aimee eyeballed her. "Right."

"Yes." Melinda marched into the kitchen. She grabbed a knife out of the block and began carving up the remains of the cake. "Like I said, it's very exciting." She slapped two plates down on the coffee table in front of her friends. "What, you're not happy for me?"

Lou scrabbled around on the floor in front of her. "I don't think I can be happy about any baby news right now, to be honest," she said, shoving her feet into a pair of scuffed mules. She grabbed her handbag. "Sorry, but I really can't take any more surprise announcements." She looked around, slightly wildly. "I have to go."

Melinda waited to feel bad, but she didn't. There was too much hurt and anger in the way.

"Lou, wait," called Aimee. "How are you going to get home?"

"Walk," came the muffled voice from the hallway. The building shook as the front door slammed.

Aimee turned to Melinda. "Oh, well done."

"What?"

"You don't think that was a bit insensitive?"

That was rich. "I don't, actually," said Melinda. "Tansy's pregnancy doesn't impact my plans."

"No, nothing ever impacts your plans."

"I'm going to wait in the car," said Nick, escaping.

Melinda, however, was ready for a fight. "And what's that supposed to mean?" Come on, say it to my face.

Aimee sighed. "Do you not think you could have waited to drop that particular bombshell?" she said. "Given how upset Lou is about Tansy?"

Melinda shrugged.

"I don't even think you mean it," Aimee continued. "So why say it? And why tonight?"

"Why wouldn't I mean it?"

"You've never mentioned children before."

"That doesn't mean I'm not interested in having them," said Melinda. "Or are you trying to suggest I'm not cut out for it? That I'm too—oh, what's the word? Self-centered. Too self-absorbed. Not *cuddly* enough."

Aimee flushed, her face and chest glowing.

"That was the nastiest shit anyone has ever said about me," said Melinda.

"I didn't really mean it," Aimee said desperately. "I'm still a bit drunk."

"Oh, I think you did," said Melinda. "I think you've probably thought it for a long time."

"I'm sorry," whispered Aimee.

She hated confrontation, Melinda knew. Couldn't stand arguments, especially if she was in the wrong. But Melinda didn't want to let her off the hook by telling her it was all okay. Because Aimee got to go home and cry to her nice husband in her cozy farmhouse, with a whole family to hug her and beg her not to get upset. While Melinda would be here all alone in her self-made penthouse with just her high-definition TV for company.

"I'm not really thinking straight at the moment," Aimee said. She was pulling at the little ringlets at the base of her hairline, a nervous tick Melinda knew well. "This accident, it's left me feeling a bit unsettled. I can't focus on anything else, not properly." She stared at Melinda, pleadingly. "You know how my head can get . . . distracted."

Melinda did. But she was also a bit sick of how much time they all spent not upsetting Aimee, because of her head. No one ever worried about not upsetting Melinda.

"There's going to be an inquiry," said Aimee, who certainly did seem distracted, now the subject of the plane crash was in the room. "I read it in the paper. They're going to look into what might have caused it, search for clues—"

"Aimee, they have an inquiry when the bloody town loos get blocked." Melinda's headache was back; she just wanted to be in bed now.

"I know." Aimee was clearly debating whether to continue. "But—"

"Aimee. Don't go there."

"But they're asking for witnesses." Aimee spoke quickly, as

though it wouldn't count if she said it fast enough. "For any-one who might have seen anything to report it. And we did, we saw a flash, and then what must have been the plane, in flames—"

"Aimee!" Melinda slapped her palms down on the kitchen counter. "That's enough. You're not a witness, you were half-pissed and on the other side of town. You're not going to report anything. To anyone."

"Even if—"

"*No one*. And that includes me." There was a harshness in Melinda's voice that surprised them both. "I mean it. I don't want to hear another word from you about this bloody acci-dent. The subject is closed."

Chapter 10

The interview room was surprisingly chilly, given the warm night. Concrete walls and floor by the smell of it, and the way sound was bouncing around. Pete's wheels squeaked with every turn. He had to stop himself from knocking the young policeman's hands off the top of his chair, from trying to take over. "You all right, sir?" the boy kept asking as he maneuvered Pete clumsily through the doorway. "You all right?"

"It's all good," Pete said through his teeth as the wheelchair bumped a piece of furniture, sending a firework of pain up his right side. "Don't worry about it." Because he couldn't even steer himself around the hospital, let alone beyond. He fought down a nauseous panic that he might be this way forever, navigating the world through sound and smell and the occasional hazy shadows that were his vision now. His arm would get better, obviously. A couple of weeks, the doctors reckoned. But would he see again? The doctors had loads of theories, about psychological stress and sensory loss, but Pete was still sitting in the dark.

Pete distracted himself by trying to guess which room he was in. He'd spent a fair bit of time at the station over the years. Kids skipping school, kids shoplifting, stuff getting vandalized. That unfortunate business with the Waltman boy. And then trouble with his own son, of course. Pete had clocked more than a few hours in the station's sterile waiting room, drinking lukewarm coffee from a Styrofoam cup and wondering where he'd gone wrong.

"Peter." The door to the room slid shut with an industrial rattle. "Good to see you again, mate. Although bloody sorry about the circumstances, obviously." A large hand squeezed his good shoulder. "How's Lincoln doing?"

Pete shrugged into the senior constable's palm. "Still unconscious," he said. "They reckon he just needs time, but . . ." Pete didn't feel he was getting the full story there either.

"Well, best listen to them." The hand lifted, a lightening that left his shoulder feeling strangely vulnerable. There was a teeth-edge squeal as the chair across from him was pulled out, a sigh of air as something heavy settled into it. Arthur had been a good two hundred and twenty pounds the last time Pete had seen him. Maybe more.

"Sorry to have to bring you all the way down here." A pen clicked. "But we need to make sure all the statements are recorded properly, so the ATSB doesn't have a fit when they take over."

"They're not here yet?" The Australian Transport Safety Bureau would have people in Melbourne, surely.

Arthur sighed. "You weren't the only New Year's crash,

believe it or not. Helicopter went down on the Mornington Peninsula early hours next day." A few more quick pen clicks. "Three American tourists, including a tennis player everyone else seems to have heard of. Pilot. No survivors. So you're not top priority, unfortunately. But for good reason."

"Bloody hell."

The door slid open again. "Sir?" The young policeman. "Anything else you need in here?"

"Coffee'd be good." A little rattle: the pen being placed down on the desk. "Peter?"

"I was thinking more about helping with the interview, actually."

"Don't be touchy, Simon." The chair creaked. "Two coffees. And a plate of biscuits, if we've got any."

The door rattled shut without comment.

"I'm going to record this, if that's okay. Procedure says you have to be able to read to sign a statement, so——"

"Of course."

There was a fumble and a click. Arthur cleared his throat, a phlegmy rumble. Did he still smoke? Probably. Heart attack on legs, Julia had called him. Fabric whispered against wood as the policeman leaned over the table; Pete could feel the energy in the air push toward him.

"Right. This recording's being made at the Hensley Police Station, Victoria. It's, ahhhhh, just after seven P.M., Friday the third of January. Leading Senior Constable Arthur Mac-Kenzie, here with——"

"Peter Kasprowicz, of 16 Gosfield Pass, Meadowcroft 3452."

The chair creaked again. "We don't need to be too formal. You're not suspected of anything. We just need to get the facts down, while they're relatively fresh. And this way I can pass the recording to young Simon here to transcribe, rather than writing it up myself."

There was a grunt as a cup was placed on the desk in front of Pete. "Thanks," he said, discovering something that felt like a Chocolate Wheaten on the side.

"Where's mine?" said Arthur.

"None left."

A shuffling, a rearranging of heavy bloke. "So let's run through the basics. What time did you guys go up?"

Pete sipped at the blessedly hot coffee as he went over the details. Letting themselves into the aero club just after sunset, the slow meander down the river. Yes, they'd drawn up a flight plan. No, they hadn't stuck to it exactly, but close enough.

"And you've got your license."

"Yes. I mean, I assume it burned up with the fuselage, my whole wallet did. But I'm qualified."

"And to fly at night?"

"I've got my full instrument rating, yes."

"Which means—"

"It means you're trained to fly using instruments, rather than sight." Pete could almost feel the wince across the table. "For nighttime, bad weather, that kind of thing."

"I see." Arthur paused. "I've got to ask. Why did you go up that late anyway?"

"It was a treat," said Pete. "A promise." Lincoln had been

pestering for months. If your marks are good enough, Pete had said. Knowing they always were.

"A promise?"

"It was his birthday last week. I said I'd take him up at night."

"But with the fireworks—"

"That was the whole point." Lincoln had seen a YouTube video of a pilot flying over San Francisco Bay on the Fourth of July. The man had set the video to opera, fireworks from dozens of individual displays blooming below him like electric flowers as the music soared. Ours probably won't be that impressive, Pete had warned, but they'd been almost serenaded by tiny pockets of bursting light from vineyards holding their own celebrations. And then the big display, the town fireworks, early for the kids. One of the last things he'd seen, period.

"Not dangerous?"

"Not really. Fireworks go off around eight hundred feet, one thousand tops. We were well above that. And you're not that close either. It's like watching something on telly, rather than being among it."

"Ah."

"It's beautiful," said Pete. It had been, all the tiny colored stars exploding, raining down on the river, straight into their own reflections. Lincoln had laughed and laughed, gurgling slightly like he used to when he was a toddler. Pure joy.

"And you didn't have any worries about the plane."

Pete shook his head. "Smithy keeps her in good nick. Always has."

"He's getting on, though."

"He's solid. I'd trust him with my life."

Arthur sucked in air through his teeth, or maybe it was coffee. Pete nibbled at the edge of his biscuit.

"So what happened?"

Pete shrugged. "I have no idea," he said. Just as he had to the doctors, his sister, Simon the statement-taking coffeemaker. "I can remember the fireworks, and thinking it was probably time to head back, then nothing. I don't even remember making the turn."

"Right."

"They say it might come back. Like my sight. But at the moment—nada."

"You didn't get distracted? By the bangs?"

"I've been up at night dozens of times. And you can barely hear the fireworks. They're little bursts of light, that's all."

"Something wrong with the engine? Was it making any noise?"

"I don't know."

"Did you stall?"

"I don't know."

Hot coffee breath as the policeman leaned forward. "You don't have to worry about liability. Your license means you're insured, regardless of fault." A pause. "Maybe you got disoriented. Confused."

"Arthur, I honestly don't remember." Pete felt for the rest of his biscuit. "I wish I did."

"Peter." There was a rattle, cup on saucer. A scrape as the

crockery was pushed across the table. "Mate. There was alcohol in your system. The ATSB is going to want to know about that."

"I'd had a beer. After lunch."

"What time?"

He'd thought about this. "Three, three thirty? I'd just finished mowing the lawn."

"Just the one?"

"Two maybe. But I don't think I finished the second."

"Funny it still showed up seven hours later."

Pete shrugged.

"Any chance you might have had another later on? New Year's, after all. Maybe with dinner, with a friend—"

There was a scuffle in the hallway, a muffled argument, and a thud on the wall.

"Hang on." Arthur pushed his chair back, but the door rattled open, banging on its rails, before he could get up. Quick steps, heavy breathing. The air became static with energy.

"Stop talking, right now." There was a foreign twang to the voice, slightly American, but the same indignant tone as ever. "You can't do this. You can't question him without a lawyer. Pete, don't say anything."

"Sorry, sir." Simon. "I tried—"

"It's okay, Cameron." Pete twisted toward the voice. "He's not really questioning me. It's just an informal chat."

"Nothing's informal with this lot. Turn that damn thing off, he's not telling you— Bloody hell!"

Pete touched his face self-consciously, waiting for his son to move toward him. But Cameron stayed on the far side of the room. Still not forgiven then. So why even come?

"Cameron." Arthur stayed seated as well. "Been a while."

"Constable."

"Keeping out of mischief?"

"Always."

Pete flushed at the sarcasm, the lack of respect.

"Glad to hear it."

"Don't worry, Constable, I'm not back to bother you." Singsong. "But if you're done with your 'informal chat,' I'm going to take my wheelchair-bound stepfather here back to the hospital. Where, as I think you know, my little brother is lying in a bloody coma."

"Don't get your panties in a bunch, Cameron. We're only trying to find out what happened."

"I don't think now's the time, do you? God, don't you bastards have any sense of decency?"

"Cameron!" said Pete. "Arthur, I'm sorry."

"Don't you apologize." There was a creak as the policeman got heavily to his feet. "Bad kids happen to good parents all the time. See it every day."

Chapter 11

Lou lay staring at the cracks in the ceiling and tried to ignore the growing realization that Melinda was probably right.

Not about everything. She was way out of line suggesting Lou had done anything wrong in the way she'd raised Tansy. Lou bunched bobbled sheets in angry fists. She'd made every sacrifice asked of her, including some she was still too ashamed to tell anyone. Nor was Lou buying the theory that Tansy had somehow been destined to get pregnant, just because Lou had. Tansy had grown up with condoms in the bathroom drawer, offers to put her on the pill when she needed it. Lou had done everything right there as well.

And yet here she was listening for clues—a toilet flush, a boiling kettle—to figure out whether her daughter had even come home last night.

Lou kicked at the bottom of the sheet, wriggling her feet free into the sticky warmth of her parents' bedroom. Maybe she should have spoken to Tansy more about her own pregnancy, how much it had turned her life upside down. How bloody hard it was. Maybe she should have been a little more honest about the facts of her daughter's conception. Lou hadn't wanted Tansy to feel guilty, or that she was a burden. But maybe it would have made Tansy more responsible. Less . . . pregnant.

Regardless, it didn't mean anyone got to criticize. Especially not Melinda, with her plush apartment, free from tantrum-throwing teenagers and unreliable plumbing. Lou stopped worrying about her own failings and turned to the more comfortable business of resenting her friends. Melinda, who was spending the weekend in a five-star hotel, surrounded by adoring groupies. Melinda of all people, who knew what it meant to work your arse off. Lou had thought Melinda understood; clearly not.

And Aimee didn't get to look at her smugly either. Aimee, who'd moved straight from her parents' house to her husband's vineyard, who was able to sit around writing bloody *poetry* all day because she'd never had to worry about how she was going to pay the rent. No, neither of them got to judge.

But Melinda was also, annoyingly, on to something. Because Lou and Tansy *were* stuck in a cycle, of bad behavior and pointless punishments. Lou tried to be strict; Tansy resented her. Lou tried to be understanding; Tansy took the piss. Lou tried to give her daughter space to make her own mistakes, and look where they were now. Lou smacked her pillow in frustration. Worst of all, she didn't know how to make it stop.

Lou glared up at the flaking plaster, the same cracks her parents would have stared at. This whole bloody house was a cycle. At least she wasn't lying in their actual bed. That had been the one change she'd made when she moved back in. The thought of sleeping on their ancient mattress, imprinted with pious late-night tossing and turning over Lou's own bad behavior, was a bridge too far, even on her budget. Lou had splurged on an IKEA special: marked down, due to shop-floor wear and tear, but at least it was new.

The rest of the room though was still exactly the same. Shiny shantung curtains, complete with pelmets and tie-backs. Spindly bedside tables, with thin gold handles that bit your palms. Textured wallpaper. Louvered wardrobes. A brown-tipped sheepskin rug at the foot of the bed that Lou had always thought looked like a run-over dog. Lou had just left it all, and so the entire house looked as though it had been pickled in 1978, down to the petrol station calendar hanging in the toilet.

God, she hated it. Lou felt her neck muscles tighten every time she walked in the front door. And yet, inheriting this house had been one of the best things that had happened to her. The whole town had given her the silent treatment after the accident, aware that no peace had been made before poor Bev and Ken passed away. And for her to still take the house with all that bad blood, move in before they were even cold in the ground? Clearly she had no shame. That month had seemed never-ending. Lou had gone to the funeral but not spoken, sat dry-eyed at the front ignoring the whispers behind her. Melinda and Aimee stuck loyally close, popping round every five minutes in case Lou needed to share regrets about things not said. But Lou had no regrets. The Cold War had been her parents' fault, and if they were too stupid to change their will, too bad. It had gotten her and Tans out of their nasty rental, put a much-needed two hundred and fifty dollars back in her bank account every two weeks. She'd thank them, but even dead, they weren't on speaking terms.

Lou shrugged her way out of bed, pulled her T-shirt down over her knickers. Tansy's room was empty; no real surprise. Lou was almost beyond caring. Almost. She shuffled toward the kitchen, with its fugly orange tiles and brown linoleum. What had happened in the seventies, to make people think clashing earth tones were a good idea? She placed the kitchen on a mental list of renovations that she'd never have the spare cash to tick off. *We'll get to it right after we install the home cinema, ha-ha.* She flicked the kettle on and fumbled in the bread bin for a loaf that wasn't there. Just two ratty crusts. Typical. Everyone else got the soft and bouncy middle slices of life; Lou seemed destined to the hard edges.

Her phone beeped with an incoming message, but Lou didn't bother reaching over to read it. Didn't have to; she knew who it would be from and what it would say. Aimee, trying to smooth over Melinda's comments. Making sure they were all still friends. There would be one from Melinda herself in about an hour, not apologizing as such, but making an oblique reference to late nights and high emotions. Maybe suggesting a trip to the city, where she'd try to buy Lou something expensive that Lou would refuse. And then they'd all go back to normal: loving and supporting and gently insulting each other, for another thirty years. They were stuck in a cycle too.

Lou took a gulp of instant and made a face. Predictable was fine, as long as the future you could foresee didn't make you want to stick your head in the oven. Although not this oven, the gas was dodgy. It'd cut out before Lou would come close to finishing herself off. She stirred the lumpy coffee with a finger, then dumped it in the sink. Melinda was going places; even Aimee, who never physically went places, had movement through her husband, her children, the vineyard. But Lou? Lou was circling round and round the plughole, a lukewarm cup of cheap granules and sour milk going slowly down the drain.

Lou rinsed out her cup—Royal Doulton with gold rims, the best china she was never allowed to use as a child and that she now shoved rebelliously in the dishwasher, not caring if it chipped. A face appeared at the mottled glass above the sink, then ducked away. Lou had the door open and was out on the steps before the figure could make it round the side of the house. "TANSY," she roared, not caring what the neighbors thought. "Get your arse in here."

Tansy slunk in, looking surprisingly fresh for someone who had stayed out all night.

"I was at Chloe's," she said preemptively, before Lou could start interrogating her. "Her parents were there. They dropped me off. You can phone and check."

Lou stared at her self-righteous mini-me. "It was my birthday," she said.

"I bought you a present. And a card."

"You disappeared, during my *birthday party*." Lou searched her daughter's face for any hint of remorse. "Do you have any idea how embarrassing that was?"

"I was there for most of it," Tansy reasoned. "And they're your friends anyway. You didn't need me hanging around."

"You didn't even say where you'd gone."

"I came back," said Tansy. "Later. And everyone had left. So technically, you bailed on me."

"I did *not*," said Lou. "I was at Melinda's. And you text if you go somewhere. Or you call. You ask permission to stay over. You know the rules." She banged her fist on the kitchen table. "For fuck's *sake*, Tansy."

"Don't swear at me!" shouted Tansy. "This is abuse. I should report you." She turned and ran out of the kitchen, short little legs pumping. Lou ran after her, their thumping feet making the watercolors lining the hallway jump and rattle. Lou caught the side of Tansy's bedroom door as she flung it open, and held on tight so her daughter couldn't slam it shut in her face.

"Bugger off," shouted Tansy, as she tugged on her side of the door. "Leave me alone."

Lou clung and pulled, but Tansy was stronger. "Tansy," she warned. "Let me in, or you're grounded."

"I'm already grounded," Tansy yelled, as she gave a final yank on the door, forcing it closed. Lou's fingers, still curled around the edge, were smashed against the doorjamb.

Holy. Fuck. Lou screamed as the door bounced back off her

flesh. The walls swung and Lou buckled, falling into a crouch over her wounded hand.

"Mum?" Tansy dropped down beside her. "Oh God. Mum. Are you okay? Show me."

Lou swallowed back vomit. Forget childbirth, this was pain. She rocked over her hand as the floor shifted, bright spots of light blinking and disappearing on the carpet.

"I'm sorry," Tansy whimpered, as Lou pushed past her and stumbled toward the bathroom. She shoved her fingers under the lukewarm trickle that counted for cold water in summer.

"Get some ice," she whispered. "Quickly."

The compress provided a few seconds of relief, but the burning was soon back. "Oh my God," Lou breathed, rocking back onto the toilet seat. There was no blood coming through the tea towel, thank goodness. She inhaled deeply until the pain lost its white heat, settling into an aching throb.

Tansy hovered, uncertain, in the doorway. "I'm sorry," she said again. "I didn't mean to."

"No," said Lou wearily. "You never do."

"It was an accident," mumbled Tansy. She took a step closer. "Do you think they're . . . broken?"

Lou peeled her hand painfully away from the towel-covered frozen veg. Her fingers were white, with ominous purple stripes, but they all wiggled when she forced herself to move them.

"Lucky," said Tansy.

"Yes, you are." Lou stalked past her daughter and into the bedroom, hand curled protectively against her chest. There was an Ace bandage somewhere, from when she'd done her ankle in at volleyball; that would probably work. She started rifling through her drawers with her good hand.

Tansy slunk in and perched nervously on the edge of the bed. Lou ignored her as she pawed through stretched-out bras, her six-pack Kmart knickers. An optimistic lace nightie. The bandage was right at the bottom, with no sign of its little metal fastener, but she could probably tape it.

"Let me help," pleaded Tansy, as Lou started winding the bandage around her hand, pulling it tight with her teeth. "I'll do a better job than you will."

Lou turned her back. "I don't really want your help," she said. "Why don't you just go out. That's all you ever do anyway."

There was a sniffle behind her. "I said I was sorry."

"Yeah, you're always sorry." Lou didn't bother turning around. "And then an hour later, you're a nightmare again. Honestly, I can't keep up with you. Yesterday you were really lovely, then you buggered off with no regard for me at all. And this morning, you're screaming like a three-year-old and slamming my hand in the door."

"I'm a teenager," Tansy said, pathetically. "I'm supposed to be hormonal."

Lou swung around. "You're a pregnant teenager," she said. "And you need to start behaving like a grown-up rather than a horrible little bitch."

Tansy gasped.

"Well, you do," said Lou. "You need to sort yourself out,

and fast. Because you've got some big decisions to make, and possibly a baby to raise, and right now you're not fit to do any of it."

Tansy took a step back.

"What, did you think we were never going to talk about it?" Lou tucked her sore hand against her stomach. "Just ignore the whole situation, until you were ready to pop?"

"You did," whispered Tansy.

"Shut up," said Lou.

"Why should I?" said Tansy, faux brave. "You can't get mad at me for getting pregnant. You did exactly the same thing. I'm as much of a screwup as you were."

Lou felt her good hand twitching as it raised itself to chest height.

"If you hit me, you're just as bad as your parents," said Tansy, nervously eyeing the door.

She had no idea. Lou saw floating black dots in front of her eyes, felt the back of her neck grow hot. She bunched her good hand into a fist and swung.

"WELCOME TO LOVEFEST!" The woman manning the pop-up coffee shop snapped to attention as Melinda approached. "What can I get you this morning?"

"Double espresso, please," said Melinda, glancing down at a flyer with her own face on it. "Actually—can you make it a triple? Is that even a thing?"

"It can be," said the barista, already working the grinder.

"Everything is possible, right?" She handed Melinda a cup of pure caffeine. "Here you go, Ms. Baker. And congratulations. It all looks really awesome."

It did all look really awesome. Melinda wandered slowly through the atrium of the Sydney hotel, admiring five months of planning made flesh. The welcome signs and goody bags, in LoveLocked's signature gold and white; the green juice and herbal tea stands, ready to refuel those, like Melinda, who'd come straight from the airport. Ideally, she'd have flown in last night, but she'd wanted to be there for Lou's birthday. Although that hadn't exactly gone to plan. Melinda took a sip of coffee. She'd send Lou a message later, smoothing things over. Maybe suggesting a spa day, just the two of them. Lou loved a massage. She'd text as soon as she was in her room.

Melinda continued through the hotel, rolling her carry-on past temporary manicure stations and blow-dry booths. She mentally added a haircut and color to the spa day; Lou would look so much better without those Hensley highlights. Although she'd have to be subtle about that. Being subtle was not Melinda's forte, she knew. Had she been too blunt with Lou last night? Probably. But it was just so *frustrating*, watching her carry on as though she had a giant red letter stuck to her chest. Lou's parents might have punished her for getting pregnant, but Lou was the one who kept making herself pay. Denying herself anything nice, refusing to move on, make a fresh start. And what the hell was she thinking, moving into their house? Melinda had strong feelings about that as well. Yes, it saved on rent, but she could have sold the damn place, bought somewhere truly her own. Rather than living in that mausoleum.

Melinda paused under a banner stretched across the entrance to the hotel ballroom. EVERYTHING IS POSSIBLE it declared—LoveLocked's unofficial slogan. The problem was that Lou didn't believe anything was possible when it came to her own life. Didn't want to, because that would mean making a change. And Lou, no matter what she said, didn't really want change. Melinda slugged back the rest of her mega-espresso. Lou didn't need her friends to give her a passport; she could leave any time she liked. She just chose not to.

"Good morning, Ms. Baker!"

"Welcome, Ms. Baker!"

Melinda waved and smiled at the Pilates instructors and personal stylists jostling for her attention. Lou hadn't even wanted to come to LoveFest, said it wasn't her type of thing. And Aimee had pleaded off last night, claiming a headache after their fight, and canceled her ticket. So Melinda was alone, at the biggest event of her year. Even her dad had bowed out. "Think I'll give it a miss, love. Couple'a hundred women selling jewelry to each other? Why don't you just tell me about it later."

Nearly a thousand, actually. Melinda sank into a gold sofa in what a little sign informed her was a "regrouping zone" and tried to get her head around the sheer size of the event taking shape in front of her. They'd had conferences before, but this was different. Nine hundred and sixty-three women were traveling from across Australia—across the Pacific, some of them—to hear how the IPO was going to affect them. Melinda wanted to spoil them, to make sure they realized how important they were. Hence the gelato carts, the free massages. And the changes to the business structure. She hadn't been sure about some of the new incentives, but Clint insisted they would reward those who'd been with LoveLocked from the beginning. "We're putting them at the top of the ladder," he'd said. "It's like promoting them, making them managers. Business owners, even."

Well, Melinda was going to make sure all her curators felt special this weekend. She took a macaron from a large display next to the sofa, a gold-and-white sign urging her to "treat herself" in LoveLocked's patented font. Classy. She smiled approvingly at the hostesses arranging welcome snacks, all wearing LoveLocked jewelry, but in an understated way. The design team had really managed to reflect the LoveLocked ethos, what Clint called "dynamic elegance." Women who were going places, but not shouting about it. Just gracefully moving on to bigger and better things.

Melinda debated a second macaron. She wouldn't normally, but there was something fizzing in her today. She felt the same sense of giddy anticipation she'd had when she first started the company—the certain knowledge that she was on the cusp of something life changing. Maybe it was better that her friends and father weren't here; they didn't really understand the scale of what was happening. And as for her mother! Melinda's mum had somehow managed to react to the news of her public offering with condescension and sympathy. "I'm just glad you're keeping yourself *occupied*," she'd said, with such a patronizing look on her face that Melinda had to turn the Skype camera off. "I felt so bad for you when things with the Verratti boy didn't work out. But there are other things in life than being married, aren't there, darling? You've managed to make a *different* kind of life for yourself, haven't you, sweetheart?"

Melinda crunched into a third macaron. There was no one she could really talk to about work anymore. It was a strange sort of loneliness. She found herself filtering what she said to friends, downplaying things, even to Lou and Aimee. Because you could hardly run around saying to people, "Hey, my company's about to raise millions. I'm going to have offices in London and New York, fly first class everywhere. And I feel slightly weird about it, so would you mind listening to me talk for a bit about the pressures of being extraordinarily fortunate?" Maybe there should be a support group: Success Anonymous.

"There you are!" Clint placed a document folder on the table in front of Melinda. "I've been looking everywhere for you. You need to sign these contracts before the delegates arrive."

Melinda swallowed a sigh. Clint was supposed to be her IPO advisor, but he'd started weighing in on all aspects of LoveLocked's business, from the sample sizes her curators received to what perfume Melinda wore at company events. "Investors are buying the whole package," he'd told her. "Everything needs to be classy as hell."

Except Clint himself, it seemed. Melinda wasn't sure why, but there was something slightly tasteless about him. He was well-groomed, but it all seemed a bit try-hard. The swished-back hair. The monogrammed shirt. The signet ring, which as far as Melinda knew, signified nothing.

She waved at a roaming hostess for another espresso and started signing. To be fair, Clint put in more hours than any of her other staff, more hours than anyone other than Melinda. He'd been hinting lately that he'd like to come on full-time, and she could see it made sense. He had a great track record. It was just that listening to him made her feel exhausted. Or maybe she was simply tired. In which case, having Clint as a second-in-command might take some of the strain off. Melinda squinted at him. He also made her want to wrap her company up in cotton wool and lock it in one of their display boxes. Although apparently that was natural. "No entrepreneur likes to hand their company over to investors," he'd told her. "Why would you? It's your baby."

"You ready to go?" he said now, bouncing on the balls of his feet. "Ready to wow them with the Melinda Magic?"

Actually, he was just bloody irritating. But he was good for LoveLocked, and Melinda could put her personal feelings aside if it meant a better deal for her company and her curators. She forced herself to smile. "Almost," she said. "Just one more coffee."

Clint dropped onto the sofa beside her. "Hey," he said, gently taking the pen out of her hand. "What's going on?"

"Bit knackered," she said. "I had to get the six A.M. flight. My alarm went off just after three."

"No, this isn't tiredness. I can tell. What's up?"

Irritating, but at least he cared. "It's nothing."

"It's not. What's happened?"

Melinda shrugged. "I managed to fall out with both Lou and Aimee last night."

"What did they do?" There was no love lost between Clint and her friends.

"Nothing," Melinda admitted. "It was me mostly. I told them I was thinking about adopting, and it just turned into this big fight."

"But that's great."

"What? No it's not. My timing was terrible. They both walked out, and even Aimee's pissed off."

"Ah, don't worry, they'll come round. They always do. But adopting—that's brilliant news. I'm so excited for you." Clint grabbed Melinda by the shoulders and kissed her—actually kissed her—on the mouth.

Melinda resisted the urge to wipe her face. "It's only an idea."

"But it's a really great one." Clint wore the same look he got when he was talking about a new distribution center, or a possible dual listing. "You're at the perfect age and stage to do this. Building a family, sharing your wealth. Giving a child who needs one a real chance. Are you thinking an Australian baby, or one from somewhere else? China, the Philippines? Or what about Cambodia? That would be ideal, given the factories."

"Look, I'm not at all sure about it. I'm just trying the idea on for size." Melinda wished she hadn't said anything.

"But it would be so good for you. Give you something beyond work."

"It would be good for the brand, you mean. Give me a softer
public image."

"Well, yes." Clint reddened beneath his fake tan. "I won't
lie, it would play really well with the press. But, Melinda," he
said, squeezing her hand, "I've been working with you for over
a year now. And you're not happy. Not really. You need some
love. You need a family. Adopting, raising a child—it'd make
you a whole person."

"I am a whole person, thank you very much."

"I just mean it's the only thing missing from your life. You've
got everything else. So why not go for the full package?" Clint
picked up his folder; women were starting to stream into the
conference hall. "Look, we'll talk about it later. Just promise
me you won't dismiss the idea."

"And you promise me that you won't mention it to anyone.
Especially not a journalist." Clint had a bad habit of sneaking
tidbits to the press. "Do you hear me? Not a word." But he was
gone, swallowed by the growing tide of LoveLocked curators
surging toward their idol.

AIMEE RIPPED A budding shoot from the ground and congratulated herself on taking action. Nick loved getting out among
the vines, preferred to do a lot of the physical work by hand.
For one thing, it allowed you to see what was going on with
the grapes; you could spot an infection, a plant that wasn't

thriving, that you might not notice otherwise. But mainly, he said, it was meditative. This was where he came to get his peace.

Moving down the row, Aimee could see what he meant. It had been years since she'd done this, but she already felt better just being outdoors. She snipped off another lateral so the tractor would be able to get through. Her old doctor used to tell her to *move* whenever she could feel her head closing in. Trouble was, that was also the hardest time to make yourself do anything. But today she had. Aimee snipped off another vine tip in celebration. Well done her.

Grasshoppers sprung out of the way as Aimee worked her way along the vines, the long grass rustling as they landed. She waved her shears in the air to dislodge spiders' webs, feeling slightly guilty as she did so. There was a pleasing repetitiveness to the work. January was all about maintenance: plucking and tucking, trimming and tidying. It was also a metaphor, she realized, as she reached over to snap off another sucker. You had to pull the new shoots out before they got established, like an obsessive thought. Stop them leaching energy from the rest of the vine. The universe was clearly trying to show her what she needed to do. Aimee tried not to put too much stock in signs—that way proper madness lay—but sometimes you had to take notice of the message that was right in front of you.

Because she'd scared herself last night, at Melinda's. The compulsive need to keep asking for reassurance, to keep going over and over the same details; that was old behavior. And she knew where it led. So here she was—rip, tug—making sure the thoughts didn't take root. Weeding her brain, so she didn't do anything stupid.

There were three gray kangaroos in the middle of the next row, lying in the shade of the leaves. Aimee moved slowly toward them, willing them not to scare and bounce off, but of course they did, staring at her reproachfully, as if to ask what she was doing in their vineyard. *My husband's vineyard*, Aimee wanted to tell them. *And I'm the one who convinced him not to fence you out, so be grateful.*

The day was starting to warm up; Aimee stopped to smear sunscreen on the back of her neck. Interesting how she still thought of it as Nick's vineyard, not theirs. Even though she did all the admin. She knew the others didn't think she really "worked," because she didn't deal with customers, didn't go with Nick to Melbourne or Sydney to sell their wine to restaurants and professional buyers. But she kept the accounts and the family and the house all up and running, and wasn't that just as important?

She came across him as she moved from the pinot into the shiraz. Collar up, hat down, the little pager that alerted him to bushfire and accidents clipped firmly to his shorts. The veins in Nick's forearms danced as he moved his hands over the vines.

"Hey," Aimee said, but softly, so as not to startle him while he was wielding clippers.

"Hello," said Nick, surprised but pleased. "What brings you out here?"

"Missed you," she said, popping a grape into her mouth. "And I was bored. Mostly bored."

"I thought you were going to Melinda's thing."

Aimee shrugged. "Didn't feel like it," she said. "Too many people. Too much noise."

"But I thought she wanted you there?"

Me, thought Aimee. *You're supposed to worry about what I want.* "She said she'd be too busy to hang out. I didn't think it was worth the ticket." Even though Melinda was paying. "I thought I could be more useful here."

He didn't press it, just tipped his hat back and surveyed the row. "We'll probably be able to get all this done by lunch then, if you're staying out."

"I'll take the left, you take the right?"

"Just remember to leave the foliage a bit thicker on your side." He gave her a quick peck. "Don't want too much sun on them. I reckon the shiraz has real potential this year."

Potential, thought Aimee, as they both worked their way down the row, Nick quickly leaving her behind. Aimee had had potential. Top marks, better than Melinda even, grades that had won her a scholarship to university. Uni hadn't suited her—too much pressure—but then she'd won an internship with a national newspaper, the only intern to be taken on without a degree. Although that hadn't quite worked out either. "It doesn't sit right with me," she'd explained to Nick. "Intruding into other people's lives." The university offered to take her back, make an exception as long as she repeated her first year—people were always making exceptions for Aimee, because of her *potential*—but by then she and Nick had other plans. "We'll build the vineyard up," he'd said. "Open a restaurant, create a proper label." Which wasn't exactly how things had turned out. The kids had arrived, so quickly, one after the other before Aimee was even out of her maternity clothes. And now she had her community obligations, her poetry. But that didn't mean she wasn't *working*—Aimee snipped off a blind bud with a little more force than necessary—or that the vineyard wasn't doing fine, just as it was. Not everyone needed to be a CEO. Not every business had to be a world leader. What was wrong with staying small? Why did everyone always want to rush on to the next stage?

At least Lou didn't. Aimee reached above her head, trimmed back a vine that was getting away with itself. Nick sometimes questioned why Lou was still part of their tight little threesome. "She's still the same as she was in high school," he'd say after a few drinks. "While you two have clearly moved on." But that's what Aimee appreciated about Lou. She wasn't obsessed with growth and goals. Aimee secretly admired Lou for not giving in to Melinda's efforts to change her—and for not trying to change Aimee either. There were no gentle suggestions that Aimee might like to look at a career now the children were older, no questions about what she was going to do next. And Lou would *never* suggest that Aimee had banged on too long about something. Aimee decimated a cobweb with one heavy swipe of her secateurs. Lou let her talk for as long as she needed. Lou was steady. Reliable. You knew where you were with Lou, and for that Aimee loved her.

SHE WOULD NOT hit her daughter. She would *not* hit her daughter. Lou unclenched her fist midswing and grabbed hold of her mother's silk curtains instead. She tugged and yanked until the entire right side of the heavy drapes came crashing to the ground.

Tansy stared at her, wide eyed. "What are you doing?"

Lou didn't answer. Instead, she grabbed the remaining curtain with her good hand and pulled, hooks popping out of casings like tiny firecrackers, until that too lay puddled at her feet. Another few rips and the prissy nets followed. Light flooded unfettered into the bedroom for the first time in decades. Lou let out a whoop. She should have done that *months* ago. She swept her arm across the glass top of her mother's dresser, and a flock of china sheep jumped from their doily fields to certain death.

"Mum?"

"Fucking *yes*!" Lou picked up a china shepherdess and lobbed her at the wall. The shepherdess fell to the floor with a crack, her separated head staring at Lou pityingly. "Fuck, I hate Lladró!"

"Mum, what's going on?"

Lou swung around, a crystal clock in her hand. "I am *breaking a cycle*," she declared, pitching the clock at a beveled mirror with a fierce underarm bowl. Glittering shards rained down on the carpet; not bad, for her left. "I am *shattering illusions*." She collapsed against the dresser, laughing at her own joke.

"I'm going to call Aimee," said Tansy, inching backward toward the door.

"Don't step in that," Lou said automatically. "You'll cut yourself." She turned around slowly, looking for something else to destroy. God, that bloody rug. Lou tried to pick the sheepskin up with one hand, but it was too unwieldy. "Oh come on, Tansy, don't be so boring. Help me throw this thing out the window."

Tansy shook her head. "You've gone mad."

"No I haven't," said Lou, wrestling with the window catch, rug tucked awkwardly under one arm. "I am having a *paradigm shift*." A Melinda phrase; she laughed again, slightly hysterically. "All this time, I've been trying to be different from my parents, while living their *same bloody life*." She rested against the cool glass. "You and I, Tansy, are in a self-perpetuating cycle, and I am going to damn well break us out of it." The window catch seemed to have been painted shut; Lou pulled back, then rammed her hip against it. "Help me get this open, will you?"

"If you throw that out on the grass it'll rot," said Tansy.

"So?"

"But it will be ruined."

"Good!" Lou stared at her daughter. "Come on, Tans. You hate this place as much as I do. Let's trash it."

Tansy took the sheepskin from her mother. "I don't think that's such a good idea."

"It's a bloody great idea. Get rid of all this old *shit*." Lou kicked at a flimsy bedside table; it toppled instantly. "All of it, gone. Just imagine!"

"I think you should stop."

"I don't." Lou kicked the table again, harder this time. Its front leg splintered. "I *won't*. It's all going. All of it."

"But what will we do for furniture?"

"Buy some. Steal some. Sit on the bloody floor, I don't know, I just want things to be *different*."

"But you can't chuck everything out the window. It'll look even worse."

She had a point. "We'll rent a dumpster then."

"You're serious."

"Deadly."

Tansy frowned. "Don't you have to order them in advance?"

"That would probably be the only perk of eight years working for the Hensley Council." Lou strode into the kitchen and grabbed her mobile. Tansy followed nervously, still hugging the dead-dog rug. "Tom? It's Lou. I need a dumpster. No, at my house. It's an emergency. Burst pipe. Yeah, exactly. Water everywhere. Oh, and I won't be finishing the accounts anytime soon. Place is in ruins. Can you let Rex know? Cheers, Tom." She flicked the phone onto silent. "Right then. Let's get to it."

Tansy didn't move, just clutched the rug to her chest like the old Barbie beach towel she used to cart everywhere. Lou put an arm around her daughter.

"C'mon, Tans," she said quietly. "Let's go crazy. It'll be fun. And God knows, you and I could use a fresh start."

Tansy considered the proposal. "Can we get rid of Granddad's birds?"

"Hell yes."

"Okay." She nodded slowly. "Where do we start?"

Lou looked around the kitchen, a celebration of Formica. "In here," she decided, dragging a rubbish bin into the center of the room. "Everything ugly, everything we hate, goes in the bin until the dumpster turns up." She grabbed a couple of black plastic bags and thrust them at Tansy. "Here you go, fill your boots."

"ARE YOU READY to hear from the woman behind it all? The woman who made LoveLocked possible?"

Backstage, Melinda winced. The warm-up act was trying desperately to whip the audience into a frenzy, but they were Australian, not American. They didn't do frenzies. "This is just embarrassing," she hissed at Clint.

"Shhh," he said. "They're loving it. Listen."

There was a faint whooping amid the polite applause. Melinda peeked out from behind the curtain; most of the ballroom was seated, but the front row, her top sellers, were on their feet and cheering obediently.

"Here." Clint poked her with something. "Take this with you."

It was a coffee mug. "Is it vodka?" She turned it round; BOSSBABE was printed on the other side, in gold letters. "Oh no, I don't do that sort of shit. You know that."

"But your curators do. In fact, one of them sent you this." He consulted his iPad. "Christie, from Adelaide."

Melinda shook her head, but kept hold of the mug.

"Five seconds," the stage manager whispered, as the warm-up act begged the audience to make some noise. "Three. Two. Melinda, you're on."

The curtains rose, and Melinda strode out onto the stage in a puff of smoke and glitter. Really? Just for a moment, she missed the days when they used to hold their annual meeting in Starbucks, free refills for all. Then she was hit by the pure adrenaline of the lights, the thumping Beyoncé, the women who were now standing and cheering, *jumping,* some of them—God bless millennials—and the intoxicating knowledge that she had built this. This was hers.

"Hello, LoveLocked!" she bellowed. "Welcome to Sydney!"

The room roared back, nine hundred and something women who loved her jewelry so much they had traveled from across the Pacific to hear what she had to say. Melinda kicked off her heels and walked to the edge of the stage, sat down on the side so she was as close to her people as possible. "I'm so stoked you could all make it," she told them, hugging a few of the more eager curators who bounced up from their seats. "All this way, from Perth, from Darwin, from Adelaide—Thank you, Christie!"—Melinda waved her mug—"from Auckland, from Wellington, from *Fiji*. And for those of you who live in Sydney, how lucky are you, right? Such a great city!" Wild applause. "I'm going to try to make sure I speak to every single one of you over the next two days so I can hear firsthand how LoveLocked is working in your life—good and bad. Especially the bad, because anything that's not working, I want to fix."

There was more applause. Clint had warned her not to

start with a negative, but Melinda knew her curators, and she knew what they wanted to hear. "Please," she continued, "if we haven't spoken before the conference ends, grab one of the organizing team, grab me, follow me into the bathroom, whatever. Because nothing, and I mean nothing, is more important to me than your opinion."

Someone rolled a bottle of water along the stage; Melinda grabbed it and topped up. "We've got loads to get through over the next forty-eight hours. There's going to be a lot of learning, and a lot of fun as well. Most important, I'm going to tell you how we're reshaping LoveLocked to help you make more money. Because we're changing, and it's for the better."

TEN THIRTY. AIMEE could feel a pleasant ache in her back muscles, a welcome weariness in her arms. Her mind was beginning to quiet as well, the way it always did when she did the things she was supposed to. "Are you looking after yourself properly?" Melinda had demanded, on her high horse in her designer kitchen. "Because you don't seem right." Aimee had taken umbrage at that. Because she was doing all the self-care stuff, exercising and meditating and checking in with her doctor. Okay, the exercise had become walking one fat Labrador, and the meditation had dwindled to mindfully stacking the dishwasher. And she'd ditched the medication, because it made her fat. But she was busy *not* doing the things that triggered her, and that was just as important.

Which included not dwelling on the past. "I think you need to take a look at yourself, Aimee, because this feels an awful lot like last time," Melinda had said. But that was exactly what Aimee didn't need. There was a drawer at the bottom of her filing cabinet that she never opened, which contained all the writing she'd done during that dreadful year. Aimee couldn't bring herself to throw it out, but she couldn't bear to read it either. Just kept it locked away so the kids wouldn't accidentally discover it.

Aimee continued to chop at the excess growth as she moved into the last row of shiraz. There was still a small buzzing in her head, the nagging thought that it might be a good idea to drive back out to the accident site and see for herself what was going on. Put her mind at rest that there wasn't some kind of federal manhunt taking place on the other side of the river. But no. Aimee put the idea firmly out of her head and forced herself to think of things to be grateful for instead.

It was an easy list to make. Aimee mentally scrolled through the usual suspects. She was grateful for her understanding husband, her lovely easy daughter. The fact Byron wasn't busy getting his heart broken by some careless lothario. Aimee genuinely didn't have an issue with her son's sexuality, but she did worry for him because of it. Australia had changed, but had it changed enough? She couldn't bear the thought of him being bullied, or beaten up, just for being who he was. Or being taken advantage of. Or catching something. Heaven forbid.

Nearly there. Aimee began snipping with gusto as she saw open sky at the end of the row. She was grateful for her friends, even if Melinda was impossible sometimes. Her pubes hadn't gone gray. The cat hadn't thrown up in weeks. None of her family was ill, Aimee included. No matter what Melinda bloody implied. She kept moving forward, snapping haphazardly, until her house came into view. Aimee dropped the secateurs on the grass. Now there was something she was truly grateful for.

Aimee liked to joke that she'd married Nick for his house. Well, his parents' house technically, but they'd already found a condo on the Gold Coast, had plans to take his dad's arthritis to a more hospitable climate. Aimee kicked her boots off and climbed up onto the porch. Nick's parents had moved within two months of the wedding, surprisingly eager to pass responsibility for the vineyard and its beautiful, impractical homestead on to the next generation. And Aimee had become the happy mistress of an early Victorian gold rush villa, an ornate wooden cake of a house, with elegant chimneys and iron filigree, wide sash windows and a deep wraparound veranda. Aimee lay contentedly on her stomach, staring out over the vines to the green-gray hills and bright sky, the kind of view that belonged on a postcard. The sheep that were supposed to keep the grass down ignored her from the shade of a cedar a previous Verratti had planted. Some of their trees were more than a hundred years old.

"Just think," said Nick's voice behind her. "We could have a dozen tables out there, full of people paying to watch our sheep poo."

Aimee rolled over. "Buses full of Chinese tourists tearing up the grass," she said. "We wouldn't even need the sheep."

He dropped down beside her on the cool stone. "A cellar

door would open us up to a whole new segment of drinker," he said. "A generation looking to discover their own wines, rather than just buy what's in the shop."

"A new generation demanding to taste everything with no intention of buying," said Aimee, falling into their familiar banter. "Asking us to pop the cork on a seventy-five-dollar bottle of shiraz, then deciding nah, they'll take the cute miniature prosecco after all."

"Extra revenue streams," murmured Nick. "Food, coffee."

"People knocking on the door at all hours, expecting to be fed."

"An insight into new trends, what people really want." He slung an arm over her.

"A reputation for not being serious, just a tourist winery." She rolled into him.

"More money for university and holidays."

"More debt."

"Word of mouth, viral marketing."

"People putting nasty reviews on TripAdvisor because we didn't tell them the quiche wasn't gluten free."

"Expansion," he whispered, biting her earlobe.

"Exhaustion," she countered, opening her neck up to be nuzzled.

"Inevitable," he stated, pushing his hand beneath her tank top, where the fat rolls had accumulated a charming coating of damp sweat.

"Inconceivable," said Aimee, gently pushing the hand away. But smiling. They'd had this argument for years, and would have it for a dozen more. She sat up, pulling her top down over her flabby tummy. "Coke?" she asked. "I'm having one."

LOU STARTED WITH the cupboards above the sink—the hated Royal Doulton. Saucers, teacups, milk jugs, it all went in the bin. The sugar bowl still had actual sugar cubes in it, perfectly square. Just like her parents. "Think how much *room* we're going to have," she said. "God, I can't believe we didn't do this earlier."

Tansy was still standing in the middle of the kitchen, contemplating the rubbish bin. "Hang on," she said. "Let's not chuck it all away." She fished out a teacup. "This is still good."

"Don't care," said Lou.

"Nah, but we could sell it." Tansy closed her hands around a stack of gilded plates before Lou could let them fall. "Stick it online. Some of this stuff is probably worth loads."

Lou paused. "Tansy, you're brilliant." She set the plates down on the kitchen table, gave her daughter's cheek a peck that Tansy didn't duck away from. "Do you know how to do that?"

Tansy gave her a look. Lou chose not to wonder how many of her own possessions had already found their way into cyberspace.

"You stack and sort, I'll photograph and upload," said Tansy, ducking into the hallway. She came back with her laptop. "I've already got an eBay account."

Of course she did. "But can I still chuck the stuff that's really gross?" Lou had found the smashing cathartic.

Tansy smiled at her indulgently. "Yes, you may," she said. "But check with me first."

They worked surprisingly well as a team, through the rest of the morning and past lunch. Lou's damaged hand meant they were moving at roughly the same pace, as she slowly cleared cupboards and drawers, keeping only the very basics to tide them over. A couple of knives and forks. A few of the less offensive plates. Next to Tansy, well-used kitchen gear piled up: CorningWare and Tupperware and Pyrex, dappled with the tide marks of a thousand shepherd's pies. "CorningWare is huge, Mum, you have no idea. People will give us thirty-five bucks a dish. Do we have the boxes?"

Of course they had the boxes. Her mother never threw anything away. Lou started to hum.

Cake stands, cruet sets, biscuit tins. Loaf pans, tablecloths, napkin rings. Laminate coasters, depicting a pastoral Britain none of them had ever visited. A heavy crystal decanter—"Mum, put it *down*"—and a set of sherry glasses so tiny Lou wondered how anyone in the house had ever gotten drunk. Tansy assessed it all with an auctioneer's eye, rescuing items that Lou had binned—"That's not junk, that's vintage"—and occasionally intervening to place bits and pieces back in drawers. "We still need to cook, Mum. We're getting rid of the memories, not starving ourselves out."

There was something almost decadent about throwing things away, after years of having to mend and make do. Even when Lou's old neighbors had left money at Christmas, on her birthday, a fifty-dollar note tucked inside an anonymous card, she'd never bought anything nice or new. She just taped the broken blender back together and put the money in her savings account.

The dumpster arrived as they started on the living room, the scene for three generations' worth of misunderstanding. Lou watched the giant container being backed into the driveway from behind heavy velvet curtains. She could have used one of those seventeen years ago. Or a couple of bin liners. Her parents hadn't left her so much as a plastic supermarket bag to cart her stuff away in. The driver set the dumpster down in the middle of the lawn, directed by Tansy. The same lawn that had once—briefly—housed everything she owned. *Déjà vu,* Lou thought, as she dragged the first black bag of kitchen rejects down the drive. Except now she had the keys, and it was their possessions she was getting rid of.

"Can we do the birds now?" asked Tansy, when they were back inside. She sat cross-legged on the floor, having convinced the truck driver to help them throw the olive velour sofa and both its matching armchairs in the dumpster. ("That couch is beyond recycling," Tansy had decreed, and even the truck driver had nodded.)

"Sorry?" said Lou, eyes drifting back to the lawn. At least all her parents' stuff was dry. She might turn the hose on it though, just to complete the circle.

"They've creeped me out since we got here," said Tansy. She tapped at her laptop, frowning. "Although I'm not sure you're allowed to sell taxidermy on eBay."

Lou eyed a green-winged duck that had been sentenced to twenty-five years in her father's trophy cabinet, no parole. "Did I ever tell you about the day I moved out?" she said. Although moved out was a euphemism.

"My bad, you can," said Tansy, frowning at the screen. "Although I don't really want to. The idea of taking money for dead stuff makes me feel kind of gross."

"We can give them to Gary at the pub," said Lou. "He likes that sort of thing." She wandered over to the liquor cabinet, fished out the ancient bottle of Cointreau that Tansy and her friends had overlooked. "I was just over five months' pregnant with you," she said, sloshing a decent measure into one of her father's whiskey glasses. "It was a Monday. First day back at school after the holidays."

Tansy eyed the glass. "They kicked you out," she said. "I know. You told me."

"They hadn't wanted me to go back to school," said Lou. "Because they didn't want anyone to know I was pregnant, and it was pretty obvious. But I insisted. Because I wanted my high school diploma"

"Right."

Lou held the amber liquid up to the light. "And when I came home that afternoon, I found everything I owned in a pile in the middle of the lawn."

Tansy stopped typing. "You never told me that."

"Everything. Every piece of clothing, every book, every CD. It must have taken them all day. Toiletries, shoes. They'd even been up in the roof space and fished out my old toys."

"So what did you do? Did Mel and Aimee come and pick you up?"

"Melinda was already off at university," said Lou, bristling slightly at the suggestion that her friends had always had to rescue her. "And Aimee was in her senior year, like me. Neither of us had our own cars." She took a comforting sip of Cointreau. "I called a taxi," she continued. "From the neighbors' house; Mum and Dad wouldn't even let me in to use the phone." She laughed, sort of. "And while I was waiting, it started to rain."

"All over everything."

"All over everything," Lou agreed. "And not a little rain either. It absolutely pissed down. And the taxi driver came, but instead of helping, he sat in the car with the meter running while I tried to stuff my things into the backseat." Lou took another drink. "My parents just stood in the window, right there, watching."

"Mum, that's awful."

"I managed about four armfuls of clothes and then gave up. He wouldn't even open the trunk."

"Who was the taxi driver? Not old Albert."

"Not Albert. It doesn't matter, the man's dead now. Lung cancer, six months later."

"Good."

"Well. Anyway, I had to leave most of it. Childhood stuff mainly, silly things, like this Cabbage Patch doll I'd absolutely adored growing up. Jean Wilma. I was going to give her to you, if you were a girl."

Tansy's eyes were sad. "And then what? Where did you go?"

Lou took a swallow of Cointreau. "I didn't want to bother anyone. So I took the taxi to the Commercial Hotel—where Melinda lives now, ironically—and asked for their cheapest room, except I didn't have enough money to pay for it." Another swallow, bigger. "And the owner suggested I could give him a blow job instead. Since I was obviously a pregnant little tart." A proper slug, this time. "And I did, because I didn't know what else to do. And then in the morning I skipped school and walked back over with a big suitcase that the hotel owner's wife had given me to get the rest of my things. Except there was nothing there. It had all gone. They'd gotten rid of it, every last trace of me." Lou drained the rest of the Cointreau and dropped the glass on the floor. "Right then. Shall we rip these curtains down? I've always hated them."

Chapter 12

"This won't take too long, Peter. I've already listened to your interview, so I've heard the basics. I just need to get a few more details from you, that's all."

ATSB, the man had said; a tired-sounding man, voice weary with decades of documenting death and stupidity and sheer bloody fate. They sat in a drowsy sunny spot in the hospital dayroom, a quiet corner away from worried parents and oblivious children.

"Sorry it's taken so long to get over here. We've got quite a bit on our plate at the moment, I'm sure you understand."

Pete nodded, perfectly happy not to be the bureau's top priority. The Peninsula crash was still all over the news; the tennis player had been a favorite for this year's Australian Open. At least with Pete's accident everyone was breathing, and no one was newsworthy.

"Here are my details." The man placed a stiff rectangle in Pete's hand. He turned it over uselessly. "God, sorry. It says—

well, I'm Steve." The man sounded embarrassed. "Look, can I get you a water or anything?"

Pete waved away both the offer and the faux pas.

"So how's your son?"

Getting there. That's what they told him, every time he asked. *He's getting there.* Although Pete hadn't been able to move in with Lincoln, in the end. His son was still too delicate, too vulnerable to infection. Lincoln's arms felt skeletal when Pete touched them, despite the calories in the IV.

"There's been a bit of movement," Pete told the investigator. "His eyelids twitch, and I swear there's pressure sometimes, when you hold his hand. That's all good, apparently."

"It's very good," Steve said, and he sounded like a man who'd know. "And you? How are you doing?"

Well, that depended on what time of day you asked. Mornings were terrible, his first thought on waking a mind-zapping panic that Lincoln might have taken a turn for the worse in the night. The terror dissipated once he sat with his son, replaced by a numb sadness as he jabbered on about nothing into the white noise of intensive care, and got nothing in return. Post-lunch, the sadness was eclipsed by frustration, as he began the day's occupational therapy with an inane task such as unlocking a door or tying his shoelaces, actions he'd performed for decades without thought, but that now took on the ridiculousness of a blindfolded party game. Pain kicked in shortly after, when they took him to physical therapy, prodded and pushed and forced him to move in ways he'd rather not. Around four he was wheeled back in with Lincoln, and he finally felt something like relief, that they'd both made it through another day. But the background music to it all, the sound track that never stopped, was guilt. "I'm fine," he said.

"You sure?" Steve's voice was kind. "It must be tough."

"It's not about me."

"No. Right." There was the click of a case being opened, a rustling of papers. "Well, let's get started. Do you want to run me through that night again, just so I can make sure I've got it clear?"

Pete fought off the narcoleptic pull of the sun through the dayroom window as he repeated the details he'd given Arthur. The promise to Lincoln, the winding route down the river. Yes, conditions had been fine. No, there hadn't been any issues with the plane. No, the engine hadn't seized, at least not that he could remember. He didn't know why they'd gone into a dive. He didn't even remember the dive. He didn't remember any of it.

"And there's been no further recollection?"

"None."

"You know I'm not here to assign blame, don't you? The ATSB doesn't look for fault, just for cause. So we can prevent similar accidents in the future."

"I'm not trying to duck responsibility. Trust me, I feel nothing but responsible. My son's in a coma, and I'm the one . . ." Pete's voice failed. Steve placed a glass of lukewarm water in his hand. "It's my fault, because I took us up. I was in control. But I don't remember the accident at all."

"What's the last thing you *do* remember?"

Pete tried to recall what he'd told the police. "The town fireworks. We'd seen a few private displays, but the main event was scheduled for ten. Late enough that it's properly dark, but still early enough for the kids. It was a big deal. It's been a few years since we've had a display." December had been wet enough that the council had decreed it safe. Pete had lain in the cockpit of his crashed plane and thanked God that at least the trees weren't going to go up in flames around them.

"And then?"

"Nothing. We must have turned, but . . . I dunno."

"And you don't reckon you were distracted. By the fireworks."

Pete thought of that one light, the glowing star that kept rising and didn't explode. "No, I was expecting them. They were the reason we were there."

Steve's pen tapped against what sounded like taut fabric. A trouser leg maybe, or the sofa arm.

"How long have you been flying, Peter?"

"Twenty-six years." Since he was Lincoln's age. But they'd know that.

"Ever been involved in another accident, even as a passenger?"

"Never."

"Ever had to make a distress call, ask for support with landing, or make an unscheduled landing?"

"Never."

"Ever run low on fuel, or miscalculated your fuel, or accidentally used the wrong tank?"

"Never."

"Ever had an incident when one of the club planes wasn't flight worthy, or refused to take one up?"

"Absolutely not."

"Ever heard any talk that maintenance was being skimped on at the aero club? Any gossip about the finances?"

"Nothing."

"Ever been refused a plane, or told you weren't in a fit state to fly?"

Pete paused. "I wasn't drunk."

"There was alcohol in your system."

"From the afternoon. Two beers. A little later than I should have, but . . . that's all."

Steve's pen tapped again. "I'm going to need your laptop," he said finally. "And your mobile phone, plus any paper diary or calendar you might keep. So we can get an accurate picture of your movements on the day."

"Sure," said Pete, brain frantically scanning. Had they written anything down? But there was no point in delaying; it wasn't as though he could go through his emails and check. "I'll get Cameron to pop over and pick them up."

"This is your elder son? He's not staying with you?"

Hell would freeze over. "Stepson, technically." Although Pete had never differentiated. "He's in a hotel."

Steve didn't push it. "And Lincoln's laptop, if he has one. And his phone."

Pete kept his face neutral. "Of course."

"Thanks, Peter. And you never know. We might find some detail that jogs your memory."

Pete forced himself to smile. "I hope so."

Chapter 13

Just a quick drive-by, Aimee promised herself. She wouldn't even stop. And if she did stop, she wouldn't get out of the car. But she definitely wouldn't speak to anyone. Aimee pulled over onto the grass alongside Maddocks Clearing. The plane was still there, a burnt-out sarcophagus rebuking her from its resting place at the foot of the ranges. Face your fears, her therapist used to tell her. Exposure therapy: if you continually place yourself in the path of what scares you, the panic will fade. Of course, the same woman had told her she had to resist the urge to keep checking, checking, checking whenever she was worried about something. That it just fed the obsession. Aimee conveniently blanked that piece of advice as she slid out of the driver's seat.

Because she needed to know. That was all. Whether they'd found anything, or if it really was just an unfortunate accident like Melinda said. If she knew, then she could respond. Either get on with her life, or . . . or . . . actually, Aimee hadn't quite decided what she'd do if it turned out they were responsible.

She had two children; she couldn't go to jail. But if she knew, then at least she'd feel more in control of the situation. Less in limbo. Her head didn't like limbo.

Aimee fingered the police tape stretched across the entrance to the clearing, sealing it off as though it was some kind of crime scene. Would it be seen as a crime, what they'd done? It wasn't as though they'd intentionally set out to hurt anyone. But maybe there were rules about where you could let those lanterns off. There were with drones, she knew, particularly around airports. Although they weren't even close to the local airfield. But maybe you were supposed to inform people, like with fireworks. Aimee's head swam with possibilities. She ducked under the tape, heart pounding. Took a few nervous steps into the clearing. Just so she could *see*.

"Help you?"

The investigator was older, a burly man she didn't recognize. Not from around here then.

"I'm only looking," she said defensively.

"You shouldn't really be out here."

"I just wanted to know . . ." What did she want to know? "Yes?"

"If you need any help. Any volunteers." Yes. *Yes.* "I could search for clues, or keep the crowds back, or . . ."

He looked pointedly up and down the deserted road. "I think we've got it covered."

"But what about food? I bake. I could bring lunches, snacks. Muffins. I make great muffins."

He shook his head. "That's very kind. But we're all good here."

There was a man crawling across the ground in front of the plane, raking the grass with his fingers. Aimee stared, frozen, waiting for him to cry out, to stand up brandishing a tattered piece of lantern or a bent wire frame. Although they'd never know who let it off, would they? And a piece of lantern didn't necessarily prove anything. Not unless it was stuck in an engine or wrapped around a propeller or something. She'd watched enough television to know that. A piece of lantern wouldn't hold up in court. If this kind of thing even went to court. Although what if there were witnesses? Someone might have seen the lanterns, watched them float away from Melinda's balcony. It was a very distinctive balcony; the whole town knew who lived in the old hotel. And half of them hated her.

"Anything else?"

"What?"

"Was there anything else?"

"Oh. No. Not at all."

He smiled patiently, waiting for her to leave.

"Good luck," Aimee said pathetically. She backed away, tripping slightly over a patch of long grass.

"You okay there?" the investigator asked.

"Fine. I'm fine. I'm sorry." And she turned and ran back to her car, aware of his eyes on her the whole way.

MELINDA HAD BEEN speaking for nearly two hours, but she barely noticed. There was so much energy in the room; with each round of applause, she felt herself getting higher. She took her time as she talked through the new collection, the key pieces that had already been featured in magazines and newspaper editorials, guaranteeing demand. It was amazing how something so simple—charms, effectively, lockets of all shapes and sizes that could house photographs, love notes, locks of hair (drugs too, more than one commentator had pointed out, and Melinda had heard stories, but chose not to listen)—could become so coveted just by slapping the words "limited edition" on them. But they did. Women swapped lockets on Facebook, had bidding wars on eBay for discontinued pieces. And it was good quality, Melinda made sure of that. Each piece was hand-finished in-house, and Melinda did random inspections of stock.

It was this attention to detail that had won her a dedicated following among her curators and their customers. People felt comfortable giving a LoveLocked necklace for a birthday or christening, because they knew it would last a lifetime. And the curators felt comfortable ordering stock, because they knew it would sell, and in the rare instance that it didn't, LoveLocked had a no-questions-asked return policy. It impacted the bottom line, but Melinda didn't care. She wanted a company she could be proud of.

She looked out over the audience as her top curators started coming onstage to share their sales techniques. Gave a quick scan for her dad in case he'd had a change of heart, bought a cheap ticket, and flown in to surprise her. Melinda squinted toward the seats at the back. Or maybe Aimee had come after all, keen to make up. Or even Lou. Although that was unlikely; Melinda had sent a text before the conference started, and hadn't heard back.

It didn't matter. Up here, Melinda didn't need anyone else to make her feel good. It was amazing, the buzz she got from simply *achieving*. Each time she strode into a meeting or gave a presentation, Melinda could feel herself becoming someone else, someone more like her true self. The words she said felt more genuine; her interest didn't need to be faked. Unlike at coffee with the local women, or the monthly Hensley Home- owners Association meetings. Melinda knew she didn't belong in town. Never had. But it was important to remember where you came from. Her dad had taught her that. Look at him, one of Victoria's top attorneys, and never tempted to abandon the town that needed him for lucrative city offers. "Bunch of wankers," he'd say in his Hensley drawl when Melinda spoke about meetings she'd had in Melbourne or Sydney. "Five min- utes in the big smoke and they think they're something spe- cial. I'd rather stay where people are real."

The house lights rose, the signal that Melinda was to start her financial presentation. She slid her shoes back on and walked to a lectern that had appeared in the middle of the stage. "I need my notes for this bit," she joked. "Don't want anyone to sue me if I get something wrong."

The atmosphere in the room changed as women took note- books out of handbags, slid on geek-chic spectacles. "The first thing I want to say is, don't worry," said Melinda. "All of these changes are designed to make it easier for you to make money. Quite simply, the better you do, the better we do."

Melinda started clicking through slides, explaining the new incentive schemes, the plan to increase rewards for those who sold the most. *Click*. The fact that they were also changing the way they set their targets, comparing curators to others within their region. "Nothing like a bit of healthy competition," Melinda said, grinning. *Click*. The social media training and product kits they'd created, all available at minimal cost. *Click*. The hefty discounts that would come with bigger orders. *Click, click.*

"Now, we know a lot of you have brought other curators into the company, whether friends and family or satisfied customers. In the past, we haven't rewarded you for that." Melinda was happy with the direct sales model, hadn't wanted to stray into anything that smacked of multilevel marketing. "Your main source of revenue is still and will always be sales. I don't want anyone to feel she has to sign up her neighbors in order to make money. But at the same time, if you're bringing in new curators, you're adding to our bottom line. So we're going to reward that." There was an excited whisper. *Good.* This was the area Melinda had been least certain about.

"That's retroactive by the way. You can claim for any introductions you've made in the whole lifetime of LoveLocked." A couple of women whooped. Melinda smiled and carried on.

"Finally, we're going to clamp down on discounting," she said. "We'll always give you your money back if you decide to leave LoveLocked, or if there are products you can't sell. That will never change, IPO or no IPO. You have my word." Another cheer, led by the loyal old guard at the front. "So there's no excuse to drop your prices. It only undercuts your fellow curators and devalues their stock. We're going to start enforcing the small print on that one. But it's going to be good for all of you. You don't need to earn pocket money by holding online jumble sales. You're better than that. We're better than that. Aren't we?"

The ballroom roared in agreement. Yes, they confirmed, with the odd high-five. Yes, they were.

CERAMIC CLOWNS. LACQUERED side tables. A freestanding velvet lamp with an actual fringe. By midafternoon, the dumpster was so full of junk that Tansy had decreed too ugly for eBay, they had to call the guy who'd delivered it to swap it for a new one.

("This stuff doesn't look very water damaged," he'd said, fingering a throw rug.

"The rot's on the inside," Lou had replied.)

"It almost feels like a normal house now," said Tansy, spinning around the half-empty living room. The dining table and chairs had been pushed up against the wall, awaiting their new owner; someone had bought them online in less than an hour. That was three hundred dollars, right there. Lou was going to be able to do the house up—well, kit it out with IKEA particleboard, at least—and it wasn't going to cost her a thing.

"I know, right?" Lou gently maneuvered a painting off the wall, careful not to put any pressure on her bad fingers. "I always found this place so claustrophobic growing up. I couldn't breathe."

Tansy took the painting from her. "That's kind of why I stay out."

"Really?" Lou tried not to feel hurt. "But I don't make you feel claustrophobic, surely?"

It hadn't just been the heavy curtains and dark wallpaper that had made her feel boxed in. It had been her parents' whole attitude, the constant judgment and questions. *Where were you, why would you, who was that?*

"It's just not very . . . comfortable," Tansy said, putting the painting in one of their "sell" piles. Horses galloping along a beach. Was there really a market for that kind of kitsch? Lou was truly out of touch.

"Comfortable?"

"At Zarah's and Chloe's you can slob out, lie on the sofa and eat toast. The furniture here just seems really . . . upright." She looked apologetic. "It's not really a hanging-out sort of house."

"So that's what you're up to, when you don't come home," said Lou. "Eating toast." Not wandering the streets with a bottle of Southern Comfort and a pack of Marlboro Lights.

"Usually," said Tansy. "Watching TV. Messing about online. You know."

Lou's parents hadn't owned a television. Lou had chosen not to buy one when they moved in, in the hope it might make Tansy more studious. But if that was all it took to keep her daughter in at night, she'd drive over to Meadowcroft right now and pick out the largest flat-screen she could find.

"Plus you're always so stressed out," said Tansy, peeling a price tag off the back of the picture. "So wound up."

"No I'm not!"

"You kind of are," said Tansy. "And it's fair enough. I know your job sucks." She bit her lip. "But it's just not very . . ."

"Comfortable?"

"Yeah. Sorry."

"S'all right." Lou wandered off down the hallway so Tansy couldn't see her face. She paused at an open door, collected herself. They hadn't attacked Tansy's bedroom yet, formerly the guest room, a mideighties nonsense of peach damask and iron bed frames. They hadn't touched Lou's old room either. Lou had given it a wide berth in the months since she'd moved back in. She peeked around the door now, breathing in the familiar scent of old wallpaper. Her mother had turned it into a craft room after Lou had gone, her sewing machine taking pride of place under the window where Lou's bed had once been. Plastic bins of scrapbooking materials lined the walls. Lou took the lid off one: stickers. Another held craft glue, another stamps and mini ink pads. Lou tried to picture her sensible mother gaily stamping multicolored frogs on fancy cards, and failed.

She opened the blinds; the room had a good view out onto the back garden and a rhododendron her dad had planted to celebrate Lou's birth. Got good light as well. They could turn this into a nursery, if they needed to. Lou swallowed back the thought. The wardrobe still sported a few faded Bon Jovi stickers on the inside walls. The closet had been a clash of civilizations once: the clothes her mother bought her on one side, the thrift shop bargains Lou insisted on wearing on the other. Crushed black velvet and Cure T-shirts versus pure wool knits and chambray skirts. God, the screaming matches over what she wore, her mother trying to dress her up for church and other functions well into high school, as though she was a child. "If you act like a child, then I'm going to treat you like one." While everyone else was in jeans and sweatshirts, their parents past caring what other people thought. None of Lou's clothes on either side remained. Instead, the cupboard looked like an old-fashioned haberdashery—buttons and wool and trimmings neatly stacked. Her mother had finally imposed control over Lou's wardrobe.

"Mum?"

"In here." Lou started pulling bags of fabric down from the wardrobe shelves. She caught her bad fingers under an old pattern book and winced. "Can you give me a hand? Last room, promise, then we'll sort out dinner."

Tansy sang to herself as she cleared, a hit Lou vaguely recognized, made famous by an underage singer who was all cleavage and feminism. Something about being the best you ever had, baby. Maybe she should have monitored what Tansy was listening to more closely. But pop music hadn't gotten Tansy pregnant. And controlling teenagers just made them rebel; Lou knew that firsthand.

"Do we chuck this stuff or sell it?" she asked. "Would anyone even want it? Some of this fabric is pretty dated."

"Donate it," said Tansy, after a pause. "Schools would use it. Kindergartens. I'll make a special pile, in the hall."

See, Lou thought. She hadn't screwed up that badly. Tansy was helping her mum. Thinking of others. But would this kinder, softer version of her daughter stick around, or would they be back to screaming and door slamming in the morning? Lou was almost afraid to hope.

"Hey, check this out." Tansy handed Lou a photo album, saccharine pink with a gingham frill. A familiar toddler stared suspiciously out at her from a padded fabric frame on the front.

Lou moved over to the window. The ring-bound album was a good forty pages, each carefully themed with sticker slogans and matching cutouts. *A day at the beach! Fun with cousins!* And marching across the colored pages was Lou: toddler Lou, sleeping Lou, first-day-of-kindergarten Lou, sandy Lou, candle-blowing Lou, up through primary and into high school. It finished with an awkward family photo, the type taken in a studio in front of a pull-down background: Lou scowling, her parents smiling proudly.

When had her mother even made this?

"It was in here." Tansy placed a cardboard box on the sewing table. Lou sucked her breath in as her daughter rifled through faded baby clothes, opened a balding velvet box to reveal the tiniest christening bracelet.

"Guess they didn't get rid of everything then," said Tansy. She pulled out a corn-haired doll with a plastic face. "And look. Jane whatsit."

She must have put the album together after Lou had gone.

Lou had never seen her mother scrapbooking; it was a post-daughter hobby. "Put the box back in the closet," she said.

"But—"

"I don't want to look at it just now. Too tired."

"Riiight." Tansy folded the cardboard flaps back in, but left Jean Wilma propped dejectedly up against the sewing machine. "You know, if they kept all your baby stuff, then they must have—"

"What say we go out and get something to eat," said Lou. "A reward for all our hard work." She marched out of the sewing room, grabbed her keys. "Come on. Last one in the car's a rotten egg."

WHY HAD SHE run? Why the hell had she run? Aimee walked back and forth across the living room, watched by a suspicious Oscar. Running would only make her look guilty. Make the investigator remember her. Why had she even spoken to him at all?

Think, Aimee, think. There must be something she could do to make her behavior seem more rational. Go back maybe, explain she was a friend of the family. That if she was acting a little odd, it was only because she was so upset. Or would that just make it worse? Give him more reason to remember her? Maybe she was overthinking. Maybe he'd forget she'd even been there. Maybe loads of people visited the site every day. The good folk of Hensley were a nosy lot. But if she didn't explain, and one of his superiors asked if anyone had been acting suspiciously, then—

"Aimee, what are you doing?"

Nick stuck his head through the open window, dirty arms resting on the sill.

"Just thinking." And thinking, and thinking, and thinking. "About Byron's birthday. Whether we should do something, or if he'll get all embarrassed if we make a fuss."

"But that's not till September." He frowned. "Are you all right?"

No. "Yes."

"Only you seem preoccupied. Like your head's somewhere else."

"I'm fine." She bent down and kissed him, hard and slow, to show how fine she was.

Nick grinned. "Should I come in? Wash some of this crap off? You could help."

"No," she said. "I need to do the books. You'll only distract me."

"Suit yourself." But he was smiling as he pulled his head back through the window.

Aimee narrowed her eyes at Oscar, who wasn't falling for any of it. Maybe she should start taking her medication again, just in case. But she didn't like the weight gain. Nick didn't either, even though he claimed it didn't bother him. That he liked her "cuddly." And sane. He especially liked her sane. Aimee collapsed on the sofa, provoking a warning hiss from Oscar. What she really needed was to talk to someone, but Nick would only worry and Lou wasn't picking up and Melinda was at her conference. Not that Melinda would listen anyway. Which was a shame; Melinda was the best at helping Aimee to see things clearly, at calming her right down. Aimee looked longingly at the liquor cabinet, remembered how calm she'd felt at Lou's picnic with a stomach full of champagne.

"We could buy him a car."

"What?"

Nick's disembodied head squinted at her. "Byron. For his sixteenth. We could buy him a car."

"Oh. Okay. Sure."

"Aimee, are you sure you're all right?"

"Of course. Everything's fine. Why wouldn't it be?"

"If we can't sell items we've bought at a bulk discount, can we still return them?"

Melinda swallowed a yawn. The question and answer session was entering its second hour. "Of course. There's always a refund on undamaged stock."

"Even if it's out of season?"

"Well, no, it has to be in season. That's always been the rule."

"But what if I order too much in order to get a discount and forget to return it in time?"

Christ on a bike. "It's up to you to manage your inventory. We don't encourage curators to buy stock they don't have orders for, or a realistic chance of selling at pop-up shows or other events." Melinda could see the shadowy forms of women sneaking out into the lobby, where there were—she knew—

cold-brew coffee and freshly made Nutella biscuits. Her stomach growled. "Is there anyone else?"

A plump woman, in the second row: "What happens if we don't hit our new targets? I've got two kids now, and I don't have the same amount of free time as I did last year."

Melinda smiled. "Nothing happens. You might not be eligible for discounts and other rewards, but you'll still get your normal commission. We're not going to punish you. The last thing I want for anyone who's juggling bath times and school runs is to have to worry about LoveLocked as well. I know what it's like to be overwhelmed. I want LoveLocked to relieve stress, not create it."

"How do you know what it's like?"

The voice came from the middle of the ballroom. Melinda squinted out into the haze beyond the footlights. "Sorry?"

"How do you know what it's like, to struggle? I mean, this is all a bit condescending, isn't it? You've been talking all day about women without qualifications, and women from tough backgrounds, and women struggling to pay the bills, and how you're the answer to all their problems. But you're an economics graduate, with a double degree from a good university and a wealthy family. You've never had to worry about money. How would you know what they need?"

There were low rumblings from Melinda's front-row fans.

"Don't be so bloody rude," one of them called out.

"That's out of line," said another. "Who do you think you are?"

"No, it's okay. Everyone gets to have an opinion." Melinda

turned to the control booth. "Can we have the lights up, please? So I can see?"

The room blinked into daylight. Standing in the middle was a familiar-looking journalist.

"Stacey," said Melinda, mentally digging up the woman's name. "Are you stalking me?"

"I live here," said Stacey, with a shrug. "And I'm not trying to be rude. I'm genuinely interested."

Genuinely trying to manufacture a headline. Melinda poured herself a glass of water as she collected her thoughts. The room was two-thirds empty; she could hear a low buzz in the lobby where the majority of her curators had already signed off for the afternoon.

"Okay," she said, deciding. "Okay. I'm going to tell you a story, about why I started LoveLocked. Why I *really* started it, not just because I'd been traveling and found this awesome jewelry, yada yada. Which is true, but it's not the reason I set up as a direct sales company, rather than simply stocking in stores. Which would have been easier and more profitable, by the way."

At the back of the room, Clint was making urgent "kill" signs across his throat. But she couldn't stop now. Melinda sipped at her water, wishing it was something stronger. "One of my best friends got pregnant while she was still at school," she said, feeling slightly treacherous, but Lou didn't read Stacey's paper. She'd never know. And Melinda wouldn't use her name, just in case. "She chose to have the baby. And almost immediately, her life fell apart. The bloke did a runner, her parents disowned her, and she failed her exams as a result of all the stress. Because she didn't have any qualifications, she couldn't get a decent job, but even if she'd been able to, there was no child care, and even if there had been child care, it would have canceled out anything she earned. It was a real catch-22. And I just got so angry." At Lou, as well as the situation. There were child care centers *and* better jobs in the city; why the hell didn't she leave?

"But it also got me thinking about what kind of job she *could* do, with a toddler, and what kind of company would need to exist to provide it. I was already planning to import the jewelry I'd found during my gap year. So I came up with a structure that could help her, and other mums like her. That would fit in around them, without any ridiculous money-up-front or minimum-order policies. She was my sounding board, as well as my first curator.

"And I've kept her in the front of my mind ever since. Obviously all sorts of women, and men, are curators now. We've got students, retirees, people with day jobs. But that's my litmus test, with any initiative. Would this have helped Lou—my friend, I mean. And if the answer is no, we don't do it."

Melinda let her eyes well up. "I wouldn't even have a company if it wasn't for her. She made me realize that I needed to think beyond myself, to create a business that actually helped women, not made money off the back of them. Her struggle might not have been mine, but I witnessed it, and it taught me the values that have made LoveLocked a success."

There was scattered but earnest applause from the women

who were left. Melinda congratulated herself on having dodged a bullet.

"It's still not the same as going through it yourself," Stacey persisted. "You don't really know what it's like to be a working mum, to not even have the time to take a shower on your own."

And something small inside Melinda snapped. "But I'm going to," she said. "If everything goes to plan."

Several women in the front row gasped; Melinda grinned at them. "No, I'm not pregnant. That's just too much dim sum." She ignored the warning bells going off in her head and smiled dangerously at Stacey. *Don't you dare try to make me look bad, suggest I'm out of touch because I don't have children.* "This is *not* for publication," she continued, "but I'm trying to adopt. So I will know what it's like to cope with a baby, on my own. Or at least I hope so."

THEY DECIDED ON McDonald's, Tansy's childhood treat. Lou's too; it was where her parents used to take her after church. For ten-year-old Lou, the reward for sixty minutes of earnest worship was never a shot at everlasting life, it was skinny fries and a small chocolate milk shake.

"But you're going to have to drive," she said, tossing Tansy the keys.

"Really?" Tansy only had her learner's license. Melinda was the one who took her out for practice, and never in Lou's car. Lou was far too worried about insurance premiums.

"Can't drive with these." Lou held up her bandaged fingers. "Plus, I've had a few." The Cointreau had been followed by a large glass of white when she'd discovered her old diaries tossed in a pile of ancient magazines in the shed.

"Okay." Tansy glowed with trust, or maybe it was just the late-afternoon sun. "I'll be really careful."

And she was, ferrying them gingerly to Meadowcroft as though there was a newborn in the back. Bang on the speed limit, using mirrors, indicating at every turn. Lou murmured encouragingly. Maybe she could rethink her not-my-car policy. It would be useful, Tansy able to get about under her own steam. Regardless of what happened next.

"You can have whatever you want," she told her daughter as they stood in front of the giant menu.

"I'm really hungry, though," said Tans.

"Me too," said Lou. "But don't worry about it. Let's just go nuts."

They carried the paper bag reeking of fat and good times over to the park and got comfortable on top of a picnic bench. Tansy fussed about with napkins and straws, but Lou just sank her face into a Big Mac. God, that was good. Better than alcohol, almost. Better than fags. Lou realized she hadn't had a cigarette all day. Hadn't needed to. She smiled over at Tansy, who was demolishing some kind of special chicken burger that didn't look any different from the regular chicken burgers, despite costing a dollar fifty more.

"Do you remember when I used to bring you down here?"

Tansy nodded, cheeks bulging.

It was one of the places they'd go after kindergarten, in that golden period when Lou thought she'd finally gotten it all figured out. Tansy had come out of her terrible tantrum phase and started talking properly, developing a quirky little personality Lou couldn't get enough of. And she was working, finally, only part-time and for minimum wage but it felt like they had a bit of money, even if really they were sliding deeper into debt. She'd finish just after lunch, pick up Tansy, and take them off on adventures. The park, with its friendly duck families, was a favorite. They'd run and swing and slide then head home exhausted, Tansy earnestly telling her mother all about the afternoon they'd just had as though she was an interested third party. Lou would fall asleep happy in the living room of her crappy flat, Tansy unconscious in the only bedroom.

Tansy stuck her hand in the bag for another burger. "You didn't want this, did you?" she said. "I feel like I didn't even eat that first one."

"Oh, I know," said Lou. "I put on thirty pounds with you."

"God, really?"

"Eating was the only thing that stopped me feeling nauseous," said Lou, remembering her toast marathons. "And I had bad fluid retention."

Tansy flicked the pickle onto the grass. "I suppose putting on weight is normal," she said. "I'll just have to make sure I'm really good afterward."

Lou held her breath.

"I don't want to be one of those women who never loses it, you know? Who looks pregnant forever? But if you didn't have a problem, then I should be fine."

Lou set her Coke down. "So are we keeping this baby then?" she asked, trying for casual.

The traffic stopped humming, the ducks quacking, waiting for Tansy's answer.

"I don't know," Tansy said finally. "What do you think I should do?" She turned to Lou with big eyes, looking so much younger than she was, which really wasn't very old at all. Too young to vote or buy alcohol or get married. To make this decision. But Lou was determined to do things differently.

"Oh no. Tansy, this isn't up to me. This is your call."

"But what do you think?"

"Well." Lou chose her words carefully. "I think it's a big decision. And it's still quite early, so you don't actually need to make it yet. You can sleep on it. Not for long, but another week or two is okay."

"But what do you think about me having the baby?"

Lou had never asked her parents' opinion, but they'd given it anyway. And not just an opinion—a pronouncement.

"Well, of course you're not having it," her mother had exclaimed, the archangel Gabriel in reverse.

"Well, I can't not," Lou had retorted. "It would be a sin."

"Sin is relative," hissed her mother, perm twitching. "Throwing away all the opportunities your father and I have worked so hard to give you is also a sin, but that doesn't seem to bother you."

"Having a baby doesn't have to mean the end of my life. I can still do stuff."

Lou's mother had laughed, a particularly joyless sound.

"Louise Marie Henderson, if you have this baby you will never go anywhere or do anything interesting, believe me. You'll ruin both your lives."

Her prediction hadn't entirely come true. Lou had been to Sydney, and Tasmania, spent a whole week once in Hobart. She was admin manager now at the council. Her own designated parking space and all the staples she could pilfer.

Lou swept aside the McCrap and shuffled closer to her daughter. "I think it's a big responsibility," she said, aiming for a middle ground between condemnation and anything that could be wrongly interpreted as encouragement. "A life-changing responsibility. And it's not really about having a baby, it's having a *child*. For the rest of your life." Lou squeezed Tansy's shoulder. "I don't want you to feel like you've missed out on anything. I don't want you to have any regrets."

"Do you regret having me?"

Oh God. "Tansy, of course not."

"But do you feel like you having a baby—not me, necessarily, but just, you know, a *baby*—was the wrong choice?"

They didn't prepare you for this at the jolly postnatal check-ups. "Not wrong, as such," Lou said carefully. "But I'm not going to lie—there were moments when it felt like I'd made a mistake. I had no idea what I was doing, and everyone else was heading off to university and starting these big exciting lives. And I was stuck here, exhausted and out of my depth."

Lou took a deep breath. "Look, babies are not fun, or cute, most of the time. They are screaming, crying, pooping, vomiting, round-the-clock energy suckers. I didn't spend my days lying on a picnic blanket gazing lovingly at you like some kind of mummy blogger. I was busy sponging diarrhea off the couch." Was she laying it on too thick? "And doing it on your own is bloody difficult. There's a reason it takes two people to make a baby. It's a two-person job to raise one. And pay for it." Wait, had her mother said that? "Look, I'm just saying being a single mum is hard. You know that. And it affects everything. We don't have a nice big house like Aimee, and I don't have a proper career like Melinda. Although," quickly, "I still think I made the right choice. Obviously."

"And you've made it work."

Had she? "I'm not sure I have."

"Of course you have. And no one's life is perfect. You're always telling me that. Aimee can be really mental, and Melinda's lonely, I reckon."

"She's thinking of adopting."

"Melinda?"

"I know."

They sat in silence, Tansy throwing fries to the ducks waddling hopefully around their picnic bench.

"But just because it was the right choice for me doesn't mean that it's the right choice for you." Lou had been practicing: an argument that was persuasive, but that wouldn't make Tansy feel pressured or manipulated in any way. Although Lou was bloody well going to manipulate her. "Our circumstances are very different. You've grown up with a lot more freedom, and a bigger sense of what's out there in the world. We barely had the internet when I was your age. I think it would hit you harder, being stuck at home with a crying baby. And you're younger than I was. That makes a difference."

"A year."

"Nearly two, and I was a lot more self-sufficient. And, Tansy, even though I don't regret having you, *at all*, I do feel that you should think very, very hard before deciding whether to have this baby. Because it will be difficult, and unrewarding, and bloody lonely, for a long time. I don't want to make you feel bad, but I struggled, a lot."

"That's kind of why I think I should have it, though."

"How's that?"

"Because you had me. Even though it was hard, and your parents kicked you out, and you've been stuck in that shit job forever because the hours are good for school. I mean, sorry, Mum, but Rex is a bit of a dick."

"Tansy."

"Well, he is. Anyway. You still had me, regardless. And if you hadn't, I wouldn't be here. I wouldn't exist at all. So I don't feel like I can get rid of it. Because how can I get rid of a baby, when you gave me a chance?"

"That's not . . . You can't really . . . Tansy, it's not the same thing."

"It's exactly the same thing."

"But—"

"It would be like killing myself."

"Oh, Tans."

"Imagine if you'd never had me."

Lou had, often. Fantasized about a life of hotel rooms and

wine bars, sexy men she met on business trips and tiny, sporty cars. But then she wouldn't have this headstrong, stroppy creature making her argument with the same stubborn stupidity that Lou had made hers, down to the jutting chin. She closed her eyes. "Look, abortion isn't the only option. If you feel that strongly, you could have the baby and put it up for adoption."

"Give it to someone like Melinda?"

"Not exactly like Melinda, no."

"What does Melinda think? Aimee? I'm guessing you've told them."

"They think I should tell you what to do. Push you into a decision."

"But you won't." Tansy wriggled around so they were facing each other. "Because you're not like your parents."

Lou sighed. "Oh, I kind of am."

"No, you're not. You wouldn't kick me out. You wouldn't throw all my stuff on the drive."

Lou rubbed her face. This conversation was exhausting, and not going at all as she'd planned. "But I'm trying to talk you out of having it," she admitted.

"I know."

"And I was totally my mother in driving you over to Fenton to see someone. That was pure Beverly, behaving as though getting pregnant was something to be ashamed of." Another cycle that needed to be broken. Lou gripped Tansy's shoulder. "I'm not ashamed of you, Tans. You know that, don't you? This is nothing to be ashamed of."

"But I've let you down."

"Tansy, half your class is probably having sex. You were just unlucky to get caught. Come here." Lou wrapped an arm around her daughter. "I'm only saying all this because I'm scared for you. I want you to have more opportunities than I've had."

Tansy snuggled in. "It doesn't necessarily have to be a bad thing, does it? Having a baby? Maybe it could be better for me than it was for you."

Lou frowned. "Maybe. But it would still be a massive sacrifice, on your part. Of your freedom. And, Tansy, you love your freedom. That's half the problem."

"But I could still have a life. I could still finish school, go to university. There are child care centers and things. And I wouldn't be doing it completely on my own. I'd have you. Wouldn't I?"

Lou watched the ducks waddling toward the lake, not a duckling in sight because they'd all left home, like they were supposed to. Not brought their own chicks back to the mummy ducks to raise. But then the mummy ducks had probably been in stable relationships, not gotten their duck selves pregnant in a messy situation that meant they couldn't even admit who the father was, denying their ducklings a solid male role model and the generous financial support of grandparents on either side.

You mustn't blame yourself, Melinda had said, but Lou knew deep down she had to. Because that was the thing about being a single parent—there was no one else to blame.

Lou squeezed Tansy tighter. "Of course you would," she said, trying not to sigh. "You'd have me. I'm not going anywhere."

Chapter 14

Pete had moved the spare key. Cameron ran his hand along the guttering as instructed, felt the little leather fob lying in a crumbly nest of bird gatherings. Three years since he'd been back but the lock behaved as it always had, sticking at first, so you had to really put your weight behind it. Inside, however, the house had undergone a personality bypass. The walls were bare of his mother's wooden signs begging someone to BLESS THIS MESS, the counters free from her jumble of nail polish and sunglasses and gossip magazines. Cameron stood in the kitchen doorway, slightly disoriented. It was as if all the color had been surgically removed. What was left looked like the rental home of two slightly dysfunctional male flatmates. A tangle of PlayStation. A giant television. He opened the pantry; a dozen packets of instant pasta propped each other up.

There was fruit in the bowl, though. Cameron bit into an apple, then spat it in the sink. He drank deeply from the tap—that hadn't changed, the cool, pure Meadowcroft water—to dislodge the taste. Right. Might as well get on with it.

The laptop was exactly where Pete had said, charging on the desk in the study. Cameron booted it up, guessing the password in less than a minute. His stepfather might be security conscious, but he was also predictable. He scrolled through emails, forwarding a couple of interesting-looking messages to himself. Lincoln's iPad was better protected, but his brother's secrets weren't what Cameron was after. He put both devices in Pete's leather holdall and propped it next to the door.

Cameron wasn't exactly sure what he was searching for, but he'd know when he found it. He went through the study filing cabinet, flicking quickly through years of electricity bills and warranties. He fished around the bathroom, free of any telltale female toiletries, but that didn't necessarily mean anything. Lincoln's room smelled of teenage boy; Cameron did a cursory search, then pulled the door shut. His own room was obviously now a guest room, and little used—same bed, same curtains, same chunky stereo system in the corner, but a new duvet cover, still creased from the package. Cameron paused, but felt nothing. He didn't live here anymore.

The master bedroom felt abandoned, and for longer than just a few days. Apart from a wedding photo next to the bed—on his mother's side, Cameron noted—it had all the human investment of a cheap hotel room. He knelt down and began to rifle through the bedside table. An unwound watch. A Lee Child. A bottle of pills, label picked off. He tucked those in his pocket. And a mobile phone.

Cameron sat back on his haunches as he turned the phone over in his hand. Pete had told the investigator quite firmly that his phone had been with him in the plane; Cameron had been standing there. He pushed at the screen, but the battery was dead. Pete wasn't tech savvy enough to own multiple gadgets. Maybe a work and a personal number? But he was a small-town teacher, not a CEO. Cameron tapped the mobile against his knee, then pocketed it, along with the charger.

There was nothing interesting under the bed, or in the chest of drawers. His stepfather's wardrobe was all white shirts and brown shoes, a stack of faded weekend polos that had long ago had the life washed out of them. His mother's closet was now storage: suitcases and tennis rackets, except . . . Cameron moved farther inside, drawn by a flash of color, as rare in this new monochrome version of their house as an exotic bird. He buried his face in a fountain of hanging fabric—his mother's scarves. Blue and purple and red and green, the silk waterfall still carried a faint trace of her perfume. Cameron began carefully pulling the fabric down. His stepfather didn't deserve to have anything of his mother. He folded the lengths around each other and placed the soft bundle in his backpack. He didn't deserve any memories at all.

Chapter 15

The ballroom was already buzzing by the time Melinda came downstairs. She'd taken her time fussing with her makeup, doing her hair, but she could delay no longer. The double doors swung open as each new couple waltzed in, giving a glimpse of the crowd inside. Women in their best dresses, fake-tanned and back-combed. Their husbands/boyfriends/partners, lots of them, getting stuck in the free bar. Melinda hung back, pretending to adjust a shoe. This was the one part of the conference she hated. Meeting people was amazing, the stage was a rush. But the dinner was a plus-one, and Melinda was arriving plus-no one. As usual.

"Joining the party?" a waiter asked. Melinda pulled her shoulders back. She was not going to feel like the odd woman out at her own event, dammit. She'd sat through too many dinner parties at the end of the table, or next to the cousin with no social skills, or worse, not even invited, because a host didn't want her to feel "uncomfortable." This was her gala celebration, and she was going to enjoy it. Or get drunk. Probably get drunk.

Clint had arranged a private tutorial, to teach her to smile in a way that would look genuine and flattering in photos: tongue pushed against her soft palate, eyes slightly crinkled. Melinda put on her photo face now and started moving through the crowd. She steeled herself for the usual questions about whether there was a Mr. Melinda, and where was her special someone tonight? But the questions never came. Instead, women gently took her elbow, steered her into quiet spaces to talk about their own battles with IVF, or hugged her and wished her luck with the adoption. Even those who didn't stop her seemed to smile more warmly. *Bloody hell,* thought Melinda. *I've crossed to the other side.*

"I thought it was so brave, what you said up there," said one woman—Stella from Takapuna, according to her name tag. "Opening yourself up like that. I've always admired you but now I feel like I *know* you."

"It must have been so hard for you, year after year, listening to us talk about our children while not being able to have your own," said Lisa from Birdwood. "I had no idea. I wish I had. I wouldn't have complained so much. I feel really selfish."

The general consensus seemed to be that she was infertile, rather than mateless. Melinda moved through the crowd, quickly growing used to having her arm touched, a kiss blown toward her. *God, this has really changed how they see me. How much they like me, even. That's . . . appalling.*

But was it really that surprising? After all, she'd done this before. The Australasian Small Business Awards, Wellington,

2014. Melinda had been feeling like a bit of a freak anyway, hadn't been on a date for over a year. She'd been the only non-partnered person at her dinner table, again. So when someone had asked, she'd said she was divorced. The change was remarkable. People had been more open toward her, men especially. It was as though she had an invisible stamp of approval: someone had wanted to marry her once, so she must be okay. It wasn't the only time she'd told that lie either. At overseas conferences, where no one knew her, Melinda had taken to intimating a recent breakup, with similar results. Her singleness was accepted as a temporary aberration, rather than the state of play. Far better, it seemed, to be damaged goods rather than left on the shelf.

At the top table Clint was waiting, looking slightly less pretentious than usual in a tuxedo, a white rose blooming in the buttonhole. He looked almost attractive, or was the kindness of strangers making Melinda herself less judgmental? She kissed him on the cheek, surprising them both.

"Well done," he muttered.

"It was an accident," she whispered back. "It doesn't mean I'm going through with it."

"Doesn't matter." He smiled, as cameras flashed at them.

God, would people think they were a couple now? What the hell. Melinda rested a hand on his shoulder as Clint put his arm around her back, both of them leaning in without discussion. The artifice just came naturally. Melinda let herself relax into the pose. She'd deal with any repercussions later. For the moment, she was just going to enjoy belonging.

"I need you to talk to that journalist, though," she murmured. "I don't want it to end up in print."

"Already did," he replied, as he pulled out her chair. There were six other people at the head table, Melinda's top sellers, but they leaned away to give the "couple" their privacy. "But," he added, as he spread a linen napkin on her lap, "I think the cork might be out of the bottle. Everyone here will be on Facebook, Twitter. That story's not going to stay quiet."

Fine. Fuck, but fine. Melinda took a balancing sip of wine and smiled, photogenically, at the woman opposite. She could play along. No one in their right mind was going to give a baby to a single woman who traveled half the month. She'd find out the names of a couple of adoption agencies, fill in the forms, and wait to be rejected. There must be some kind of consultant who could help her with that. She'd get her assistant to find one in the morning. Melinda took another sip of wine, calmer now. The paperwork alone would take a hundred years, and if it gave her an edge in the meantime, so be it. Look at all the press those power mothers got, the I Don't Know How She Does It articles, the praise for merely having a working womb and someone willing to fill it. How was that fair? It didn't take a genius to have a baby. Teenagers got pregnant all the time. Like Tansy. Melinda felt a pull of conscience at the thought of Tansy's frightened face, of Lou's permanently tired one. She quieted it with another slug of wine. Because it wasn't a complete lie. She was considering adoption. She just planned to consider it for a long, long time.

BY THE TIME Lou and Tansy left the park, the light was starting to go. They drove back to Hensley in silence, apart from the odd instruction from Lou. "Watch out for that van." "It's green, Tans, you can go." Tansy was too busy concentrating on the road to talk. Lou was concentrating on not being her parents.

Because her attitude, so far, was exactly the same. She could tell her daughter that pregnancy was nothing to be ashamed of, but look at the way she was acting. Sneaking off to another town for tests, hoping Tansy would decide not to have the baby. Or if she had it, not to keep it. Pushing her toward the "right" decision, however much she claimed she wasn't. Which was even worse: hypocrisy. At least her parents had never hidden their position. *Enough,* Lou told herself firmly, watching her daughter bite her lip as she negotiated the hills that led into Hensley. If she wanted to break this cycle, she had to stop perpetuating it. It was that simple.

"Tansy," she said quietly, once Tansy had passed through the dense tree cover and was looking more comfortable with the clear visibility of wide country roads. "Whatever you decide to do, I'll back you one hundred percent, okay? Promise me you'll think about it properly first, but—you've got my support, no matter what."

They were approaching Maddocks Clearing. Where Pete's plane had come down, Lou realized with a start. The man's son was lying in a coma; she should be thankful her daughter was only pregnant.

"One hundred percent," she repeated, staring at the flapping accident tape ahead. "I love you very much, Tans, and this doesn't change that, not at all."

Tansy gave a sob.

"Oh for God's sake, don't cry." Lou put her hand out to steady the wheel. "Okay, this is no good. You're going to have to pull over."

Tansy steered the car onto the side of the road a few yards short of the crash site. Lou could make out two men standing at the base of the ranges, a tarpaulin over what must be the remains of the aircraft. She turned her attention back to her daughter, who was slumped over the steering wheel. "That's it," she said, rubbing her back. "Let it all out. Good girl."

"I—just—don't—want—to make things *worse* for you," Tansy choked out.

"Oh, Tansy, you're not," Lou lied.

"But I know you want to travel. You want to go off and *do* things. And I've messed it all up."

"You haven't," said Lou. "This is a . . . postponement of plans." Like Aimee had said. "You don't need to worry about me."

"Because I don't think I can do it on my own," Tansy wailed. "I need your help."

"And I've said I'll help," said Lou. She made her voice softer. "But, Tans—do you want to tell me who the father is?" There wasn't a boyfriend, Lou was fairly sure. But that didn't mean whoever he was couldn't shoulder some of the responsibility. Him and his parents.

Tansy stared vacantly toward the corpse of the plane but didn't speak. Lou's stomach turned over. "Tans?" she whispered, frightened. Because what if it wasn't another kid? She was assuming a teenager, someone drunk and stupid, but— what if it was a friend's father? Someone they knew. An authority figure. A teacher. It happened, didn't it? Especially at private girls' schools. You saw it in the papers all the time. Tansy quivered, and Lou bunched her good hand into a fist. She would fucking kill him.

"I can't say," Tansy whispered. "Not yet."

"Is it . . . an adult?"

She shook her head. "It's just a big mess."

"Do you need to tell him first?"

Tansy nodded slowly.

"But you know who it is, right?"

"Yes." Tansy looked indignant. "There was only one. I was at a party." She leaned her forehead against the steering wheel. "But I can't talk about it right now."

And Lou found she couldn't push her. Because she'd hardly been forthcoming in that regard herself, had she? Lou sighed and shunted her seat back into a reclining position.

"You understand, don't you, Mum?"

"Oh yes."

Tansy adjusted her own seat so she was lying beside Lou. "Did you ever tell my father about me?" she asked, so quietly it was almost a whisper.

"You know I haven't. I don't know where he is."

"I just thought you might have found him at some point. Tracked him down over the internet. It would be easier to do now."

There was a fly buzzing in the car. Lou turned the engine on so she could crack a window and let it out.

"He was just passing through," she told Tansy, as she had done for sixteen years. "Backpacking. I don't even know how to spell his last name, or where exactly he was from. He was French. It's a big country."

"We could try."

Lou twisted onto her side. "Do you want to? You've never been bothered before." Tansy had barely even asked about him, the only emotional button she hadn't pushed in her teenage rebellion. As though she realized Lou wouldn't be able to take it.

"Nah," said Tansy, chasing the fly through the gap on her side. "I don't really need a dad now. Besides, the timing might be a bit off. Bonjour, Papa. Meet your pregnant daughter."

She gave a loud, inappropriate laugh, and Lou found herself cracking up as well. They rolled together, bumping the gearshift as they snorted and shook.

There was a tap on the windshield. One of the accident investigators. "Everything all right in here?"

"Fine, Officer." Lou straightened herself up. "Nothing to see here."

He nodded, unsmiling, and moved back toward his field, his shrouded plane.

"Fuck," said Lou, wiping mascara out of her eye. "What are we like?"

"Each other," said Tansy. "We're just like each other. Sorry, Mum."

THE ELEVATOR DOOR slid closed softly.

"Alone at last," said Clint. "What a fantastic evening."

Melinda smiled, swaying slightly. It *had* been a fantastic evening. And Clint had been a surprisingly big part of that. Keeping her glass topped up, his arm on the back of her chair. Melinda knew she was setting feminism back a thousand years, but there was something about having a man beside her that had made her feel . . . accepted. Bulletproof. As though, finally, there was nothing about her to criticize.

There'd been only one sour note in the whole evening. Somewhere between the fish and the sorbet, there was a rustle next to her. The Sydney journalist woman—Sarah? No, Stacey—pulling out a seat that had recently been vacated.

"I want to apologize," she said. "For giving you such a hard time earlier. I didn't realize what you'd been going through."

"It's all right." Melinda had smiled magnanimously. "You weren't to know."

"It's nothing personal," Stacey continued. "I'm just really interested in LoveLocked. My mum used to sell it. It was how she managed to raise three kids on her own." She frowned slightly. "Although I'm not sure what she'd make of all these changes."

Melinda bristled. "Well, you have to move with the times," she said. "Our current curators seem to love them." She dropped her voice. "Look, Stacey, can I ask you—"

"I won't write about the adoption," Stacey promised. "Clint's already spoken to me. I understand it's private."

"I'd appreciate that."

They'd chatted about the IPO, Melinda hinting daringly at potential big-name investors. And then Stacey had said, as she was getting up to leave, "What's happening with the plane crash, by the way? The boy who was in the coma? How's he doing?"

Melinda had been thrown, and her half-pissed face had shown the shock.

"Gosh, I'm not sure," she'd bumbled. "I haven't been following the story."

"Really? I thought it was such a close community. Your friend Aimee was telling me how well you all knew the pilot."

Melinda had nothing to say, just an open mouth that definitely wasn't photogenic.

Clint had come to the rescue, kind of. "We don't know him personally, but obviously we're concerned. Anything that affects Hensley affects us. LoveLocked is going to make a big donation to help the pilot and his family with their recovery."

We are not, thought Melinda. She didn't want anyone making a connection between her company and Pete Kasprowicz's plane.

"That's strictly off the record, of course," Clint added. "We don't talk about charity work."

Stacey said she understood, smiling up at him in a way that lots of women had been all evening. And why not? He was a good-looking man. Just a little . . . pushy. But ambition could be attractive. Melinda had begun to feel the first spark of something toward Clint, a little flare of attraction ignited by another woman's interest. Competition did it for her, always had. She'd leaned closer, closed the gap between them. "No, we don't," she told Stacey. With a slight but obvious emphasis on the "we."

The elevator pinged.

"My floor," said Clint.

Should she?

"After you," he said.

And Melinda found herself walking unsteadily toward her IPO advisor's hotel room, his hand on the small of her back.

"St. Margaret's Hospital, Intensive Care, good evening."

"I'm calling to ask about a patient."

"Sorry? I can't hear you."

Aimee pushed the door of her study shut. "I'm calling to ask about a patient," she repeated, as loud as she dared. "Lincoln Kasprowicz."

The woman on the other end of the phone sighed. "It's a bit late for that, isn't it?"

"Oh my God." The bookshelves tilted as Aimee sat down hard on her desk. "Is he . . . dead?"

"What? No. But it is nearly midnight." The nurse sounded impatient. "Who's calling please? Are you a relative?"

"I know it's late. I'm sorry. I couldn't sleep." That was true enough. "It's Lincoln's aunt. Peter's sister. Mary Kasprowicz. Well, Waters now, but I was Kasprowicz." She was babbling, she could tell.

"He's still the same, Mrs. Waters, as the last time you called. No change."

"Thank you so much. I'm sorry, I was just—"

"I know you're worried. But you only called three hours ago. I told you, someone will phone if there's any change."

"Email, please. I'm not always home."

"Yes, email. There's a note here." Another sigh. "Try and get some sleep, Mrs. Waters. I'll speak to you again tomorrow, no doubt."

"I will. Thank you. I'm so sorry to bother you. Thank you again."

Chapter 16

It was like falling asleep in class—the vivid daydreams that you'd get as you nodded off, the kind that felt so real you were shocked and confused when the teacher caught you and shouted you back awake. Mixed in with long periods of black nothing. Nothing that sometimes had a voice shot through it, harsh and unintelligible, a foreign language. Nothing that would then be cut with another image, a sudden memory, like accidentally coming across an old photo on your phone.

Lincoln lay in the black and enjoyed the memories, smiling inwardly when they appeared. His mother reading, the bulk of her covering the couch. Cricket with his dad, in the backyard. Sitting on their concrete front step with Cameron, sucking on a Popsicle. His throat was dry, in the blackness, his head heavy, as though it had somehow been weighted down.

The images started coming more often, and lasting longer. Weekend flights, the toy-town views of the cellophane river from up high. His dad's hands, steady and confident, on the controls. Dad smiling in the cockpit, explaining, pointing.

The stomach-dropping freedom of gaining height, the same nauseous excitement when it came time to land. His own first few lessons, just the basics. Dad watching proudly from the ground.

More Mum. Cooking. Singing. Swimming, at the beach, the bottoms of her two-piece disappearing between thighs and stomach. Mum sick. Getting smaller. Grayer. The hospital. Drips, tubes. So real he could smell the place, hear the beep of the machines.

Lincoln tried to open his eyes, but they refused. Instead he watched the painful pictures of his mum's last days. Asleep, most of the time. In pain when she was awake. His dad panicking, running across the hospital parking lot. The funeral. The coffin. Cameron. Then no Cameron.

And sex. Many of the flashes were sex. Lincoln had only done it once, and not that long ago. But those memories seemed extra real, and he could feel the same giddy disbelief that someone was actually going to let him. The girl's mouth, smiling. His head, arching back. The thrust, thrust, thrust, too quick probably. It hadn't lasted long.

The blackness began feeling softer, lighter, mixing with the memories now. His own face, begging for the night flight. Dad, finally giving in. The two of them pulling the plane out of the hangar in the fading sunlight, like something from an old Tom Cruise movie. The sunset, setting the river on fire. Lights rising, exploding, falling. Growing closer.

And then just the one light, brighter than all the others. Floating in front of them like a luminous jellyfish. The ground, swinging toward them. His father yelling. Lincoln, hands over his eyes, not wanting to know. Like a child. Like a bloody child. His dad, leaning over him. Shielding him. The flame in the engine like a beautiful, deadly firework, ready to explode.

The blackness turned to gray, then to gritty beige, then to full-on fluorescent buzzing white. Bright. Loud. Lincoln tried to move an arm, his hand, but nothing obeyed. His head. He could roll his head. The foreign words came closer. Faces. Too close. He closed his eyes again, forced his tongue free, seeking water. Thirsty. He was so, so thirsty.

Chapter 17

"I'll take two vanilla cannoncini. The nice fat one at the front, and the big one there in the second row." Aimee pointed out the pastries, careful not to leave smudgy fingerprints on the display case. She normally made her own cakes, but the custard horns at Elisabetta's were Lou's favorite. "Extra icing sugar, if you don't mind."

"Takeout?"

"Please." Lou was letting her phone go straight to voice mail, obviously still bruised. Aimee placed the cake box carefully on the passenger seat, tucking her handbag in front so it wouldn't fall off. Poor Lou. Melinda had been horribly bossy, when Lou needed understanding, not instructions. Aimee picked the pastries off the seat and placed them in the footwell instead. Safer. And the whole adoption idea was simply insane. Not just the thought of Melinda with a baby, which was ridiculous enough, but throwing it at Lou five minutes after she'd told them about Tansy? Aimee normally approved of Melinda's refusal to censor herself, but that was going too far.

But then Melinda was being more insensitive than usual at the moment. Cold, almost. Look at the way she'd delivered her ultimatum on the accident. Her refusal to even have a *conversation* about it. Aimee turned the ignition on, then off again. She walked back into Elisabetta's and ordered Lou a cappuccino, large. What Lou needed now was a good heart-to-heart. She might not think she wanted company, but Aimee knew better. Hence the expensive pastries and cappuccino, treats Lou rarely allowed herself. They'd sit out on the back step, and Lou would finally have a chance to really talk about everything that was going on. Aimee drove a little faster in anticipation. Lou would be grateful for the chance to speak honestly about how freaked out she was, like she'd tried to before Melinda had shut her down. And then Aimee would share a few of her own fears as well, so Lou didn't feel alone.

Aimee puttered down the main street toward what counted for suburbs in Hensley. Poor old Lou. And bloody, bloody Tansy, letting her mother down again, when Lou gave up so much for that girl. It must feel like one blow after another. Aimee thought briefly of the whole shoplifting phase, the tongue piercing. Shelley had been told nothing but earlobes while she was still using their water and electricity, but really, they hadn't even needed to say that. Shelley had asked permission to start wearing nail polish.

Elegant verandas gave way to squat brick bungalows, the houses becoming smaller, the front yards sparser the farther Aimee got from the town center. Lou needed gentle handling, not harsh home truths. She needed to be bolstered, to be

convinced she'd still be able to travel, see the world. Although
Aimee wasn't entirely sure that was true. Tansy had about as
much natural ability to raise a baby as Melinda; Lou was going
to have to downsize her ambitions dramatically. Maybe Aimee
should suggest a small trip for the two of them before the baby
arrived. Get them both out of Hensley. For the first time she
could remember, Aimee desperately wanted to be somewhere
else as well.

A couple of sun-bleached magazines lay in the middle of
Lou's lawn, next to a ripped cardboard box. God, she was
really letting the place go; she must be even more upset than
Aimee realized. She clutched the pastry box as she trotted
evangelically toward the front door, secure in her belief that
she was bringing salvation and solace to the troubled family
within.

Except no one was answering. Aimee knocked again, rang
the bell. There was music, Lou's car in the drive—they were
blatantly home. She knocked harder. This was no good; the
coffee was getting cold. She stooped to fish the spare key from
inside the gnome that sat beside the front step, but the gnome
was gone, along with his plastic wishing well. She tried the
door. Open. It was never open. Aimee gripped her mobile
phone.

"Lou?" She took a cautious step into the hallway, ready to
run if necessary. The bare hallway, its paintings and trophy
cabinet missing, a dark square on the carpet where Ken's precious birds had once lived. Had they been robbed? Although
what kind of burglar took taxidermy? "Lou? Is everything

okay?" She walked through the living room, empty except for two beanbags and a scattering of takeout cartons. Maybe everything had been repossessed. Maybe Lou was in financial trouble. Aimee poked her head into Tansy's bedroom as she passed. Empty as well, only a mattress on the floor. This was just weird. "Lou!"

"Out here." They were in the backyard, throwing shoes into a dumpster filled with old clothes. Aimee hovered at the kitchen door, uncertain.

"I called the council, but they said you were working from home. I wanted to check you were okay."

"We're spring cleaning," Lou called, emptying a washing basket of men's trousers on top of the pile. Bruce Springsteen blared from an old tape player perched precariously in the open kitchen window. Lou gave a little twirl as the trousers fell, a dozen corduroy legs spinning as though they were dancing as well. "You're just in time for the bonfire."

"It's not spring," said Aimee, feeling a little silly with her box of pastries.

Lou just laughed, as though she'd said something hysterical.

"Where's all the furniture gone?" said Aimee. "There's nothing here."

"I know," said Lou, wiping dirty hands down her jeans with no thought for stains. "Isn't it great? We're starting over."

Aimee didn't know what to say. She thrust the box toward her friend. "I brought cannoncini."

"Amazing." Lou balanced the box on one knee. "And coffee. Thank goodness. We accidentally binned the kettle." She turned toward the garage. "Tansy!" she hollered. "Aimee's brought food."

Tansy was also filthy, dirt tattooing her face and arms. She ran across the lawn, dodging the dumpster, and thrust a greedy hand into the pastry box. "Vanilla, my favorite," she said, shoving the biggest one straight in her mouth. Aimee waited for the reprimand, but Lou just ripped the other horn in half. "Want to share?" she asked, waving the fatter end, custard dripping.

Aimee shook her head. "I came to see how you were," she said, staring meaningfully.

"We're fab," said Lou. "Having a long overdue clearout. We're going into Melbourne tomorrow, getting all new stuff. Even a TV." She looked younger, lighter. *Happy.*

Aimee pulled at the neck of her mumsy tunic. "Well, there should be New Year's sales on, I guess."

"Oh, Tansy's made us a load of money selling everything online." Lou waved at her empty house with bandaged fingers. "She's amazing. You wouldn't believe what people will pay for old clothes. Mum's crocheted minidress, the lemon one? Two hundred and fifty bucks. No joke."

"That's—Lou, your hand!"

"Oh." Lou looked down. "Yeah. I bumped it."

"Bumped it?"

"Against a door. Long story. It's better than it was."

"Right." The fingernails peeking out the end of the bandage were an unhealthy shade of blue; Aimee felt as if she'd tumbled down the rabbit hole.

"But we've made thousands, Aims. Well, Tansy has. Honestly, she's a genius. Knew which stuff to phone antique shops about, what to auction online. She made more in three hours than I would in a week at work."

"Maybe she should come round and go through our house," said Aimee, remembering the missing necklace. She could never prove anything, but she'd always known.

"Nah, your stuff's the wrong kind of old." Tansy licked custard off her thumb. "No offense."

"None taken."

Lou slung an arm around her daughter. "Anyway, we're going to set fire to this lot. Toast some marshmallows over the final evidence of my parents' bad taste. Fancy it?"

Aimee shook her head. "I have to get back. I only popped in to drop these off, a little treat."

"They were a big treat." Lou smiled generously. "Really lovely of you."

"Well." Aimee looked from Lou to Tansy, leaning against each other, grimy and content. "Do you want to walk me out?"

"Sure." Lou untangled herself. "Tansy, wait for me before you let loose with the lighter fluid. I don't want you breathing the fumes."

They didn't speak as they walked through the house, Lou bouncing ahead of Aimee toward the open front door.

"Sorry," said Aimee. "I must have forgotten to shut it. I was just a little shocked."

"No worries," said Lou. "Nothing to take anyway." She laughed, a new, looser laugh.

Aimee reached for her friend's unbandaged hand. "Lou, are

you okay? I was worried, after the other night. Melinda was really off, and you haven't been answering your phone—"

"My phone?" Lou shook Aimee's hand away, reached in the pocket of her skinny jeans. "Oh, it's on silent. I didn't even realize."

"Well, if you want to talk, I'm here. We can sit in the car if you want, go over everything."

"Nah." That dismissive wave of the hand again. "I'm done with talking. Moaning really, let's be honest. I'm all about action now. Although—"

"Yes?"

"I want to book a plane ticket. For three years from now. It's largely symbolic, but—would travel agents even do that?"

"Lou, you don't need a travel agent. You can do it all online. Although I don't think they issue tickets that far out."

Lou laughed. "Guess I've got a lot to learn."

"Is this a ticket because Tansy will be in university?" Aimee did the maths: Lou was obviously giving Tansy a year to settle in.

"Not really. I mean, she will be at some stage, hopefully, but she's having the baby. She's quite certain about it."

"Oh. Oh, Lou. I'm so sorry."

"No, it's fine. Like you said, she won't need my help forever. And I've made some calls and she's eligible for benefits, even if she's living here, and more if she's studying. There's loads of support. So you were right. It doesn't have to mean the end of things."

"I see."

"Honestly, it'll be fine. She's more capable than we give her credit for. And it's her choice. I'm not going to push her into anything. You know how I feel about that."

Did she? "Yes."

There was an impatient shout from the backyard. "Tansy, wait!" Lou turned back to Aimee. "But I do want to book a ticket, or do something to feel like I'm still moving forward, you know?"

Aimee wasn't sure she knew anything about Lou anymore. "You could probably make a hotel reservation."

"Brilliant." Lou squeezed Aimee's arm with her good hand. "You sure you don't want to stay? We're getting Lebanese for lunch later."

Aimee shook her head as she fumbled with her car keys. "I'm just glad everything's okay."

"Thanks for coming. It was really sweet of you."

Aimee climbed into her car, but she didn't start the engine. Instead, she watched Lou saunter back into the house, head high, arse swinging. *Jaunty.* She hadn't even asked how Aimee was doing. There was laughter from the backyard, a crackle as the flames went up. The smell of petrol made her gag; she had to wind up the window. Aimee sat staring at the smoke for a good five minutes, watching the black clouds billow and spread across the neighborhood. Then she put her foot down and headed for the hills.

"Good morning, Ms. Baker."

Melinda shut her eyes, as though that would block out the

warm breath in her ear, the hand tickling its way down her stomach. Clint. She was in bed with Clint. And not for the first time either. Every night of LoveFest she'd wound up drunk on her increased popularity and sparkling Australian wine, and in bed with her IPO advisor. A man she now knew had a scorpion tattoo on his shoulder, a hairy lower back, and a predilection for a manicured finger in his anus.

"Not ready to face the day? Shall I order coffee?"

His erection wriggled hopefully against her bottom. Melinda nodded, and arched subtly away from his bobbing penis. "Black," she croaked. There had been a lot of wine.

Clint opened the curtains a crack as he rang down for room service. He had a good body at least—long, lean. Nice arse. He was considerably younger than her. Twenty-nine, he'd admitted; he'd lied to HR at his first consultancy firm, and no one had checked since. Melinda quite admired that. She'd do the same. But he was *Clint*. A man who used the word *onboarding* as a verb. Although the sex had been . . . interesting. Borderline kinky, which was new, and made her feel a little younger as well. She'd even taken a pill last night. A pill! Without even asking what it was. He'd told her it would set her "on fire," and she'd just gone with it. The thought of Melinda, control freak extraordinaire, swallowing something without checking its provenance and chemical makeup was so out of character she wanted to phone someone and boast about her newfound recklessness. Lou, probably. Not Aimee. Aimee would have a heart attack.

It couldn't continue, obviously. Both the drug taking, and

the Clint fucking. They had to work together; Melinda needed to be able to pull rank. Hard to do with someone who knew you swore when you came. And there was the fact that she didn't actually *like* Clint. Fancied him, obviously more than she'd realized, although that could be 50 percent prosecco. But in terms of being interested in what he had to say, what he was up to other than driving her company forward? Not really, if she was honest. He could be a bit of a dick.

Melinda listened to Clint pee, flush, brush his teeth. The everyday sounds of cohabitation that other people took for granted. The only sounds in Melinda's flat were those she made herself, or that came from electronic devices. Melinda generally appreciated the peace and quiet, but there was also something infinitely depressing about knowing that every human interaction was yours to arrange. If she wanted to speak to someone, eat with someone, or go to a movie, she had to initiate it. And accept the crappy time slots. When you were the only single left, you got used to meeting people for coffee or lunch rather than dinner—family time!—and obviously weekends were out. Which left an awful lot of lonely, empty evenings, wondering where you'd gone wrong. Melinda had spent thirty-eight years waiting for the right man to show up. And he hadn't. At what point did you admit to yourself that this *was* your life, and that it only took up one side of the bed?

And yet. Here was a firm impression next to her in the mattress, a man gargling in the bathroom. A man who hadn't casually mentioned a not-quite-ex-wife, or a criminal record, or asked for a loan. A man who asked her what she was into, rather than just trying to push her head toward his crotch. Melinda had once slept with someone who'd asked if she wanted foreplay, as though it was optional.

The coffee arrived. Clint answered the door with a towel around his hips, paid, and tipped. Melinda had waitressed through university; she approved of people who tipped. There were many good points to Clint, she reminded herself. He was very considerate with his oral hygiene. He could discuss a profit and loss statement for hours. He automatically reached for the bill and kept hold of it, even if she insisted. Melinda had had enough of men who expected her to bloody pay for everything, just because she could.

"Hey, check out the story on page five," he said, kneeling up beside her. "I knew they were in trouble."

And he brought her the business pages in bed. Maybe he understood her better than she thought.

"Want me to pour the coffee?" he asked. "Black, two sugars, right? I told them it had to be strong."

She reached beneath his towel.

"It'll get cold," he warned, warm and growing in her hand.

"Don't care," she said. "Come here."

"Well, well." It was the first time she'd initiated anything; he was pleased, she could feel. "But what about——"

They'd run out the night before. Gone through a full box, in less than three days. God, what was she *doing*?

"Don't worry," she said, tugging his towel off. "I'm on the pill." Melinda pulled Clint down on top of her and welcomed him inside.

"You again."

Aimee smiled nervously. "Sorry?"

"You were here yesterday, weren't you?" The investigator tipped his hat back. But he didn't seem annoyed, or suspicious. He sounded pleased, almost. It must be lonely, standing by the side of the road all day. "You're the muffin lady."

"Muffins? Oh, right."

"So did you bring any?"

"Sorry, I didn't think. I just came to—" What? Confess? *Come on, Aimee. Stay calm. You've got this.*

He waited, the sun at his back shining right into Aimee's eyes. She shifted closer toward him, into his shadow, so she didn't have to squint.

"To explain," she said. She'd been practicing in the car. "What I was doing here. What I am doing here."

"Yes?" There was a smile now, small and amused, that Aimee had to tilt her head back to see.

"I'm a friend of the family. Of the Kasprowiczes. So I wanted to see what was happening, to make sure—" Her mind went blank. "To make sure it's all being done right."

"You mean you keep turning up here, driving past all the time, to check that I'm doing my job properly?" He chuckled. "And there I was thinking you just wanted to see me."

Aimee felt her face explode a guilty red as she tried to calculate how many times she'd scoped the field out, how often she'd slowed down to get a better look. Dozens. Two, three times a day, at least. Oh God. She might as well be wearing a T-shirt that said WE DID IT. "You noticed me drive past?"

"Course. Good-looking woman, great hair. Terrible driving. Who wouldn't notice?" He grinned. "Your left taillight's gone, by the way."

Hang on. Was he *flirting* with her? "I don't think . . . that's not . . ." Aimee drew herself up to her full five feet, which brought her nose about level with his neck. "I really don't think that's appropriate."

His voice changed. "You're right. I'm sorry. You're here because you're worried about your friends, and I'm hitting on you. It's very inappropriate." But he was still smiling. "Shall we start again?" He held out a hand. "Damien Marshall, Australian Transport Safety Bureau."

Oh bugger. "Aimee."

He kept hold of her hand. "Do you have a last name, Aimee?"

"Yes."

"But you're not telling."

"No."

He laughed. "Right. So then, Aimee Not Telling, how can I help you?"

Leave her alone. He could just leave her alone. Aimee yanked her hand back. All she'd wanted to do was explain herself, to make her actions seem less suspicious, and now this man, this *official crash site investigator*, knew her name and her car and that she was effectively stalking the place.

And he was making fun of her.

"Hey. Shit. Don't cry." He stooped down so their faces were level. "I was only teasing."

"I'm just—"

"Worried. You're worried. Of course you are. Your mates are in the hospital and some arsehole is flirting with you." He tipped his hat back again, wiped his forehead. "Last thing you need. Forgive me. I'm being a jerk."

Aimee wiped her own cheeks. Her hands came away black with mascara. "Forget it."

"Nah, but seriously. How can I help?"

"You can't." No one could.

"Well, I might be able to. You said you were worried the accident wasn't being checked out properly. It is, but . . . shall I explain what we're doing? So at least you feel like something's being done?"

The offer shimmered in the hot air between them, almost tangible, as though Aimee could reach out and grab it. This was the moment, she knew—the jumping-off point. She'd had moments of clarity before, described them to her doctors even, when her brain gave her a lucid choice: to walk away, or dive further into the crazy. It was never an easy decision. Her brain craved reassurance like a six o'clock gin and tonic. But she also knew that if she stopped feeding the craving, then the merry-go-round in her head would eventually grind to a halt. She just needed to resist.

"Aimee?"

She could resist.

"Aimee?"

It was like an itch. If she gave in, she'd only need to scratch it again, and again.

"Hello? Anyone home?"

She looked at him with genuine regret. "I'm sorry. I shouldn't even be here. Talking to you. I have to go." And once again, she turned and ran to her car.

They'd only been in the shop ten minutes, but Lou had already lost her sense of perspective. The televisions covered every surface, shiny screens all showing the same cricket match. Dozens of men in white leaped silently for a ball to the left. Thousands of fans jumped to their feet in mute celebration. Lou had stopped going into shops that sold things she couldn't afford years ago; it was the best way she knew of saving money. In the interim, televisions seemed to have undergone some kind of revolution. She had no idea what any of the initials meant, whether HD was better than LCD, let alone why anyone would want a curved screen. Worse, she couldn't even tell which televisions were big anymore. Thirty-two inches sounded large, but compared to some of these wall-mounted monsters, it looked positively tiny.

"You really don't want anything under fifty inches," the salesman said. "Not if you want a comfortable viewing experience."

"We do," she heard herself saying back. "We want the most comfortable viewing experience going."

"What are you watching, Netflix? Foxtel? Movies?"

Aimee had Netflix, didn't she? "That's it."

"Then I know exactly what you need." He directed them to a television the width of her car. "Sixty-five inches, smart capabilities, Ultra HD 4K. Netflix and all the rest are already programmed in." He pushed a few buttons, and *Gilmore Girls* flicked up on the giant screen.

Over a thousand dollars for a television. It sounded obscene.

"We can't buy that," Tansy said quietly.

We shouldn't, thought Lou, watching Lorelai drink coffee. These must be reruns, surely. The show was as old as Tansy. Lou had had a boxy TV for the first few years in their old flat, left behind by the previous tenant. *Gilmore Girls* had been one of her favorites, proof that you could do it alone.

"Let's look at some smaller ones," said Tansy. "Or I can find us something secondhand online."

The old television had blown up one evening, the ancient tube finally giving out with a puff of actual smoke. The repairman Lou called had laughed. "Not worth fixing that, love," he'd said. "Cheaper to buy a new one." Lou, who hadn't bought a new anything for three years, quietly paid his call-out fee and shoved the *TV Week* in the bin.

"If cash flow is an issue, we can help with that," said the salesman.

"We're fine," said Tansy. "We don't need it."

"We do actually," said Lou. "Tell me."

There was an app, apparently. You entered the amount you wanted to borrow, and the purchase was either approved, or not. "Six months interest free. Have you got something with your address on it?" She did. They didn't even need to go back to the counter.

"But you hate debt," hissed Tansy.

Which was true. But where had that attitude gotten her?

A house that her daughter didn't want to hang out in, and that Lou didn't want to either. On the oversize television, Lorelai and Rory hugged. Lou decided that was a good omen.

"We'll take it," she said. Because didn't she have a PayPal account full of cash from the old furniture, and a steady job, and a mortgage-free house? "Show me how to download this thing."

SHE HAD A plan, Aimee reminded herself, as she flew down River Road, darting across the one-way bridge when it wasn't even her turn to go. She gave a wave of apology to a visibly startled Sharna as she passed. But Aimee had a plan, with numbered steps to follow, all logical and prescribed. Literally prescribed—it was in a booklet she'd been given by a clinical psychologist to prevent her brain from spinning. You could argue it was already in motion, but that didn't mean Aimee couldn't slow it down.

She didn't bother to pull into the garage, just abandoned her car outside the house, blocking the truck, but she'd worry about that later. Aimee strode down the hallway to her study. The booklet was locked away at the bottom of her filing cabinet. She grabbed it and sat down at her desk.

"Mum?"

"Not now, Shelley."

"But, Mum—"

"I'm writing!" The kids knew her writing time was sacrosanct. And it wasn't even a lie. Aimee turned to the first fresh page. WHAT'S THE WORST THAT COULD HAPPEN? it asked.

She wrote the date in the top-right-hand corner, as she had a dozen times before.

Thinking on paper. That's how the psychologist described it. When the brain knows there's a plan, a solution, it calms down. Pros and cons lists don't work—a really obsessive mind will always manage to create an even score—but writing out a worst-case scenario forces the brain to acknowledge that everything is manageable. That the worst-case scenarios are, in fact, in your head.

It was a process Aimee believed in, because it had worked for her before. She turned her attention to the first column. THE SITUATION.

Well, that was easy. She wrote quickly, describing the accident.

MY FEARS.

Keep it simple, that was the key. *That we caused the crash*, Aimee wrote in tiny letters. *That we put a man and his son in the hospital. In intensive care.* They said in town that Pete had lost his sight. So they'd have blinded him as well, a widower, living alone, raising a teenager. Aimee gripped her pen.

WHAT'S THE WORST-CASE SCENARIO?

This bit was always the hardest. *We get found out. Everyone hates us. No one ever speaks to me again. I go to jail. I get sued. We lose the vineyard. I never forgive myself. Nick never forgives me.*

WHERE AM I BEING IRRATIONAL/FORTUNE-TELLING/ CATASTROPHIZING/EXAGGERATING/DISTORTING/JUMP- ING TO CONCLUSIONS/USING MAGICAL THINKING/DOING OTHER PEOPLE'S THINKING FOR THEM?

Aimee couldn't remember what magical thinking was, but it didn't matter. There was enough here to get on with. She sucked the end of her pen. This was usually the eye-opening bit, where the flaws in her thinking became apparent. But she couldn't see any here. She wasn't being irrational. She wasn't catastrophizing, or imagining things. A *plane* had come down. That wasn't in her head. And people who caused accidents, especially those who hid them, got into trouble. Fact. So she'd need a lawyer, and they couldn't afford one. They didn't even have enough money this year to fix the roof. Pete could sue them; that was a very real possibility. In which case they'd have to sell the vineyard. The land that had been in Nick's family for generations. Nick would be heartbroken, and his parents would never speak to her again. Aimee stared miserably at the blank box in front of her. Obviously, this technique worked better on abstract fears, rather than things that had *actually happened*. She drew a big question mark in the middle of the page.

WHAT WOULD I DO?

And this was the part that was supposed to make her feel better. Where she wrote a practical answer to her worst-case scenario. *I'd move into an apartment with the children. I'd fly to Adelaide and nurse Mum until she died.* All answers she'd given to her fearful *What If?* situations in the past. Aimee stared at the little notebook. But there were no answers for this one. No plan B to reassure her. Because this problem was real, so clever psychology questions to stop her head *making things up* didn't work.

There were only two questions that mattered and neither of them was printed on this sheet of paper. Aimee tore the double page from the booklet and started ripping it into tiny strips. One: Did they cause the accident? And two: If so, did anyone know? Those were the questions she needed answers to, and she needed a new strategy to get them.

IT WAS AMAZING how just walking through the door of your childhood home stripped years off you in a way the fanciest face creams never could. Melinda twisted her watch, the first really expensive thing she'd ever bought, to remind herself she was an adult as she vied with the cricket for her dad's attention.

"Two more minutes, Mellie, I want to see if—YES! YES! Oh, well *done!*"

A successful adult. Melinda let out a small sigh, loud enough to be heard but not to be reprimanded for.

"Why don't you come into the kitchen with me," whispered Polly. "We can have a glass of wine and a gossip, leave him to it."

"I'm fine," said Melinda, slouching farther into the sofa. She had no desire to hang out with her father's latest girlfriend, a chirping parakeet of a woman who'd be replaced in a few months anyway. "I've only got a few minutes."

"Hold your horses," said her father. "They'll be done in a— oh YES! Nice one!"

Melinda scrolled through her emails as her dad slapped the side of the armchair. She should have called instead. But she'd been driving past, and in such a good (post-orgasm) mood that she'd thought why not? She stared at the back of her father's bushy gray head. This was why not.

The last wicket fell and the crowd erupted. Melinda's dad nodded appreciatively. "So what can we do for you today then, Miss Mellie?" he asked as he searched for the remote control.

"I was on my way back from the airport. I came to tell you how well it went."

"How what went?" He jabbed at the mute button.

"The conference. LoveFest."

"Right, right." The batteries in the remote were clearly dead. Her dad got stiffly to his feet and started rummaging around the TV console. "Well go on then, tell me."

Melinda tried to recapture some of her former excitement. "It was fantastic," she said, the words sounding hollow to her own ears. She'd been so looking forward to describing the packed ballroom, the cheering crowds, the positive news coverage—"television too. It's still online if you want to watch."

"Mm-hm."

"I've emailed you the links. There was a particularly flattering segment on *Weekend Breakfast*." Australia's Bobbi Brown, they'd called her. "I've had two more offers to buy me out."

Her dad nodded, distracted. "Polly, where are the batteries? I'm sure I bought more."

It was like being twelve again. Melinda followed him into the kitchen. "We're already looking at spaces for our first American conference. New York probably, or maybe L.A. We might even have to hold two."

Her dad nodded again, forehead wrinkling as he scanned a supermarket receipt. "America, eh? Fancy."

"And I'm going to be on the cover of *Forbes*."

The email had been sitting in her inbox when she landed. Melinda had actually hugged a flight attendant, then apologized in case it was harassment. "No worries, Ms. Baker," the woman had said, fingering her "eternity ring" locket. "We all find you such an inspiration." Melinda had promised to send her the matching earrings.

"Mm-hmm. See, Polly, I did buy them, three packs it says here. Where've you put them?"

"Dad!" Melinda could hear the whine in her own voice. "Did you hear me?"

"I did. *Forbes*. Very nice."

"It's the Asia issue, not the international one obviously, but that's actually perfect because we've earmarked Singapore and Hong Kong for expansion. And the magazine is really well respected, lots of people in the finance industry read it—"

"I do know what *Forbes* is, Melinda."

"You don't seem very excited."

"Don't be silly, of course I am."

Polly smiled nervously. "Your dad's super proud of you, Melinda. He talks about you all the time."

For fuck's sake. Polly was what, ten years older than she was?

"It's a sign that we're being taken seriously," said Melinda. "That we'll get a strong reception if we go for a secondary listing."

"That all sounds great, Mellie. Really." Her dad rubbed his

hands together, made a little clapping sound. "So what else have you been up to?"

Other than preparing to expand my company in seven countries across three continents while raising ten million dollars? "Not much, funnily enough. That's about it."

"Being in the paper will be exciting," said Polly.

"It's a magazine, actually."

"Hey," her dad said mildly. "Don't be rude."

"Sorry." Melinda dug her nails into her palm. *Adult*, she reminded herself. "But enough about me," she said. "What have you guys been doing?"

"Oh, we've got loads going on," said her dad, coming to life again. "Polly's all go with the shop, aren't you?"

Melinda searched her brain to remember what kind of shop Polly ran. A florist? A dress shop?

"And the firm's flat out. I keep talking about taking a week off, finally getting a bit of a holiday, but the clients keep knocking on the door. Harrisons' have a girl suing them for wrongful dismissal, got pregnant in her probation period. Silly mare."

Melinda said nothing and hated herself for it.

"And we've got Matthew coming down from the Gold Coast, which'll be great, won't it, Polly? Don't see enough of him. Sounds like this new DJing gig of his is going well. Very well. Going to be a nice little earner that one, I reckon."

Melinda had a check for Matt in her handbag, the second she'd written in three months.

"Just need him to meet someone nice now, settle down and give me some grandchildren."

"Actually, I'm thinking of adopting a baby."

"There was one girl he was dating, we got all hopeful, didn't we, Pol, but she didn't seem to last long."

"Dad, did you hear me?"

"Sorry, what?"

"I'm thinking of adopting a baby."

Melinda's dad stared at her for a few seconds then roared with laughter. "What, you?"

Polly glanced at her boyfriend then started to titter as well.

"What's so funny?"

"Come off it, Melinda. That's hardly your sort of thing. You're not going to fit a breast pump in that now, are you." He waved a hand at her Prada saddle bag. "Express your milk between conference calls." He started laughing again.

"I said adopt one, not have one." Melinda walked quickly over to the sliding door and stared out into the safety of the garden. She didn't really believe in crying. Just like she didn't believe in blaming your parents for anything after the age of eighteen, or allowing other people to dictate your emotional state. Her father was still chuckling, Polly giggling. Melinda focused hard on a blurry row of spinach. She wouldn't normally care what they thought. She was just tired, with all the late nights recently. And maybe a little hormonal. She went for a subtle eye swipe with the top of her index finger as her father pulled her into his side.

"Ah now, love, don't cry. We're just having a laugh."

"I'm not crying," she mumbled.

He leaned down, wrapped her in a surprisingly bony hug.

"Don't get your knickers in a knot." He patted her hair. "We're just a bit surprised, that's all. You're not the kind of woman who wants a *baby*." He said the word slightly incredulously, as though she'd expressed a desire to start an alpaca farm.

"I might be."

"No you're not, Mellie." He gave her another squeeze. "Don't be silly. That's not you at all."

THEY'D BOUGHT A houseful of furniture, but Lou didn't mind. Not even when they veered away from the IKEA plan and ended up in Freedom Furniture. Or when they upgraded from Freedom, and found themselves buying a posh department-store sofa, large and deep and soft. The type of sofa you could collapse into. Comfortable.

Nothing bothered her today. Not the Hensley Town Festival go-kart race they'd gotten stuck behind leaving town, the buggies that had taken over the main street, adding an extra half hour on to their journey. Not the growing stack of receipts in her wallet, as they charged everything from a dining room table to a barbecue on her magic app. A *barbecue*. Imagine. A flash one too, with infrared burners and a warming rack. She had images of Melinda and Aimee and the kids all hanging out in her backyard, Tansy walking around with a tray of steaks, Lou being the hostess for once, rather than the ever-grateful recipient of everyone else's generosity.

"What should we bring?" they'd ask.

"Nothing," she'd say. "Just bring yourselves."

Lou was beginning to realize that she hadn't had to scrimp

and save so much over the years. Other people bought stuff on credit. Other people let themselves have nice things. And a lot of them earned less than she did.

Lou and Tansy wandered down Bourke Street, sipping their Starbucks like everyone else. Just one stop to go, then they'd call it a day. Lou's feet were going to kill her later, but too bad. She ignored the blister forming on her right heel and enjoyed her five-dollar macchiato.

The baby shop was an older one, its facade dated among the trendy clothes shops. There were newer chains they could have gone to, but this was the shop that Lou had wandered through more than a decade ago, belly distended, rubbing the handles of buggies she couldn't afford. Tansy's buggy had been a gift from an anonymous well-wisher, dropped off in the stairwell of her building during the night. It was black and gray and a bit ugly, but she didn't care. She was just glad it hadn't been nicked.

The buggies, however, had gone the way of the televisions: instead of two or three plasticky upright models, there was a veritable fleet of all-terrain vehicles. Some of them even had *gears*.

"Isn't it a bit early?" whispered Tansy.

Lou kissed the top of her head. "We don't have to," she said. "But I thought you'd made up your mind."

"I have," said Tansy. "But it makes it all feel a bit . . . real."

"We can just look then. It'll be fun to look."

And it *was* fun, the most they'd had in ages. Better than stripping the house even. Lou and Tansy fondled tiny onesies and miniature booties, Tansy asking Lou's advice on fabrics and sizes as though Lou was a font of knowledge, rather than a nuisance. Lou felt a brief flutter of excitement. This baby was her own flesh and blood, after all. We'll just buy one, they agreed, picking out an adorable mint green suit with a sleepy stegosaurus on the breast. Well, maybe two.

"Aren't these precious?" said the saleswoman as she wrapped up their pile. "And these are for——" She looked uncertainly from Lou's midthirties bloat to Tansy's teenage flatness.

Tansy stuck her chin out. "Me."

"My daughter," confirmed Lou. "I'm going to be a grand-mother."

"Well, isn't that exciting?" said the woman.

"Hugely," said Lou. "We're over the moon."

And do you know what, she thought, as she carried their over-size bags back to the car. *I think I'm even starting to mean it.*

AIMEE PULLED AT the neck of her slippery shell top and tried not to feel like a complete idiot. It's really only a T-shirt, she told herself. A bit of makeup. And a skirt. You're not that dressed up. Melinda wears this kind of thing every day. So why did she feel like she was going to a wedding? Aimee wanted to turn the car around, drive back to the house, and pull on her jeans. Instead, she smeared on another coat of lip gloss and took a quick swig from her water bottle. Right. Showtime. She forced herself out of the car.

The muffins were warm against her shirt as Aimee trotted across the field, her wedges catching as she ducked under the flapping plastic police tape. They weren't the ideal shoes, but she'd wanted the extra height, and heels would have made her look ridiculous. If she didn't already.

Damien spotted her and waved, strode toward her smiling as he checked his phone. He wasn't a bad-looking man. Probably ten years older than she and Nick were, a bit florid in the face. She'd heard the accident team was putting in as many hours at the pub as they were on the crash site. His wedding ring caught the sun as he shoved the phone into his pocket. Harmless banter then, she told herself. For both of them.

"I thought you might be back," he said.

"Well, I had to deliver on my promise."

"And which promise was that?"

"The muffins." She held out the plastic container. Their hands brushed slightly as he took the box from her.

"Homemade?"

"Of course."

He cracked the lid. "Smells delicious. Banana?"

"Carrot. Sorry."

"Even better." He grinned. "So what do you want in return?"

Aimee hadn't flirted with anyone since she was a teenager. "Reassurance that you're not just out here chatting up the local women," she said, looking up through her lashes. "That you're doing your important job properly, to protect everyone." God, she sounded like a bad Harlequin romance. "And I wanted the chance to see you again, of course." Actually, Harlequin had better lines.

"Well, someone's in a good mood. You must have heard the news." He grinned at her confusion. "What, you don't know?"

"Know what?"

"Your mate's son is awake. Hasn't anyone told you?"

Lincoln was awake? Aimee wobbled on her stupid shoes. She grabbed Damien's forearm to steady herself.

"Opened his eyes this morning. Not able to speak yet, but he's conscious, and looking good." Aimee tightened her grip, not trusting herself to stand. "Hey," he said. "Careful. People will talk." But he was smiling.

Awake. That was amazing. Aimee felt twenty pounds lighter, everything felt lighter, the sun, the heat, her head. Because if Pete's son was awake, then none of this was as bad. She could live with what they'd done if they hadn't killed anyone. Aimee took a deep breath of wonderfully fresh air and sent a silent thank-you upward.

"Made your day, haven't I?"

Aimee grinned. "You have no idea."

"You won't need me anymore then, I guess." He squinted at her. "To tell you about the investigation. Remember? Or are you not bothered about that now?"

Was she? Strangely, not as much. That all-encompassing need to *know*, the urge to check and ask and just *be* there, in case she could influence things, had dissolved in the shimmery heat of the January sky. If they found part of a lantern, well, what did that really prove? Anyone could have let them off. Aimee felt as though she'd been given a second chance.

"Not that anything I could tell you matters that much anyway," Damien continued. "Not anymore. Important thing now is going to be what the boy has to say. He's the one who'll be able to tell us what happened."

MELINDA'S DAD INSISTED on seeing her to her car.

"You're sure you're okay?" he said, as they strode across the lawn. "Don't want you driving if you're upset."

"I'm fine," said Melinda. "I need to get back and start dealing with emails."

"You don't want to stay for tea?"

"I really can't."

"Well, make sure you put your shades on. You'll have the sun in your eyes heading into town."

It was only twenty minutes to Melinda's apartment, but her dad always behaved as though she was crossing the Nullarbor. They stood shoulder to shoulder staring out toward the hills, the sun starting to play peekaboo behind the purple ranges.

"Never get tired of that view," he said. "You don't get a view like that in the city."

Melinda nodded, mentally prioritizing the work she had to do when she got in. It was all very well spending hours rolling around naked with her IPO advisor, but it would take her the week to catch up.

"Terrible thing what's happened to that boy, though," her father continued. "Poor old Pete. That's got to be killing him."

"Mmm-hmm." Melinda placed her handbag on the passenger seat.

"There'll be some lawsuits with that one, mark my words."

Melinda straightened up. "What makes you say that?"

"Lawyer's intuition." He tapped his forehead with a wrinkled finger. "You've got a competent, experienced pilot, ditching a plane for no reason? With his son strapped in next to him? I don't think so. Something happened. Either with the plane, or with the fireworks. None of those vineyards will have had permission for a display. And I'd be surprised if that Cessna was being kept up to spec. Finances at the aero club have been tight for years." He shook his head. "Someone will be liable. Someone always is."

Lou slipped into Tansy's room, pulling the door quietly shut behind her. Tansy still slept like she had as a toddler: on her back, arms flung sideways, hair sweat-stuck to her forehead. The sheet had been kicked free from the mattress she was using till the new furniture arrived. Lou rested her bum on the windowsill and watched her daughter breathe.

Lou hadn't breast-fed Tansy for long, hadn't spent months gazing lovingly at her suckling child. Not because she didn't want to. Tansy had turned her head away after the first couple of weeks, rejected anything that didn't come in a bottle. Bloody-minded. Her mother's daughter. So Lou was used to sneaking these quiet moments of adoration. She slid down the wall and sat on the floor hugging her knees. Secret adoration that Tansy would never countenance awake. Although Lou wasn't the type of mother to engage in gratuitous child worship anyway. She'd never been a helicopter parent, hovering over her daughter in case of splinters or accidental nut ingestion. She'd never been one of the health Nazis, sending Tansy off to birthday parties with a printed list of what she wasn't allowed to eat.

No, Lou had been pretty laissez-faire, making things up as she'd gone along. As if she'd had another choice. She leaned over and pushed Tansy's damp hair away from her face. Would things have worked out differently if she'd given Tansy a father? Pointed a finger at someone in town and forced him to take responsibility? You heard so much about the importance of male role models. But Lou hadn't wanted to lie. It didn't seem fair.

And they hadn't done that badly, not really. Yes, Tansy was pregnant, and Lou looked fifty at thirty-five, but they were alive and healthy, and they didn't steal or cheat or hurt others. Lou took stock of her sleeping daughter, better behaved in the past forty-eight hours than she had been in the last ten years. Maybe she could choose to look at this baby not as the end of everything, but as a fresh start. Lou knew she hadn't made much of her life so far. But she could be a fantastic grandmother. Modern. Hip. She pictured Tansy and herself taking a toddler on road trips, family holidays to Bali or Fiji. They could all get passports. It wasn't quite the big European trip Lou had dreamed of, but it still sounded pretty good.

The room lit up, the moon scanning the floor like a searchlight as it broke free of the scattered clouds. They'd pulled Tansy's curtains down as well, even though they were an inoffensive beige; the curtain pulling had become a little addictive. Lou started to fold T-shirts now, to stack fashion magazines into neat piles on the floor. She leaned over to grab a dirty sock and accidentally knelt on Tansy's hand.

"Mum? What are you doing?"

"Shhh. Go back to sleep."

Tansy squinted at her. "It's nighttime."

"I know. I'm just having a tidy. Shut your eyes."

Tansy obeyed. Lou kept sorting, the way she had when Tansy was a baby, grabbing random bursts of time for chores while her daughter slept. She started chucking dirty laundry toward the door.

"Mum—"

"It's okay, it's okay. I'm going now." Lou leaned over and kissed Tansy on the forehead, breathing in sweat and skin and a hint of Allure, Lou's only good perfume that had mysteriously disappeared a few months ago. She said nothing, just snuck another kiss while she could. "Love you," she said.

"Love you too," muttered Tansy, and Lou sat back on her heels in surprise. As she did, she knocked a photo off a stack of books next to the mattress. She moved to put it back, then paused. It was one of her dad's seventies shots; Lou recognized the rounded corners, the yellow and brown tones, the Kodak branding on the back. She held the photo up to the moonlight. Her mother stared blankly back at her from a hospital bed. Her arms clutched a baby Lou, too tightly. She wasn't smiling, but no wonder. The photo must've been taken straight after Lou was born; her hair was still damp, her face red. There were no flowers or congratulations cards yet. Just one exhausted new mother—Lou was a fifteen-hour labor, she'd continually been reminded—and a nervous young father, capturing the moment with his trusty Pentax.

"Tansy," she whispered. This had to be the earliest photo of herself. So why hadn't she seen it before? "Hey, Tansy, where did this come from?"

"Mm-hm?" Tansy rolled over.

"The picture. Where'd you get it?"

Tansy opened one eye. "It was in the album. In an envelope." She smiled sleepily. "You look like me. Same nose."

Her mother probably hadn't thought it was flattering, but Lou liked the photo. It looked real. It looked like what motherhood was: hard work.

"Leave it," whispered Tansy. "I want it here next to me."

Lou rested her hand on top of her daughter's damp head. Her daughter, who had all that hard work to come. "I'll get you a frame," she promised.

The December sales figures were better than forecast. And what perfect timing, just ahead of their investor road show. Melinda poured herself a glass of wine to celebrate and tried to appreciate the numbers parading proudly in front of her. Except that she didn't feel like celebrating. She felt like crying. No, she felt like howling. Throwing herself onto her eighteen-hundred-thread-count white Egyptian cotton sheets face-first, mascara be damned.

Beyond her balcony Hensley was coma still; the town had already tucked itself into bed. Melinda tried to focus on her spreadsheets, but the house was too silent to concentrate. The peace that she usually loved—double doors flung open to the summer night, the only noise the gentle rustling of her curtains, the chirp of distant cicadas—was suddenly too much. Her beautiful, sparse apartment felt as empty as she did.

Post-event comedown, that's what this flatness was. Melinda took a slug of wine. She'd had three days surrounded by noise and excitement, everyone treating her like some kind of guru. It was only natural to feel a bit low. She picked up her phone. Nearly twelve. Too late to speak to Aimee or Lou. And there was no way in hell she was phoning Clint. You didn't booty-call someone on your payroll, even if they had licked prosecco from your vagina. Hensley prosecco, of course. Even drunk and horny, Melinda was loyal to her friends.

Outside the building, a car alarm went off; inside, Melinda logged on to Instagram. She felt her shoulders loosen as she began to scroll through dozens of photos of herself. Melinda speaking, Melinda laughing, Melinda dancing with her dress hitched up around the top of her thighs. God, she didn't remember that. On and on she scrolled, switching to Facebook when the feed ran dry. Her curators had wasted no time and no emoticons in letting the world know just how awesome LoveFest had been. She smiled at the images of herself, a more relaxed version than usual, hugging her curators, posing for selfies. There were more than a few photos with Clint; they looked good together. Natural. She poured a little more wine, unsure if the warmth and relaxation she was finally feeling were coming from the bottle, or the memory of how *happy* she'd been in Sydney. Part of the stream of life, rather than merely an observer. Could you tell in the pictures she was having sex? Yes—there was absolutely a glow.

There was also an adoption conversation. Melinda clicked on the comments under one photo, captioned "Sexy Mama— yes, really!" Her curators were discussing her "announcement." Well, Clint had warned her. She leaned back, trying to decide if that was a good thing. Or more important, whether other people felt it was a good thing.

Melinda had thought carefully about this on the short drive into town. It didn't matter whether her family felt she was capable of raising a baby or not. (Matthew had left a charming voice message while she was in the shower, hooting about the whole adoption idea and calling her Melinda Jolie.) But it did matter what the public thought. Potential investors, fund managers, analysts. Her defensive blurt about adopting might well put them off. Who wanted to invest in a company where the CEO had other priorities?

Melinda opened a fresh browser and searched for "Melinda Baker" and "baby." Then "Melinda Baker" and "adoption." Unsurprisingly, the story had leaked. She pulled the laptop closer, back in work mode now. Beyond the curator gossip, a couple of investor forums were discussing the idea. A few users— male, by the looks of it—had questioned her commitment, but they'd quickly been eaten alive. Interesting. Several Women in Business blogs were supportive to the point of being giddy, but you'd expect that. Only one mainstream newspaper had picked up the story. There was a sidebar in the paper's Investor Notebook. Melinda clicked through.

Melinda Feels the Love, it stated, running quickly through the statistics from LoveFest, the new incentive structure. And then at the end:

> *It seems LoveLocked may not be Ms. Baker's only baby for long. In an emotional speech, the popular entrepreneur revealed that she was infertile, and looking to adopt. AustraStock analyst Phil Shepherd said the news didn't alter his buy recommendation for her upcoming IPO. "If anything, the opposite," he told Investor Notebook. "This brings Melinda much closer to her sales and customer demographic, and might make her more relatable to her core constituency. And if there is one woman who can juggle both a multimillion-dollar business and motherhood, it's Melinda Baker."*

Melinda sat back in her chair. The chances were zero, less than. Single woman, working fifteen-hour days, six days a week, across three time zones. No family support. An impractical glass-filled, sharp-edged apartment, not even safety locks on the windows. There was no way in hell anyone would give her a baby. But it would look good to try. And she really had to now. She didn't need anyone accusing her of lying, any clever journalists wondering why there was no paperwork. Melinda leaned forward and started to type.

Chapter 18

Pete sat next to his son, his miracle child, awake from the dead, and felt nothing. All around him, people were quietly celebrating. Doctors, nurses—even Cameron had grabbed his arm, the first time they'd touched in years. The air was fizzing with barely contained excitement, a World Cup goal scored in intensive care. "Awake," people kept whispering to each other, marveling. "Awake." But this wasn't awake. This was bullshit.

They'd come and fetched him from physical therapy, two nurses bursting through the door like a firecracker, and he'd lumbered blindly back down the hallway with them. Pete had almost run those last few steps, his stick sliding across the hospital floor, had to be told to slow it down. But when they'd reached Lincoln's room, everything was the same as it had been at breakfast. His son wasn't sitting up, asking confused questions about where he was. His son wasn't doing anything. The machines were still doing it all. It took Pete a few moments to realize, to hear the devices beeping and humming and feeding and emptying his child. And then he'd collapsed, his shocked breath setting his chest on fire.

"You can't expect him to be right as rain straightaway," said the neurologist. "It's not like flicking on a light switch." Lincoln's eyes were open, apparently; he could focus, had turned his head. But still, Pete felt cruelly tricked. The five-minute stumble down the corridor, the word twinkling in his ear—*awake!*—had been the only bright moment since the accident. And now he sat with a limp hand in his, faking a smile that the doctors could clearly see through.

"He's not so much awake as aware," one said quietly, pulling a chair up alongside. "Completely normal with head injuries. It's a gradual process, coming round. It's not like the movies. You need to be patient. He'll come back to us, in his own time."

I'm not impatient, Pete wanted to say. *I'm fucking guilty.* With that one word—*awake!*—Pete had begun to feel the impossible: absolution. Now he just felt as though the universe was playing a trick on him. Teaching him a lesson, letting his hopes fly high, before bringing them crashing and burning to the ground.

"Give me a moment," he said. "I want a bit of time alone with him, if that's okay." The room murmured understanding, amid a flurry of scraping furniture and padding feet. Pete pulled his chair up right next to the bed, so close he could feel Lincoln's breath.

"Mate," he said when they were gone, his hand on top of

Lincoln's head, cupping it like he had when he was little. "I'm so sorry."

People spoke about what they'd do for their children, if they had to. If they could. Offering to die in their place, to take the pain on themselves. Hang around a hospital like this and you heard it all the time. *I wish I could have the chemo for him. If only I was the one who was sick.* There was a woman who got a new tattoo every time her daughter was brought in for treatment, so she could feel the needles and burning as well. That was love, that was. But what Pete was feeling was more complicated. He let the tears come, not bothering to wipe them from his useless eyes. Because he'd done this, he'd put his son here, and for just a few bloody minutes it had seemed like the world was going to forgive him.

There was a trolley rattling down the hallway. Pete waited until it passed, then laid his head carefully on his son's chest. "This is all my fault," he said, feeling the determined heartbeat beneath his cheek. "I should've known better. I messed up, mate. I really messed up."

The crying felt strangely cathartic. Pete wasn't religious, but his confession took on the cadence of a prayer. "I'm sorry," he choked out. "I'm sorry. I'm sorry. Please. I'm sorry."

A curtain whispered behind them. "Who's there?" Pete called, but no one answered. He waited, making sure, then went back to his pleas. "I'm sorry," he continued, voice low. "Please, I'm sorry."

And maybe someone did hear, maybe there really was

someone up there who answered the prayers of the desperate, because in the middle of Pete's chant, an arm knocked gently against the side of his head. There was a grunt, not even particularly human, but still. Pete sat up so fast he sent an IV pole reeling.

"Mum," said a hoarse voice in the bed.

"He's awake," Pete called. "Someone, anyone, he's really awake."

HE DIDN'T REMEMBER until later, didn't even think about the noise he'd heard until the nurse came in to turn Lincoln. "Miracle or no miracle, we don't want him developing bedsores," she said, bustling around the room. Lincoln was asleep again, but that was fine, he could take his own sweet time now that Pete knew he was going to be okay.

"You've got a visitor," the nurse continued. "Out at reception. Why don't you go chat with her, maybe get some fresh air." Her tone was light, but forceful. "Leave us to do his exercises in peace. We don't need an audience, do we, Lincoln?"

An audience. "Was there someone here earlier?" Pete asked casually. "About half an hour ago? I thought I heard someone in the room."

"Must have been Cameron," the nurse said. "He's been in and out all day. Like a cat, that one—you just turn and he's there." There was a whir as the bed was lowered. "Lovely for him, isn't it, his brother coming round? You two have really got something to celebrate."

CAMERON STOOD IN the doorway, taking stock of the woman perched beside his stepfather. She looked vaguely familiar, but then so did all the women in this town. Dark curly hair. Plump. Sexy, if you liked older women. Which he didn't, particularly. He could see why Pete would fancy her, though. They were speaking quietly, heads close together. Intimate.

She must have felt his eyes on her, because she looked up with a start.

"Don't mind me," he said easily. She wore a lot of jewelry, as the better-off women in Hensley tended to. Quite a bit of makeup too. She was clearly making an effort. For a blind man?

"You two carry on," he said, leaning against the door frame.

She stumbled to her feet, flushing pink. "I was just leaving." She bent down to kiss his stepfather—on the cheek, Cameron noted, but with a lingering hand on his arm. "I don't want to take up your time. Today of all days."

Cameron didn't move aside as she passed, forcing her to brush against him, reeking of sweat and an overly sweet perfume. Nervous. That was interesting. And bolting like a horse. He followed her slowly out into the hallway, stood and watched as she jabbed at the button for the elevator.

"Who was that?" he asked the duty nurse, as the elevator began its descent.

"That? Oh, that's Aimee Verratti." The nurse held up a basket. "She brought muffins, look."

"The two of them are friends?"

"Dunno. Assume so." The nurse rooted around beneath the

tea towel. "Everyone's friends with everyone out here. Ooh, look, carrot. Lovely."

He held out his hand. "Has she been before?"

"Don't think so," said the nurse. "Although I'm not always the one on duty. I could check with the others." She looked up from the basket. "But why don't you just ask your dad?"

"Stepdad." Cameron tore his muffin in half, straight down the middle. The inside was sticky-soft and still slightly warm. "Don't worry," he said, sinking his teeth in. "I will."

Chapter 19

Most of the children had chosen to paint the gold rush. Aimee wandered around the post office, hmming appreciatively at endless misshapen figures holding outsize pans and the sort of nuggets that would have given Hensley a GDP on a par with that of Switzerland.

"Aren't they darling?" called Sharna, from behind the counter.

"Darling," agreed Aimee, raising an eyebrow at a blue ribbon attached to a particularly average painting by the mayor's favorite grandson. "What was the theme?" she asked, placing her handbag on the counter.

"Town slogan, of course," said Sharna, jerking her head at the banner on the far wall. HENSLEY: THE LUCKY TOWN it read, in clashing football-team colors of maroon and gold. "Same as last year."

"Creative," murmured Aimee, although she personally loved the slogan, agreed with it completely. "So what's been going on?" she asked, pulling a couple of fifties from her purse. "Can you break some notes for me?"

"Well, we've all been talking about you," said Sharna, taking the money.

Aimee's breath caught at the bottom of her throat.

"Whole town's looking forward to hearing this poem of yours. Maxine's even recording it for the radio. But no pressure!"

"Oh God," said Aimee, reaching for her water bottle. "Don't tell me that." She screwed the lid back on, tight. "Surely there are more interesting things to talk about than my poetry though."

"Well, you know the Reillys are leaving, moving to the city. Hensley's not enough for them anymore." Sharna sniffed her disapproval.

"Is that so."

Sharna bit her lip as she counted Aimee's notes. "The cupcake shop's closing down. No great surprise. I said there wasn't enough business to keep that store going, but when did Deidre ever listen to me?"

For God's sake. "Have you heard about Lincoln?"

Sharna paused, keys dangling. "About him waking up? Sure did." She dropped her voice, even though they were the only people in the building. "Course, there are a lot of unanswered questions. Let me get this sorted, and I'll bring you up to speed."

Aimee leaned against cool plaster while Sharna bustled out back to the safe. Nick never understood why she didn't just use the local bank, but Sharna's wooden post office was the beating heart of Hensley. If there was a job going or a car for sale, it was on the notice board, internet be damned. If you needed to make a phone call without your number popping up on someone's mobile, her tin roof sheltered the only pay phone left in town. And if there was a rumor doing the rounds, Sharna would've heard it. The trick was to get what you needed without divulging your own family secrets, which would be halfway to Melbourne before you were out the door.

"Here you go, couple of twenties and the rest in tens and fives." Sharna tucked the little plastic bag of notes inside Aimee's handbag herself. "Oooh, this is pretty," she said, opening an eye shadow compact. "Dior, fancy. Melinda give you this?"

"Birthday present to myself," said Aimee, taking the compact back and zipping it firmly away. "So, what were you saying about the Kasprowiczes?"

"Well." Sharna settled her elbows into a pair of grooves worn into the post office counter by decades of gossip and judgment. "You know the boy's woken up, obviously. Which is great news."

"Yes," said Aimee, who wavered almost hourly when it came to whether the news was great or not. Obviously, she was glad Pete's son was doing well. But the idea that Lincoln might have seen something had thrown her. She'd sat outside the hospital for nearly an hour, convincing herself that she didn't need to go in, that she'd be intruding on a family she barely knew, but in the end she couldn't stand not knowing whether he'd said anything incriminating, if she'd be met with frosty stares from the nurses and naked hatred from Pete and a police officer saying, "Aimee Verratti? What a coincidence. Can we have a moment?"

"He's floating in and out of consciousness, apparently. Was able to say a few words to his dad last night, but not, you know, sentences. People reckon he's going to be fine, but I dunno. He was out for almost a week. You can't tell me that's good for things upstairs." Sharna tapped her own head knowingly.

Aimee nodded back. She'd been horribly relieved to find Lincoln was sleeping, that he'd only been awake for a few minutes. And then instantly disgusted with herself. How could she be pleased that a teenage boy, the same age as Byron, was lying unresponsive in a hospital bed? What kind of terrible person would hope this child stayed alive—of course she wanted him to stay alive—but that he also might conveniently have his father's memory loss?

Although if he was going to have brain damage, and that's what she was hoping for, wasn't she, really, then maybe he'd be better off— *No, Aimee. Don't even go there.* She took a swig from her water bottle.

"So they did some tests." Sharna leaned over the counter. "Little bird at the hospital told me. And there was alcohol in Pete's system. He'd been drinking before he went up." Sharna's chest gave a self-important quiver.

"Are you sure? That doesn't sound like Pete."

Peter Kasprowicz was the type of man who'd been forty-five since he was seventeen. Earnest. Community minded. The kind of man who volunteered for the Clean Up Our Riverbank drive, then actually stayed to pick up rubbish, rather than duck off to the pub with the rest of them. "I've never even seen him drunk."

"Arthur's been asking around. No one saw him at the pub, and he wasn't at the river barbecue. But he'd certainly had a few. Maybe at home alone." Sharna nodded to herself. "Can't say I'm surprised. He hasn't been the same since Julia died. Maybe he turned to alcohol to blot it out."

"Maybe," said Aimee, taking another sip from her water bottle. "I can see why you would."

"Well, he's certainly medicating." Sharna tilted Aimee's bag, admired it. "And there's more. I don't want to gossip, but I once ran into him over in Meadowcroft picking up a prescription. I was just close enough to see the form on the counter, you know, when they go off to fill it. And it was for antidepressants. And everyone knows you're not supposed to mix the two."

"You can, actually," said Aimee.

"Well, I wouldn't know about that." Sharna didn't like being corrected. "I just know it's a lot to have in your system." The little bell on the veranda tinkled as someone walked up the post office steps. "And I know that if you're flying you're not supposed to drink at all. It's not like driving." Sharna closed Aimee's bag with a decisive little click. "Say what you like, that man's going to have some explaining to do."

MELINDA HAD JUST begun stuffing the thick A4 envelopes through the infuriatingly small mailbox opening when Aimee came barreling into her. "Hey," she said, quickly turning the envelopes over. "Watch it."

Aimee looked confused to see her. "What are you doing here?" she asked. "And what are you posting?"

"Nothing important." Melinda willed more envelopes into the gap, but the forms were thick and plentiful. "God, you'd think they'd widen this. What's Sharna going to do when Hensley discovers eBay?"

Aimee reached over and took the last couple of envelopes from her. "Adoption agencies?" she said. "In Bulgaria? Really?"

Melinda shrugged. It seemed incredible that these places couldn't be dealt with online, but more than half a dozen still insisted on a physical inquiry, with photos and photocopies. The more forms Melinda had filled out, the more strangely excited she'd become about the whole project, and the more important it seemed that she didn't let a single foreign possibility go unexplored. By 3 A.M. she had an empty bottle of wine, a stack of envelopes, and a possibly unwise photograph of her labor on Instagram: *Taking my first baby steps toward growing our LoveLocked family.*

"You're really going to do it. You're really going to adopt."

"Oi!" said Melinda, glancing through the open post office door, where Sharna was tacking a large banner. HENSLEY: THE LUCKY TOWN. Well, let's hope so. She pulled Aimee off the veranda steps and onto the footpath. "Keep it down. I'm not ready to take out a front-page ad in the *Hensley Echo* just yet."

"Sorry," said Aimee, but she didn't lower her voice. "But why didn't you just get your PA to post them? You don't do mail."

Because Melinda had wanted five minutes picking Sharna's brain, although now there was no chance. "Because I'm on my way to watch you speak. Two birds, one stone." She gave Aimee's arm a squeeze. "Are you excited?"

Aimee didn't seem to hear. "Guess what," she said. "Lincoln's awake."

Melinda checked over her shoulder. "That's nice," she said cautiously. "I'm glad to hear that."

"Even better, he doesn't remember anything!"

"There's nothing to remember." Melinda squinted at her suspiciously animated friend. "Have you been drinking coffee? You know you're not supposed to."

"No," said Aimee, indignantly. "Have you been shagging Clint?" She pulled out a copy of *The Age* and waved it in the air accusingly.

Blimey, that was quick. "We're seeing each other, actually," said Melinda, reaching for the moral high ground, and the newspaper.

"But you don't even like him," said Aimee, holding both out of reach. "You said he was boring and money-driven and full of himself."

"Well, maybe I was wrong."

Aimee held the paper higher. "He talks about himself in the third person."

"He's stopped doing that, actually." Melinda swiped again.

"He eats with his mouth open," Aimee reminded her. "He makes quote marks in the air with his fingers."

"Well, sometimes you have to compromise."

"But you don't compromise."

"Well, maybe that's the problem," said Melinda, exhausted.

Aimee was hyper, which meant she'd crash later, the town crier was in earshot, Melinda was riding on four hours' sleep, and they still had this bloody concert to get through. "Maybe I need to." She held her hand out. "You're being really fucking annoying, Aimee. Just give it to me." The paper was lowered; Melinda grabbed it. "*Thank* you."

"They call you a power couple," said Aimee petulantly.

"Really?" Melinda started flicking. "That's good." One of the pictures was extremely flattering. Maybe she could get a copy.

"No it's not."

"Aimee, just leave it."

"But you once caught him picking his nose when he didn't think anyone was looking!"

"I KNOW!" Melinda roared. "And I don't care. I'm just enjoying myself, all right?"

"O-kay," said Aimee, making the sort of face she'd tell Byron off for.

"For fuck's sake," Melinda snapped, feeling uncharacteristically teary and slightly out of control. "I'm allowed to have sex, aren't I? I'm allowed to have fun, aren't I? Don't worry, I'm not going to do anything stupid like marry him, or give him half the company."

"You don't sound like you're having fun," muttered Aimee, but she was interrupted by a loud "yoo-hoo" from the post office steps.

"Melinda," hollered Sharna, waving one of the stuffed envelopes jubilantly above her head. "This package, to China's International Child Foundation? Insufficient postage, love. You need to give me another dollar fifty."

BLOODY HELL, WHERE were they? Lou tried to keep her eyes on the door, but every two minutes she had to stop an over-excited Hensleyite from stealing her seats. "I'm saving them," said Lou, earning herself glares and tuts from exactly the sort of people who'd glared and tutted at her all her life. "My friends are coming."

"You can't save seats," one woman said indignantly. "It's against the rules."

"There are no rules," said Lou. "It's free seating, at a free event."

"But I'm live-streaming!" pleaded another.

"I don't care," said Lou. "And neither will anyone else. It's not the fucking Oscars."

Honestly, what were these people like? True, Lou had nabbed great seats: halfway down, right on the aisle, away from the village elders and overenthusiastic parents at the front, and perfect for quietly ducking out when you got bored. And you would get bored. Lou flicked through the badly photocopied program. Speeches from Rex the mayor, the Rotary president, the head of the local Country Women's Association. Numerous musical items and one-act plays. Good thing Aimee's poem was fairly high up; Lou wasn't going to last more than half an hour.

The hall was nearly full now. Lou spread the contents of her handbag across her spare seats so there could be no mistake. She ignored the evil looks and studied the front of her program. HENSLEY: THE LUCKY TOWN. Lucky for some. But the slogan didn't invoke the rise in blood pressure that it normally would. Even this hall, the site of so many snubbings and small humiliations, was beginning to look almost charming, with its wood paneling and homemade bunting. Lou watched a frankly adorable row of kindergarten kids with recorders being marched onto the stage. Well, maybe in some ways it was lucky. It was a safe place to raise children after all. Grandchildren. One little rascal began stealing the show, playing his recorder as though it was a saxophone and he was Kenny G. Was it wrong to hope Tansy had a boy? Lou had never raised a boy. She secretly thought she'd be suited to them.

Melinda and Aimee arrived at the start of a second-grade play depicting the gold rush.

"Where the hell have you two been?" asked Lou, clearing her stuff off their seats. "And why do you both look so weird?"

"Aimee's a bit caffeinated," hissed Melinda.

"Melinda's sleeping with Clint," whispered Aimee.

"Really?" said Lou. "Oh well. At least someone's getting some."

"*Thank* you," said Melinda.

"Shhh," said the woman sitting next to them.

"Lou, he's a dick," said Aimee.

"Well, yeah, of course," said Lou. "Biggus Dickus." She turned to Melinda, curious. "Is he, by the way? Biggus Dickus?"

"Fairly largish dickus, yes," said Melinda. "Above average dickus, certainly."

"Lucky you," said Lou. "I don't remember the last time I saw a dickus of any length."

"Behave," murmured Aimee.

"Oh, I've come across my fair share of dickus lately," said Melinda, clearly enjoying herself. "In both senses."

There were a few sniggers; the ears of the heavyset man in front began to go red. "Do you mind?" asked the woman sitting next to them, motioning to an oblivious child.

"Not really," said Lou. She might be feeling friendlier toward the town as a whole, but not its individual inhabitants. "So, did he do anything especially interesting with this dickus?"

"Oh God," said Melinda. "You know, he did this thing where he raised my legs over my head, like right over, so my feet were flat against the headboard, then piled pillows under my arse and entered me on his knees. It was incredible."

The woman next to them got up and moved.

"And then," said Melinda, not bothering to keep her voice down, "he tried to pour prosecco inside me and drink it out. It didn't exactly work, but it was weirdly sexy. I kept thinking of Mum's copy of *Lace,* remember? All that was missing was the goldfish."

Heads began to turn. The neck of the man in front of them was virtually purple. "*Stop* it," hissed Aimee.

"I don't even know if my legs still go over my head," Lou said wistfully. "Probably not. My stomach would get in the way."

"You two——"

"You could try yoga," came a voice from behind them. "My husband says it's like shagging a new woman."

"That's a hell of a lot better than him actually shagging a new woman," Melinda said loudly. "Which far too many men around here seem keen to do."

Aimee grabbed her handbag and pushed past their knees. There was a spare seat two rows in front. She settled into it, face turned pointedly toward the stage.

The second-grade gold rush finished; the third-grade depression began. Melinda leaned toward Lou. "I love you," she said quietly, giving her a squeeze. "And I'm sorry about the other night."

Lou squeezed back. "Me too."

"I was insensitive."

"I was oversensitive. Forget about it."

"So how are you feeling about everything? Any better?"

Lou gave Mel a genuine smile. "Really good," she said. "Honestly. I feel like it's all going to work out for the best."

MELINDA MONITORED THE back of Dave Tolford's neck as the mayor made his way toward the stage. It was slowly becoming less purple, like a nervous penis draining of blood and color. But the tips of his ears were still bright red, his shoulders tense. Good. Let him be the one to feel like a bloody idiot.

Biggus Dickus. Dickus Majora. Melinda scrolled quickly through her emails as the mayor arranged himself behind the lectern. Three from Clint, all work-related. And why wouldn't they be? He might not be quite the Dickus Twatus she'd initially thought, but he wasn't her boyfriend either. Melinda had no illusions about that. This wasn't a relationship, no matter what she told the others; this was a mutually beneficial arrangement between two busy, horny adults.

Melinda dropped her phone back into her handbag as the mayor began to acknowledge everyone who'd made this morning possible. Would all her relationships be like this, going forward? Unspoken understandings, reciprocal itch scratchings? The kind of sex where you thanked the other person afterward, as though they were doing you a favor. Even worse—how long had things been like that? Too long. Melinda's last real relationship, she realized as she watched Aimee swig from her water bottle, had probably been Nick.

Well, she'd messed that one up. Possibly—probably—her one chance for a proper family life with children and pets and weekly date nights that she could post on Facebook to prove the romance was still alive. He'd gone down on one knee in the middle of his parents' vineyard, spelled out the life they'd have together. The kind of life that made Melinda inwardly recoil. Devoid of any variety or growth, unless you counted bloody grapes. "No thank you," she'd said, as though she was turning down a job offer. "I don't think this is for me." He'd begged her to think about it, dropped the ring in a drawer, and taken her to bed, as if to remind her of what he could do for her. And he certainly could—that was one thing she'd never needed any convincing about. Melinda shuffled in her hard plastic chair as she remembered just how good the sex had been. How desirable and fun he'd made her feel, as opposed to the ageing spinster she'd somehow become. But sex was not enough. And once you'd said you didn't want to marry someone, the relationship was pretty much over, no matter how much you both tried to pretend you could carry on as normal. She'd broken up with him the week before she flew to Europe. "Don't wait for me," she'd said, shutting down his promises. "You need to find someone else. I'm going to." She hadn't expected him to find someone quite so soon, or so close to home. But when you were the one who left, you didn't get to dictate the terms.

THE MAYOR BEGAN to speak about the town's latest achievements, but Lou wasn't listening. All she could think about was Clint and Melinda in bed together. Melinda's small breasts bouncing gently, her pale thighs pushed wide to either side. Lou's bits began to tingle; she squeezed her legs together.

"New dividers for the town hall," Rex droned, "meaning it can be used by multiple community groups at the same time."

Had Clint made her come? Almost certainly. Lou felt her face heat up, like the poor bloke in front. She snuck a look at Melinda, perfectly composed, tried to imagine her with her jaw slack, her breath shallow. Lucky bitch. God, when was the last time Lou had shagged someone? A year ago at least. Probably two. Hell, *Tansy* had had sex more recently than she had. The tingling feeling disappeared. That was it, Lou vowed. The next person who asked her, the next person who so much as looked at her funny, she was going to sleep with.

The mayor moved on to this year's fund-raising plans. Tansy had been sick that morning; Lou had left her tucked in bed with a pot of ginger tea. Not so long ago she'd have dressed her up and dragged her out, paraded her in front of the old guard dotted around this hall, the churchgoers and committee members like her parents, including her parents, *especially* her parents, to show that she wasn't ashamed. She and Tansy had gone to every town event for fifteen years, just to make a point. School prizegivings, carol services, music recitals. It was the one time Tansy behaved.

Fifteen years. A decade and a half of passing her parents on the main street, of sitting just a couple of picnic blankets away down by the river, and never, ever saying a word. Her mother not so much as glancing down at Tansy in the kiddie seat of the supermarket cart as she reached over her for a tin of own-brand baked beans. And how the town had loved it.

The mayor started talking about community spirit and Hensley's deep-rooted Australian values, and Lou started snickering. All these good honest folk, the Harolds and Sonias and Carols, they all loved the drama. Lou glared at the gray heads sitting, innocent, in the front row. Hypocrites.

And yet without the standoff, Lou felt slightly lost. If it wasn't for Aimee's poem, she wouldn't even be here today. There was no point in making a point without anyone to make a point to. The anger had given her a reason to get out of bed every morning and face her mediocre life. To put on makeup and go to work in the soul-sucking office where *they* had to come to pay their property tax. Lou's adult life so far had been one giant Fuck You.

But that was the past. She had a new life now. A new role as a grandmother to look forward to, a new relationship with Tansy. A new house, sort of, to enjoy it all in. And sex. She was bloody well going to have sex. With anyone who had a penis.

NOT AGAIN. WHAT were they like? Aimee ignored the snickering behind her and concentrated on the mayor's speech. Lou and Melinda might not care what the town thought of them, but she did. What was the point of living in a small community if you didn't want to be a proper part of it? Why come to an event like this if you were just going to make a scene?

But Aimee knew why they were both here, today at least. She sat up straighter as the mayor began to introduce her.

"Our poet laureate," he intoned. "A leading light of this community. Not just for what she contributes in terms of her literary talent, but also the sheer amount she does to keep this town together behind the scenes. I'm not sure there would even *be* a Hensley if it weren't for Aimee Verratti."

Aimee smiled modestly. She *did* do a lot to keep the town together. And she was doing an okay job of keeping herself together, considering. Aimee mentally patted herself on the back as the mayor continued lavishing praise. "Girl Scouts, the Junior Baking Club, founding member of the Hensley Garden Committee." She'd only asked three people for reassurance since the accident. Well, four. Ish. But that was incredible progress. A couple of years ago, a situation like this would have floored her.

There were a lot of things she was handling well at the moment, actually. A long list of things she was keeping in perspective. She wasn't freaking out about their finances. She wasn't worried about how often Nick seemed to bump into Melinda. Shelley had broken her arm last year, in two places, and Aimee had calmly driven her to the hospital, made all the decisions about surgery and anesthetic without a moment's hesitation.

"Her poetry book, *A Light on the Vine,* was a local best-seller, now stocked in Melbourne and Sydney."

And all that without her pills. She'd been right to come off them; she'd lost ten pounds already, and her libido had come bouncing back. If she lost another ten, Nick's might as well. He said her weight didn't bother him, but Aimee could tell. They'd become more lights-off-duvet-up than midafternoon-on-the-winery-bench. Aimee missed the winery bench.

But that was the only issue in their relationship, in fact the only real problem in her life right now. Aimee remembered writing the little card for Melinda's letting-go exercise, how hard it had been to come up with anything wrong. Even the accident didn't seem like such a big deal anymore. Because the boy was okay, and that was a blessing. Whatever he saw and whatever he said, it didn't matter. Aimee smiled at Shelley and Byron, slipping through the stage curtain to hear her read, at Nick standing beside them, holding Shelley's double bass. The things that really mattered in her life were rock solid. She wasn't even bothered that the mayor had gotten the title of her book wrong.

Someone else obviously was, though. Another council member darted up to the stage with a folded piece of paper and an apologetic glance at Aimee.

"Reciting a poem she's written especially for Hensley's anniversary . . ." The mayor paused, confused, and patted for his reading glasses. "Excuse me a moment."

Aimee smiled patiently and gave her family a little wave. Nick spun the double bass, jazz style, and winked at her in return. That man was as hot at forty as he had been at twenty-three. Aimee felt a familiar tug deep in her stomach. Once she lost the rest of this weight, she was buying new underwear. *And* getting everything waxed. Nick wouldn't know what had hit him.

"Ladies and gentlemen, if I could just have your attention." The mayor was back, but without his Hensley Town Festival smile. He frowned as he smoothed the creases out of the piece of A4 he'd been handed. "I'm afraid I have to make an announcement. It's about the plane crash on New Year's Eve. Sorry, Aimee"—he looked grimly at her—"but I'm afraid this impacts you."

Oh God. They'd found a lantern. With her and Nick's bloody initials on it. Aimee's head whirred.

"I know you've all been following news of the accident, and that your thoughts and prayers are with the Kasprowicz family. As the deputy principal of Hensley High School, Peter Kasprowicz is a pillar of this community. He and his family may technically live in Meadowcroft, but they're still very much part of Hensley. We consider them our own."

She was going to be publicly admonished. Verbally flogged. The mayor was going to call her out in front of everyone for causing the accident and putting the entire community at risk of bushfire.

"This isn't easy to say." The mayor paused, scanning the crowd.

And then she was going to be marched off to the police station and charged with public endangerment and grievous bodily harm and destruction of public property and God knows what else. Aimee placed her water bottle in her handbag, ready for her exit.

"I'm very sad to have to tell you that Lincoln Kasprowicz passed away last night at St. Margaret's Hospital."

The room gasped in shock. The mayor rubbed a beefy hand across the top of his face. "Complications, from the accident. There'll be an announcement in tomorrow's paper." He stared directly at Aimee, whose heart gave a single, heavy thud. "So I don't think—well, given the circumstances, it doesn't seem appropriate to go on with the reading this morning, or the concert. I'm sorry, Aimee. I know you've been preparing for this."

Two hundred faces swung round to gawp at her. Aimee swallowed back the bile rising in her throat.

"I'm sure you agree it wouldn't be right to celebrate. Not now. But maybe you could lead us in a moment's silence instead."

The faces grew blurry as Aimee stumbled to her feet. She clutched the chair in front of her for balance, opened her mouth to speak. "Please bow your heads," she managed. And then she vomited, straight into her handbag.

Chapter 20

Shameful how much crap you could accumulate in barely a week. Pete sat numbly on the edge of the bed as nurses bustled around him, questioning what he wanted to take home. Surely he'd want to keep the little portable radio, the rest of the chocolates, what about the nice tin those biscuits had come in? All of it from misguided well-wishers; Pete had arrived with barely the clothes on his back.

And now he was leaving without the one thing that mattered most. "None of it," he said. "I don't want any of it."

What about the cards, they asked, surely he'd want the cards, the more personal gifts? There was a lovely photo album someone had put together.

"Leave it," he snapped, and rolled onto his back. Stared at the ceiling, or at least he would have if he could see.

"Mr. Kasprowicz—"

"I said LEAVE IT."

"I'll do it." Cameron's voice, smooth and assured, with that newly acquired accent, impossible to place, like his motives.

The nurses disappeared quickly—grateful, probably—and there was silence, apart from the quiet rustling of the remains of a life being packed into a nylon sports bag.

He'd have to get used to silence. There'd be no more mindless American rap to roll his eyes at, no PlayStation battles to block out as he prepped in his study with World War III raging on the other side of the wall. "You could get a bird," the hospital's chaplain had suggested. "A lot of people enjoy the company." Pete had made short work of him as well.

And now it would be just him and Cameron. Well, in theory. "We wouldn't let you go if you didn't have someone to look after you," his doctor had said, after Pete requested—demanded—to be discharged. Because there was no bloody point in his staying here. There'd been a flurry of consultation between specialists: Pete could return home, if Cameron stayed with him for at least three weeks—ha!—and he came back daily for dressing changes and occupational therapy. A nurse would visit, periodically and unannounced. He'd consider counseling. He'd refused the chair, was lurching about with a stick that made his ribs ache and his arm spasm, but maybe that was justice. Pete had never felt religion as keenly as his wife, but he was beginning to understand those guys who flogged themselves. Pain was an amazing distraction.

They all saw him off, what felt like every nurse in the place, each with a hug and a quiet word of encouragement. Tears, some of them. Pete tried to respond, went through the motions. Murmured appreciation. But there was nothing left of him to give. He was as dead as his boy.

Chapter 21

The first rule of damage limitation: remove yourself from the situation. Melinda tried to hustle a hyperventilating, vomit-flecked Aimee away from the whispering crowd, muttering bullshit as she went about nerves and grief.

"Excuse me," she ordered, elbows out. "Coming through, *excuse* me." Christ on a bike, what was wrong with people? Melinda could feel Aimee's embarrassment radiating from her bowed head. She pulled her friend close to her chest, sod the stains. "Out of the way," she hissed at a small child clutching a recorder. "How'd you like it if you were sick and people were staring at you?"

Aimee began dry heaving, and the curious onlookers of Hensley finally parted like the Red Sea. "*Thank* you, excuse us. Yes, probably shock. Yes, of course, we all are. A mother herself obviously. Thank you." Melinda held Aimee's puke-filled handbag in front of her like a talisman to ward off the more persistent vampires. "Coming through, coming through. Get out of the bloody way."

Just a few more steps and they'd be in the relative safety of the hall kitchen, and no longer the reluctant stars of this unscheduled entertainment. Melinda felt for Aimee, she honestly did, but God, her timing was awful. Nick caught up with them just as Melinda put her shoulder to the swinging door.

"What's going on?" he asked, reaching for his wife. But Aimee ducked away.

"No," she gasped. "Don't."

"Panic attack," whispered Melinda, stating the bloody obvious. "Maybe leave us for a bit. Fewer people the better." She could see Shelley and Byron behind their father, eyes wide. "Why don't you get the kids out of here," she suggested, then let the door swing shut on the gossip already swelling behind them.

IN. OUT. IN. OUT. Aimee tried to picture the breath expanding in her lungs, flowing through her body, but all she could see was Lincoln lying in his hospital bed, his narrow teenage chest never to rise again. Another wave of nausea flooded through her, leaving her bent double over the steel bench.

"Breathe," Lou instructed, like some kind of birth coach. Aimee gasped. "Come on now." Lou started rubbing Aimee's back, small circles of relief that she didn't deserve. All these people worrying about her, all this *caring*, when she was basically a murderer. Aimee began to cry, the tears making her hiccup. She gulped for air, and started to choke.

"Christ, Aimee," Melinda's voice sounded very far away. "You've got to calm down."

"Go easy on her," said Lou, guiding Aimee toward the sink. "I think she's in shock." Lou maneuvered Aimee's wrists under the tap. "Don't worry, darling," she murmured. "Everything's going to be okay."

The water squealed and spluttered through ancient pipes, but the cooling dribble on her skin did the trick. Aimee felt her breathing finally begin to slow, although her head was still a whirlpool.

"That's better," said Lou. She handed Aimee her water bottle. "Here, drink this."

Oh God. Aimee leaned forward and heaved again, splattering bright yellow bile into the sink.

"AIMEE?" LOU SPOKE softly, so as not to spook her further. She'd never seen Aimee this bad before, not even when her mother died. Aimee's shoulders were spasming, her whole torso convulsing as she retched.

"Come on, love." Lou took the water bottle back and opened it herself, held it up to Aimee's mascara-stained face. "It'll make you feel better."

Aimee turned her head away, mouth clamped shut.

For God's sake. "Don't be silly," said Lou. But she couldn't help feeling slightly smug. Because it wasn't Lou heaving her guts out, or Tansy making a spectacle of herself. It wasn't her family the good people of Hensley were whispering about in the town hall. Lou was on the right side of the sink for once. She took a deep breath and tried again. "Darl, you need fluids. Come on. Aimee!"

"GIVE ME THAT," said Melinda, grabbing at the water bottle. The second rule of damage limitation: be sure of the facts. She took a sniff, then a cautious sip. "Oh, you have *got* to be kidding me."

"What is it?" asked Lou.

"Guess," said Melinda, tipping the bottle down the sink. She turned back to Aimee, sympathy well and truly evaporating now. "What the fuck are you playing at?" she demanded. "How long've you been walking around with half a liter of vodka in your handbag?"

Lou gasped.

"Well, I don't know why you're surprised," said Melinda. "You should be good at spotting that sort of thing."

"Hey," said Lou.

"Sorry," said Melinda. "But really? Aimee?" She leaned back against the pegboard wall, working her temples with her fingers. *Bloody hell.* This was a bigger disaster than she'd realized. Outside the kitchen, Melinda could hear the delighted rise and fall of unsubstantiated rumor. Inside the kitchen, Aimee began to shake.

"IT'S ONLY SINCE the picnic," Aimee said defensively, remembering the ease and comfort she'd enjoyed down by the river, the glorious numbness of the champagne. "It makes me feel better." She wrapped her arms around herself to try to stop the trembling.

"For Christ's *sake*, Aimee. You know it'll only make things worse."

"Don't yell at her," murmured Lou.

"Things couldn't be any worse," snapped Aimee. It was all going to collapse, she could see that now. Her wonderful, too-good-to-be-true life was going to crumble to the ground. These people were going to crucify her. We'll have to move, she thought randomly. That's assuming Nick would stay with her, once he found out. Or let her have the kids, if they split up. She'd killed a child; no judge in his right mind would award her custody. Aimee's breathing began to speed up again.

"They could be worse," hissed Melinda. "And they will be, if you keep falling apart like this. Drawing attention to yourself. People will talk."

"They'll talk anyway," insisted Aimee. "They'll find out it was us. It's only a matter of time."

Lou stared at them both. "Are we talking about the accident again?"

"Yes!" shouted Aimee.

"No!" shouted Melinda.

The door to the kitchen swung open. Nick, his handsome face both angry and confused. "What's going on?" he said. "Why are you guys yelling? Byron and Shelley are freaking out, Aimee. I don't know what to tell them."

Neither did she. Aimee didn't know what to say to any of them. She stared hopelessly at her upright fire-volunteer husband, the love of her life, who hated dishonesty in any form. Stupid, she'd been so bloody stupid. "No," she said, shrinking away as he reached for her. "Just leave me alone." Aimee put her face in her hands, waiting until she heard him walk away. Even Melinda murmuring reassuringly to Nick as the door swung shut didn't bother her. She just wanted him gone. One less person to feel guilty about.

THE THIRD RULE of damage limitation—or crisis management, as this was swiftly becoming: control the information.

"She's so embarrassed, bless her," Melinda told Nick, and Sharna, who was loitering near the kitchen doorway with intent. Melinda dropped her voice, leaned in toward them both. "She was nervous about the reading, so we had a drink at mine beforehand." The fourth rule: include enough of the truth to keep things credible. "A stupid idea, in this heat, but I thought a bit of Dutch courage might help." Rule number five: accept responsibility. Melinda held her hands up, palms spread wide. "My fault. But then with the news about the boy—well, it was all too much."

Nick looked her in the eye. "She's always had a nervous stomach."

"She puked before your wedding," Sharna said helpfully.

"Exactly," said Melinda. "And she was too wound up this morning to eat anything. So prosecco, in the sun, with no breakfast? Then this kind of shock? It's not surprising."

"She was asking about Lincoln just this morning," said Sharna, eyes bright with the sheer thrill of the drama. "Wanted to know all about how he was doing."

"Well, that's Aimee for you," said Melinda. "Always concerned about the community."

"I've had a text from a friend at the hospital," said Sharna. "They've let Pete go home. Maybe I should go and tell her. Might make her feel better, to know what's going on." She eyed the wobbling door hopefully.

Melinda put her hands firmly on Sharna's shoulders and turned her away from the kitchen. "The only thing that's going to make Aimee feel better is a couple of Tylenol and a liter of water," she said. "And knowing that people aren't talking about her. Sharna—can I trust you not to tell anyone that we were *all* a little tipsy this morning? She'd be mortified. And I really don't need people thinking I'm some kind of lush. It's hardly going to convince them to give me money."

"Or a baby," said Sharna.

Bitch. "Exactly," said Melinda, walking Sharna back toward her audience. "As I said, stupid of me. But it seemed a nice idea at the time, to celebrate."

"Not much to celebrate now," said Sharna.

"Oh I know," said Melinda. "You don't need to tell me."

Lou HAD JUST gotten Aimee calmed down when Melinda came swinging back into the kitchen.

"Right," said Melinda, her face so stony even Lou felt a bit intimidated. "Here's what's going to happen. Nick's going to take the kids out for lunch. Lou's going to take Aimee home, put her to bed with a bottle of Gatorade. And I'm going to speak to the mayor, explain that we all had a few glasses before the concert, and that you're a lightweight." She held out her hand. "Give me your phone."

"Me?" Aimee clutched her iPhone to her chest. "No. Why should I?"

"Because you can't be trusted not to call someone and say something stupid."

Lou could feel her own phone vibrating in her back pocket. She slid it out, but she'd missed the call. *Damn.*

"It wouldn't be stupid," said Aimee. "It would be the truth."

"You don't even know what the truth is."

"For God's sake," said Lou, squinting at the unfamiliar number. "Can't you two drop it, for one afternoon?"

"We need to drop it, period," said Melinda.

"We can't," said Aimee. "Not now." She yanked off the tea towels Lou had draped over her shirt. "I'm going to go fix this," she muttered, clambering awkwardly down off the bench.

Melinda put her arms out, blocking the doorway. "Where do you think you're going?"

"I'm going to speak to Damien."

"Dami-who?"

"He's one of the investigators."

"And you know his name *how?*"

"We're friends," said Aimee, chin up but voice wobbling. There was a vomit-coated curl poking stiffly out of the side of her head. Lou had to stop herself from reaching to smooth it down.

"Oh my God," said Melinda, looking as though she was about to throw up herself. "What have you said to him?"

"Nothing," said Aimee. "But I have to now. I have to come

clean, explain that we might have had something to do with the crash. So he can investigate properly."

"Keep your voice *down*," hissed Melinda. "Ow!" She pitched forward as the swinging door thumped into her back. "Bugger off," she called. "We're busy. Get a glass of water somewhere else."

"ONLY ME," CALLED a strident, unwelcome voice. Sharna. Melinda squeezed her eyes shut, trying to block her out, along with the industrial pale green walls, the rows of smoked-glass coffee cups, the washing-up roster, the whole claustrophobic small-town nightmare.

"Is everything okay in there?" asked the postmistress. "Can I help?"

"Everything's fine," Melinda called back. "We just need a moment to clean up." The door moved against her back again. "Aimee's naked," she warned. "We're washing her down in the sink."

"Thanks a lot," muttered Aimee, as the footsteps receded.

Melinda took a deep breath and tried for a calm, reasonable tone. Even though she felt anything but calm or reasonable. She felt uncharacteristically panicked. Aimee wasn't just unstable, she was a bloody time bomb. Melinda dug her nails into the palms of her hands.

"What," she said quietly, "do you think you're doing, befriending one of the investigators? For that matter, what the hell are you doing talking about the accident to Sharna? That's just asking for trouble."

"I wasn't," blustered Aimee. "I needed stamps."

"No one goes to the post office for stamps. They go for gossip."

"Then what were you doing there?"

"Damage limitation," said Melinda, gritting her teeth. "Now you listen to me. You are not going to say another word about this, to anyone. Not your investigator friend, not Sharna, not even a bloody priest."

"Why shouldn't I?" said Aimee, sounding brave but not looking it.

"Because you don't know all the facts."

"Like what?"

"Like that Peter Kasprowicz has a history of severe depression."

"I do know about that, actually," said Aimee. "And his depression has nothing to do with this. He was medicated."

"No. He *should* have been medicated. He hasn't filled a prescription since August." Melinda narrowed her eyes. "Like someone else we know."

Aimee turned to glare at Lou. "Thanks a lot."

But Lou was looking at her phone. "Shit. I need to make a call," she said. "Can you two try not to kill each other for five minutes?"

"Don't go," said Aimee, grabbing at Lou's top. But Lou shrugged her off. The kitchen flooded incongruously with sunlight as Lou stepped out into the parking lot.

MELINDA SPOKE VERY slowly, as though to a small child. "There are a million things that could have happened to that plane that have nothing to do with us," she said. "Pete was depressed. He was off his meds. There was alcohol in his system—not much, but enough. And it's an old plane, 1970s. It could have been technical failure, the carburetor icing up, anything."

"Ice?" Aimee stared at her. "What are you talking about? It's eighty-something degrees."

"Not at night. And you only need a drop of twenty seven degrees for ice to form, which could easily happen if they were high enough——" Melinda broke off. Aimee was looking at her as though she'd grown another head. "What?"

"Oh my God, you think we did it. You think we caused the accident."

"I do not."

"You do. Or you think we might have." Aimee gripped the bench behind her. "You wouldn't know any of this otherwise. Carburetors!"

"I'm just gathering facts," said Melinda.

"And how do you have access to Pete's medical records? Are you *spying* on him?"

"No," said Melinda. She wasn't doing a thing. Clint, on the other hand . . . "It's just in case."

"Just in case they find out our lanterns were involved."

"Actually, it doesn't matter if the lanterns were *involved*. Legally, they'd have to prove that they were the sole or main cause. And there's no way——"

"Have you spoken to a *lawyer*?"

"No." Technically, Roger was a paralegal. "The only reason I have to think about any of this is because of you, Aimee, not because of those bloody lanterns. If you go around town mouthing off about how we might have done something, how this might be our fault, then people are going to believe you." Perception was as bad as guilt, especially in the papers. "People are upset. They want someone to blame. Listen to them."

FOR THE FIRST time, Aimee became properly aware of the hubbub on the other side of the door. The babble of shocked voices, the wailing of children who'd obviously been told that one of their old friends was dead. Her community, shocked and hurting. Aimee took a few steps toward Melinda, determined not to be intimidated.

"But we don't need to construct some kind of legal defense," she said, trying to stop her voice from shaking. "We'll just admit what we were doing, and let Damien and his team figure out what happened."

"No we bloody won't."

Courage, Aimee. "But it's the right thing to do."

"Not in this case." Melinda put a hand on Aimee's arm. "Listen to them, Aimee," she said quietly. "None of those people are thinking rationally." And neither are you, Melinda's eyes said. "It wouldn't matter what the inquiry found. The accident would be our fault in everyone's minds from the moment you opened your mouth."

"But maybe it is."

"And maybe it isn't. Pete wasn't taking his medication, he'd been drinking. Maybe he was trying to end things."

Aimee felt the air in her lungs go cold. "Are you suggest-ing . . . that he would . . . with Lincoln—"

Melinda shrugged. "I don't know. And neither do you."

"Of course I know. Peter Kasprowicz loved Lincoln. He'd never do anything to hurt him." Aimee crossed her arms. "Melinda, that man's *son* is *dead*."

"And you confessing won't change that."

Was she made of stone? "His life is in ruins."

"So why do you want to ruin three more? Six, if you count Nick and your kids. Seven, with Tansy, eight with her baby. Come on, Aimee. You've got a depressed, drunk, amateur pi-lot, flying at night through a bloody hailstorm of fireworks, and you want to sacrifice all of us because of a couple of tiny lan-terns on the other side of the river? What's wrong with you?"

"I'm trying to act like a decent human being, rather than a sociopath. What's wrong with *you*?"

BLOODY HELL, THEY were still at it. Lou walked back inside to find her two oldest friends glaring at each other.

"Thank God," said Melinda. "Talk some sense into her, will you?"

"You understand, don't you?" pleaded Aimee. "You're a mother."

"Understand what?" said Lou, texting. Tansy was at a friend's house, and didn't want to leave. Too bad. *Picking you up in ten*, she typed, and pushed send.

"Why we have to say something," said Aimee. "About the accident."

"Why we bloody can't," said Melinda. "It'll ruin all our lives. Including yours, Lou."

"But it's fine to ruin Pete's, is that it?" Aimee was getting teary. "He doesn't deserve justice?"

"His is already ruined," said Melinda. "You said so yourself."

"Lou," bleated Aimee. "Help me."

Do I have to? asked Tansy. *Yes,* said Lou. But she didn't want to upset her daughter. So she added a smiley face and a promise of *McDonald's*.

"Lou." Melinda had her do-what-I-say voice on now. "Tell her."

But Lou didn't feel like falling into line. "Buggered if I know," she said. "And to be honest, I don't really care."

"What?"

"Lou—"

"And neither do either of you." Lou glanced back down at her phone, where there were real problems. "You're both only worried about yourselves."

"Well, Melinda is, but I—"

"Aimee's not even thinking about—"

"Stop it, both of you." Lou had had enough now. Enough of Melinda's power games, enough of Aimee's whining. Enough of looking after everyone. Because that was all she bloody did. Ironic, given how everyone questioned the quality of her mothering. Lou shook her head. She had her own family to look after, now more than ever. She didn't have time for this. "Come on. Let's be honest. Neither of you are really worried about Pete, or Lincoln. You never have been."

That shut them up. "You don't want the truth, Aimee. You just want to feel better. You want someone to tell you it's all going to be okay, to *absolve* you. To take over. It's like when you call me in a spin, asking for advice. You're not actually after my opinion, you're looking to outsource the worry. You use people like a pacifier."

Aimee's face went blotchy pink as she gaped at Lou like a newborn searching for a nipple.

"You're not trying to give Pete *justice*," said Lou. "You're trying to make this someone else's problem."

"*Thank* you," said Melinda.

"As for you." Lou turned to Melinda, somehow not covered in vomit or sweat like Aimee and Lou, but looking cool and righteous. And angry. Well, Lou didn't care anymore if she was angry. "You're not worried about them either. Or us, or our families. You're worried about yourself, and your precious company, and what might affect your bloody IPO. Do you think we're stupid?"

"And you're the only one who's not thinking about herself, is that it?" Melinda had her hands on her hips, looking very much like she used to in the playground when someone didn't do what she wanted. "The only one who's not a bad person."

"I'm the only one who's not being a hypocrite."

"You are, actually," said Melinda. "Because you're as much a part of this as we are. You can't just wash your hands of the situation and say it's got nothing to do with you."

Lou shrugged. "Doesn't mean I have to waste my time arguing about it," she said. "Trying to control everything. What will happen will happen, regardless." Her phone vibrated. Lou checked it, and shoved it back in her jeans. "Honestly, I've got bigger things to worry about than your insecurities, or your reputation."

"Easy for you to say," said Melinda. "It's not your money that's going to end up paying for this."

Lou gave a snort. "That would be one of the benefits of not having any."

"Think of the effect it will have on Tansy," said Melinda, changing tack. "The baby."

Lou whirled around. "Don't you dare bring Tansy into this. You don't care about her, or what might affect her. God, you don't even ask how she's doing."

"I do," said Aimee, pathetically. "I ask."

"Only so you can feel smug about the fact that it's not your perfect daughter," said Lou. "Only so you can sit there thinking, 'My Shelley would never do this.'"

Aimee groped along the bench for her water bottle.

"Oh, for God's sake." Lou grabbed her handbag. "Fuck the both of you. I can't be dealing with this."

Neither Aimee nor Melinda stopped her as Lou strode toward the door. They just stared at her, looking stunned.

"Tell," Lou said. "Don't tell. I don't care. Do whatever suits you. You always do anyway. Both of you." And she banged out the fire exit and into the glorious peace of the parking lot.

IN THE QUIET of the kitchen, Aimee began to cry. She didn't bother to wipe the tears, just stood there with snot and mascara dripping down her face, leaving tracks in what little foundation had managed to survive the morning. There were flecks of white tissue on her black shirt where Lou had tried to scrub the vomit away, and a roll of escaping fat where her Spanx had clearly given up. She looked pathetic and vulnerable, and it was all Melinda could do not to bustle her out the door after Lou and safely home. But she couldn't. For all their sakes, she couldn't make Aimee feel better. She had to make her feel worse. Melinda reached out and grabbed Aimee's wrists.

"Listen to me," she said quietly, feeling like the biggest bitch who ever walked, but this had to be done. Aimee was self-destructing and taking them all down with her. "If you start telling people about the lanterns, if you talk to *anyone* about us potentially having *anything* to do with the accident, I'll make sure no one in this town ever listens to you again." She squeezed Aimee's wrists, hard, to drive the point home.

"Like you, you mean," said Aimee.

"They don't like me, but they respect me," said Melinda. "They'll listen to me. They're not going to listen to you, Aimee, because you're not credible."

"I am," said Aimee. "I'm school council president. I'm practically a local."

"You have a history of making things up."

Aimee gasped. "Don't say that."

"You imagine things," said Melinda. "Convince yourself they happened. You've done this before."

"I was ill," Aimee whispered, twisting in Melinda's grip. "And that was a long time ago."

Melinda's heart twisted with her. But still she kept her hold tight. "You convince yourself that you're responsible for events you have nothing to do with."

"I was unwell," Aimee repeated. "And it doesn't mean I'm sick again now. It doesn't mean I'm imagining this."

"Aimee, you weren't *unwell*. You didn't have the flu. You had a *mental breakdown*. You were in a *psychiatric hospital*."

The harsh words bounced off the steel surfaces around them. No one ever said it, Melinda realized. But someone had to. And as usual, it was her.

"If you tell anyone . . . ," Aimee said shakily.

"I won't say anything," Melinda promised. "As long as you don't. Deal?" She squeezed one more time. "Aimee? Do we have a deal?"

Aimee yanked her hands away and wiped them down the front of her skirt, as though to get any trace of Melinda off her.

"Come on, promise me."

Aimee backed toward the door, looking at Melinda as though she didn't even recognize her. "You're supposed to be my friend," she whispered, as she fumbled for the handle, then ran, stumbling slightly, out into the sun.

Chapter 22

Cameron lay on the floor of his brother's room and stared at the model planes dangling from the ceiling. They hung completely still, their wings held aloft by a funky teenage mix of sweat and sneakers and spray deodorant. But Cameron didn't open a window. Didn't want a single molecule of his brother to escape before he'd had a chance to properly say good-bye.

He took a deep breath, as though he could absorb the last few years of Lincoln's life by breathing in stale air. The walls were covered in Blu-Tacked pictures of a teenager he didn't quite recognize: the same toothy grin, but taller, thinner. More confident. Lincoln had been a shy and overweight twelve when Cameron left. "But I had no choice," Cameron angrily told the room. He couldn't stay here, watching Pete get on with his life like nothing had happened, watching him go off every day to work at the same place as *her*, knowing what he knew.

Through the thin wall, Cameron could hear Pete banging around in his own bedroom, becoming familiar with the newly dark space. He didn't get up to help. Just watched the planes shudder slightly with the reverberation. Had Lincoln really loved the idea of flying that much, or had Pete pushed it on him? Wanted his real son to share his passion? "I'm your dad too," Pete had insisted, when Cameron started calling him by his first name, but that was bull. Pete was Lincoln's father and Cameron's stepfather, and there was a world of difference. Pete had never bothered to take Cameron flying.

There was a painful-sounding thump next door, but Cameron stayed put. He had a real dad, in Sydney, the first place he'd run to, but he'd been just as useless. Hadn't wanted much to do with him. Cameron had spent a week on his old man's couch then taken off again, working odd laboring shifts until he lucked out and got a job crewing on a superyacht. Went wherever they sent him. Traveling was a bloody good way to deal with pain.

But in turning his back on Pete, he'd also turned his back on Lincoln. Cameron stood up and fingered a yellow Tiger Moth. Kid probably thought he didn't care. He yanked on the plane, feeling a satisfying pop as the string gave up its grip on the plaster. And when he finally did return, it was too late. He pulled down another plane, then another, and another. Cameron wasn't one for apologies. But he could make a promise. He went to chuck the planes in the bin, then realized it was probably Lincoln who'd painstakingly glued them together. "I'll make sure no one gets away with anything," he whispered, stacking the models carefully in a desk drawer instead. "I'll find out what happened, and I'll make sure people pay." First his mum, now his brother. Cameron felt a wave of emotion so overwhelming he had to drop onto Lincoln's narrow single bed. "I promise," he said again, trying to stay angry. Anger was easier to deal with than grief; his grief might just bury him. Justice, Cameron told himself, as he clutched Lincoln's pillow to his chest. Retaliation. Payback. It was the only thing that had kept him sane last time. He shoved his face in the pillow so Pete wouldn't have the satisfaction of hearing him fall apart.

Chapter 23

Aimee ran down the main street, wishing her family away.

Not forever, obviously. But just for the day, the next few hours even, so she didn't have to face them like this. Embarrassed. Filthy. Thoughts bouncing painfully up and down like her under-supported double Ds in the bra she'd outgrown years ago.

She ran past the newsagent's, the butcher's, the hardware store, all thankfully closed for the town concert. Ignored the curious stares of parents hustling tearful children into SUVs, the hesitant half waves from people she sat on committees with.

"Just getting a bit of exercise," she huffed to old Marjory, sitting outside the post office in the sun. Sharna, praise the Lord, was nowhere to be seen. Still out spreading the news of Aimee's humiliation, no doubt.

Aimee ran faster.

Over Hunter's Creek bridge, past the bowling club, the

town swimming pool. Up the hill that led to the petrol station. The teenage attendant on the forecourt gaped at her.

"I'm in training," Aimee snapped, aware of the skirt riding up her knees, her pointy leather flats biting into her feet as she lumbered along. The picture she must be painting: a middle-aged fat woman, puffing along in her Going Out clothes, all failed deodorant and sweat patches.

A crazy woman.

"I'm not crazy," she told herself as she turned onto the wide grass verges of Old School Road. "I'm not crazy. I'm not crazy." Heading out of town now, the space between houses growing. Miles from their own property, but Nick had taken the car and it wasn't as though she could've asked Melinda for a lift. Aimee yanked off her shoes and continued barefoot. "I'm not crazy," she repeated, the mantra giving her focus and rhythm as she ran. The exercise she was supposed to be doing anyway, to keep her head from turning on her.

Forget her head turning on her. Look at her friends.

The houses disappeared, giving way to fields, the occasional vineyard. Long dirt driveways. Aimee slowed to a walk now that the danger of people wanting to talk to her had passed. And it wasn't as though she was in any hurry to get home. She had nothing to say to Nick or her children, no explanation except the truth. Aimee felt a little sick again. Please let him have taken them out to lunch like Melinda ordered. Please let her have a bit of space, to sort herself out in private. Except Aimee knew her husband, and knew that he'd be at home, waiting for her. Worrying about her.

Thinking it was happening again.

It wasn't happening again.

It couldn't happen again.

Aimee hitched up her skirt and began to run.

"BEFORE YOU OVERREACT, remember, this is not a definitive diagnosis. It doesn't necessarily mean there's something wrong."

Lou eyeballed the doctor. "Overreact?!" The bloody nerve. "You message me to say we need to come in ASAP, tell us there might be some kind of *problem* with the baby, and you're telling me not to overreact?"

The doctor—cool, calm, *expensive*—looked at Lou with exaggerated patience. "Mrs. Henderson, you're not helping."

"I'm not married." But Lou took her point. In the armchair next to her, Tansy looked as though she'd been shocked with a cattle prod. Lou put an arm around her rigid daughter and forced her voice to remain even. "All right then. What does it mean?"

The doctor put her pen down on the pile of test papers. She walked around the desk and pulled a third chair in toward Lou and Tansy, so close her bare knees were almost touching theirs. "The important thing to remember is this is only a first trimester screening," she said. "It can give an abnormal result, even when there's nothing wrong. On the other hand, it could be the first sign there's an issue."

Under Lou's arm, Tansy flinched.

"So what do the results suggest?" asked Lou.

"There's an indication that the baby might—*might*—have a chromosomal condition called trisomy 13," the doctor said.

"Is that bad?" asked Tansy.

"It's serious, yes." The doctor spoke gently. "Babies with this condition have quite severe abnormalities. Parts of the baby, like its eyes or its spine or its heart, might not develop properly. There would almost certainly be intellectual disability. A lot of babies with this condition don't live very long after they're born. And those who do struggle to have what you and I would call a normal life. They need a lot of extra care."

"But you said you didn't know," said Tansy.

"I don't know, you're absolutely right."

"So why even tell us?" Tansy demanded. "Why would you say something like that, if you weren't sure?"

The doctor flicked her eyes toward Lou. "Because you're very young, and you're also very early in your pregnancy. Eight weeks now, am I right?"

Lou nodded. "We think so."

"We know so," said Tansy. "I've only slept with one person. I'm not a slut."

The doctor winced slightly. "Anyway. You need to be aware that this is a possibility. Because it might alter the decisions you make, going forward."

Tansy whipped her head around. "Is she talking about abortion?"

"Tansy." Lou tightened her hold on her daughter to keep her in the chair.

"Because I'm not having an abortion. I've already decided. No matter what."

The doctor nodded. "And I wouldn't try to influence you. I'm just giving you all the information. That's my job."

"We don't need any more information." Tansy wriggled out of Lou's grip. "I don't want to know any more."

"I would recommend further testing." The doctor moved back behind her desk, pulled the little keyboard toward her. "Even just so you can prepare."

"I don't want to walk around for the next seven months thinking there might be something wrong with my baby."

"Which is why we're going to find out one way or the other." Lou turned her attention back to the doctor. "What kind of tests?"

The doctor clicked at the keys. "I'm going to arrange for chorionic villus sampling," she said. "Because it's still a little early for amniocentesis. We take a tiny bit of the placenta—"

"No!"

"And the cells are tested for any chromosomal or genetic disorders. It will tell us whether the syndrome is present, although not how severe it might be."

"Is it risky?" asked Lou.

"It does carry a slightly higher risk of miscarriage, yes."

Tansy had tucked herself into a small ball, shoes leaving scuff marks on the pale leather seat.

"Is it painful?" Lou nudged her daughter's feet off the chair.

"Not particularly. More uncomfortable. I'll do another ultrasound now though, look for any excess fluid behind the baby's neck. That will give us a further indication of whether CVS is necessary."

Lou eyed the sleek silver Mac. "How much?" she asked. "For the tests."

"You'll have to speak to reception, but I think the CVS is around six, seven hundred dollars. Plus the ultrasound and consultation, of course."

Of course. "Only we were thinking of transferring to St. Margaret's. It's closer to where we live."

"That's entirely your choice. I'm happy to send your notes over there, if that's what you want. It might delay things a bit, that's the only thing I'd say. I don't think they do CVS. It's quite specialist. You might have to go down to Melbourne."

They'd already spent four hundred on the blood tests, two hundred and fifty on the last consultation. Lou quickly tried to do the sums.

"Mum?"

"Sweetheart?"

"I don't want to talk to any more doctors. I don't want anyone else to know."

"They're not going to tell anyone, love. They're not allowed." But Lou turned back to the sleek blond bob in front of them, the empathetic yet unlined face. "How soon would you be able to do it? How soon can we have the test?"

As AIMEE RAN, she remembered.

It had started with a simple—but colossal—mistake. A

heartwarming article she'd written about a terminally ill toddler, a town rallying around a struggling family, funds raised
to bring grandparents over from England for one last visit.

Except there was a question mark over whether the little
girl was actually dying.

"Did the doctor confirm the prognosis with you?" the news
editor had asked as Aimee hyperventilated in his office, the
whole newsroom craning to see what was going on.

"He said that survival rates were negligible," Aimee said
miserably. "He said children with this kind of cancer generally
didn't make it."

"But did he actually say she was going to die?" The news
editor looked wearily at his intern reporter. "Look, technically, you're probably right. But technically isn't going to cut
it with this one, I'm afraid." There was talk of a lawsuit. The
paper's legal team was summoned. A retraction would only
make things worse, they decided; the paper ended up making
a big donation to the hospital, in the child's name, and Aimee
was sent home for a week.

"Go clear your head," the news editor said kindly. "Get
some rest. Come back raring to go."

But Aimee hadn't come back raring to go, she'd come back
nervous. She began double-checking, reading interviewees
back their quotes. Offering to let them see the story before it
went to print.

"Absolutely not," the news editor said, when one of the other
interns told on her. "We don't give anyone copy approval."

So Aimee began making her inquiries in secret: mobile

phone conversations in hallways, emails she deleted immediately. Another journalist got a big budget story wrong and
Aimee began worrying about numbers, asking other reporters
to check her copy. Another quiet word to her boss, and Aimee
was moved off the news desk and on to entertainment.

Which should have made things easier, but somehow, they
got worse. Within six months, Aimee had gone from promising young intern, the first hand up for assignments, to hiding
at the back of the morning meeting. She began obsessing about
punctuation. Had she put the right accents over crème brulée?
And what if she accidentally libeled one of the restaurants she
was reviewing? She started going back at lunch and ordering
the exact same meal she'd eaten the night before, to make sure
the pavlova really was chewy. Taking photos of the menu, the
prices on the specials board, so she could look at them over
and over again.

Aimee became tired, and paranoid, and broke.

Unsurprisingly, her writing began to suffer. Anything con-
troversial, anything negative, she struck out. If an interviewee
said something newsworthy, Aimee wouldn't include it.
Wouldn't even pass the tip on to another journalist to follow
up, just in case she'd gotten it wrong. The entertainment editor began to sigh when Aimee filed her copy. She got moved
again, to proofreading the crosswords.

The first one took her half a day.

"So what are my chances?" Melinda leaned toward the silent woman who seemed to hold so much power, even though

she didn't work for the government, didn't have any official involvement in the adoption process whatsoever, was merely there to advise and maybe—*maybe*—increase the odds through tips about clever interview techniques or smarter form filling. Yet there was something deeply authoritative about Claudia Lang, with her crisp white cotton shirt, her surprisingly old-fashioned briefcase, set carefully on one of Melinda's acrylic chairs. This must be how couples waiting to hear if they were candidates for IVF felt, or older women desperate to know if their eggs were viable. Older women like Melinda. She smiled, even though the adoption consultant wasn't the one she'd have to impress. "What do you think?"

Claudia Lang shuffled through her papers on the other side of the table. "They're not as bad as I would have thought," she said finally, surveying Melinda's living room. "You obviously have the means to do this."

You wouldn't have come all the way out here otherwise, thought Melinda, or at such short notice. Her PA had found the consultant just twenty-four hours before, and here she was making a house call. Out in Woop Woop. Who said money didn't talk?

"Your timing is very good as well." Claudia Lang nodded at her laptop. "There's been a recommendation that the law in Victoria be changed, which could give single people the same adoption rights as couples. You could end up being a pioneer."

A pioneer. Clint would like that. Melinda pictured herself in the papers, fighting for the rights of single women like herself, a special line of jewelry even, where a dollar from each piece would go to a foundation to help people access their very own Claudia Lang.

"It might be easier in other states. But I don't suppose you want to move."

"No," said Melinda. And then quickly, "Although I would, of course. If it was the only way."

"Of course."

Melinda scanned her notes, the directives to put proper locks on the balcony doors, to remove sharp-edged sculptures and heavy glass paperweights before interviews, to lay down sheepskin rugs. "We want an *illusion* of softness," Claudia Lang had murmured, eyeing Melinda and suggesting she invest in some leggings, maybe a sweatshirt. "You have a partner?" she asked, spotting the tie that Clint had left behind and Melinda had deliberately slung over an armchair.

"I can do," Melinda had answered, looking Claudia Lang firmly in the eye. "Would it help?"

Not particularly, it turned out, unless they could prove long-term live-in stability. It wasn't just the local laws she had to worry about; Australia's partner countries had their own eligibility rules. Melinda looked down at the surprisingly short list in front of her. South Korea wouldn't consider un-married people as adoptive parents, neither would Sri Lanka. "What if the law doesn't change?" she asked.

Claudia Lang folded her hands neatly beside her laptop. "There are other avenues—" she began.

"No," said Melinda. "Everything has to be aboveboard."

"Well then. Single women are allowed to adopt here, in special circumstances."

"Meaning?"

"Generally, taking a child with additional needs."

Melinda took a quick breath. "No," she said, faster than she meant to. And then felt her face catch fire. Because it was so embarrassingly shallow and narrow-minded. Women had children with disabilities every day and loved them fiercely. Said they wouldn't swap them for the world. But Melinda, who wasn't even sure how to parent a child with average, everyday needs? "No," she said again, embarrassed at herself, and then angry at this stranger in her living room for making her feel ashamed. "I'm sorry, but I can't."

"It will make it harder. And the wait much longer."

"I don't care." Melinda knew she sounded bad, but this woman didn't make the decisions, did she? Although Claudia Lang had connections, would hold influence. She needed her on her side. "Can we somehow say that I don't want to, without actually saying that? Without making me sound . . . nasty?" Melinda tried to regroup. "It's just the time, the dedication it would involve—not that raising a child doesn't take time and dedication, but—"

"I understand," said Claudia Lang.

Don't look at me like that, thought Melinda. *Don't judge me against those parents who would gratefully take any child as long as it meant a baby of their own. I'm paying you, remember.* "That can't be made public," she said, feeling horrible as she did so. "I know that sounds hypocritical, but it would look really bad."

Claudia Lang nodded.

"But a foreign baby is fine. I mean, I'm not worried where it comes from, what color it is. I don't have any prejudices. Obviously."

"Obviously."

In the silence, Melinda's phone began to vibrate. She forced herself not to turn it over.

"Do you need to take that?"

"Well, I—" Melinda snuck a look at the screen. Clint.

"Just answer it."

There was too much information: investor concerns about the new incentives, their impact on profits. Clint's voice came streaming down the line, a river of recommendations to raise, lower, tighten. Really, she needed to sit down, go through this with him, but . . . "Do whatever you think is right," Melinda said smoothly, a woman who didn't take work home with her. Who would prioritize a child. "I trust you."

Claudia Lang made a few notes on her yellow pad, like a lawyer.

"Seriously, Clint, it's fine. You should probably be making these kinds of decisions anyway." Melinda smiled at Claudia Lang. Balance. Boundaries. "Just make sure you cc me." She put her hand over the phone. "Sorry," she mouthed.

But the woman was already eyeing her watch; Melinda's ninety minutes were up.

"Is there anything else I can do?" she asked, as the adoption consultant began tucking her laptop into her briefcase.

"Just wait," said Claudia Lang, as she pushed her feet into a pair of highly polished heels. "Make the changes to your apartment. I'll be in touch with a list of our best options."

"Sounds good."

"And stay out of trouble."

Melinda laughed as she guided Claudia Lang into the hallway. "I'm coming up to forty," she said. "My days of getting into trouble are well over."

"I'm serious. There's often controversy in these cases, when children are taken overseas. You're a high-profile person. That will help, but it also means there can't be any suggestion you're jumping the line or taking a baby you might not be eligible for." She glanced over at Melinda's business awards, lined up along the windowsill. "You need people to be talking about you for the right reasons. There can be no scandal attached to you at all."

AIMEE TRUDGED UP the driveway like an old horse heading for the glue factory. She had serious sunburn and plenty of blisters, but still no reasonable explanation for what had happened—and worse, why she'd shut her poor husband out. There'd been nothing in her head for the last hour except replayed conversations and accusations.

You had a mental breakdown.

But maybe Nick wouldn't want to talk about it straightaway. Maybe he'd wait until the kids were asleep.

You're not ill.

At the very least, he'd give her time to clean up, have a cup of tea.

You're crazy.

It wasn't like he was going to interrogate her.

You imagine things.

Aimee took a brave breath and pushed the door open. "Hey," she called. "I'm home."

You make things up.

Silence.

Aimee hobbled down the hallway, noting the lack of shoes. Into the empty kitchen, the quiet living room. Checked the kids' bedrooms, the den, but the whole house was deserted except for a sleeping Lucinda, happily shedding all over the clean laundry.

You've done this before.

There was a note on the kitchen table: Nick had taken the kids to the skate park. *Give you some space.* Oh. Well, good. Aimee grabbed a fresh towel out of the hot water cupboard, stripped her clothes off where she stood and shoved them in the washing machine. She turned the dial up as hot as it would go. Too late, she remembered the skirt was dry clean only, but it didn't matter; Aimee couldn't imagine herself wearing it again. Wasn't sure she'd ever leave the house, actually.

Aimee walked naked through the kitchen, no Byron to embarrass or Shelley to horrify. Only Oscar stared at her disapprovingly as she limped past him in the hall. "Bugger off," she muttered. She left the door to the bathroom open, turned Nick's waterproof radio on so it wasn't *quite* so silent. Space was nice, but—wasn't it a bit strange that they'd left her all alone, knowing how upset she was? That Nick hadn't even called or messaged to see how she was doing? A note was a little . . . cold. Aimee stepped into the shower, emotions tumbling like her underwear in the old Whirlpool. She didn't want people around, but she didn't want them to abandon her either. Leave her to cry alone in the shower. Aimee turned her face up to the flowing water, eyes stinging. She wanted love and reassurance and herbal tea. A husband who would completely understand, but ask no questions. And friends who didn't throw her weaknesses in her face.

You use people like a pacifier.

Aimee scrubbed furiously. The whole point of having friends, of being married, was that you had people to lean on. Who you could turn to, when you needed help or reassurance. Not too much reassurance, she understood that. There were boundaries. She'd spent hours in group therapy sessions learning all about boundaries. Which was probably why she was the only one of her friends capable of having a meaningful relationship. Of raising good, honest children who actually spoke to her. Melinda didn't even have a bloody pet.

You were in a mental hospital.

Yes, and it was wonderful. Aimee raked the razor up her shins, small dots of blood blooming in the foam. Apart from a frustrating ban on harmful objects—blades, belts, her favorite fountain pen—it had been like staying at a health spa. Not a posh one; there was far too much vinyl for Aimee's liking. But there'd been a gym and a lap pool and a masseuse who

came once a week. People who listened to her. Taught her
meditation and other head-calming techniques. If it was run
by The Ritz-Carlton, people would be lining up to go.

You don't want my advice.

And one of the main things she'd been taught at the clinic
was to listen to her own intuition. To trust herself. And what
her intuition was telling her was that she needed to do something.

You only think about yourself.

Well, that was just unfair. Because Aimee wasn't thinking
about herself at all. Aimee was willing to sacrifice herself so
another human being would have answers. The very opposite
of selfish, thank you very much.

You've done this before.

But this wasn't like the other times. There was a real accident here, with a real dead body, and a very real chance that
Aimee had caused it. Aimee and her so-called friends.

You're not credible.

No one will believe you.

They'll believe me.

And if her friends weren't going to help, if they weren't going to take her seriously—if they were threatening to *discredit*
her—then Aimee was clearly going to have to sort this mess
out by herself.

Lou sat in the hallway, listening to her daughter throw up on
the other side of the bathroom door.

"Tansy," she said, when the retching finally stopped. "Let me in."

No answer, just the gurgle of water as the cistern emptied and refilled.

"Sweetheart?" She picked at the flaking wallpaper. "Tans? Talk to me."

Silence. Which at least wasn't screaming or swearing or accusations. The drive back from Fenton had been twenty-five minutes of hell. Tansy had left the clinic hiccupping with misery, tears rolling down her face. Lou had tried to reassure her as they drove out of town, convince her everything would be okay, no matter what. "And who knows," she'd stupidly said while negotiating a tricky intersection, "it might all be for the best."

"What's that supposed to mean?"

For God's sake, it was her right of way. "Well, maybe it's nature's way of taking care of things."

She might as well have thrown a match into the petrol tank.

Lou leaned her head back against what was left of the wallpaper. Tansy had become hysterical. Yelling, crying, claiming Lou wanted to kill her baby, was plotting with the doctor to make her have an abortion, that the tests would make her miscarry, "which is what you want anyway, isn't it, go on, admit it." She'd worked herself into such a state that she'd started hyperventilating, and Lou had nearly driven into a truck trying to calm her down.

"Tansy?" Lou rapped her knuckles gently against the bathroom door.

Nothing.

We're back here again, Lou had thought desperately, as the truck driver screamed at her, Tansy screamed at her, and Lou pulled frantically at the wheel. *I knew it was too good to be true.* And worse, they were back there with a baby, and not just any baby, but a baby that might have something terribly wrong with it, and Tansy was behaving like a child herself, which was fair enough, because that's what she bloody well was. Lou had wanted to pull over onto the side of the road and howl along with her daughter. Instead she'd put her foot on the accelerator and wound down the window so Tansy's screaming would at least be drowned out by the rushing air. *The moment I get in the door*, she'd promised herself, *I'm having a bourbon and Coke, a bloody big one.*

But Lou had never gotten her drink, because Tansy had started dry heaving as they pulled into the driveway. She'd run into the house, Lou hot behind her, and slammed the bathroom door so hard a large lump of plaster from the ceiling had come crashing to the ground. Lou stared blankly now at the clumps of white sprinkled up the hallway. *No one else*, she thought. *No one else is going to pick this up but me.* Lou crawled across the carpet, gathering the pieces in her hand. She'd cleaned up vomit this morning, and she'd be the one bleaching the toilet this afternoon. This was her life for the foreseeable future: bodily fluids and breakages. And she was too old for this. She didn't have the energy to make sure the cleaning products were locked away, or the patience to answer endless questions about why the kitten couldn't come home with them and where farts came from. Although it was unlikely this child would ever ask bright, inquisitive questions. Lou heard a sob from the other side of the wall and swallowed down one of her own.

And the worst thing was, Tansy was right. It would be easier for everyone now if she lost the baby, if she woke up in the middle of the night all cramps and blood. Lou clambered awkwardly to her feet, knees cracking. Had her own mother wished the same thing, standing outside this very bathroom door? Almost definitely. *But this is different*, Lou thought, as she dumped the plaster flakes in the bin. *Totally different. This baby's not going to have a proper life. And neither are we.*

Chapter 24

"Why'd you stop taking the pills?"

Pete twisted the beer bottle around in his hand, as though he could read the label. Just here to pay my respects, Arthur had said when he'd turned up, clinking. Cameron had told the policeman to bugger off—"Are you fucking kidding me? He's not even bloody cold"—but Pete intervened. Although more to remind Cameron whose house it was than out of any desire for conversation. He placed the bottle carefully down on the concrete step. "Thought you said you were here as a mate."

"Oh, I am," said Arthur. "Trust me, this is the friendly conversation."

"Now that sounds like a bit of a threat."

Arthur sighed. "Not a threat, Peter. More a warning. Because I've seen the paperwork, and they're zeroing in on this. And given the circumstances—well, I wanted to give you a heads-up. That this is going to be a thing."

The door was open behind them; Pete could feel the colder

air on his back, a stark contrast from the afternoon sun on his face. "Let's walk," he said, reaching for his stick.

He led the senior constable down to the bottom of the garden, steps slow but fairly sure. "You've got the hang of that pretty quick," said Arthur. Pete waved away the compliment, even though he'd been quietly pleased at how he was getting around. He'd ditched the sling as soon as he'd gotten home, preferring the stability of two arms and the punishment of the burning in his shoulder.

"Fig trees?" Arthur said, as they stepped off the path. His words were muffled by the long grass, the leaves whispering above their heads and crunching below their feet. "You've got quite an orchard down here."

"Just half an acre," said Pete. "Figs, apples. Kids used to have a stand outside." But he wasn't down here to make small talk. "So tell me then. What are they going to ask?"

Pete paused to catch his breath, pressed a hand into his aching ribs. "Sure you're up to this?" Arthur said. Pete nodded. "All right then. They want to know about the antidepressants, why you suddenly stopped taking them. A new prescription, unfilled. Follow-up appointment canceled."

"I felt better." The inertia that had weighed him down since Julia died had finally lifted. Pete had become interested again, in flying, in his job. In life.

"But that might have been the pills."

"It wasn't. It was just a matter of time. Time sorts everything, eventually." Although Pete doubted time or pills could help with this one. He almost missed the numbness that had come after Julia's death.

"Did your doctor know? That you were planning to stop taking them?"

Pete shook his head and heard Arthur sigh.

"You saw a psychologist. As well as getting the prescription from your GP."

"For God's sake, my wife died."

A pause. "You told him you wanted to die too."

Could the psychologist disclose that? "A figure of speech. Overdramatic. I was grieving."

"Pete, you talked about deliberately crashing a plane."

Pete reached for a branch that wasn't there, pushed his hand through a thick patch of leaves that offered no support. "Once," he said. "I mentioned it maybe once. And that's all confidential," he added. "He shouldn't have told them that."

"Your psychologist has a duty of care to report it, now that . . . well." A thick hand on his shoulder. "I'm sorry, Peter. But you can see why it has to be followed up."

Pete shrugged the hand off. "Are they saying I killed my boy?" he whispered. "Is that where you're going with this?" He grasped his stick. "You know I didn't. I wouldn't. This is ridiculous."

"You have to admit, it doesn't sound great. Under the circumstances."

"It was *years* ago." Three easily, just before Cameron left. "And it wasn't how it sounds. There wasn't any plan. It was just a . . . fantasy. To escape everything. I was never going to do anything."

"So explain that to them. Because with the alcohol—"

"Oh, for heaven's sake, I'd had a couple of beers. I thought they'd be out of my system."

Arthur was somehow closer, in their chamber of leaves and tree. "The important thing now is to be honest. For Lincoln's sake."

"I *am* being honest. I wasn't drunk, and I'm not suicidal. I was, at one point, depressed, which is why I went and saw someone. I was being responsible." He hadn't really wanted to hurt himself. It was more the absence of want, the lack of desire to do anything at all. "It's what we tell the kids to do. Act before there's a crisis." Pete had found himself looking at the controls, thinking, *I could just keep flying. I could just keep going until I ran out of fuel and then it wouldn't even be my decision.* "I needed help, so I went and got it. It was a *good* thing to do. Christ."

Arthur was standing beside him now, leaning against the same branch, which dipped under the strain. "Saying you don't remember the accident, well, it sounds like you're hiding something. Or that there was nothing *to* remember. Nothing out of the ordinary. Everything fine. No logical reason for you to crash."

"It wasn't fine." The words were out of Pete's mouth before he knew he was going to say them.

"No?"

Could he do this? "The engine was running rough. Vibrating. Just before we came down."

"So why didn't you say something earlier?"

"My memory was hazy. I couldn't be one hundred percent sure. And I didn't want to dump Smithy in it, if I wasn't absolutely certain." Pete pictured the shambling old mechanic and waited for a tug of guilt, but there was nothing. The man must be near retirement anyway. It wasn't as if he was ruining a career.

"But now you are."

What the hell. "Yes. We were only getting a partial amount of power. I couldn't keep altitude. I don't remember the actual crash, but I remember struggling, that the nose kept dipping. And that must have been it."

"Straight into the side of a hill."

"I think we probably clipped some trees on the way down. But yes."

There was a creak as the branch released its heavy burden. "Right. Well, I'll let them know. That you've remembered." Arthur's voice came from a slightly higher place, now that he was standing, and had a different tone. Disapproval? "You know they've recovered the engine, don't you. And that they'll test it." Skepticism. Maybe a bit of disappointment. "Don't worry, if there was a fault or a maintenance issue, they'll find it."

"I don't want—"

"You don't want what?"

"Smithy and the guys who run the club. They do a good job. With limited resources. I don't want anyone to get in trouble."

Arthur's big hand was firm as he took hold of Pete's arm. "It's not about getting anyone in trouble," he said, as he led them both out of the cool thicket of trees and back into the sunlight.

"You're a teacher, you should understand that. It's about taking responsibility. And if someone's caused this accident, then they need to be held accountable, no matter who it is."

PETE FOUND CAMERON lurking in the kitchen, back door wide open. All the better for eavesdropping. "You don't need to hang around," he told him as he leaned against the bench to get his breath back.

"Sorry?"

The kettle had boiled half a dozen times that day already for sympathetic visitors. Pete felt along the bench until he found it, still warm and half full, judging by the weight. "Here in Meadowcroft. You can head off now." He patted the top of the cups, selecting a bumpy clay mug one of the boys had made in primary school. Cracked and mended a dozen times, the glue running over its surface like Braille, but it had outlived half his family. "You didn't come back for me, just for Lincoln," he told the window. "So you don't need to stay."

"Oh, I'm staying," said Cameron. Standing behind him, but not bothering to hand him a tea bag, or get the milk. "I might even move in for a while. You can't see, you have to stop and rest every few minutes. You won't be able to cope on your own."

"They're sending a nurse," said Pete, rummaging awkwardly in the fridge. A container of something tipped over; he ignored it. "And the entire female population of Meadowcroft seems to be rostered to bring me lasagne. I'll manage."

"Maybe I want to be here."

"You've barely been here. It took you three days to even get here." Pete filled the mug the way he'd been taught, one finger curled over the top so he could stop pouring when it hit the sensitive skin at the tip. So many tricks, just to survive.

"I was working."

"Good to see you've got your priorities straight."

"At sea. I couldn't exactly just leave." The voice hardened. "At least I was there when it mattered. Where were you when Mum died?"

"You're never going to forgive me for that, are you?" But there was something comfortable in the familiar argument, the old hatred. It felt right, being hated.

"Where is Suzanne these days? I haven't seen her around town."

"She's gone. You leave her alone."

"So who is it now?" Cameron followed Pete into the living room, sounding exactly like the angry teenager he'd been when he left. The broken boy kicking out at the world, wanting everyone to hurt as much as he did. "The dark-haired woman? The fat one? Aimee whatsit."

Pete felt for the dining room table, put his tea down carefully.

"The two of you seemed very cozy at the hospital. Cozy enough to drag you away from Lincoln anyway."

"He was *asleep*," said Pete. "And she's an old friend. We used to be on committees together. She does a lot for the community."

"Does she do a lot for you?"

Pete didn't bother to answer that.

"She's not in your phone, this Aimee. Or is she there under a nickname? A pet name?"

Which was more disappointing—the fact that Cameron had gone through his things, or that Pete wasn't surprised? He stared sadly out the sliding door at a garden he could no longer see. "Do you still have it?"

"Might have," said Cameron, from the reclining chair. Pete's chair. "Or I might've given it to the police. Does it matter?"

Did it? Pete wasn't sure, couldn't remember what was on it. A genuine memory lapse.

"Or is it one of the others in there? Like Fionna, who's Fionna?"

"She's my assistant."

"And Melinda?"

"A local businesswoman. She came in to talk to the tenth-graders about entrepreneurship."

"Right. Then what about—"

"Cameron, what do you want?" Other than to punish him, again. Which Pete perversely welcomed. Was he after money? But Pete was hardly taking round-the-world cruises on his school salary, and Cameron hadn't tried to hit him up for the flight home. Pete realized he didn't even know what his son was doing for a living. He'd ask, but it didn't seem like a cozy chat kind of moment.

"I want to know what happened," came the voice from the recliner. "The police obviously think there's more to it. So do I. I'm here to find out what you did."

Chapter 25

Melinda had never really thought about babies before, but now she'd started, she couldn't stop.

It didn't help that half of Hensley was knocked up. What was the old saying—that when you were pregnant, you saw pregnant women everywhere? Obviously it was the same when you were trying to adopt. Melinda followed the curve of the river, enjoying the hard thud of the packed earth under her feet, the satisfying crunch of dry eucalyptus leaves. So far on her run, she'd passed numerous waddling basketball bellies, and three—three!—women with strollers, including one who was running almost as fast as Melinda. Melinda had dug in, put on some speed, left the woman back at the rail crossing. There was no way she was being beaten by someone in a maternity bra.

But. *Trying* to adopt. Melinda ducked to avoid being hit by a low branch. Was she? Really? She'd felt relieved when Claudia Lang had first mentioned the kind of waiting period they were looking at. Two, three years. At least. Visits and assessments and approvals and reports. Melinda's application would be safely tied up in admin for the foreseeable future, with no danger of anyone presenting her with an actual live baby.

But at some point during their meeting, her feelings had changed. She'd wanted to beat the system. To make this happen. To get the damn baby already. Was that her natural competitiveness, or something else?

One mile to go, and she could tick off her thirty for the week. Melinda ignored the cramping in her calf as both she and the river headed back into town. It didn't really matter either way. She couldn't lose. If this took forever, if it ultimately failed, at least she'd look good trying. And she wasn't going to feel bad about capitalizing on that. Melinda had put up with discrimination for years because of her childlessness. Constantly overlooked for Inspirational Women awards in favor of supermoms; people intimating that she somehow had it easy because she wasn't juggling meetings with school runs. It wasn't on a par with racism or anything, but it still wasn't fair.

And if she didn't fail, if she actually managed to adopt— well. There it was again, an unexpected excitement fluttering in her stomach, just below her navel. A gut feeling, as it were. Maybe she wasn't as hard-boiled as everyone thought. Maybe, deep down, Melinda actually wanted to be a mother.

Either way, it proved she'd been right to go all tough love on Aimee. A small, sick, guilty feeling joined the happy flutter, but Melinda chose to ignore it as she picked up her pace on the home stretch. Because she needed to control the situation. Claudia Lang had virtually said so. *The last thing you need is a scandal.* Aimee thought Melinda was worried about her money, the company—*and you are, let's be honest*—but it wasn't only that. There was more at stake here.

And there was no way they'd caused that bloody accident.

Although Aimee seemed convinced.

And they all knew how Aimee could get when she was convinced about something.

You're doing it for her own good, Melinda told herself as she turned off the river track. *She'll thank you, when all this is over.*

Melinda jogged down the road, slower now. Hensley's main street was almost deserted, shopkeepers shutting up for the day even though the sun was still high. "How does anyone make any bloody money?" she'd exclaimed when she first moved back, but she'd secretly grown to love the early closing. The peace and quiet. There were a few tourists, window-shopping; Melinda made a big show of swerving round them. She knew she should be on the side of progress, pushing the town to open up more. But she'd also spent hours stuck in long weekend traffic in Echuca, crawling along behind a procession of Jet Skis and motorboats. If Hensley stayed an anachronistic throwback, if the ban on tourism lasted forever, she wouldn't mind at all.

Melinda fumbled for her key in her shorts pocket, not that there was any real need to lock up out here, but she'd promised Clint. Insurance. All that stock on the premises. Blah blah blah. She leaned against her front door—deep glossy cream, to match the iron railings, a magnet for graffiti but totally worth the hassle—and promptly fell through it.

Because the door was already open.

Burglars. Arsonists. Rapists. Kidnappers. Melinda's heartbeat thudded in her ears. *Don't be ridiculous*, she told herself, as she picked herself up off the spiky rattan mat. There hadn't been a break-in in Hensley for nearly a decade. But beyond the whoomp-whooping of her own pulse, she could hear muffled thumps above her, like furniture being moved. Televisions being taken. Melinda grabbed an umbrella from the stand and began creeping up the stairs.

The footsteps were man-size, heavy and flat. They were coming from her stockroom. Of course they were. She crept up to the first-floor landing, back against the wall. The door to her mini-warehouse was ajar, the light on. Melinda paused. *Maybe I should just call the police*, she thought, but then the door was pulled open and Melinda, shocked, swung the old-fashioned wooden umbrella into the face of the only other person in Hensley who had a key to her flat.

"Bloody hell, Melinda," Nick said, as his knees buckled. "Are you trying to kill me?"

No one at the newspaper had been surprised when Aimee quit. Everyone at home, however, was horrified.

"But you love writing," said Melinda. "This is your dream job."

"And after you gave up your degree and everything," fretted her mum.

"Won't you miss the city?" said her dad.

But Aimee didn't want to go back to the city. She wanted to stay at home, where she felt safe. She took casual work picking grapes with the local gray army—no responsibility, no worry about messing anything up.

"But of course you'll go back to uni now," said the retirees, ex-teachers mainly.

"Take a few months to clear your head and give it another bash," advised her dad.

"Careful," said her mum. "You don't want to get stuck in bloody Hensley."

But Aimee refused to listen. She shook her head when Melinda suggested joining her in Europe, turned down the university when they offered her another place. Nick's parents put a note up in the pub asking for help with the harvest. Aimee wore low-cut vests and short shorts, her figure shapely from all the manual labor, her cleavage brown. Melinda had never had breasts.

Aimee started hanging round the house at the end of the working day, having a few glasses and listening to Nick rant. "You don't have to bugger off to London to be a success. You don't have to go overseas to have a career. There's loads you can achieve right here."

Aimee refused to comment, saying she didn't want to be disloyal, and began working on the reception desk at the local dentist.

"All your *potential*," wailed her mother.

"Straight As and you're reminding people to floss?" said her father.

But any woman Nick married would need to have a job. He spoke approvingly of other winemakers whose wives worked in town. Teachers, shop assistants. "A safe second income." Because he had so many dreams, about buying more land and planting new varieties. Turning his father's hobby winery into something commercially viable. They'd need other money coming in. Aimee allowed herself to be poached by the local GP for a twenty-five percent pay raise. A bit more responsibility than she was comfortable with, but it seemed worth it.

Yet by the time Nick finally asked Aimee out, the nervous checking had returned. Only small things: phoning patients to make sure she'd told them the right appointment time, repeating Dr. Malcolm's requests back to him. But with it came the worry that the whole circus would start up again. That her thoughts would start looping like a Ferris wheel, and she wouldn't be able to shut them down.

She downplayed it to Nick, said the job was making her a little anxious.

"I'd hang in there," he said. "The money's good, you won't make that anywhere else in town."

Aimee had said she'd try. They'd only been dating a few weeks; she didn't want him to think she was a nutter.

"Good girl," he said, and took her to Adelaide to celebrate the end of the vintage.

At the doctor's office, things got worse. Aimee began taking

children's temperatures in the waiting room, in case of unde-
tected meningitis. She rubbed in sanitizer after every patient,
to her elbows, so she didn't accidentally pass something on.

"You keep using that stuff, you're going to have no skin left,"
Nick joked as he held her poor, chapped hand at the movies on
their fifth date.

Dr. Malcolm gave her a written warning after she turned
up at a patient's house to check that they were taking their
medication correctly.

"I'm sorry, Aimee," he said, "but there's a line."

But it didn't matter because by then there were actually
two lines, blue, at the end of a stick. She was pregnant.

THE FRAME WAS clearly her mother's work. More puffy
gingham—apple green this time—surrounded by white rick-
rack and hardened pearls of escaping glue. Lou picked up the
photo and sat down heavily on Tansy's bed. *Are you enjoying this?*
she challenged the picture. *My turn, to deal with the hard decisions
and the willful pregnant teenager? You'd say it served me right, if you
were here.* But the photo contained no secret messages. Just her
exhausted, overwhelmed mother, looking improbably young.
And baby Lou herself—red and angry, but perfect. The right
number of chromosomes, all doing what they should be.

Tansy had stuck a similar maternity ward picture of herself
and Lou up on her new bulletin board. Lou reached over and
unpinned it, held it next to the yellowing seventies shot, comparing. Would Tansy's baby have the same features? Would it
even live long enough for them to take a photo like this?

"Mum?" Tansy appeared in the bedroom doorway, looking nothing like any of the Henderson women. Her eyes were slits from crying, her face blotched and puffy. Lou braced herself for the explosion—*get out of my room, stop going through my stuff*—but it didn't come.

"What are you doing?"

"Sorry, love. I can't stop looking at it." Lou glanced down at the photo again, trying to figure out why it bothered her so much. Was it because her mother looked human for once? Scared, uncertain. Like Lou felt, but couldn't let Tansy see.

"Are you wondering what my baby will look like?"

Careful, Lou. "Well, of course I am. Everyone does."

Tansy shuffled farther into the room, arms wrapped protectively around her stomach. "I don't want to have the test," she said.

"Tansy—"

"But I will, on one condition. Well, two conditions."

Her chin was jutting forward—another family trait. Lou had a sudden flash of her own pregnant self, telling her parents what she would and wouldn't do, her mother laughing in her face at the gall. *Like you're in any position to dictate terms. You've got two choices,* Lou had been told. *If it goes, you can stay. And if it stays, you have to go.* "Tell me," she said, patting beside her on the duvet.

Tansy continued to stand. "If there's anything wrong with the baby, we don't tell anyone. Till it comes."

Till it comes. Lou took a silent breath through her nose.

"Not Aimee, not Melinda, no one."

"And?"

"And you don't try to talk me into getting rid of it. No matter what. You need to promise."

"Why don't we wait and—"

"I mean it. Or else I'm not doing the test."

The second ultrasound had been inconclusive; the baby was still too tiny to give up any of its secrets on the screen.

"Promise?"

Lou nodded.

"Say it."

As though Lou was one of her school friends. "I promise."

"And no googling. No freaking ourselves out."

Lou had already used up half her phone battery, finding out all she could about what they were facing. She pulled herself awkwardly up off Tansy's bed. "No googling," she agreed. "Good idea. No need to drive ourselves any crazier than we already are."

Tansy hugged her, hard. "Thank you."

"But, Tansy, you and I need to have a proper talk now. You have to tell me everything."

THE CUT ABOVE Nick's eyebrow wasn't deep, but it was long—a good inch where the tip of the umbrella had caught it; the skin had split over the bone. "I think you might need stitches," Melinda said as she dabbed at it with a makeup remover pad.

"Don't be ridiculous," said Nick. "It'll be fine. Just stick a Band-Aid on it."

"Like I'm the type of person who has a first aid kit." But she did, under the sink, bought in anticipation of an inspection by Claudia Lang. It even had tiny butterfly Band-Aids. "Hold still," Melinda said, as she doused the cut in alcohol, careful not to get any on the furniture.

"Fuck," muttered Nick. But he didn't move as she carefully pulled the edges of the wound together, just breathed deeply as she worked the Band-Aid up and over. His breath still smelled the same, of mint and carrots. Melinda moved her face so it wasn't so close to his.

"Nearly done," she promised, working as gently as she could. "There." She sat back on her calves, pleased with her own practicality. "Who says I'm not bloody maternal?" The skin around the Band-Aid was slowly turning purple, all the way to his hairline. "You're going to have one hell of a bruise though."

"Bugger," said Nick, as he struggled to sit up on the sofa. Melinda pushed him back down, her palm on his chest. There was a dizzying sense of déjà vu with the gesture, a sense that it should be followed by her swinging a leg over him, straddling him on her Irish linen couch, kicking the carefully coordinated neutral cushions to the floor. Melinda pushed herself back up onto her feet instead. "What are you doing here anyway?" she said as she made her way over to the sink.

"I told you," he said. "I came to sort out your store cupboard."

"Your boxes were all over the place," he'd claimed, as she helped him off the floor. "I noticed when Byron and I carried your stuff up the other day. I was scared one of them was going to fall on you."

"But why now?" Melinda said, as she washed his blood off her hands. "Surely you should be home with Aimee, given everything this morning." She placed a beer on the coffee table next to him. "Careful, don't knock that."

"I'm giving her a bit of space," he said. "Besides, I wanted to talk to you."

"What about?"

"Oh come on, Mel, what do you think? Aimee! What's going on with her?"

Melinda wandered back into the safety of the kitchen. "You know, I'm not the one you should be—"

"Because it's not just today. She's been really twitchy."

"Twitchy?" Melinda pulled her head out of the cupboard. "Why, what's she done?"

"She's edgy. Preoccupied. A bit like—"

"Like what?"

"Like she was before." Nick grabbed the bowl of nasty cheese puffs she held out. "Awesome, you still buy these."

"Yeah, I developed a taste for them."

"I'm worried it might be coming back. The panic stuff."

"She hasn't said anything to you?"

"About what?"

His fingers were yellow with fake cheese dust; she passed him a paper towel. "Get that on my sofa and I'll kill you."

"Do you know?" he said. "What's going on? Has something happened?"

It was weird, discussing Aimee with Nick. Uncomfortable. Usually there were three of them, or four, or more. The protection of a crowd. These days, on the rare occasions Nick and Melinda were alone, they talked about safer subjects. Business. The economy. And back in that golden period when they were often alone, they sometimes didn't bother to talk at all. Melinda fiddled with a coaster. She didn't want to be disloyal. But on the other hand—

"She's stopped taking her medication," she said finally.

Nick paused, cheese curl suspended in midair. "Shit."

"Yeah, I didn't know either till Lou mentioned it."

"When was this?"

"Last year, I think. A good few months ago, anyway."

"So this could be about anything." He wiped his mouth with the back of his hand, a habit Melinda used to find disgusting, but that now seemed raw and masculine. Her stomach flipped.

"Anything or nothing." She stopped herself from reaching over, wiping a glowing smear of cheese dust from his cheek. "Anything *and* nothing. You remember."

"Bugger," he said, but softly. He shuffled forward on the sofa, his leg inches from where Melinda sat cross-legged on the floor. "What do I do?"

"Talk to her?" *Don't talk to her.*

"Do I make her go back on her medication? I mean, can I insist?"

Melinda leaned back, head resting on the sofa next to him. The day was just starting to lose its heat. Wine o'clock. Melinda had a sudden urge to get crazily, irresponsibly drunk. She took a swig of Nick's beer, her lips cool on the glass where his had just been.

"Easy, tiger," he said, as she took another. His old pet name for her. Her ginger curls. Or giraffe, he used to call her, because of her freckles, his giraffe. Nick was the first man to make her feel truly beautiful.

Melinda set the empty bottle down on the floor. "Shall I get us some more?" she asked. Nick looked down at her, considering. "Sure," he said. "Why not?"

SIX THIRTY, AND still no family. Aimee stared blankly out into the vineyard. At some point over the past few days, Nick had put the nets out; the vines were swathed in funeral-black mesh. A pair of cockatoos glared accusingly at her from a wooden post: *How dare you spoil our fun?* But their early evening squawks were the only sound. Aimee pulled the window shut. Normally the nets reminded her of Halloween, cheap fun fair spookiness that didn't scare anyone. The kids used to play hide-and-seek among them; Aimee and Nick had had sex under them even, for a laugh. Not anymore.

He could have asked her to help. It used to be a family activity—Nick slowly driving the tractor, her and the kids feeding the nets out of their old wool bales, pulling and straightening, shouting "stop, stop" when things got tangled. It was good, therapeutic work. Rough on the hands, and you finished up a bit stiff. But there was a satisfaction in it, of knowing you could ease off after this. The grapes had begun to change color, the training and spraying had been done. All that was left was to keep them safe and watch them grow. Like pregnancy, after the all-clear scan. But Nick hadn't even mentioned he was doing them. He clearly didn't expect her to take an interest.

There was a warm softness at her ankles; the cat twined between them, meowing pitifully. "Oh, Oscar," said Aimee. "You're the only one who cares. And you don't even like me that much." She bent down to pick him up, but he slipped out of her way. "Come here, show me some love." Maybe she could curl up on the sofa with a good Netflix series and a glass of wine. Or something stronger. There was still half a bottle of vodka in the freezer. "Fancy it, Oscar? I'll mince you some chicken livers." As she was supposed to be doing anyway, for the cat's IBS. I can tell you what the BS stands for, Nick had said when he heard the vet's diagnosis, but Aimee was secretly fixing the special food anyway, or at least when she remembered, and it did seem to be helping. "Some of us just need a bit of extra care," she told the cat. "And there's nothing wrong with that."

Oscar lifted his tail and shat on the bottom of the curtain.

"Oh you're *kidding* me." Not an accident in weeks, and *now* he decided to have diarrhea?

The cat looked at her unapologetically, then scooted his bottom along the floor, leaving a pale brown trail on the wooden boards.

"No!" cried Aimee, as she chased him into the kitchen. "No, Oscar, outside." Another small torrent was released under the table, where the cat was trying vainly to hide. "Oscar! Outside!" The phone rang as she shooed, trying not to get too close to the sticky mess that was Oscar's backside. "Out!" She nudged him with her bare foot as she grabbed the receiver. Oscar bit her toe in retaliation. "Ow! SHIT! What?"

"Is that Aimee Verratti?"

A broom would do it. Oscar yelped as he was brushed onto the back porch. "Maybe. Yes. Unfortunately."

"It's Damien. Damien Marshall."

Aimee slammed the door shut behind her incontinent cat.

"From the ATSB? We met a few days ago. At the accident site."

A clatter as she dropped the broom. "How did you get my number?"

"You guys are in the book."

"I didn't think I'd told you my last name." She bloody hadn't.

"I asked the receptionist at the police station. Don't worry, I didn't tell them about your taillight."

"That's quite an invasion of privacy, don't you think?"

"Is it? I didn't mean to be creepy. I only wanted to say how sorry I was. And check that you were okay." He sounded genuinely concerned. "Are you? Okay?"

Aimee looked down at the trail of cat shit tracking across the kitchen floor. "Not really, no."

"No, I didn't think you would be." His accent was broad. It made everything he said sound a bit like laughter. "Is there anything I can do to help?"

He was the only person who'd phoned to see how she was doing. No one else had called: not Lou, not Melinda. Aimee gave a little shudder at the thought of Melinda, who would be horrified by this conversation.

"I could try and make you muffins in our crappy communal microwave," he said.

Melinda, who had virtually *blackmailed* her.

"Or I could fix that dodgy taillight. If no one else is going to do it for you."

Aimee looked around her silent kitchen. "Could you meet me?"

"Now?" Flustered. So he didn't mean it then. Was just enjoying the banter. Fair enough. "I can't right now. We've got to get some preliminary notes together, now that the accident is . . . well."

It was probably for the best. Nick wouldn't love it either.

"But I could see you tomorrow."

Aimee felt her heart rate pick up, a familiar flutter of nervous energy in her chest. Warning signs. But someone had to do something.

"How about lunch?" he said. "I'll buy you that muffin. Safer."

Melinda was going to kill her. "Okay, but in Meadowcroft. Not here in town."

"Really?" She could hear him breathing, his voice closer to her ear somehow. "Sure, we can do that. If that's what you want."

"Thanks. It's just off the——"

"I know where Meadowcroft is. That's where we're staying. The Princess Royal Hotel? They do a good chicken parma. Why don't I meet you there?"

HONESTY, LOU TOLD herself firmly, as she carried their mugs out onto the back step. It was the only way. She'd encourage Tansy to be honest with her, and then Lou would tell her the truth in return. Like she should have years ago.

"Ew yuck," said Tansy, brushing off the concrete. "Someone's been smoking and flicking their butts into our backyard."

"Gross," agreed Lou, as she got comfortable against the rough brick wall. "You need a cushion?"

The scrubby garden looked almost pretty in the fading light. Lou and Tansy had bought a picnic table to go with their new barbecue, strung tiny lights through the trees that came on with the dusk. "Solar," the salesman had said. "Commercial grade. Bit more expensive, but they'll last for years." The little lights made the garden look like something out of a magazine, like somewhere life happened. Next weekend, thought Lou, we'll invite everyone over, cook some sausages. Although whether anyone would want to come was another story. Maybe it would be easier to have Tansy's mates around instead.

"Who are your friends these days?" she asked. "I haven't seen Zarah for a while."

Tansy shrugged. "Don't have much to say to her."

"Does she know you're pregnant?"

Tansy shook her head.

"Have you told any of your friends?"

"Nope."

Lou shuffled closer. "Have you told the baby's father?"

Tansy didn't answer, just stared into her ginger tea.

"It's okay," said Lou. "It doesn't matter who he is, it really doesn't. I'm not going to get upset. But you do have to tell me. It's important, especially now."

"Do you think maybe he passed something on to the baby?"

"Not like a disease, no. But there might be something hereditary, in his genes, that we need to know about."

"So this might not be my fault."

"Tansy, *if* there's something wrong with this baby, it's no one's fault."

"I think it might be, though." Tansy twisted her mug round in her hands. "I was drinking, when I went out. Loads. Cider mainly, but we also nicked your brandy, and I drank most of that." Her voice got even quieter. "I was hoping it might . . . fix things."

Lou put her arm around her daughter's shoulders, for what felt like the hundredth time that day. She'd held her more in the last week than she had in the past year. Two years. Who'd have thought?

"And I smoked a couple of joints. And sniffed some glue. Only once, but—what if that made the genes change? Mutate or something?" Tansy's voice rose and carried on the still night air.

"That's not how genes work. Nothing you've done could have caused this." Lou had spent the final weeks of her own pregnancy worrying about her former fondness for Southern Comfort, had cried with relief when the disturbingly purple Tansy was pronounced "absolutely perfect."

"But I imagine the doctor will have questions for him."

Tansy fiddled with her tea bag.

"And we're going to need to speak to him about money. Well, his parents. You heard what the doctor said. This baby might need a lot of extra care, and it's only fair they contribute." Lou squeezed her daughter. "You need to be brave and tell him."

"I can't talk to him though."

"Tansy, you have to. I'll come with you if you want."

"No, I mean I can't talk to him at all." Tansy looked up from her tea, her eyes miserable. "I can't say anything to him because he's dead."

MELINDA LEANED BACK against the sofa with the top button of her shorts undone and tried not to feel disloyal.

It wasn't as though they were doing anything. They were only talking. But oh, the talking. She'd forgotten how easy Nick was to confide in. She rolled to one side, crushing a nacho into her mohair throw, and didn't care. They were surrounded by food—delivery pizza, hot chips, more junk than Melinda had eaten in a decade, all scattered across the floor with no place mats, sticky bottle rings tattooing the blond wood. If she was going to raise a baby, she'd have to learn to live with mess. Melinda rubbed her beer-bloated belly contentedly. Maybe she should take a photo and send it to Claudia Lang.

"You could kick out the baker downstairs," said Nick. He sat among the crumbs and cushions next to her, legs outstretched. "He's not local, so no one will care, and his cannoncini are rubbish. Then you'd have some decent space to store your boxes, rather than piling them up like a death trap."

He was still worried about her hurting herself, even though he was the one with a goose egg on his forehead. Melinda gazed out her open balcony doors, blinking away unexpected tears. Not like her to get emotional. And a bit embarrassing, as Australia's third-most inspiring female, as voted by *Women's Weekly* readers, to get sniffly because a man had gone all protective on her. She was supposed to be beyond that. But it was just so nice to be looked after, for a change. Someone had taken the time to drive over and rearrange her shelves because they cared what happened to her. Someone thought she was worth caring about. Melinda escaped to the bathroom so she could have a proper sob. This was why she never watched rom-coms—they reminded her of what she was missing. What everyone else had. A husband to sit on the floor and eat crap with, a partner to give you advice when you needed it. It was so bloody ordinary, and yet it felt like visiting a foreign country, one she'd never had a passport for.

Although she had, once. Nick had been hers first. And she'd given him away.

"Well, that was stupid," she muttered at the mirror. "Didn't think that one through, did you?"

The face that stared sadly back at her was just starting to line. She'd be thirty-nine at the end of the year. Almost forty. Past the point where you could fool yourself that your love life might still be about to take off. This was her life; borrowing someone else's husband for an evening, and drunkenly pretending it meant something.

"It wouldn't have worked anyway," Melinda reminded her mirror self. She'd wanted to do things, and he hadn't. She'd had ambition, and he didn't. She probably wouldn't have even started LoveLocked if she'd stayed here with Nick.

And it wasn't really about him. Melinda carefully patted concealer under her eyes as she tried to convince herself. There was nothing special about Nick. He could be any guy. It was just the sheer male closeness that was making her a bit weepy, because she was lonely.

"Can I tell you something?" Nick asked, as she walked hesitantly back into the living room.

"Sure." She stayed behind the couch so he couldn't see her red eyes, and so she couldn't accidentally grab hold of him.

"I've missed you," he said.

Melinda clutched the back of the couch instead.

"Just to yabber with. This has been really nice." He was a bit drunk, she could tell; he was bobbing his head around like a newborn calf, as he always did when he'd had a few. "I can't really talk to Aimee anymore," he said. "Even without the anxiety. We don't really understand each other at the moment."

"Nick, I don't think we should be having this conversation."

"Oh, I don't mean anything like that. I love her. She's my wife. But when it comes to the vineyard, the business, we're not on the same page."

Melinda could talk business. Business was safe. She sat

down among the congealing remains of their feast, but with a moat of cushions between them. "The cellar door?"

"She won't even talk about it. Won't look at the plans I've had drawn up, nothing. She treats it like this big joke, but it's important, Mel. It's the only way we're going to stop being just another hobby winery, the only way people'll take us seriously. And I can't do it on my own."

"Have you put a business plan together?"

"Of course." He looked vaguely insulted. "We'd have to borrow a bit, but it works out."

"Are the banks going to lend to you?" They'd had a tough year, Melinda knew.

"Maybe. Maybe not. I'd kind of thought——"

"You thought you'd ask me."

"Actually no. I thought we'd do some crowd funding."

Melinda leaned over her cushion barrier. "Do you have the plans? On your phone?"

There was an easy silence as she flicked through the architect's drawings—tasteful, clever, expanding the old stables but keeping an authentic feel—and his preliminary costings.

"This is really——"

"I know."

"And the new labels——"

"Neat, eh? I've taken the shapes from Granddad's war medals. I thought we could display them in the cellar door."

"Which might make you eligible for some government money, a local history grant."

"Exactly."

"You could even do up a proper museum." There were whole albums of photos that Nick's grandfather had taken in the war, Melinda knew, as well as uniforms, letters. "I bet there's a load of old guys around here who'd lend you their stuff, who'd love to see it exhibited. And then you've got an instant drawing card for tourists, and you'd totally pull in the baby boomers. They're the ones going on wine tours anyway."

"I knew you'd get it."

"This is really cool." Melinda flicked through the plans again. "So why doesn't Aimee want to do it?"

He shrugged. "There's a new reason every day. Time, stress. Money."

It would be so easy, to gently character-assassinate her friend. Point out the money they'd spent on Aimee's health care over the years, the hours she found to put into community activities outside the vineyard. Melinda didn't even need to say anything. She could just sit here agreeing with Nick, enthusing over his project. Being the one who got it. "I'm sure she'll come round," she said.

He shook his head. "She doesn't want to do anything new. Says she likes everything the way it is. But I want more."

"That must be difficult."

"You'd have been up for it though, wouldn't you, Mel?" He leaned over and grabbed her wrist. "I wouldn't have had to convince you. You'd have already lined up the shareholders." He laughed, a little bitterly. "Shame I didn't wait a bit longer for you to come back."

"But you didn't, and now you have a wife who adores you,

and two gorgeous children, and the world's most expensive cat." Melinda shook herself free and started stacking plates decisively. "Everything's worked out exactly as it was supposed to."

"You forgot the dog," Nick said, watching her with a funny look on his face.

Drunk. He was drunk. They both were. "Come on, soldier," she said, nudging him. "Time to go home."

But he was staring over her shoulder. "Who's the tie belong to?"

"Oh that." Melinda had forgotten it was still out. She wound it around her fist, the shiny fabric padding her hand like a boxing glove.

"You're seeing someone."

"I am."

"Is it serious?"

"Mmmm."

That look again. "Lucky guy."

Melinda examined the little misspelled label promising "100% hand-stiched" silk. This wasn't at all what she'd imagined it would feel like, finally flaunting a partner in front of Nick. Watching the regret move across his face as he realized he'd made a mistake.

"I'll let myself out."

And Melinda was left standing in the middle of her living room, clutching her fake boyfriend's fake Prada tie, while the man she'd said she didn't want, who she'd *told* to marry someone else, but didn't expect to bloody well go off and do it, walked slowly backward to the door. She didn't need a mirror to know her face would look exactly the same as his.

"OH, TANSY," Lou said sadly. "I didn't even think you knew him. You haven't seen each other since you were toddlers."

"We met at a party," Tansy said, between sobs. "Well, a couple of parties. But it only happened once."

"It only takes one time," said Lou, her mother's words slipping out of her mouth before she could stop them. "Sorry. Not helpful." She searched her scrambled brain for something to say. "Did you like him? I mean, were you . . . close?"

"I didn't even really know him." Tansy was gulping now. "Oh God, that sounds so bad."

"No it doesn't," said Lou, stroking her back. Because who was she to judge?

"But he seemed really nice, you know? He's not one of those guys who hassles you to send dodgy pics or anything. He's really respectful."

Lou winced. "So when was this?"

"Angela's birthday." More tears. "It just kind of *happened*."

All that worrying about her daughter roaming the streets, about inappropriate friends and older guys, and Tansy gets pregnant at the local GP's house. Lou leaned her head back against the rough brickwork.

"I'm sorry," said Tansy. "I've made a big mess of things, haven't I?"

"No more than the rest of us," said Lou, heart breaking for her daughter.

"But we don't have to tell them, do we? Lincoln's parents? It'll only make things worse for them."

Lou had told the boy's parents, seventeen years ago. And yes, it had only made things worse.

"We could just not say anything. Keep it a secret. Make something up. Please?"

Lou had made something up, in the end. A French backpacker, in the days before email and mobile phones. A summer romance. A man that no one could question, a story no one could disprove.

"We don't need their money. We'll be fine."

Lou had taken the money, in the end. Let them buy her silence. *Do you really want this to go to court? For everyone you've slept with to be made public? Because you don't really know whose baby this is, do you? You're just going after the family you think is wealthiest.*

But she'd known.

At least, she thought she'd known.

A small icy doubt slid down into Lou's stomach. Chromosomes. Extra genetic material. Oh God. She reached over and grabbed Tansy's shoulder. "Are you sure? Absolutely sure? That this baby is Lincoln's?"

Tansy twisted away. "I *told* you."

You've got no idea. You've slept with everyone in town, and now you're trying to pin it on my son.

"He was the only one!"

Lou had screamed the same words at her parents. She'd been lying. She was still lying. And now, as her mother had promised, it looked like her chickens might be coming home to roost.

THE STARS SEEMED very far away, much farther than usual. Aimee lay on the trampoline beneath the vast southern sky and tried to feel insignificant. In the grand scheme of things, she reminded herself, *my little thoughts and actions don't even register.* Cicadas hummed their agreement from the trees. *When you consider the size of the universe,* one of her counselors used to say, *we're really not that important. Look at the order, look at the science. Do you really think you have the power to disrupt it? Are you actually telling me you can control the cosmos, just by checking?*

Jeff had been her favorite counselor. Not a proper psychologist or psychiatrist, just a trainee who ran the group sessions, he was the one person who could make her laugh at herself. Yes, it was probably unlikely that she'd poisoned a group of senior citizens by leaving a container of biryani out overnight. (Although reheated rice was the perfect vehicle for bacteria.) Yes, it was slightly ridiculous to take notes when she watched the evening news, just in case there was an accident she might have been involved in.

Yes, there was a small chance she hadn't set fire to a light aircraft, even though she'd let off a lantern with an open flame in a residential area on the same night that the plane crashed with an experienced pilot at the helm in an unexplained accident the police were treating as suspicious, barely ten minutes from her house.

But only a very small chance.

A shooting star fizzed across the sky, and Aimee's heart gave a thump. Once upon a time she'd have taken that as a sign, that what she was thinking was true. But she was better now. Wasn't she? *Yes*, she told herself firmly, as a plane—a real, unexploded, safe-in-the-sky plane—blinked red and white above her, and she ignored that sign as well. *Much better.*

"Mind if I join you?"

The trampoline rolled beneath her as Nick climbed onto the mat. A wave of beer fumes followed him.

"Where've you been?"

"The pub."

"What about the kids?"

"Claire's. She promised fish and chips and a sleepover in a tent. They thought it sounded cool."

Nick's sister was a forty-five-year-old orthodontist; the kids didn't think anything she did was cool. He'd gotten rid of them so they could talk. Aimee held on to the thick edge of the matting, body as tense as the springs supporting her.

"So what happened?" he asked.

"Oscar had another episode, all over the kitchen. I really think we should take him back to the vet, maybe get a second opinion."

"Aimee—"

She had to be honest with him. He was her *husband*. He wasn't going to tar and feather her. He'd promised to love and protect her. And who knew, it might even make things better. "I'm a bit worried," she said finally, stating the obvious.

Nick reached over and took her hand, his skin warm against the cool webbing. "What about?" he asked, squeezing gently, and she remembered all the reasons why she'd chosen him.

"I think I might be responsible for Pete Kasprowicz's accident."

Aimee felt rather than saw him nod.

"We should never have let them off," she said miserably, staring at the little pinpricks of light above, lights that were not exploding into balls of flame and killing innocent children. "I should have known better."

"I thought that might be it. I wondered if you were blaming yourself."

A wave of relief washed over Aimee. "You did? How?"

"Aims, I live here. You've been a wreck since New Year's Eve. You've rearranged the pantry three times."

"Don't joke." She pulled her hand away. "I'm serious. There's a very good chance I caused that boy's death."

"That's not possible."

She opened her mouth to tell him just how possible it was, but he kept talking.

"Look, I was worried as well, if I'm honest. I didn't think it was a brilliant idea, but I didn't say anything. I knew you were trying to do something nice for everyone. But I had my eye on my pager the whole time. I thought they were going to burn the bloody riverfront down, rain or no rain. And instead— well, the only small consolation is that the fuel from the crash didn't set the bush alight. Can you imagine?"

The fireworks. He thought she was talking about the fireworks.

"But you didn't bring that plane down. Look, I had a quiet word with Arthur. Pete was flying at a completely different height. And he was a good pilot. He wouldn't have flown into a bunch of fireworks."

"But what if someone let something else off? Their own stuff? Thought it was safe, because we'd gotten approval?"

"Yeah, there were a few unauthorized displays. Arthur's going to have a word. But again, fireworks wouldn't have hurt the plane."

"But what if it was something bigger? A sky lantern or something?"

"A what?"

She gripped the edge of the matting. "Like we had at our wedding. You know, the paper balloons, with the candles inside them."

"But those lanterns are illegal now. You can't buy them. No one would even have them."

Aimee's heart stopped. "They might," she whispered. "There were some here. In the cupboard. Left over."

Nick sat up. "What, you think Shelley or Byron got into them? Aimee, come on now. You're just making up scenarios."

"But—"

"Neither of them would be that bloody stupid. We've raised them better than that. They know the risks."

"But what if—"

"You know what I'm worried about?" Nick ran his hands through his hair—a warning sign that his patience was fading. His wedding ring shone in the darkness. "I'm worried about you. What's going on in your head. This all sounds a bit familiar."

Aimee scrambled to sit up as well. "It's not in my head," she said, but quietly, because she didn't want to admit to being that bloody stupid.

Nick sighed, and more beer fumes puffed out from him. "You didn't cause the accident," he said, but this time it sounded admonishing, rather than reassuring. "Look, I know you've stopped taking your medication. I think you need to start again."

"How——" *Melinda.* It could only be Melinda. Nick never really spoke to Lou, and besides, she wouldn't be that much of a bitch.

"It doesn't matter how I know. What matters is we get you sorted."

But it didn't sound like a "we" type of statement. It sounded like a "you" type of statement. You get yourself sorted. Aimee hugged her knees into her chest. "You know from Melinda," she said. "The same way she knows we might remortgage."

"Oh for fuck's—yeah, if I run into her, I talk to her, okay? You know that. No different than I'd talk to anyone. She and I are friends, you and her are friends. Best friends, remember?"

Not anymore. Aimee held herself tighter. The universe might be big and vast and powerful, but at the end of the day, you were all alone in it. No matter who you married, no matter how much you tried to build a safe and happy life for yourself. You could never truly ward off disaster.

"Aimee, what are you not saying?"

Where to start. Where were you the night after you checked me into the hospital? How do you know where the plates in Melinda's house are kept? She turned toward him, and— "Oh my God, what have you done to your face?"

"It's nothing. I slipped on the pub steps. Someone spilled a drink."

"But—Nick, you're bleeding."

"I said it's nothing. Just leave it." He pushed her hand away. "Look, it's late. I'm going to bed." He started crawling toward the edge of the trampoline.

Aimee put her hand out to steady herself. "Aren't you hungry? Don't you want something to eat?"

"I ate at the pub." And he disappeared into the dark.

Lou SLID OUT into the warm night, moving quietly so as not to wake Tansy. She held her breath as she pushed open the rusty garage door, but the only sound she could hear was their voices. *Are you sure, Louise? I don't think you really know, do you? You're just trying to pin it on my son.*

"I do know," Lou whispered into the dark. "I am sure." But here she was, on her knees, digging through ancient copies of the *Women's Weekly*, searching desperately for confirmation. Because the statistics didn't feel very much in her favor. A chromosome disorder. A lip-biting coincidence. *We know you've slept with other men.*

Lou tried not to think about snakes and spiders as she gingerly pulled books and magazines from the pile. They'd tried to gaslight her, read out a list of names. But Lou had been insistent. Her diaries were right at the bottom, where she'd spotted them in their clearout. Lou reached for the most recent. She'd never really hoped for much for her life. Just the chance to escape it. But right now, she wished more than anything that she'd gotten her dates right.

The moon was bright as Lou carried the fabric-covered notebook over to their nice new outdoor table. The cheap lock gave easily as she pulled it apart. *You've not exactly discriminated. How could you possibly know who the father is?* She flicked through pages dotted with initials, until she found an entry with PK circled at the top. Then another. And another. And then, gloriously, two weeks later, page after page marked with tiny red stars.

Lou looked up at the dark country sky and thanked a God she didn't believe in. She knew. She *knew.* It wasn't Bob Farrier, who dropped off the firewood, and it wasn't Larry the butcher's apprentice, now Larry the butcher. Or Andrew Simons, or Cooper Murphy. And it wasn't Peter Kasprowicz, even though she'd managed to convince herself, for one long horrible moment, that her mother was right and Lou was, finally, being punished.

Chapter 26

The flowers just kept coming. Every morning saw a funeral pyre of lilies and white roses covering the front step. Some people rang the doorbell and quickly dropped them off in person, but most just quietly laid them on the mat, bland condolence cards tucked among the Gypsophila. *Thinking of you. Please know you're in our hearts.* Cameron was tempted to leave them there in the hope his stepfather would trip over them, but Pete rarely went outside.

The food was starting to slow down, though. The women from the church still came, with their shepherd's pies and banana bread, but there were fewer neighborly casseroles, fewer blokes from the aero club clutching an awkward six-pack, just come to see how you're doing, mate. Cameron swore as he carried in that morning's offerings. There was a time limit on people's sympathy, he knew, but for God's sake, you'd think it would last longer than a week.

Cameron's own grief was still glowing, a hot coal of anger that kept him awake at night. Pete might not notice the lack of visitors, might be content to spend his days pacing the house, counting footsteps, memorizing the position of light switches, but Cameron wanted answers. For Lincoln's sake. Few tragedies occurred without human error, Cameron knew. Even when it seemed there was nothing to blame for your loss except a malfunctioning GPS or a mutating cell, someone, somewhere would be culpable. If only for making things worse.

One woman still came though, nearly every day. The dark-haired woman from the hospital. *Aimee.* Constantly creeping down their driveway with a biscuit tin, jumping up from their sofa if Cameron arrived home before she'd left. She was the only one who wanted to talk about the accident, what happened. Cameron sometimes hid in the hallway, hoping Pete would let something slip.

She's just an old friend, his stepdad insisted. *I haven't really spoken to her for years.* But Cameron knew there was more. Old friends didn't park across the street and sit staring at your house. They didn't drive slowly past, taking note of other cars, checking who was inside.

Cameron knew he should be grateful Pete had company, that someone was around to help, but he wasn't particularly interested in the old man's well-being. Hadn't been since Pete had left his mum to die alone, surrounded by machines. Wondering where her family was. Why her husband didn't answer the hospital's frantic calls. *She'd never have known,* the nurses said, *she had very little cognizance at the end.* But that was bullshit too. You'd know you'd been abandoned. You'd sense it.

Someone had left a tub of bougainvillea, no card, no name.

Cameron lugged it down the driveway and settled it next to the mailbox. He waved at Mrs. Verratti in her four-wheel drive on the other side of the street, wearing a pair of sunglasses as though maybe they'd stop him from recognizing her. And when she was startled and fumbled for her keys, he was ready. He let her make her way down the street, then hopped in his stepfather's trusty Corolla and followed her out of town.

THE VISITORS HAD stopped coming. Oh, Julia's old friends still turned up, and those who had to be there: nurses, occupational therapists. Tradesmen fitting new handrails everywhere, making his sightlessness seem more permanent with every hole they drilled. And the aero club members still phoned, one a night; Pete suspected a roster. But he could hear the distance in their voices. Things had changed.

They're not sure what to say, Aimee suggested, but Pete knew it was more than that. There'd be divided loyalties, now he'd pointed a finger at one of their own. *Don't be ridiculous,* Aimee said, *you lost your son. They want to know the truth as much as you do.* But Pete knew he'd broken the code. You didn't do the dirty on your mates, especially when it wasn't true.

Pete fumbled in his wardrobe for a pair of trousers, now conveniently hung from light to dark so he could tell what he was putting on. They'd know it was bullshit as well, the people he'd been flying with for years; they all knew those planes inside and out. They weren't so crass as to call him on his lies while he was grieving, but they'd be wondering why he'd done it. What he had to hide.

Pete patted along the wardrobe floor for his shoes. He didn't care if people avoided him. He didn't care if they hated him, if he was left alone for the rest of his life, if the doorbell never rang again—he probably deserved that. But he did care about implicating someone else in his mistakes. Pete shoved his feet into a pair of sneakers. He might feel dead inside, be numb to the core, but he wasn't a complete arsehole.

It had been a moment of weakness, that was all. A bad judgment call. But at least he could set this one right. Pete fumbled around the nightstand for his phone, now set to voice command, and instructed it to ring Cameron. His son wasn't keen on his company either, but he was nosy enough to want to keep an eye on him.

"Cam," he said, as the phone went to voice mail. "Can you come back to the house, mate, soon as you can. I need a favor. I need you to take me somewhere."

"I MADE A mistake."

Pete kept his hands in his lap, where they shook slightly. Nerve damage, the doctors said, but the truth was that accidents aged you. The physical trauma, as much as the emotional pain. The body could only withstand so much shock.

"What sort of mistake, Peter?" Arthur's voice was kind, too kind.

"About the accident. It wasn't the plane. There was nothing wrong with the plane. The engine was running fine."

"Then why . . . ?" A heavy wheeze from Arthur's barrel chest. "Are you saying you remembered wrong?"

Pete grabbed the generous interpretation the policeman was offering him. "Yes. Yes, I remembered wrong."

"So what have you remembered that's right, then?"

There was no offer of coffee this time, with or without biscuits. Pete swallowed, the noise loud in the concrete interview room. "If I tell you, can you keep the other stuff back?"

"Your concerns about the maintenance? The condition of the plane?"

"I don't have any doubts about the condition of the plane. The plane was fine. I was confused." Pete could feel Cameron's silent stare from the back of the interview room. He'd insisted on coming in, gripped his dad's elbow as though daring him to refuse.

"Well, that'll be a great relief to Smithy. He resigned, you know. Even before you'd said anything."

Pete ducked his head in shame.

"But it won't make much of a difference to the investigation. The ATSB will still inspect the plane. That's their job."

"I know. But if you could amend what I said, about the engine seizing. Make it clear I was mistaken."

"I'll make a note." The scratch of pen on paper. "They've probably got you on some heavy painkillers."

"They do, yes." Pete shot the policeman what he hoped was a grateful look.

"But, Peter . . ." Arthur's voice moved closer toward him, and the desk moved forward as well, knocking Pete's chest, setting off a flash of fire all the way down his right side. "If it wasn't the plane, people are going to wonder what happened.

They're going to look at the lab reports"—a meaningful pause—"and consider what was and wasn't in your system."

"I know about the alcohol," Cameron called from his corner. "Don't censor yourself on my behalf."

"I'm not talking to you," bellowed Arthur. He lowered his voice. "You know what I'm saying, don't you?"

Pete nodded as he gripped the desk, his trembling hands setting off a little earthquake that traveled down the table legs. "I can't have them saying that, Arthur. I can't have them saying I deliberately—" His throat caught. "They're probably already thinking it though, aren't they? Aren't they?"

"Do you want to tell me," Arthur said softly, "what really happened up there? Do you want to tell me why the plane came down?"

"I made a mistake." Pete lowered his head, ashamed. "I got distracted by the fireworks, disoriented, and I cocked up the navigation. I saw a bright light at the far end of the river and thought it was a star. I thought it meant we were higher than we were."

"And you flew into the hill."

"I pulled the nose down. Deliberately lost altitude. A stupid, stupid mistake. By the time I realized what was happening, by the time I could see we were headed into terrain, it was too late to pull up." He crumpled the tissue that was placed in his hand. "I killed him, Arthur, not on purpose, but I might as well have. The accident was entirely my fault."

Chapter 27

The red floaty top was extremely flattering. Not just because it was expensive, although it was a bit, or because it was American, shipped through a fantastic new service that redirected your shopping from a false address in the U.S. Aimee tugged on a pair of her old jeans, which—miraculously—actually did up. The top looked great, even the jeans looked passable, because she was another four pounds down. It was true, the medication had been making her eat more. It had taken a while, but now it was truly out of her system she was finally starting to look like herself again.

She was beginning to feel more like herself too. The fact that the big parcels didn't fit in their rural letter box—an old milk can Shelley had converted for a school project, the road was full of them—meant she had to pick them up in town. Which gave her an excuse to check in with Sharna, find out what was happening. Aimee felt okay, as long as she knew what was happening.

"Bye," she called toward bedrooms where the children no

doubt sat in the dark on a glorious day staring at screens and not caring whether she was there or not. "I'll be home in a couple of hours!"

No answer. But she hadn't expected one.

"Bye, Oscar," she said to the resentful cat, curled up on the front step where he'd been banished until his bowels started behaving. "Bye, Lucinda." The Labrador at least lumbered over and shoved a wet nose into her hand, licked off a probably toxic dose of Wild Peony moisturizer.

"You off again?" Nick was rolling a barrel into the sun to dry, ready for the next vintage. It was important, Aimee knew, that the barrels were kept in top condition, that nothing happened to the expensive, imported oak. When she'd first learned how much they cost, she'd nearly choked. And if one turned, got infected, if there was the slightest hint of taint, it was all over. "Nick takes better care of those barrels than he does of me," she used to say to the girls. Joking, obviously. Although here he was running his hand lovingly along the curved wood, and he hadn't even looked up at her.

"There's a music rehearsal at the retirement home," she said. "We're practicing for the festival closing ceremony."

Nick didn't argue, and Aimee felt guilty. "I'll give you a hand moving them back in when I'm home," she promised. "Help you get them up on the racks. I can be back by three."

Nick lumbered to his feet. "I'm not going to put them back in the stables," he announced. "I'm going to try them under the house instead."

"Why would you do that?"

"So I can clean this place out, get a proper look at it empty." There was a familiar set of plans poking out of the back of his jeans.

"I thought we wanted to keep things as they were for a bit. Wait for the right moment."

"You wanted to keep things as they were. I wanted to give this a try."

"But I'm not ready."

"Aimee, you're never going to be ready." Nick turned the barrel carefully onto its side. "And I want to get started. I've arranged for Tommo to come give me a hand, shift everything before we need to get this next lot off the vine."

"But the money—"

"I've done the numbers. It'll work. If we're careful."

Aimee squinted at her husband. He'd never ignored her wishes before. *Anything you want, Aimee,* was his usual mantra. *Whatever you need.* "But you know how I feel about this," she said.

"Yeah, I do." He ran his hands through his hair. "Question is, do you care how I feel about it?"

Dozens of people, every day, that she'd have to feed and water and be responsible for. All those toddlers she'd have to keep away from fertilizer sprays, all those pregnant women she'd have to make sure didn't accidentally order anything with raw egg. All those disasters, just waiting to happen. Maybe she just wouldn't play. Force him to hire someone else, see what that did to his precious numbers. "I won't come back early then. If you don't need me."

"Oh, Aimee, I'm going to need you, don't worry. This cellar door isn't going to run itself." He stepped over the damp concrete between them, planted a kiss on her forehead. He smelled of wine and wood and sweat, smells she loved. "We'll talk about it tonight, okay? Don't get yourself into a twist. It's all doable. You might even enjoy it."

She nodded, not trusting herself to speak.

"You look nice, by the way. Lucky pensioners!"

Lou MADE SURE the office was empty then pulled her mobile out of her bag. She'd felt terrible leaving Tansy at home, her little face white with worry and pain. But what could she do? She wasn't Aimee, with a nice husband providing for her so she didn't have to work. She wasn't Melinda, who worked from home the whole summer, every summer, just refused to go down to the city. Which you could do when you were the boss. Lou wasn't the boss of anything except the stationery cupboard. Sometimes she denied people extra notepads, told them they'd hit their monthly quota, just because she could.

"Come on, Tans, pick up." But it was probably better she was sleeping. The test had looked brutal, despite the doctor's assurance she'd feel nothing more than a bit of cramping after. Lou had to look away as the needle went through Tansy's pale stomach. But at least she'd finally agreed. There'd been one aborted attempt, two days earlier, when Tansy had fainted as they explained the procedure to her. They'd given her an ECG instead, just in case there was something wrong with her heart, which was ridiculous for a healthy, if slightly underweight teenager. Ridiculous and expensive. Lou'd had to pay for an extra doctor's appointment, and a cancellation fee for the CVS.

Lou was starting to feel a bit sick herself every time she handed over her card. It hadn't been refused yet, but— *Nonsense*, Lou told herself as the call rang out. This was just some weird debt phobia, a hangover from when she was younger. She had a steady job, no mortgage. What was the worst that could happen? She tapped a quick message to Tansy, reminding her there was custard in the fridge, her latest obsession.

She'd have a quick peek, though, while Rex was out. Lou logged on to her bank account. Four unread messages. Lou bit her lip. She'd taken her eye off the ball, what with Tansy and then all this stupid Aimee and Melinda stuff. Not paid enough attention to the day-to-day. When had she last even checked her balance? Lou braced herself as she reentered her password to access her bank messages. But they weren't final demands, or however people told you they were going to come and re-possess your compact disc player these days. Lou let out a little laugh. The last time she'd been in debt, people actually sent you letters, physical letters, with actual red writing on them. The last time she'd been in debt, people bought compact discs. She clicked open the top statement, the one for her current account.

Holy. Shit.

Lou had never seen that many zeros. And they weren't on the good side either. She scrolled down, the account summary going on forever. Lou's bank statement usually contained the same boring four or five entries. Power. Rates. School fees. The cash she took out every week to live on so that they never spent more than their budget. This list was just insane. Lou clicked to go over the page—over the page! She'd never gone over the page before. But then, she'd never bought a satellite television subscription before. As well as Netflix. Because Netflix didn't have *Game of Thrones*, and she and Tansy wanted to know what all the fuss was about. The same way they'd wanted a rocking chair, and a dishwasher, and a microwave that didn't stink, and a proper coffee machine, and a bassinet. The money they'd raised selling the old stuff didn't cover a third of it.

Her hard-won savings were all gone. She was in overdraft, for the first time in a decade.

Lou paced around the council reception area, tapping her fingers on filing cabinets and copy machines. Okay. Okay. This was manageable. She'd get paid at the end of the month, and she and Tansy would have to be extremely careful, and they'd have to leave the nice posh clinic and transfer to St. Margaret's, and Tansy would just have to understand.

Except that the bank account wouldn't be the worst of it. Because most of their big purchases—the television, the sofa suite—she'd put on the magic ask-and-we'll-lend-it-to-you app on her mobile phone.

Lou made herself sit back at her desk, made herself log into the account the man in the electronics shop had set up for her. Six months interest free, he'd said. So at least if her chickens were coming home to roost—God, she had to get that dreadful phrase out of her head—they wouldn't do so until the middle of the year. The statement came up, another frighteningly long list of purchases, but yes, there was a little note saying that she didn't need to start paying interest till July.

It didn't mean she didn't have to start paying *anything* till July, though. Lou swore, loudly, in the empty office. Because of course there were still monthly payments, of the balance; what did she think it was, free money? And then, just to scare herself more, she clicked on the small print—the link actually said *The Small Print*, in that horrible comic book writing—and looked at the rate of interest she'd be liable for if she didn't clear her balance in time.

No wonder it was so damn easy to use the app. This made credit card charges look reasonable. Lou put her head down next to her keyboard. How could she have been so *stupid*?

THEY'D NEARLY WORKED their way through the hotel's chicken parma menu, from Hawaiian to Hibernian. Parma and a pint, nineteen dollars; they were getting a bit of a routine going now, ordering two flavors and going halves. The Italian worked, they both agreed. Aimee was less sure about the Greek.

"Feta cheese does not belong on a parma," she said, waving her fork. "It doesn't melt."

"But the eggplant's good," said Damien. "That feels authentic." He pushed his chair away from the table. "So how's Pete doing?"

"The same," said Aimee. "Getting around a bit better, and

his arm's healing well. Still no improvement in his sight, though. The doctor says it's psychological, the shock of the accident, but he's convinced it's never coming back."

"What about his memory?" Damien folded his hands over his stomach. "Anything new?"

"Nothing," said Aimee. "Or at least, nothing he's mentioned." She placed her knife and fork together. "He doesn't really like to talk about it."

"You need to keep him talking about it," said Damien. "It's good for him. And it might jog something, help him remember."

Aimee wasn't sure she wanted anything jogged in Pete's memory. But the visits were good for her. Like these lunches with Damien. She smiled over the table at the investigator, but with her mouth closed, in case there was parsley in her teeth. Nothing new to report, he'd said as he pulled her chair out in the Princess Royal's little pub garden. They were running the engine from the plane in a special bath, or at least that's what she thought he'd said. To see what condition it was in. So far, they hadn't found anything suspicious.

It might just be, Aimee thought, that the person who knew what was best for Aimee's head was Aimee herself. Forget their books full of lists, their little tricks to push her out of her comfort zone. Aimee didn't need to be forced out of her comfort zone, that was only going to make her crazy. The doctors were clearly in cahoots with the pharmaceutical companies, pushing her until she had no choice but to take pills and lie in private psychiatric hospitals. What Aimee needed was to feel safe. And the closer she kept to the investigation, the more she knew, and the safer she felt.

Damien started to make a little bill-signing motion to the waitress, then stopped. "Sorry," he said. "Did you want coffee?"

It was also nice to spend time with someone who didn't treat her like a mental patient. Just offered her coffee like a normal person, without worrying what it might do to her nervous system.

"Maybe a cake? They do a good ginger crunch. Or do you have to get back?"

And who wasn't mentally comparing her to his skinny ex-girlfriends.

"I don't have to be anywhere," Aimee said.

"Hensley Council, Lou speaking."

Lou had gone through the motions all morning. Answering the phone, dealing with the mayor's Post-it demands—he loved a Post-it—updating the council website. Her head whirring the whole time. What the hell was she going to do?

Because there were two things Lou knew for sure. One: this wasn't her fault. She might have gone slightly overboard buying things, but it was only the stuff everyone else had. It wasn't like she'd gone out and installed a Jacuzzi, for God's sake. Lou was just trying to live like her friends did, in a comfortable house with furniture that didn't hate you and beds you actually wanted to sleep in.

And two: it was only going to get worse. They could change

doctors, but the real costs would arrive with the baby. Lou had been secretly googling chromosomal disorders, and among the heartbreaking pictures and testimonials, she'd discovered there was a very real chance that this baby could live, for a few years at least. Which was a wonderful thing, of course it was, but she couldn't imagine a minute of those years was going to be cheap.

Seven to ten days, the doctor said. Let's not leap to any conclusions until we've seen the results. But even if the test came back clear, they'd still need money, more money than they were currently living on. Lou had been fooling herself, she could see that now. Their finances were already tight, and their little family was about to grow by 50 percent. Yes, there would be benefits and assistance and whatnot, but Lou knew firsthand that you always went over. Babies were expensive.

So what were her options? Lou waved the equality campaigners the mayor had specifically asked her to get rid of toward his office. "Go straight in," she said. "You don't need to knock." She could ask for a raise, but there was about as much chance of that as her finding a winning Lotto ticket tucked down the back of her new couch. She could sell the house. She'd only moved in because she knew it would've upset her parents. But how much would they get for a run-down brick bungalow in the wrong part of a country town? And then where would they live? She could get a better job, but she didn't exactly have a stellar CV, or the energy to even look. Lou eyed the petty cash box, wondering if she'd get away with it.

"Louise." Rex came bustling into reception, followed by the campaigners. "Could you make our friends here a follow-up appointment, in around six months?" The women started to protest politely but the mayor just flapped his hands. "Progress takes time, ladies, progress takes time." Lou could hear him locking his office door as he closed it. She booked the women in for early February, blocked off the whole morning. "Bring your friends," she said. "I've reserved the conference room." And she went back to worrying about money, a habit she thought she'd finally outgrown.

There was three hundred dollars in petty cash. Not even the price of an ultrasound. Lou stole a bottle of ibuprofen from the first aid kid and left the money untouched. Less than a month ago, she'd been convinced she'd be on a plane to London before she turned forty. Lou pictured herself on Melinda's balcony, holding that stupid lantern, planning her escape. Ha. Three weeks later and all her careful savings were gone. Her running-away fund had gotten her as far as the Fenton Women's Clinic. The only way she was leaving this office was in a coffin.

Lou fiddled with the little badge the equality women had given her. IT'S ONLY FAIR. There was one thing she could do. If she was brave enough. "Keep fighting," one of the campaigners had whispered, as the mayor stuck a Post-it to her computer screen, asking for COFFEE, even though she was sitting there. Lou tore it in half. She'd stopped fighting years ago. The teenage Lou had allowed herself to be scared off by legal jargon and empty threats. By the time she realized that what they were doing was wrong, her stubbornness had taken over. She'd gone from *You owe me* to *I'll show you*.

But now she needed money, proper money. She pinned the badge to her Kmart shirt. Seventeen years ago they'd been able to buy her off. Seventeen years ago, they'd been able to bully her, to make her doubt herself. *You don't really know, do you?* But she did. She always had. And now it was time to stick up for herself.

"Louise." The mayor stuck his head around his office door, frowning at her equality pin. "I thought I asked for coffee."

"Get it yourself," she said. "I'm going on my break."

"AND YOU?" DAMIEN said. "Forget everyone else. How's Aimee doing?"

"I'm all right," said Aimee, licking the froth from her spoon. The iced coffees here were excellent; they made them with condensed milk. She'd had two. "Still horribly sad about everything, but it's not about me."

"Don't be silly," he said. "You're so close to the family. It's only natural you're upset."

Aimee fiddled with her teaspoon.

"I can't get over how well everyone's keeping it together," Damien continued. "Pete especially. I splashed boiling water on my youngest once, dropped a kettle when she was little, and it ate me up for months. I can't imagine what it's like to think you might somehow be responsible for your child's death."

It came out of nowhere. Aimee felt a rush of adrenaline

down her arms, and then she was trembling uncontrollably, heart pounding, her breath coming in little gasps.

He was at her side in a flash. "Aimee?" He pressed a glass of water into her hand, held it steady so she didn't drop it, his big fingers curled around hers. "It's just a panic attack. Have a drink of that, you'll feel better." She took a small sip, then another. "Good girl." He dampened a paper napkin, pressed it against the back of her neck. "What's going on with you, Aimee Verratti? What aren't you telling me?" He smoothed the hair back from her forehead. "Talk to me. It'll make you feel better, I promise."

MELINDA TRIED TO stay focused on her emails, but it was impossible. Every few minutes her mind would float away from press requests and prospectus drafts and toward the unanswered questions that kept rising and exploding like fireworks in her brain.

Could a sky lantern actually set an engine on fire?

Weren't planes designed so that things couldn't randomly fly into them?

Weren't there two engines anyway, just in case?

This is the last time, Melinda told herself, as she opened a new browser window. It was amazing how much she now knew about aviation. Accident statistics, health and safety regulations, the complete training and certification requirements for pilots in Australia. Melinda could probably land a light aircraft if she had to, just from what she'd read on the internet. She watched the unread emails pile up as she googled. Engine mechanics. Previous incidents. There were a few former pilots on Quora who looked useful; she created an account under a fake name and posted a carefully hypothesized question.

This must be what it felt like to be Aimee.

They'd only spoken once since the incident in the town hall. Melinda had been researching the range possibilities of sky lanterns—instead of dealing with a pile of curator concerns about their new targets—when she'd discovered they'd been illegal in Australia for nearly a decade. *Wow, your blood really can run cold,* she'd thought, as she stared at the Consumer Protection Notice permanently banning them. The notice was aimed at retailers, said nothing about actually using them, but even so, Melinda could see this made everything a hundred times worse.

Aimee hadn't answered straightaway, and when she did, her voice was as cold as Melinda's veins.

"Did you know," Melinda said, not bothering with any niceties, "that they were illegal?"

"I didn't then," said Aimee. "Obviously. But I do now."

"But you *bought* them," hissed Melinda.

"In 2001!"

The rest of the lanterns had still been at Melinda's place, helpfully put away in her hall cupboard by the twice-weekly cleaning lady. Melinda yanked them out and threw them in the recycling. Yanked them out of the recycling, and put them in an empty bin bag. She'd dump them later, on her run.

"It means we committed a crime, doesn't it?" said Aimee, voice wobbling. "Even if we didn't hit the plane."

"It's only a crime if you get caught," Melinda had said, and then instantly regretted it. "Oh God, Aimee, I don't mean that. No, we haven't done anything wrong. Of course we haven't. Loads of people must still have lanterns hanging about. Just best not to mention it to anyone, you know? No point in confusing things."

But Aimee had hung up.

Melinda turned back to her search query. God, the rate that private planes came down, it was amazing anyone used them. She wouldn't, even if she had the money. When she had the money. But she wasn't going to get this IPO off the ground looking at images of horror crashes. Melinda thought sadly again of Aimee. Her cousin could have been anything she wanted. But her head had decided to self-sabotage, and Aimee had chosen to hide away in poetry and children.

Emails began to ping up on the side of her screen from Clint. URGENT, they claimed, and NEED YOUR SIGN-OFF ON THIS. Well, Melinda wasn't going to sabotage her business just because Aimee hadn't kept up to date on product recalls. Although she felt for Aimee, she really did. After all, the lanterns had been her idea. Melinda had originally planned to burn their resolutions in her (probably also illegal) chiminea. "No," Aimee had said. "I've got something better." No wonder she felt guilty. It really was a miracle she'd managed not to burst forward with some kind of public confession. Maybe she was coping with everything better than Melinda thought.

She was actually keeping very quiet, considering. Even Nick didn't seem to know anything.

Melinda pulled her keyboard back toward her and entered "Aimee Verratti" and "Hensley."

A million links about school fairs and poetry readings and how to sign up for the local gardening club.

She took a deep breath and added "accident" to her search query.

The internet yielded just one result. A video, on a news website. Melinda kicked her office door closed and turned up the volume.

"Everyone's very upset," Aimee told the journalist holding the shaky camera. Melinda checked the number of views: over five thousand. Really? "We'll find out who caused this," Aimee vowed, tugging at the hair at the base of her neck. The video cut out just as the lock of hair came free, and Aimee looked confused and upset and, quite frankly, bloody guilty.

"FUCK," yelled Melinda.

"I NEARLY KILLED my daughter," Aimee said quietly. "Shelley. She almost died."

They'd been visiting the Mulligans, down off Gully Road. Aimee had left five-year-old Shelley in the car while she ran up to the door to drop off a cake mixer Sarah Mulligan wanted to borrow. She'd been handing Sarah a couple of fresh eggs when the woman gave a scream. Aimee turned around to see her HiLux and her daughter disappearing down a steep bank toward the lake on the edge of the Mulligans' property.

"My God," said Damien. "That must have been terrifying."

It had taken Aimee several seconds for her brain to realize

what was happening and her limbs to follow. She'd sprinted down the bank after Sarah, fast but not fast enough to stop the pickup from barreling through a low wire fence and into the water.

"But she was okay, wasn't she?"

Shelley barely remembered the accident. But Aimee would never forget wading through that thick sludgy water, Sarah hoisting her up so she could pull her daughter out through the truck's open passenger window. Thank God for the open window. If the window had been closed, Shelley would have died.

"I really don't see how that's your fault," said Damien. "If anything, you saved her life."

"It is my fault! I left a child in a vehicle, unsupervised. A child I'd had to tell off before for playing with the hand brake. I should have known!"

"Aimee, I have to say, I think you're being a bit hard on yourself."

Which is what everyone else had said. Nick, Lou, Melinda. The ambulance staff, who she'd insisted come out to look over a confused Shelley. The local GP, who Nick had taken Aimee to see when she couldn't stop crying a week later. The nice trauma counselor who'd been brought in specially when the double-checking started yet again, and Aimee couldn't leave the house without making sure the pilot light was out, all appliances were unplugged, the sitter had their numbers, both their mobile phones were fully charged, they had a full tank of gas, and even then, she'd make Nick turn around before they reached the end of the driveway.

"I can see why you'd feel responsible, but it's a mistake anyone could've made."

"But it was *my* mistake. I made it."

And things had spiraled from there. All the old behavior Aimee had thought was behind her, the anxiety she'd hoped she'd outgrown. If Nick didn't answer the phone, she became convinced he'd been in an accident. She hid the keys to the tractor, so the kids—and Nick—couldn't find them. She evacuated the Hensley Retirement Home, twice, because she smelled smoke while volunteering. (Birthday cakes, both times; the staff used to put on the full complement of candles.) Worried herself sick because a girl she saw crying in the street might have been a victim of abuse, and Aimee hadn't stopped to speak to her, and therefore anything that happened to that little girl would be *her fault*.

She'd tried to get the local school shut down because Byron had come home happily chatting about a bat.

After the bat incident—Aimee had called the State Education Department when the local authorities wouldn't take her seriously, and Byron had stayed home for a week out of shame—Nick convinced her to get professionally assessed.

"Classic OCD," the nice psychiatrist had said. "You think if you don't obey these urges to take action, something terrible will happen and you'll be responsible."

No one had ever explained her thought process so clearly before.

"We'll start you on medication," he'd said. "And refer you

to a cognitive behavior therapist. There is light at the end of the tunnel, don't worry. We're not going to lock you up."

But then Aimee had noticed a crack in a support beam at the town hall, and the struggle not to say anything, not to warn the council that the whole building was about to come down on the population of Hensley, had been more than her poor embattled head could stand. Nick came in from bottling one night to find her sitting in the corner of the living room, thumping her skull against the wall, over and over, to try to make the thoughts go away.

They found her a bed the next morning, and Aimee was in the hospital for nearly three months.

"Aimee, I get it." Damien took her hand, rubbed his thumb over the top of her knuckles. "I understand why you'd blame yourself. And I understand now why you want to know what's going on, with this investigation. You didn't feel you had control over your daughter's accident. You want to feel like you've got some control over this one."

Was she an awful person, to let him think that?

Damien placed her hand gently back in her lap, but stayed crouched next to her seat. "Look, the first draft of the accident report is making the rounds at the moment," he said. "When I get hold of it I can show it to you, if you'd like."

THE FRONT DOOR to the law firm was open, so Lou let herself in. Last time she'd agreed to meet him after hours—rookie error. She'd made it too easy for him. There was less chance of being bullied if she was standing in his office in broad day-light. He couldn't shout at her if there were clients sitting in his waiting room.

Except there was no one in the waiting room. No secretary even. Lou took in the yellowed Venetian blinds, still hung with Christmas cards. The poky rooms, which once felt so grand and intimidating, but now just looked dated. She felt her nerve grow, and with it the certainty that she was right.

She knew who'd gotten her pregnant. Yes, there had been others; not "half the football team" as he'd insinuated, but a few. Lou had been rebelling. Teenagers, especially those from strict households, often did. It hardly made her the town slut. But there had only been one who'd refused to wear a condom. Said he couldn't perform in a sleeping bag, claimed he wouldn't be able to keep it up if she made him. *I just want to feel you, Lou. Come on, don't be boring.* Only one who'd worn her down with begging, pleading, mild threats, and some quite nasty emotional blackmail, until she'd agreed, okay, just the once.

It only takes one time.

Lou could see, through the old-fashioned frosted glass separating his office from the reception area, the silhouette of a man at work, bent over his desk. Lou steeled herself to knock on his door, but the old man was already rising.

"Louise," he said. "What can I do for you? Is there something wrong with Melinda?"

Like he didn't know.

"No, Mr. Baker," said Lou. "I'm here to talk about your son."

Chapter 28

"Well, that was quite a performance," Cameron's voice was calm, cheerful almost. "I don't believe a word of it, by the way."

Pete stared pointlessly out the passenger window. He'd tried to keep a mental tally of turns and intersections, but he'd quickly lost count as they sped through town.

"You're one of the most methodical people I know. You don't misjudge altitudes. You don't get *distracted*. That's not you."

Pete thought they were near the supermarket, but he couldn't be sure. Cameron could be taking him anywhere.

"And you're not suicidal either. That's the gossip around town, in case you're interested. That you never got over Mum's death. Did something stupid in a moment of madness." Cameron made a hard left and Pete was jolted painfully into the car door. "Of course, you and I both know how quickly you did get over her, so we also know that's bullshit." The car thumped over a speed bump. "Although I'm not against you topping yourself. Just in case you were thinking about it."

They'd never had a great relationship, but this was a new

low. "Cameron." Pete braced his arm against the glove compartment and his shoulder screamed. "Slow down."

"So the question is, why are you lying?" Again, the casual tone, as though they were discussing cricket. "Were you drunk? Was that it? It didn't sound like much alcohol to me, but maybe you were topping up from the night before. Or sleep deprived, from a night of shagging. Your dick getting you into trouble again. Is that it?"

"I'm a widower, Cameron. *If* I was having a relationship, it would be none of your business."

"It is when members of my family die. This is becoming a trend."

They were on the highway, Pete could tell that much. There were more cars now, moving faster beside them. He could try to signal, but what good would that do? He wouldn't be able to see if anyone even noticed. The car shook as they weaved from lane to lane. "Cameron, *slow down*."

They came to a screeching halt on the hard shoulder, and Cameron leaned across him. There was a shock of hot air as the passenger door popped open. "Don't like my driving? Think you can cope on your own? Get out then. Let's see how you manage."

The noise from the highway traffic was dizzying; the open passenger door flapped violently each time a car flew past. Pete grabbed hold of it, tried to pull it back one-handed so it wouldn't be blown off. God, he was the one who'd taught the boy to *drive*.

"Didn't think so." Cameron leaned over and wrenched the

door the rest of the way in. "You should be pleased I'm here to give you a lift," he said, as he started the engine. "I can remember one evening when you couldn't be bothered."

"I know how upset you still are about your mum's death, Cameron. And I understand. You two were incredibly close. But I wasn't responsible for it, no matter how much you like to think I was."

"You were responsible for us not being there. Me and Lincoln, not just you. We never got to say good-bye."

"I made a mistake. One I'll never forgive myself for." They weren't heading north, Pete could tell that much from the sun streaming in the side window. Where was he taking them? "But you need to forgive me, if only so you can move on. You're the one it's damaging. You're the one who's suffering here."

"Like Mum suffered, thinking none of us cared about her?"

"You know that's not true."

Cameron pulled them off the highway with a shriek of rubber and a blare of outraged horns. "What I know isn't true is what you told old Arthur back there. I know there's more to this. And if you killed my brother because you were out all night, or up late on the phone to your girlfriend, or messaging her while you were flying, or doing anything at all that would have clouded your judgment, believe me, I will find out."

He's just an angry young man, Pete reminded himself. *A messed-up kid. He doesn't really mean you harm.* Pete sat on his hands so Cameron wouldn't have the satisfaction of seeing them shake. "Cam, where are we going?"

The car was moving slower now, along country roads. Pete could hear livestock, the low rumble of tractors.

"Cameron, please. Can you just take me home?"

Cameron laughed, tapped a jaunty little beat out on the steering wheel. "Never thought I'd see the day when it was you begging me to take you somewhere." He turned on the radio, soulful country music about driving through a hungry little town at midnight. "We're going to my hotel, *Dad*, so I can grab my bags and check out."

Pete let himself relax, just a little, into the worn vinyl of the passenger seat.

"And then I'm coming home with you."

Chapter 29

Lou had mentally rehearsed her argument in the short walk to the lawyer's office. Logical, persuasive, firm. But the moment she was back in that building, with its intimidating diplomas and cloying scent of Pledge, all reasonable adult discussion left her head.

"I need more money," she blurted out.

Maxwell Baker LLB, OBE raised a slow eyebrow. "Louise," he said. "I thought we'd dealt with this." He looked at her sadly, as though she'd let him down by even raising the subject. "But, if you want to have the discussion again——" He motioned toward his office.

"No," said Lou. Because she wasn't stepping back in there, the scene of her former capitulation. She was nervous enough as it was, stomach dancing as though she'd been called into the principal's office, even though she was the one doing the calling. *You're not a teenager anymore*, she told herself. *Don't let him intimidate you.* "I want to talk out here," she said, voice embarrassingly high.

"Whatever makes you comfortable. No difference to me." He made an expansive I'm-not-hiding-anything movement with his hands, his face mildly amused, as though he was humoring her. But he also took a few steps toward the door and flipped the open sign to closed.

"Can I at least offer you a seat? A glass of water? We've got some chocolate biscuits somewhere, from Christmas. They're rather good." He was acting as if this was a social call. Lou felt her temper flare.

"I'll stay standing, thanks." She dropped her handbag on a chair. "I'm just here to tell you that I intend to go after what's rightfully Tansy's. Child support from Matthew, and back payments for all the money he should have given us and hasn't."

"But we don't know for certain he's the father, do we? You've never been able to prove it."

"I've never tried to prove it. You made me feel too ashamed. But I don't care anymore. I'll get a DNA test, I should have done it years ago."

"People will wonder why you didn't." Melinda's father sounded as though he was thinking out loud, as though he was analyzing the flaws in her decision for her benefit. Like he was on her side. "People will wonder what you had to hide."

That worked on her last time, but it wouldn't now. "You want to read a list of my ex-lovers out in court, put a notice in the paper asking for anyone who may have 'made my intimate acquaintance' to come forward, you go for your life." She really didn't care, Lou realized. She never should have. The people of

Hensley didn't like her anyway, so what was a bit more stigma? "My parents are dead now, Mr. Baker. They were the only people I was really concerned about embarrassing." Because she'd done enough to hurt them, the lawyer had convinced the teenage Lou as he shoved the papers toward her. You don't want to drag their name through the mud any more than you already have.

And despite her anger, she hadn't wanted to. A legal battle, "and a scandal this town will never forget, I promise you," naming half a dozen potential fathers, including unsuitable men, married men, church members, would have hurt her mother beyond measure. Lou had given up because Mr. Baker had worn her down, certainly. But also because underneath it all, she wasn't a bad person.

"We had an agreement. You signed a contract absolving Matthew—"

"In exchange for ten thousand lousy dollars. I'm pretty sure any court would see that as buying me off."

Melinda's father eased himself into one of his own waiting room chairs—"You'll have to excuse an old man, I don't have the stamina your generation does"—and regarded her carefully.

"Louise," he said finally. "What is it you actually want?"

What did she want? In her five-minute dash down the road, Lou hadn't gotten much further than broad concepts. Responsibility, justice, money. She certainly hadn't thought about actual amounts.

"Why are you really here?"

"I'm here because you need to do right by me. By my daughter."

"No, you're here because my son shot through to Queensland and earns bugger all pissing about in nightclubs at the age of thirty-six."

"It's your responsibility."

"Actually, it's not. It's Matthew's. I looked out for him when he was too young to know better, but he's an adult now. Go talk to him. Go chase him for your money." He closed his eyes briefly. "There's a whole system set up to help you do just that."

"You're not even trying to pretend Tansy's not his." Lou had come expecting a fight; without one, she wasn't quite sure what to say.

The older man shrugged. And he was older, Lou realized, much older. Melinda's dad had always been tall, but now he was starting to stoop, his wiry frame gaunt in a suit that was too big for him. Everything in the office was a bit worn, a bit past its prime. The dated gold lettering on his signage, the little bell on the reception desk. Even the Venetians needed a good dusting.

"I had wondered over the years, looking at Tansy. She looks a bit like my ex-wife, round the mouth."

Lou gaped. "Then why didn't you ever say anything?"

"Not my job."

"Or push your son to step up? To take responsibility."

He raised an eyebrow.

"You could have made him. It might have been good for

him." Matthew spent his time dating a revolving door of younger women with fake breasts and dodgy hair extensions, she knew from Melinda. *Still behaving as if he's twenty-three*, Melinda would sigh as she fell for the latest hard-luck story. "Might have made him grow up."

"Louise, you've come to me now for the same reason you came to me years ago. Because Matthew is, quite frankly, pretty bloody useless."

"Then why were you so horrible about it? Why be so *nasty*?"

"If I was heavy-handed, I apologize. But you weren't the one who needed looking out for, as I saw it. You and Melinda have always been able to look out for yourselves." He sighed. "Matthew, on the other hand, can barely tie his own shoelaces."

"You thought Matthew needed *protecting* from me?"

"You got pregnant when you were old enough to know better. You were unhappy at home. You can't tell me you didn't pick the one boy in town with a bit of money behind him."

"That's—I was seventeen!"

"Interesting that you never got pregnant from any of the troublemakers you were running around with."

Lou fingered her little equality pin. IT'S ONLY FAIR. "That's bullshit and you know it," she said. "But you're not going to embarrass me into silence anymore. You're not going to deny me what you owe us."

"Like I said, feel free to speak to Matthew." He waved a hand, dismissing the whole mess.

But . . . "The contract," Lou said, remembering. "I want

you to tear up that contract. You should never have made me sign it."

For a moment, he looked as though he was about to argue.

"It wasn't fair, and you know it." She'd been six months' pregnant and crying when she put his heavy fountain pen to the bottom of the thick document, most of which she hadn't understood. Just knew that she needed to sign it to get the money. Ten thousand dollars had seemed a fortune at the time, and just for not making a fuss that she hadn't wanted to make anyway.

It was probably illegal to make someone sign a document when they were distraught.

"You took the money."

"Ten thousand is nothing," she said. "I know that now. Not for a child." Lou had thought they'd be able to live off it for years, maybe put a deposit on a little house. Ha.

"You seemed happy enough with it at the time."

"Well, I was young and stupid. We've established that." Lou picked up her bag. "The contract," she reminded him. "You need to destroy it."

Melinda's father shrugged. "I don't want to make things difficult for you. I've only ever wanted to help." He pulled himself awkwardly out of the chair; Lou didn't move to assist him. "I just did what I thought was best for everyone."

Best for you. Lou snorted as he made his way slowly out the back. But his era was over, she realized, looking around at the old black-and-white football club photos, the yellowing news-paper clippings of cases won. The whole Hensley network of old-time locals who ruled the town with antiquated expectations and enforced silence—it was done. It had died out with her parents, maybe long before.

"Here you go," he said. "Will you do the honors, or shall I?"

The contract looked slightly ridiculous. Typed—imagine!—on a couple of thin sheets of A4, not the dozens of pages of sub-clauses she remembered. Lou reached out and tore it straight in half, then half again, and again, before dropping the pieces on the floor. *I've won,* she thought. *I've actually won.*

He didn't say anything. Just stood, his jacket hanging from his shoulders, in the middle of his empty office. Not one person had knocked in the half hour she'd been there. No one was banging the door down for legal advice from Maxwell Baker LLB, OBE.

"Interesting," he remarked, as she headed for the door, "that in all these years you've never told Melinda." He sounded more like himself again: condescending, a touch smug. "It sounds as though you are still ashamed of your behavior after all."

Oh, Mr. Baker, you really are a dinosaur. An impotent, unimportant dinosaur. "I've never been ashamed of my behavior," Lou said, chin out, but for the right reasons this time. "The only thing I've ever been ashamed of was allowing you to pay me off."

MELINDA KEPT WATCHING the video, over and over. Aimee pulling at her hair, looking nervously away from the camera. Speculating as to whether the accident was really an accident or not, in the national media. What was she *thinking*?

Well, if Aimee was going to start talking, so was Melinda.

She bowed her head for a few moments, then pushed herself away from her desk. "I'm just going down to the post office," she told her assistant as she headed for the door. "I'll be back in half an hour."

The young woman looked up from the prototype baby lockets she was fiddling with. "You don't need to go," she said. "I'll do it."

"No, I want to," said Melinda. "I need some fresh air."

EVEN THE HENSLEY sun felt lighter as Lou made her way back along the main street. Ridiculous, that she'd allowed herself to be silenced all these years because of a couple of pieces of paper and a few thousand in her bank account. Lou smiled at Sam the newsagent, at Sandra the butcher's wife standing gloriously unaware behind her display of lamb chops and green plastic grass. She'd won. She'd actually won. No wonder Melinda got so damn fired up about all her empowerment stuff. Lou had never really stuck up for herself before, she realized. She'd wanted things to be different, but never actually done anything to change them. Until now.

Lou swung into the council building. The weird thing was, nothing had actually changed. Matthew had no money, she knew that. She'd watched Melinda write out dozens of checks, rolling her eyes as she did so. Cash checks. She couldn't even put the money in his bank account, because it would get swallowed up by his overdraft the moment it landed.

No, she'd get bugger-all out of him, and there would be nothing more out of his dad. Lou probably wouldn't even tell anyone; getting pregnant from Matthew Baker wasn't anything to be proud of. But what she'd gained instead was more important. Confronting the man who'd threatened her, tearing up that damn document—it was worth more than money. That's how she'd explain all this to Tansy. The importance of not being pushed around. Maybe the equality women would invite her to come and speak.

Lou waltzed into reception, unfazed by the phalanx of Post-its she knew would be stuck all over her computer. Heaven forbid Rex should deal with a phone call himself. But that was okay as well. She'd just spend the afternoon meandering through them, instead of doing any real work.

There was only one Post-it, smack in the middle of her monitor. PLEASE SEE ME. Lou looked at it and laughed. Had the printer jammed and sent him over the edge? Had they run out of toner? (Lou was the only one who knew where the toner was kept; the secret allowed her to wield an astonishing amount of power.) Surely he couldn't be annoyed that she'd left the front desk unattended. It was January; most of the council—most of Australia—was still on holiday. Lou had volunteered to come back *early*, for the money. Really, she was doing him a favor. He should be grateful she was even here.

She didn't bother knocking, just pushed his door open and poked her head around. "I was only gone forty-five minutes," she said. "The shire isn't going to come grinding to a halt because there's no one to give directions to the car-trunk sale."

But the mayor wasn't smiling. "Close the door would you, Louise."

Lou had had enough of old men calling her by her full name. "Just tell me," she said. "I'm busting to go to the loo."

Rex let out a huff. "That's exactly the kind of thing I'm talking about. It can't continue. Your flippant approach to council affairs. Your insubordination."

"Insubordination? Is this because I didn't get you coffee? That's not insubordination. That's feminism."

"It's intolerable, is what it is."

"Don't be ridiculous." But the mayor just stood there, red-faced, not quite making eye contact. "What, you're going to give me a written warning, is that it? Seriously?"

"Louise, I appreciate everything you do here, but the fact is, your attitude is showing us up."

"Is this because I yelled at Father Brian? Because I'm sorry, but he has to wait in line like everyone else. Being a God-botherer doesn't mean you get to skip lines."

"There've been complaints. I have to take them seriously."

"Fine, whatever. Write out a warning, and I'll sign and file it." Lou knew the drill. This wasn't her first time.

"I'm afraid we're past that point." Rex fiddled with his shirt cuff. "I'm going to have to let you go."

"You're *firing* me?"

"If you could pack up your desk. I'll handle things for the rest of the day."

"You? You don't even know where the toner is."

"Louise." The mayor took a step forward, obviously expecting her to move as well, to shuffle meekly out the door. His voice grew sterner when she didn't budge. "Louise, I gave you this job because your father asked me to. But I think we can both agree your heart's not in it. Look, at the end of the day, you'll probably be happier somewhere else."

"You're firing me."

"I'm sorry, Louise." He opened the door.

"You can't do this. I'll . . . lodge a complaint. With the rest of the council." Who were all related to Rex. Lou looked around his office, took in the Rotary crest, the Lions badge, the lovingly framed photos from the football club. "Did you get *told* to fire me?"

He didn't meet her eye. But he didn't have to. Once again, the people who really ran Hensley were getting one over on her. Lou let out a little sob and pushed her way past him. Once again, it wasn't bloody fair.

MELINDA'S PHONE STARTED buzzing as she made her way up the post office steps. She flicked it to silent; let Clint deal with any nervous curators. The changes were his idea, after all. *Hang on.* Melinda stopped short in front of a row of iron post office boxes. Was she actually delegating, like every life coach and performance advisor she'd ever employed had begged her to? *I know it's hard to believe, Melinda, but the company might actually run better if you didn't micromanage every piece of it.* Melinda chuckled to herself as she pushed open the post office door. Out of adversity came progress. Who knew.

"Well, you look cheerful," Sharna said disapprovingly. "Practically glowing."

The Hensley Town Festival regalia had disappeared. Instead

of children's paintings and bunting, the post office was now decorated with black ribbon. A book of remembrance stood in the corner, under a picture of Lincoln in his school polo shirt. "Just pleased to be out of the office," she said, lowering her eyes appropriately.

"So what can I do for you?" Sharna didn't really approve of Melinda. She didn't really approve of anyone who'd dared to leave her precious town, even if they did return. And plow thousands of bloody dollars into it, creating jobs and funding main street beautification schemes. Sometimes Melinda wondered why she bothered.

She dropped her envelope on the counter. "Just a stamp on this, thanks."

Sharna examined it as she reached for her little book. "How is your brother doing?" she asked as she held the envelope up to the light. "You should really use registered mail if you're sending a check, love. Safer."

"I'll risk it."

"Always did think it was a shame he left. Handsome, your brother. A real charmer."

But Melinda wasn't in the mood for bullshit. "Sharna, you know as well as I do Matt was up to his eyeballs in gambling debt when he legged it." Borrowing to play the slot machines mainly, but also the horses. Their father had given him twenty grand to start over, stay out of trouble; Melinda was still a little bitter. "Although he seems to feel safe enough coming back here with his hand out." She eyeballed the postmistress. "Did Dad pay his debts off, Sharna? You'd know." But Sharna just kept carefully writing Melinda's address on the back of her envelope.

Melinda wandered around the post office, picking up charity calendars, examining a collection tin next to the book of remembrance. They were planning to build a memorial to Lincoln at the airfield. She rattled the little tin at Sharna. "This is a nice idea," she said. "Yours?"

Sharna's chest puffed self-importantly. "It seemed like the right thing to do."

Melinda stuffed in a couple of twenties. "I agree."

"They're moving ahead with the inquiry," Sharna said. "Early next week, I'm hearing. I think they're keen to give people some resolution. Shut down the old rumor mill."

"Good," said Melinda. The sooner everyone stopped talking about the damn accident, the better. "That'll make it much easier for Pete, I imagine."

"Much easier for everyone." Sharna dropped Melinda's letter into a bag behind the counter. "Whole community is affected, something like this." She handed Melinda a receipt. "Speaking of which, how's Aimee doing?"

And she hadn't even had to bring it up. "Mmmm," Melinda said, pulling a worried face. "Not sure."

"Because she got herself into a right old state, didn't she? I know you'd all had a few, but I did wonder if something else was going on."

"Well," said Melinda, dropping her voice. "It's just . . . well, you know how Aimee went to stay with her mum that time. When Shelley was little."

"I do remember. Just before Patricia got ill." Sharna made a cross-like motion. "Bless her."

"And Aimee was gone for ages."

"Months."

"And Nick and the kids stayed here."

"Yes."

"Well, the truth is—" *I'm sorry, Aimee.*

"Yes?" Sharna leaned forward in anticipation.

"The truth is," Melinda said then paused. She could picture Aimee on the video, visibly squirming. Aimee in her kitchen, clearly in turmoil, unable to stop going over the story. Desperate for Melinda to reassure her that everything was okay. "The truth is, I wish her mum was still alive. My aunt. I feel like it would do Aimee good to have her around at the moment."

Sharna looked at Melinda as though she was the one who was slightly crazy.

"You know, to help with the kids and the property and . . . stuff."

"Right."

"Family's important, especially when people are grieving." Melinda was burbling now. But she couldn't do it. She just couldn't do it. "But Aimee will be fine, she always is. Just sensitive. Anyway, always lovely to see you, Sharna. Good luck with the collection." She pulled a note out of her wallet; a fifty, but too bad. "Here, stick this in as well. Anything to help."

IT TOOK LOU less than twenty minutes to clear her desk. To wash out her coffee mug, the one that said WORK IS FOR

OTHER PEOPLE, to pack up the photo of her mother she'd taken from Tansy's room. *I bet you're bloody enjoying this,* she told the exhausted woman in the ugly frame. *Enough chickens roosting for you yet?*

Rex watched as she moved around the office on autopilot, logging out of systems, stacking jars of instant coffee and artificial sweetener into the box he'd thoughtfully provided. "What?" said Lou. "Are you worried I'm going to steal your precious Post-its?"

She turned her back, and heard him shuffle off toward his office.

She would not cry. She would not cry. She rubbed at her eyes, her nose, skin suddenly sensitive as it always became when she got really upset. She'd hated this job, for years and years and years. She wasn't going to bloody cry over it. But what on earth was she going to do without it?

Lou gave the reception area another sweep, just to check there was nothing she'd missed. The room was bare, apart from one last stack of papers Rex had left on top of the photocopier, Post-it firmly attached: PLEASE. Obviously placed there before he decided to sack her. Before he was told to sack her. Lou tore off the Post-it and carried the papers over to the shredder. Hopefully they were really important.

She'd have to go back on the dole. Lou ripped the plastic binder comb out of Rex's stupid report. Fill out a hundred forms, prove to some spotty teenager that she was actively searching for another job. She switched on the shredder. She'd fed in half the top page before she noticed the title on the second: COLLISION WITH TERRAIN INVOLVING CESSNA 182, VH-QDK, 12 KM NORTH HENSLEY, VICTORIA.

And below it: CONFIDENTIAL.

Lou kicked the shredder's power cord out of the socket.

"Louise?" The mayor's voice floated out from his office. "What's going on?"

If nothing else, reading it would give her something to do. Now that she had all this unexpected free time. Lou shoved the remainder of the report into her handbag and slammed the door on her way out.

AIMEE PULLED UP outside the house, hours later than she'd promised, but she didn't care. If Nick wasn't going to respect her feelings about not opening up their home—her sanctuary—then she wasn't going to cut her day short by rushing back to make him dinner. She strode indoors carrying two big bags from the Thai takeaway in Meadowcroft. Nick was allergic to lemongrass.

"Back," she called out. "With food. Pad Thai and green curry and extra spring rolls." But not even the animals came to greet her.

"What, no one's hungry?" said Aimee, as she pushed open the kitchen door with her shoulder.

The children were in the kitchen. But they weren't alone. Standing at Aimee's stove, wearing her apron and expertly twisting her carefully seasoned wok above a high blue flame, was Pete's stepson. Cameron.

Chapter 30

Pete lay on his bed and spoke to his dead wife.

Cameron was still out; Pete hadn't heard the car come back. Not that he'd care if his son was eavesdropping. It'd probably do him good to hear a few home truths.

"We messed up with that one," he told Julia, or at least the ceiling. As always, he imagined her floating somewhere above it, watching him pityingly, but not too pityingly. Julia had never cut him any slack. Cameron, however . . . "You were too soft on him," he told his wife. "Let him get away with too much. It's all very well having favorites, and I did too, but you mothered him beyond the point a boy needs to be mothered. So when you died, it just blew him wide open."

Pete kept a photo of Julia next to the bed. He groped for it, but there was nothing on top of the bedside table but dust. He rolled back onto the duvet, defeated. He could guess who'd taken it.

"I thought he'd grow out of it," he said. "I thought it was a phase." The bullying, the petty intimidation. "But he's started to frighten me, Julia. This isn't just a teenager behaving badly anymore."

Pete pictured Suzanne's scared little face as she loaded up her Suzuki Swift. *He's a stalker, Pete. Well, I don't know what else you'd call it. He's behind me in the supermarket, he's waiting outside my classroom in the morning. I've found him going through my mailbox. That's not grieving, Pete. That's not acting out. That's something else.* She'd taken a temporary teaching job in Western Australia. He'd written to tell her when Cameron left town, but by then she'd met a nice washing-machine repairman, had made herself comfortable.

"And I don't blame her," Pete said. "I half think he's going to come in here and hold a pillow over my face, finish me off in the night." Which might actually be a relief. Pete slept with his bedroom door unlocked.

"I know what you'd say. He's still a child. But he's not, he's nearly twenty. He's a man, even if he doesn't act like one." Pete thought of Cameron's broad shoulders, his thick forearms. "I'm worried the anger has poisoned him. That he still hasn't recovered from your death, and worse, that he doesn't want to."

Chapter 31

Aimee gripped the takeaway bags. "What's going on?"

"This is Cam," Shelley said importantly. "He's *Lincoln's* brother." She stared at her mother meaningfully.

"I had a flat tire," said Cameron. "Made it just to the end of your driveway. These guys rescued me."

"I changed it," Byron said. A happy, flushed, confident Byron. Aimee gripped her bags tighter.

"He did. Made a damn good job of it too." Cameron reached across and cuffed Byron's head. But it wasn't the head ruffle you'd give a younger boy. It was a fond, almost loving gesture. Aimee turned away and started slapping foil containers down on the bench.

"And then we said to Cam that we didn't know where you or Dad was, and he said what were we having for tea, and had we ever had Vietnamese pancakes." Shelley was falling over her words, almost giddy. "Cam lives in Vietnam."

"Sometimes," said Cameron. "I move around."

Aimee ignored him. "I said I'd be back before dinner. You should have waited."

"You said you'd be back hours ago. We were hungry."

"You're not helpless. You could have sorted yourselves out with a snack to tide you over." Aimee started bundling the takeaway containers back into their bags. "Well, that was a waste of time and money. It won't be as nice tomorrow." She tried to shove the bags into the fridge; there wasn't room. "Maybe I'll just feed it to Oscar and Lucinda."

Cameron put a hand on her forearm, forcing Aimee to look up at him. He was dangerously good-looking. Smooth skin and dark, unreadable eyes. "Don't worry, Mrs. Verratti," he said. "The pancakes are really light, and we've only had two between us. Everyone's still got plenty of room for dinner."

Shelley was rescuing the spring rolls. "Prawn!" she said happily.

"My favorite," said Cameron. He reached over and helped himself, digging around in Aimee's food, food that she'd bought home for *her* children. "Hey, these are good."

"Cam can stay for dinner, right?" said Byron. He eyeballed her, daring her to say no.

"Please, Mum!" said Shelley.

"Please, Mum," said Cameron. "Ah come on, Mrs. Verratti, it'll be fun."

AIMEE CORNERED CAMERON as he came out of the bathroom.

"So how'd you end up all the way out here?" she said, willing her voice to sound natural.

Cameron smiled as he ducked under the door. The gold prospectors who'd built the house were short; Cameron was tall, over six feet. "Stroke of luck," he said. "Burst a tire, and I end up with a delicious meal, great company—"

"But what were you doing out here in the first place? We're not on the way to anywhere."

"Why, does it bother you?"

Aimee forced herself to meet his eye. "Not at all. It's just a bit of a coincidence. All the houses on this road, and you end up in mine."

"You've spent enough time in mine, don't you think?"

Aimee froze.

"I see you. Parked across the street. Walking your dog down our road when you live miles away. And I know how often you visit Pete when I'm not there. He's not a great secret keeper, my stepdad."

"I'm only—"

Cameron put his arm around Aimee, stooping slightly to do so. He walked them back toward the bright light of the kitchen. She could hear Shelley and Byron squabbling happily, see Lucinda sniffing around for leftovers. "Calm down, Mrs. Verratti. I only wanted to see where you lived. You're so involved with my family, it seemed only fair that I met yours." He stopped next to the back door. "Hey, you've got a cat," he said, fumbling with the rusty lock.

"He's not allowed in," said Aimee, as Oscar took advantage of this unexpected turn of events and shot between them.

"Well, that doesn't seem fair."

"He has health issues. He's outside till they're sorted."

"Banished," Cameron said sadly. "Poor cat. I like cats. Well, I hope you don't banish me." He put his arm back around Aimee. "Whoa, tense. You need to relax, Mrs. Verratti. If you don't mind me saying so, you seem very highly strung."

THE INVESTIGATION REPORT was surprisingly readable. Lou made herself comfortable on two thousand dollars' worth of unpaid-for sofa and continued flipping. She'd expected it to be impenetrable, technical. Pages of analysis of wing flaps, and whatever else kept planes up in the air. But it read like a good mystery. If the executive summary had been the description of a new movie, Lou would have gone to see it.

> On December 31, at approximately 9:30 P.M. Australian East-
> ern Daylight Time (AEDT), the pilot of a Cessna 182 aircraft,
> registered VH-QDK, taxied for departure from runway two at
> Meadowcroft Airport.

It was amazing how hindsight made everything sound more meaningful. Like reading a good book where you know something awful is going to happen, and every line could be a clue. The description of Pete's movements before the flight, of Lincoln's fascination with the airfield, the reference to "witnesses" when really they meant normal Hensley people who'd let their kids stay up to see the fireworks and had accidentally found themselves with ringside seats to a tragedy.

Several witnesses reported seeing the aircraft undertake a right turn toward the ranges.

There were no witness reports of any smoke emanating from the aircraft, nor of unusual engine noise as heard from the ground.

A video shot on a mobile phone (iPhone 6s) shows the aircraft flying apparently unhindered above the firework display in an east-north-easterly direction.

That was interesting. Lou didn't know there'd been a video. Although it made total sense; Tansy and her mates filmed everything. There were probably dozens of videos of the fireworks online. Lou hoped Aimee didn't realize that; she'd never sleep again.

Lou kept reading. An exhaustive—and slightly dull—analysis of the plane's single-operator control system gave way to "Section 1.24: Medical and Pathological Information." She sat up straighter, turned on her new floor lamp.

The pilot's medical records showed no evidence of any preexisting disease or condition that may have impaired his performance. However, the pilot had been treated three years previously for depression and prescribed the selective serotonin reuptake inhibitor Lexapro (escitalopram) at a daily dose of 10 mg. Toxicological analysis of the pilot's blood did not show any presence of Lexapro (escitalopram).

Julia had died almost five years ago. Lou had gone to the funeral, sat quietly at the back. Pete, Lincoln, and Cameron had walked behind the coffin, reminding her of the princes at Diana's funeral. Lincoln, the little one, confused and hurt like young Harry. Cameron, sullen, staring at the ground, an angry William. And Pete—Pete had cried in a way Lou had never seen a man cry before. As though he would never recover. Lou had felt embarrassed witnessing his grief.

> Toxicological testing indicated the presence of alcohol in the pilot's blood.

Well. Lou was so surprised she put the report down in her lap. Pete, flying drunk? He was the straightest man she'd ever met. That had to be a mistake. Lou read the paragraph again, the careful accounting of how much Pete had likely drunk and when. They couldn't be sure about amounts and times, but it was clear—Pete had not been completely sober when he'd hopped in that plane.

Lou got up and switched on all the lights. Why did she want Pete to be innocent? Not because they had history, surely? They hadn't even had a relationship, just been two people who got on well and needed a bit of affection. Really, she should be rooting for Pete to have made some terrible but undeniable mistake so that Aimee would calm down and life could go back to normal. Lou read on, hoping for a freak wind, a broken altimeter that would absolve them all.

"Mum, I'm going to go to bed now."

Tansy emerged from the bathroom in Lou's fluffy new robe. Wet hair and big eyes. There'd been tears earlier, when Lou had to tell her she'd been let go. "Made redundant" was the term she'd used. Cost cutting. "What are we going to do?" Tansy had whispered. Lou had tried to reassure her—"It's only a job, Tans, there are plenty more out there"—but Tansy hadn't been convinced. Lou had run her a bubble bath and left her to calm down in their cracked narrow tub.

Tansy came and sat at Lou's feet, dripping water on their new (two-hundred-and-fifty-dollar) ottoman. Lou quickly turned the report over; no need to upset her further.

"I've been thinking," said Tansy, so quiet Lou had to bend down.

"What's that, love?"

"I won't have the baby if we can't afford it."

"Oh, Tans," said Lou. "No. You don't need to worry about that."

"But I do." Tansy looked up at her mother, eyes shining. "I read the brochures about all the stuff the baby will need. And we don't have any of it."

"I'm not even having this conversation with you."

"But we don't have enough money anyway. I'm just making things harder for us."

"Tansy, no one should have to decide whether or not to have a child because of money. If they did, the population would die out."

Tansy didn't laugh. "But you said you'd rather die than go back on benefits. And if we—"

"We're not talking about it." Lou rubbed at her neck, which was starting to itch. Stress. "Not. Talking. About. It. You're having this baby, and we're getting the results back next week, and it's all going to be fine, no matter what." She kissed Tansy's slippery head. "Go to bed. Stop worrying."

And amazingly—it still felt amazing, every time—Tansy obeyed.

Lou turned back to her report. Section 1.27: Damage to Aircraft.

> *The condition of the engine could not be established due to the substantial damage suffered by the aircraft's components as a result of impact forces and postimpact fire.*

Hmmm. That was interesting.

"I just want you to know that I realize how much having a baby costs. And that I don't expect—"

"Bed, Tansy." Lou didn't even look up.

"HEY, DO YOU want to meet me? I've got something you might want to see."

It was Damien. "Now?" Aimee glanced at her children. They were lying on the floor in the den, Cameron between them, half watching *The X-Factor*. Byron and Cameron were playing some complicated game that involved throwing popcorn into the plants and punching each other when they lost, and Shelley was gazing at them adoringly.

"I can't now," she said quietly. "It's not a good time."

"Ah, sorry. Nick there?"

Actually, that was a good point. Where was Nick? Aimee checked her watch.

"No worries. I just got hold of the accident report, is all. Thought you might want to take a look."

Her husband would be round at one of his mates', or at the pub, poring over the plans for his precious cellar door. Figuring out how many hours they'd have to keep it open to make it profitable. How many thousands of tourists they'd have to entertain, each one giving Aimee a mini nervous breakdown.

"It's not a big deal. It can wait."

Why should Aimee have to stay in just because Nick couldn't be bothered to come home for dinner?

"Give me a bell when you're free, yeah?"

And it wasn't as though the children were *children*.

"Maybe lunch later in the week? I'll try to keep hold of it as long as I can."

Plus she had a built-in babysitter. Aimee took another look at the cozy scene in the living room and swallowed her misgivings. She didn't have any actual *reason* to mistrust Cameron. And he was certainly good with them. "Where are you?" she asked.

"At my hotel."

What was the worst that could happen? "Give me half an hour, and I'll be with you."

"Great. I'm room 203, on the second floor."

"Can I come round?"

Melinda looked down at herself. Boxer shorts, stretched-out vest top, no bra. No need. Filthy hair pinned on top of her head. She looked a mess, but it was probably safer that way. "Sure," she said, reaching for her cardigan. "Let yourself up."

She hadn't even put on deodorant before she heard the key in the lock.

"How——"

"I was downstairs." Nick held out a bottle. "I brought wine."

"The pinot," said Melinda, but she didn't move to take it. "My favorite." As though he was wooing her. As though they were going on a date.

"I'm sorry," he said. "Showing up like this. It's just been an intense couple of days, you know?" He wandered into her kitchen. "And I was in town, so——" Nick busied himself uncorking the wine, pouring a generous slosh into two glasses. He carried them into her living room, placed them next to each other on the coffee table. "God," he said. "I don't even know where to start." He drained half his glass, not even bothering to appreciate his own wine. "Tell you what, I needed that."

Melinda watched him from the far side of the room. "Nick," she said, "why are you here?"

"I decided to take the plunge with the cellar door," he continued, as though she hadn't spoken. "Partly because of you. Mainly because of you. I thought, bugger it, I've wanted this for so long, I'm not going to put it off any longer. Aimee's just going to have to become comfortable with it."

Melinda shut her eyes.

"Because life needs to continue, you know? I don't mean to sound insensitive, but I can't put everything on hold each time she has a bad spell. Or in case she might have a bad spell. I'd never do anything."

"Can we not talk about Aimee?"

"Shit, sorry," said Nick. "Like you're not up to your neck in plans of your own." He patted the sofa. "Come here, tell me what's happening with LoveLocked."

Melinda let herself sink into the cushions beside him. The couch seemed more comfortable, more balanced somehow, with the extra weight. "Why are you here?" she said again.

Nick looked sheepish as he ran one hand through what was left of his hair. "Because it was so good to talk to you again," he said finally. "I didn't realize how much I'd missed it. Being able to say what I was thinking without having to worry about upsetting someone. Without having to censor myself, you know?"

She did know. Melinda had no shortage of people to talk to, as long as she didn't call them during bath time, or school pickup, or at weekends. She censored herself too, tried not to sound needy or lonely. Upbeat, always. Like she wasn't sitting at home with Netflix and a miniature bottle of prosecco, waiting for the workweek to start.

"I'm scared, Mel. I'm scared she's going to disappear down the same black hole as last time, and we'll have to tiptoe around worrying about what might accidentally set her off. And the kids are older now, so they'll realize what's going on, and fuck, Mel, I'm not sure I've got the energy to carry us all through it again." Nick banged his head lightly with the heels of his hands. "I know I shouldn't say it, but it's really shit to live with, you know? I mean, it's horrible for her, but it's bloody awful for us too."

Melinda sighed. "Let me get the rest of the wine."

And just like that, they were back in their old routine. Feet up on the coffee table, heads tipped back against the edge of the couch. Confiding, understanding, talking in low voices even though there was no one else in the room. Their Aimee-is-in-the-hospital routine. Their only-stopping-by-for-one routine. Their Claire-has-the-kids-and-I-needed-to-get-out routine.

"It's heartbreaking to watch, you know? But it's not just about Aimee this time. I can see Shelley developing similar habits." Nick reached for his glass. "I don't want her growing up thinking the whole world's an accident waiting to happen. I found her surfing a load of medical websites the other night, and I thought, shit, here we go."

Nothing was happening, Melinda told herself. They'd never crossed that line. All those evenings spent at hers, while Aimee lay in her narrow hospital bed. They'd cried and ranted together, freaked out about what it all meant. Aimee was her cousin; Melinda had been truly petrified for her. Was worried she'd never get better. Melinda and Nick had been blown back together, like small ships in a rocky bay. But they'd never let things get out of hand.

"I feel like a real jerk, Mel. Selfish. Because I should be there for her, one hundred percent. And, I'm like, sixty-five percent. Seventy. While the rest of me is thinking, do we really have to do this again? Can you not just read a self-help book or go see someone and get over it already?"

"You're not selfish," murmured Melinda. And neither was she. At least, that's what she'd told herself, every time he'd turned up after visiting hours. Because Nick had been hers originally, and yes, she'd let him go, but she also hadn't made any kind of fuss when Aimee scooped him up. Melinda had only been gone a month. But she could tell how bad Aimee felt, even from the other side of the world; she hadn't wanted to send her already fragile cousin over the edge with guilt. So Melinda had smiled and told everyone how fine she was with it all. Through the wedding, the pregnancies, christenings, birthdays, every celebration of Aimee's perfect family life. Absolutely fine.

"I think the fireworks were the trigger. Because she helped organize them, you know?" Nick eased his shoes off. "The responsibility thing again. And now there are no matches or candles anywhere in the house. She's even gotten rid of the gas from the barbecue."

She was only listening, Melinda told herself. Just providing a safe, neutral sounding board. Nothing wrong with that.

"So what do you reckon? Should I call the old guy she saw last time? Make an appointment and have a quiet word?"

Melinda shrugged.

"Come on, I need to know what you think."

"I can't," she said. "It's not fair." Because she was never completely neutral, was she. Melinda had enjoyed Nick's company just a little too much during those hospital months. Having someone to sit up talking with, to veg out next to on the sofa watching crappy television. She could reach out her hand, only a few inches, and they'd be touching.

Nick rolled toward her. "Shall I open another one?"

Melinda nodded, despite herself. She watched his tall, slightly awkward body move around her kitchen. He looked good in there. Like he belonged. Melinda bit down hard on her lip to bring herself back to her senses.

They might not have crossed the line, but they'd pressed right up against it. Long hugs hello, longer hugs good-bye. Nights they'd accidentally fallen asleep on the sofa, the floor. That one night she'd been crying over some bloke she didn't even remember, and Nick had pulled her head into his lap, stroked her hair until she was quiet. That night he'd been too drunk to drive and she'd let him stay over and they'd woken up in her bed. Clothed, him on top of the duvet, her under it. But still.

He was rummaging through her cupboards. "Where do you keep the decent stuff these days?"

Intimacy didn't have to be physical. Melinda and Nick had been in love once. And even though they weren't anymore, it gave a charge to their conversations she didn't feel with anyone else. With Nick, there was always what they were talking about, and what they weren't talking about.

He reappeared carrying something Argentinian she'd bought in duty free. "Hey, this looks bloody good."

And what they were talking about wasn't fair. Because it was Aimee. In words and tones they wouldn't use if she was in the room.

You didn't have to take your clothes off to cross the line.

Melinda stood up and gently took the bottle from Nick. "We're not drinking this."

"But I've already opened it."

"We shouldn't have." She set the bottle carefully down on the floor and handed him his shoes. "You need to go home."

He looked down at his Adidas, and then up at her. "We didn't . . . we're not—"

"Yeah, we kind of are." She walked him, regretfully, to the door.

"I didn't mean—"

"I know." Melinda held out her hand. "But I think you'd better give me back my key."

It felt as though she was losing something as she closed her hand around the key ring. There'd be no more Nick letting himself in to take a look at the pipe under her sink, no more coming home to find the guttering had magically been cleaned out. She was giving all that away. No, Melinda reminded herself. Giving it back. She held him close, one last, long hug.

"Go home to your family," she said into his hair.

THE KIDS WEREN'T bothered in the slightest. Didn't even look up. "I'm heading out for a bit," Aimee had said, poking her head into the den. "Fund-raising drama at the nursing home. I'll be back in a couple of hours."

The only person who twisted around to say good-bye was Cameron. "Don't worry, Mrs. Verratti," he'd said with a wide smile. "I'll take good care of them. Least I can do, given how well you've been looking after my stepdad."

That smile was bothering her now, as she drove toward Hensley's main street. First thing tomorrow, she'd tell the kids not to have anything more to do with him. She didn't have to give them a reason. She was their *mother*.

Aimee turned at the pharmacy, headed onto the main drag. The streetlights were haloing in her dirty windshield; she turned the wipers on, gave it a quick wash. And was left with crystal-clear glass, just in time to get a nice, good look at her husband, letting himself out of Melinda's building.

MELINDA SAT ON the edge of her bathtub and howled.

She'd never really cried over Nick. She'd been so busy pretending not to mind, then so genuinely busy with the business that she'd never stopped to grieve. Just moved on to the next thing. The next goal, the next house renovation, the next go-nowhere relationship. *You're so resilient, Melinda. Nothing ever bothers you.* But she'd been carrying a torch, just a small one, her own little shining lantern, all these years. And now it was time for a private letting-go ceremony.

Melinda let herself cry, the sort of embarrassing wailing she hadn't done since she was a child. Mouth-gaping, nose-running, chest-heaving cries. Thank God her tenants had all gone home for the day; it meant she could mourn in peace. She turned the taps off and tipped a jar of expensive oil into the hot water. Melinda had never been a bath type of person; she'd installed the claw-footed tub simply because it looked good. Five-minute showers with the news turned up loud, that was more her style. But tonight she was going to have one of those long pampering baths that women's magazines always banged on about. Not that Melinda read women's magazines, unless she was in them. But she occasionally flicked through one on a plane. Melinda grabbed her copy of *The Economist*, and the good Argentinian wine, and a block of Swiss dark, salted caramel. She was going to have a proper, old-fashioned wallow, just a couple of decades too late.

God, that was good. *Necessary.* Melinda sank lower, let the hot water soothe her. Because it wasn't just Nick she was mourning, she realized as she flicked through an article about the ageing population in Europe—it was all her younger expectations about how her life was going to turn out. Yes, she was successful, and well-off, even semifamous, in certain circles. And that was all only set to increase. But the whole idea of a husband, two kids, and a dog? Melinda needed to put it to bed.

It will probably never happen, she told herself, as she ducked her head under the water. She might manage to adopt, but if she did, motherhood was more than likely going to be a solo endeavor. Life was not a movie; the perfect bloke was unlikely to pitch up while she was effortlessly raising an adorable small child. And she had to be okay with that. Just like she had to be okay with the fact that, yes, she might still meet Mr. Right, but she also might not. She might be single for the rest of her life, and she had to accept that, and be grateful for what she had. Because she could feel herself getting bitter, and God knows, that never suited anyone.

And acceptance was not the same as giving in, Melinda reminded herself, as she came spluttering to the surface to the sound of her mobile phone. It wasn't giving up. She'd keep waxing, keep plucking, keep going to business conferences with favorable male-to-female ratios. Melinda padded naked and dripping to the phone. But she would also do her best to enjoy her life *right now*, and not keep thinking how much better it would be if only there was someone else in it.

"Hey, Clint." Melinda tucked the phone against one damp shoulder as she searched the kitchen for more treats. "Yeah, all good. Just in the bath."

She hadn't meant it as a come-on, but he took it as one. He was on the highway, only ten minutes from her turnoff. Did she want company? There was an unattractive leer in his voice. He could stay the night, head back down to Melbourne in the morning. It'd be no problem.

You wait hours for a bus, and then two turn up at once.

"I don't think so," she said, grabbing another bar of chocolate from her secret stash. She took a deep breath. "In fact, I don't think this is a great idea, period. You and me." Now that she'd remembered what it felt like to really be into someone, there seemed little point wasting time with someone she could barely stand to have a conversation with. "Nothing personal," she added. How many times had she heard that? "I think we're probably better just as colleagues."

Clint expressed surprise and regret while Melinda tore the wrapper off. Yes, she agreed, the sex had been fun. No, she didn't want to talk through it. There was nothing to talk about. Melinda would rather have no man than the wrong man. She took a large bite of chocolate in celebration of something that everyone else had probably figured out in their twenties.

"Well," Clint said, slightly huffily. "If you don't want to talk to me, you need to speak to Stacey Manning at least. The journalist. She keeps calling."

Melinda pictured Aimee in the video again: Stacey's video. The best way to shut down a story was to not fuel it. "You talk to her," she said. "There's nothing I need to comment on." And she switched her phone off.

She'd just topped up the water, was settling into a fascinating article on the future of North Korea, when the doorbell rang. "I told you both to go home!" Melinda yelled, and ducked her head under the water.

The bell was still ringing when she came up for air. "For fuck's sake," she muttered, pulling a pair of jeans up her damp thighs. When she actually wanted a night alone . . .

Melinda made little puddles across the hallway as she padded to the door. Puddles she'd have to be careful to clean up later; her floorboards didn't like water.

"I told you it wasn't happening," she said, but kindly, as she opened up the door. No need to hurt anyone's feelings. But it wasn't Nick or Clint. It was Lou.

DAMIEN OPENED THE door in his undershirt. "Hey," he said, slightly flustered. "I wasn't expecting you so quickly."

"I drove fast," said Aimee, still feeling as though she'd been hit by something heavy across the back of her head. Eighty miles an hour, all the way to Meadowcroft. She hadn't even realized until the speed camera caught her coming into town.

"Nice place," she said, wandering around as Damien pulled on a shirt. The hotel room was dark and depressing, the kind of place you'd choose to top yourself in. Cheap laminate furniture. Heavy curtains. There wasn't even a view. There was a miniature fridge though, under a foggy mirror. Aimee knelt down and started going through it.

"We can go down to the bar, if you want a drink," said Damien.

Aimee pulled out a miniature bottle of chardonnay from a rival vineyard. "Do you mind if I open this?"

"Is that what you want?"

She didn't really, but she also didn't want to feel anything, and she could hardly down a couple of miniature vodkas in front of the man. "Please," she said.

Damien seemed uncertain as he took the bottle from her, but he screwed the cap off anyway. "I don't think there are any wineglasses," he said, fumbling around in the wardrobe. He emerged with a single coffee cup and a drinking glass. "These'll have to do, I'm afraid." He handed her the larger measure. "Cheers."

Aimee sat on the sloping edge of the hotel bed and tried not to gulp.

"Don't you want to take a look?" he asked.

She stared at him blankly. "What?"

"At the report." He held out a thin ring-bound document.

"Right." Aimee wasn't sure she even cared anymore. She tried to remember why it had felt so vital to know what was happening, to stay on top of everything. What a joke. Aimee didn't even know what was happening in her own home. She tipped the rest of the wine down her throat. Everything had exploded, not just the plane.

"It's just the preliminary findings," said Damien, flicking through the document. "But if it makes you feel better to have a quick read, go for it. Although you can't take it with you, obviously. And for God's sake, don't tell anyone I showed you. They'd have my head."

He held the report out again, but Aimee didn't move. Just stared glassily at this kind man who was risking his job for her. Who'd made her feel attractive and interesting, for the first time in years. He was going through a separation, he'd told her over one of their lunches. Chasing accidents around the country didn't really help a marriage. Two kids, grown up now. He wasn't that bothered about being single. Meant he got to have lunch with a beautiful lady like Aimee, without any guilt.

She waved her empty glass at him. "Can we open up another one of those?"

"Are you sure you don't want to go downstairs?" he asked. But he pulled out another little bottle. "Not bad this, I have to say."

The wine was terrible, but Aimee didn't care. Finally. She who cared too much, who never did anything without worrying about the potential impact on her husband and her children and her bloody community, no longer gave a damn. She stood up and clinked her glass against his coffee cup. They made a hollow clunk, like something broken.

"What are we drinking to?" he asked, watching her face closely.

"Whatever you want," she said. "Whatever the fuck you want." And for the first time in sixteen years, Aimee Verratti leaned forward and kissed a man who was not her husband.

Chapter 32

The absolute bugger about being blind was that he couldn't read the labels. He could find the bottles easily enough. Vodka and gin beside the root vegetables on the pantry floor. Aspirin in the junk drawer with the spare keys and batteries, as it always was. But the mother lode, Julia's pain medication, was mixed up among every other pill and gargle and elixir they'd bought or been prescribed since Lincoln was born.

Pete leaned against the bathroom wall, getting his breath back as he felt the shapes of bottles and rattled containers. Cameron was out, had disappeared with the car earlier in the evening. Pete needed to get this done and dusted before he returned. Not because he thought Cameron would stop him; he probably wouldn't even bother to call an ambulance. But Pete didn't want to spend his last moments at the mercy of his angry son, Cameron whispering poison in his ear.

His son. Pete still thought of Cameron as his own, even if Cam didn't. He'd raised him since the age of three; the loser Julia had been married to before could barely remember Christmas. Pete shuffled through the medication, moving as quickly as he could. He'd truly thought Cameron would straighten out. That he'd find himself in Sydney, or wherever he ended up. But he was still the same angry young man, inflicting pain on others so he didn't have to feel his own.

Well, Pete didn't fancy feeling pain anymore either. The public inquiry had been set for the beginning of next week—three days away. "Let's see if we can help you and your family find some closure," the bloke from the ATSB had said. Closure. Exactly.

Pete decided to take all the heavy glass bottles and the small pharmacy-issue plastic vials. They seemed likely to do the most damage. If he ended up swallowing a few dozen vitamin E along the way, then he'd just be a well-preserved corpse. Pete piled the bottles in the bottom of his polo shirt and carted them over to the bed.

How he actually wanted to spend his last moments was with his wife, clutching one of Julia's scarves, breathing in what he could imagine was left of her scent as he drifted out of his body and toward wherever she was. Religion had always been more her thing than his, but for the first time Pete hoped that she was right, that there was something out there after death. And also that she was wrong—that they let you in regardless of whatever you'd done on earth.

Chapter 33

"You look like shit," Lou said, staring.

"You don't look so hot yourself," said Melinda, and it was true. Lou's nose and chin were red, as though she'd been rubbing at them, and her eyes were tired. She was still wearing her work clothes, even though it had to be nearly eleven. "Bit late for you to be out, isn't it? You've got to be up at six."

"No, I don't," said Lou, as she walked straight past Melinda and into her apartment. "I don't have a job."

"You're kidding." Although truthfully, Melinda had been waiting for this day for years. Both she and Aimee agreed it was only a matter of time. Lou had the worst work ethic in Hensley; she did the crossword in council meetings instead of taking minutes. But even so.

Melinda pushed the door shut and gave her a big, wet hug. "Oh, Lou, I'm sorry."

Lou stood stiff in her arms. It was the first time Melinda had seen her since their fight in the town hall. Their big argument, the most serious the three of them had ever had. But she must be over it if she'd come here for sympathy. Melinda rocked her from side to side; it was like rocking a plank of wood. "I'm so sorry," she said again.

"Yeah, so am I," said Lou. There was no emotion in her voice; she must be in shock.

Cold bathwater dripped down the back of Melinda's T-shirt. "Give me two minutes," she said. "I'll just sort myself out. Stick the kettle on or something, whatever you want." She nearly slipped on the damp wood as she ducked into the bathroom. "There's chocolate in the freezer!"

Melinda felt almost jolly as she pulled her wet hair up on top of her head, not even taking the time to apply hair oil. *The sacrifices I make,* she thought, but cheerfully. She'd missed the others. Melinda knew her life was empty, that she was all work and no play, but she'd not realized she didn't have any other female friends in Hensley until this week, not a single person she could call and say, "Let's go for a drink." Which was entirely her own fault. Melinda had never bothered to make any other friends because Aimee and Lou had always been there. There was no need for anyone else.

But now drama was bringing them back together, as always. Melinda smiled to herself as she quickly rubbed in moisturizer. How many times had they sat up late at night, listening to Lou's outrage, Aimee's worry, Melinda's big plans? When Aimee's parents got divorced Melinda and Lou had all but moved in, sleeping on the floor of her pink-and-white bedroom, wearing each other's uniforms to school. When

Aimee's mother died twenty years later, they'd done the same thing again, only with proper bedding. They were the kind of friends who rose to the occasion, Melinda thought, as she went humming into the kitchen. Who were able to put the nonsense behind them when it mattered. She shoved a couple of slices of nice thick wholemeal into the toaster. Tomatoes on toast and a cup of tea—Lou's favorite comfort food.

"So what happened?" she called. "Don't tell me you lost your temper and walked out."

Lou was wandering around the dining table, flicking through papers. Melinda set the plate down. "Sit," she said. "Tell me all about it. Did you finally tell Rex to shove his Post-its up his arse?"

"I didn't, no," said Lou, not touching the toast. "He fired me."

"Never!" Melinda made a shocked face, wishing Aimee was there to hear this. She'd call her now, get her to come over, but Aimee liked an early night. And Aimee was properly angry with her, unlike Lou. Lou was too busy being angry at the world to hold an individual grudge for long. "How come?"

"My attitude, apparently," said Lou.

"Well, that doesn't make any sense at all," said Melinda. "He's put up with your attitude for years. It's not like he didn't know you had one." She tore a piece of toast in half. "Was there something specific?"

"Nope. I think I just upset the wrong person."

"Oh, you can totally sue for wrongful dismissal then," said Melinda, munching toast. "Use the company lawyer if you want. Or Dad would give you a hand, I'm sure. He's known Rex for years. Want me to ask him?"

Lou gave a small snort. "No thanks."

Something was wrong here; Lou wasn't ranting and raving, threatening to burn the council building to the ground. She wasn't even blaming anyone, which was totally unlike Lou. She sat fingering a little button on her blouse, staring at Melinda's chandelier as though making her mind up about what to do next. *Shock*, Melinda thought again, as she finished off the toast. But Lou could easily get another job. She wasn't stupid, she was just a bit lazy. The fact she'd stayed in that silly office role for so long was testament to that. Lou complained about her lack of qualifications and options, but the only thing she really lacked was ambition. *Look at Richard Branson!* Melinda always told her. *He's dyslexic! Steve Jobs was a dropout, and so was the Facebook guy!* Getting fired could be a gift, if Lou looked at it the right way.

"So let's talk about what you're going to do next," said Melinda, sucking crumbs off her fingers. "I'd say come and work for LoveLocked, but I don't want you to take the easy option. This could be a real chance to grow, Lou. Do something different, make some real money."

"I didn't actually come here for advice," said Lou.

"But this could be the start of something big," said Melinda. "Your next chapter! I'm so excited!"

"I came to show you this." Lou pulled a crumpled bunch of papers out of her handbag.

AVIATION SAFETY INVESTIGATION REPORT, the mangled top sheet read. Her hands shook slightly as she handed them over.

"Bloody hell," said Melinda. "Where did you get this?" She flicked through the pages, ominous phrases jumping out at her. *Warning systems. Stall speed. Emergency checklist. Impact fire.*

"Doesn't matter," said Lou. "The bit you'll be interested in is on page twelve. Halfway down."

It was only a short paragraph, but Melinda read it three times.

"Pretty definitive proof, don't you think?" said Lou. "That we were involved?"

No wonder she looked shell-shocked. Melinda read the paragraph a fourth time, walking around her living room. "Only if you were us," she said finally. "This wouldn't mean anything to anyone who wasn't with us that night."

"True. The only people that would mean anything to are you, me, and Aimee."

Aimee. Melinda could only imagine the panic attack if Aimee were to find out about this. There weren't enough sedatives in the world. "Please tell me she hasn't seen it."

"Nope, just us."

"Thank God for that." Melinda let out a slightly shaky breath. "Fuck. Well, if we're the only two who know about it, or at least what it means, then we're safe, I guess."

Lou stared at her, looking uncharacteristically nervous.

"What?" said Melinda. *Don't freak out on me now, Lou, that's not going to help anyone.* "Do you expect me to do something? I think the best thing here is that we do absolutely nothing. Say nothing. I've thrown everything out, anyway." God, this was the kind of conversation you had when you'd actually committed a *crime.* "Don't worry. There's no way they'll associate what they've found with us. Why would they?" Lou still wasn't speaking. "What are you looking at me like that for? What do you want me to do?"

"I want you to pay me," Lou said quietly.

"ARE YOU *BLACKMAILING* me?" Melinda stared at Lou, open-mouthed.

"I guess so," said Lou, hardly believing it herself. She'd come up with so many euphemisms on the short drive over. *I'm asking you to help me. I'd like you consider a kind of permanent loan. I'll sell the report to you.* She'd sat in her car outside Melinda's building, and tried to do the visualization exercises Melinda had been pushing on her for years. Tried to picture a conversation in which she'd hand over the report, and Melinda would say, unprompted, "You know, I'd really rather this didn't get out. Please don't take this the wrong way, but could I maybe give you something, to keep this between ourselves?" And Lou would graciously accept, and they'd both go off to bed, friendship intact.

"But why?" Melinda said, in disbelief. "Why would you do that?"

Lou tried to focus on the sculpture behind Melinda's shoulder, tried to get angry that Melinda was able to buy tasteful modern art while her daughter thought she needed to abort a baby to stop their television from being repossessed.

"You're my *friend*," said Melinda.

Lou had to grip her little pin just to keep her nerve. *You're not my friend,* she told herself. *You're Tansy's aunt. And you write countless checks out to your waster brother and never give a thing to us.* Although that wasn't true, and she knew it. Melinda tried to give them things all the time—hand-me-downs and furniture and fancy toiletries she'd bought extra of "by mistake"—but Lou didn't want to take anyone's charity.

Because blackmail and being paid off were fine, but charity would go against her upstanding moral code.

"Lou." Melinda walked toward her but stopped at the end of the dining table. She grabbed the top of a chair. "Come on. You don't want to do this."

But the brief moment when Lou could have laughed, and said, "Don't be silly, I'm only joking," had passed. *Stay angry,* she reminded herself. *This woman spends more on her gym memberships—plural—than you do on groceries.* Lou took a deep breath, and felt a small spark of rage that she tried to mentally fan. *And don't forget whose family is responsible for the fact you no longer have a job.*

"I want you to pay me," she said again.

"But pay you for what? This is a public document, or will be." Melinda was struggling for composure, Lou could tell. She was putting on her "confidence cloak"—shoulders back, head high. As though she was wearing a garment that made her invincible. It was something Melinda did before meetings;

she'd told Lou all about it. Which meant that Lou could see straight through it, and see that Melinda was completely naked underneath.

"You need to pay me not to tell anyone what that section really means," said Lou. "And not to tell Aimee. Which is the same thing really."

"But we don't even know what would happen. What the consequences for what we did even are."

Lou shrugged. "Does it matter?"

"It'd be the same for you," Melinda tried again. "You let off the lanterns as well. If I'm guilty or liable or whatever, then so are you."

"Except I'm at an interesting stage in life where I have nothing to lose."

Melinda eyeballed her. "You wouldn't say anything. You wouldn't drop yourself in it. You're bluffing."

Lou stared back. This was the second Baker she'd faced down in less than twenty-four hours. "Try me."

Had they ever really been friends? True, proper friends? Melinda was Aimee's cousin, and Aimee had been in the same class as Lou, and their parents used to get on, so they'd all been conveniently thrown together. But would they have chosen each other? There'd always been that age gap, Lou told herself, except that she'd been five steps ahead of her own year group, and Melinda had liked bossing them all around, and none of it mattered once you left school anyway. They didn't have anything in common, she thought, except for the same sense of humor and three decades of shared history. Melinda kept judging her, she tried again, kept trying to fix her, with all her helpful little "suggestions." When there was nothing wrong with Lou or her life. Although if that was true, what was she doing here?

Melinda dropped her gaze first. "How much would you want?" she asked, looking at the table.

"A hundred thousand dollars." Enough that she'd never have to bother any of the Bakers again.

Melinda gave a barking laugh. "That's crazy."

"You've got it." Lou waved her hand at Melinda's designer living room. "Sell a painting or something if you have to."

"This is ridiculous." Melinda shoved the chair she'd been holding toward the table; the sound of banging wood was harsh and loud in her minimalist apartment. "We've been friends for nearly thirty years. You used to sleep in my bed. I helped bury your *parents*. I don't understand why you're doing this."

And Lou couldn't tell her. Because it felt so grubby, the way she'd snuck out of Melinda's room, sleepover after sleepover, into the more exciting bed of her brother. They all used to joke about Matthew—what a total sleaze he was, what a sexist pig. Even as a teenager Melinda had nothing but disdain for her younger brother and the girls who hung around him "like flies." "He's got no respect for any of them," Melinda used to say. "The way he treats them is just gross." They had names for the girls as well, terms Lou was ashamed of using now. Because it was all true: Matthew was a jackass and she'd been one of the idiots who'd fallen for it. Fucked him at the end of the hallway while her friends were asleep two doors down. A boy she'd known since she was eight, had virtually grown up with. "It's all just a bit nasty," Melinda's father had said, and deep down, Lou agreed.

"Just do it, Mel," said Lou. "Just do it, and we can all get on with our lives."

"And how am I supposed to pay you? Assuming I'm going to."

She was going to, Lou could tell. "The inquiry starts next week," she said. "If the money isn't in my bank account by then, I'll stand up and tell everyone exactly why Lincoln was found lying on the charred edge of a bright pink-and-gold notecard." The only word that had been visible on the card was *happy*. Any one of them could have written it.

"You should have left," Melinda said, as Lou headed for the door. "You should have gotten out when Tansy was small. You might have had a life. You might have actually done something with yourself."

"You can talk," said Lou. "You only stay here because you're trying to impress your father. God knows why. You make out like he's this mover and shaker, but he's not. He's just a big fish, in a small, polluted pond. He's not worth it. And neither is your brother."

LOU LET HERSELF out of Melinda's apartment, heart racing, her face on fire. *Bloody hell. That was . . . awful.* She'd expected to feel jubilant, like some kind of warped justice had been served, or even relieved, but instead, she just felt like shit.

Lou forced herself not to run back to the glossy cream

door—three coats on that, they'd spent all weekend painting it—and ring Melinda's bell, claim some kind of temporary insanity. Beg for forgiveness. But it was too late now. All she could do was wait.

Hensley's main street was deserted, not even a loitering teenager getting high in the pub parking lot. Lou hopped in her car and pulled down the rearview mirror. Hopped in her ancient Nissan Bluebird, parked next to Melinda's shiny Range Rover. The comparison made Lou feel slightly less guilty about what she'd just done. Slightly.

What if Melinda didn't pay? What on earth would she do then? But Melinda would pay, Lou knew. Aimee would have gone to pieces, but Melinda could see the bigger picture. No one would invest in a company where the CEO was involved in a child's death. And it would be the end of all those fawning magazine spreads and documentary appearances. Melinda liked being a minor celebrity, no matter what she said. She was very comfortable being a big fish in a small pond as well.

Lou switched the light on in her car and examined her burning skin, the sensitive raw patch under her nose. Eczema. Damn. She'd had it chronically as a child, rarely as an adult, but it came back from time to time when she was particularly wound up or run-down. Lou flipped the mirror back up. Well, it was hardly surprising. They probably had some Sudocrem in the bathroom. Or she might even buy herself a big jar of something nice. Something organic, with goat's milk. Why not?

It was only fair, Lou told herself, as she drove guiltily down the main street. Melinda wouldn't miss the money. She was about to make millions. And Lou was doing this for Tansy. Tansy and the baby. Melinda would do exactly the same, if their roles were reversed.

None of it made her feel any better about herself.

Lou killed the headlights before she turned into her driveway, so they wouldn't shine through Tansy's bedroom window. Crept into the bathroom and pulled out an ancient tub of cream, predictably crusty on top. She examined her nose in the mirror. Definitely eczema. Which meant she'd have it around the sides of her mouth by tomorrow, all flaky and gross. Ah well, it wasn't like she had to go to work and see anyone.

Lou tucked her hands under the covers so she wouldn't scratch in her sleep. Her mum had made her mittens, ultrasoft, out of an old crib sheet, to keep her face safe from her nails when she had an attack. Maybe she should run some up on the machine. But that was ridiculous. She wasn't a child anymore. She should just cut her—

Lou flicked her eyes open and stared at the crack in the ceiling.

She'd been born with eczema. Scales, all over her face and arms. *Like a baby crocodile,* her mother used to say. *I didn't let anyone take any pictures of you for the first month, your face was such a mess.*

There were no newborn photos of Lou. Her first photo had been taken at home, on a sheepskin rug, skin finally calm. Lou scrambled out of bed, tore through the cardboard box of work things she'd left next to the dining table, searching for the green frame. Turned on the light so she could see the picture properly. Although she already knew. The baby in the photo was red and angry, but its skin was shiny smooth. Perfect.

Lou was not the baby in the photo.

Chapter 34

Aimee drove through Meadowcroft, head strangely calm, considering. Not particularly proud of herself, but justified, on so many levels. *Look how far I've come,* she mentally told her old psychologist, the procession of doctors and therapists who'd tried to make her well. *I'm doing things I know are wrong and coping just fine. Where's my excessive sense of responsibility now, eh?*

Although . . . she *was* only a few streets away from Pete's house. Aimee felt a familiar prickle on the back of her neck, heard the car's indicator come on almost by itself. Just a quick check that all was well. She took a left, then a right. It was the friendly thing to do, given she was in the area. In the area, at a quarter to one in the morning. How was she going to explain that? Well, it wasn't like she was going to talk to him. Just drive past, check everything looked okay. Almost like Neighborhood Watch. Aimee had been instrumental in setting up Hensley's "nark patrol," as Lou liked to call it. Looking in on Pete was virtually her duty.

Aimee slowed down as she approached the Kasprowicz

house. There was no car in the driveway. No Cameron. Aimee let out a small sigh of relief. There was something dodgy about that boy. She'd already decided to check on the kids when she got home, something she hadn't done since they were small. Paranoid, but she'd sleep better. There was a light on in Pete's bedroom though. Now that was odd. She parked and trotted down the driveway, the night air alive with cicadas. Pete didn't turn lights on; no need. Aimee climbed the steps to the front door, just to check it was locked. Pete often left it on the latch, for visitors. Aimee worried about unwanted guests taking advantage of a man who couldn't see them coming.

"Pete," she whispered, rapping lightly on the door. Not loud enough to wake him, just loud enough that he might hear if he was up, getting a cup of tea. "Pete, you good?"

There was a crash from the other end of the house.

Aimee rapped harder. "Pete!" She scrabbled around all the usual hiding places for a spare key: beneath flowerpots, under the mat. Nothing. She stepped back into the drive, triggering the security light. There was a cricket ball in the garden she could use to break the window. Drastic, but this was an emergency, a real one. Pete could have fallen, slipped in the shower, been lying injured for hours. The crash could be him trying to get her attention. Aimee was deciding between the ball and a garden rake for breaking and entering when she noticed a lawn chair, pulled up next to the house. And above it, a patch of guttering rubbed free of dirt. She smiled, despite her thumping heart. Her dad had done exactly the same.

The door was sticky; Aimee almost thought she had the

wrong key. She crept into the kitchen holding the rake for self-defense, careful not to make a noise. Although that was pointless; any intruder would know she was there. "Pete?" she called again.

There was another thump, fainter. Aimee ran through the house, dropping the rake. "Pete!" He stood at the end of the hallway, startled, bent over slightly, but 100 percent not lying in a pool of his own blood.

"Oh my God. Pete." Aimee clutched the wall. "I thought something had *happened* to you." And so she'd let herself into someone else's house, in the middle of the night. Aimee flushed; this was exactly the sort of behavior that had gotten her into trouble in the past. That made people think she was crazy. And she wasn't, she bloody wasn't, but she also wasn't entirely sure how she was going to survive the soap opera that was her life now. Every day seemed to bring a new disaster. She'd lain next to Damien in that lumpy hotel bed having flashbacks of her room in the clinic. Not scary *One Flew Over the Cuckoo's Nest*—type flashbacks, but loving memories. Aimee could think of nothing nicer than sinking into a cool hospital bed, sequestered from the world and all her mistakes, and pulling the sheets over her head for at least a month.

"It's Aimee," she said, in case he was confused. "I know it's late but I was driving past, and thought I'd check on you. And then I heard a crash—"

"I kicked over a stool," he said.

Aimee looked over his shoulder. And yes, there was the

stool, lying on its side, on the bedroom floor. And behind it, a bed covered in alcohol and pills.

"Oh my God," said Aimee. "Pete, what have you done?"

"I HAVEN'T TAKEN anything," Pete promised. He could feel the panic radiating off her, hear her fumbling with something— her phone? "Honest, Aimee, you don't need to call anyone. I swear, I've had a drink, that's all. No pills." He patted his hand around in the air until he found hers, which yes, was clutching the cold edges of a mobile. "Don't. Please. There's no need."

"I interrupted you," she said, sounding dazed.

"Actually, I couldn't get the safety tops off any of the containers." He tried to laugh, but it came out a bit more like crying. "Oh shit."

She walked him over to the side of the bed and held him as he sobbed. She was crying too, quietly. He could feel her chest quaking, the dampness of her face on top of his head.

"I'm sorry," she kept saying. "I'm so sorry."

"Don't be sorry," said Pete, trying to pat her back and getting an elbow. "You don't have anything to be sorry for. I'm sorry you had to find me like this." He'd assumed Cameron would discover him in the morning, but it could have been Aimee, popping in to check on him with a batch of muffins. Or the district nurse. Or any of the neighbors, or even the neighbors' children. Unforgivable, how much pain he kept causing.

"But why?" Aimee whispered. She was propped up against

the headboard; it knocked the wall gently. A sound he hadn't heard in years, no matter what Cameron thought.

Pete shuffled backward so he was sitting beside her. She reached over and took his hand. "Because I'm a coward," he admitted.

"You're not a coward. God, the opposite. Look how well you're—"

"I am," he said. "A total coward. You want to know why I was doing this? Because I don't want to stand up there in front of everyone and admit I let my boy down." Even though they knew. "I don't want everyone to judge me." He was squeezing her hand; he let it go. "Better I judge myself. Save everyone the hassle." But he couldn't find any of Julia's scarves, even though there'd been dozens of them. Cameron must have taken them, like the photo. Stolen them. Pete had kicked the stool over when he'd realized.

Aimee was taking deep breaths, the air whistling in and out. Pete tried to picture her face. When was the last time they'd sat on a committee together? Years ago. And yet she'd been his most constant visitor.

"I'm sorry I scared you," he said. "You don't deserve any of this. You've been a really good friend."

"I really haven't."

"No, you have. You kept showing up, when the others were avoiding me. You're a good person, Aimee Verratti." Pete shifted so he wasn't sitting on a bottle of who-knows-what. "Can I ask you to do one more thing for me? I know I don't have the right, but . . . could you help me clean this up? I don't want anyone else to find it."

She didn't move.

"Don't worry," he said. "I'm not going to do anything. It was stupid. *Selfish*." Just leaving his mess for someone else to deal with. "You can take it all with you, if you want." He swung his legs over the side of the bed and knocked a bottle of spirits to the floor. It made a dull but intact-sounding thud. "It's just, I'd have no idea if I missed anything. And I don't want Cameron to know."

Aimee stayed on the far side of the bed. "What are you going to say at the inquiry?" she asked. "What are you going to tell them?"

Pete clenched a box of aspirin. "I'm going to tell them the truth. That I'm responsible for the crash."

"But how?" Her voice was unnaturally loud in his closed-up bedroom. He didn't even bother to open the windows anymore. "How are you responsible?"

"I made a mistake," Pete said, exactly as he'd told Arthur. Same as he'd tell the rest of Hensley. At least he wouldn't be able to see the disapproval on their faces, a small mercy. "I saw this bright light and I thought it was a star. Thought it meant we were higher up than we were. I misjudged. And I pulled us down. Right into the hill." He gripped the painkillers in his fist. "I know what you're supposed to do when you fly at night, I know all the rules and regulations, how to use my instruments. And I didn't follow them.

"And then," he said, "I tried to blame one of my mates. Which is unforgivable. So actually, all of this—" He made a sweeping movement across the bed, heard another bottle roll off and across the floor. "This is a complete fucking cop-out. I'm *glad* you turned up. I deserve to stand there and be held accountable."

Aimee stayed silent. Disgusted as well. Fair enough. Pete did his best to scoop the containers of pills into a clinking, rattling heap.

"Can you help me?" he asked again. Begged, almost. "I don't want my son to know about this. He's . . . a bit messed up. Angry. At me, mainly."

"You're not responsible for the accident," said Aimee.

"Oh I am," said Pete. "There were only two people in that aircraft, and one of them was supposed to know what he was doing. Make the right call."

It was a way of atoning, for everything. Aimee crawled across the bed and grabbed Pete by the shoulder. "Did you hear me?" she said. "You're not responsible. You didn't cause the accident. I did."

She felt no fear as she spoke. None of the usual prickly skin or adrenaline surge. Just the certainty, deep in her gut, that this was the right thing to do. This must be how normal people felt, when they talked about having the courage of their convictions. But it was obvious. This poor man was not only facing the rest of his life without his son, and probably his sight, but also with the misguided belief that he'd killed his child. Aimee could live with a lot of secrets, more than most people realized. She would probably never tell Nick about her night with Damien. She'd never confessed to him that neither of her pregnancies was an accident, and had no intention of doing so. She'd never told Melinda that she suspected Tansy was actually her niece, even though Lou had never said a word. She didn't have to. You only had to look at the girl's face—she was the spitting image of Melinda's mum.

Actually, she might tell Melinda. Wipe some of that smugness off her face.

But she had to tell Pete that this wasn't his fault. Anything else was unforgivable. "I caused the accident," she said again. "I let off a couple of sky lanterns, to celebrate the new year, and one of them caught fire, not far from where you crashed."

I, not we. Because no matter what the others thought, she wasn't going to drag them all down. They were her lanterns, and this was her choice, to speak up. The others could do what they wanted; this was Aimee keeping herself sane.

It helped that she no longer gave a damn what her husband thought.

"It exploded," she said. "I wanted to call emergency but there were already sirens. So I thought someone else had. But that bright light you saw, that confused you? That's what it was. My lantern."

"You don't know that. It could have been anything. A stray firework. Your lanterns weren't the only distraction in the sky."

"But I do know," said Aimee. "I have proof." She reached

across the floor to where she'd dropped her handbag and pulled out the stolen page. "Listen to this."

Finally, she was doing something right. As Damien had sat up in bed and read the report to her, so Aimee read it to Pete. He lay back against his pillows, hands folded on his chest like the corpse he'd nearly become. Aimee's voice wobbled as she got to the incriminating paragraph, but she kept going.

"So you see," she said at the end, "there's not really any doubt."

"But what does it mean for you? What are the consequences?" He still sounded stunned.

"I don't know," said Aimee. The internet had been disappointingly silent, creating an unfortunate space in her head for a million worst-case scenarios. "But it doesn't matter. The point is, I caused your accident. And I'm going to stand up at that inquiry and say so. No—" She pushed Pete's protesting hand away. "I have to. I couldn't live with myself if I didn't."

Chapter 35

Aimee woke up as far on the edge of her bed as she could be without tumbling to the floor. Only her tightly tucked sheets were keeping her in, suspending her over the side as if she was in a hammock. It was as though she'd tried to flee, subconsciously, in the night.

She and Nick had hardly spoken to each other when she'd finally made it home.

"Where were you?" he'd asked curtly as she crept into the bedroom.

"Pete's," she said. "There was an emergency. Where were you?"

"Pub," he said. And they'd both rolled over and slept on opposite sides of the bed, hugging their respective resentment and guilt.

Did she feel guilty? Aimee stared out the window at her lovely garden, the dog trotting happily among the vines, her husband, tanned and fit in his dorky shorts, striding down the driveway to the sauvignon in the far corner. Aimee mentally shuffled through her emotions, naming them as she'd been taught. She felt exhausted, certainly. Drained. Emotionally spent. But there was also an unexpected lightness, as though the craziness of the evening had somehow been necessary. Cathartic. She'd been involved in ending a life, but she'd possibly saved a life, and she'd made a decision to own her part in things regardless. So there was relief, as well. But not guilt. How strange.

There was definitely hunger, though. Aimee pulled on her old robe, tied up her hair. Eleven thirty, according to the alarm clock. She'd slept till nearly lunchtime. She walked slowly down the hall, the cat weaving between her ankles.

"Who let you in?" she grumbled, but she didn't mean it. She gave Oscar a friendly pat. "Let me wake up properly, and I'll fix you up with some livers." She'd cook up a big batch of the smelly meat and freeze it so the cat's stomach could finally have a chance to calm down, and he could live inside with the rest of them. It wasn't like he'd done anything to deserve to be kicked out.

Would they ever really talk about it? Aimee wondered as she stopped to pull the living room curtains open, let the light flood into the living room. Dust motes escaped from the chintz and danced in the air, like daytime stars. Or would they just pretend last night never happened, neither of them asking the other where they really were? Lots of people lived with unspoken agreements, deep secrets. Look at Lou. If you never told, then people stopped asking. Aimee could easily picture herself and Nick slowly putting their anger aside as they got on with the day-to-day, never confronting each other head-on. Maybe he'd build his cellar door, as revenge for something he could sense but didn't know for sure. Maybe she'd get a job in town again, make herself unavailable to help with the new venture, to punish him for Melinda. Aimee picked up the popcorn bowls that littered the living room floor. So much to look forward to.

At least her head was calm. In all her years of therapy, why had no one told her that doing the right thing would quell the panic? That the way to discern between a paranoid thought and a problem that genuinely required action was the lack of chaos in her head. Aimee breathed deeply, appreciating the silence. Her marriage could wait. She was going to enjoy the peace.

The only other person in the kitchen was Shelley, drawing. "Put the kettle on, will you, love?" said Aimee, as she dumped the leftover popcorn in the bin.

"You do it. You're closer."

"Excuse me?" Shelley didn't talk back. Aimee eyed her daughter; there was a definite sulk to the lips. "Oh God, Shelley, don't you start giving me grief. The last thing I need is two hormonal teenagers to worry about. You're supposed to be the easy one." She pulled out a kitchen chair. "Just get me a cup of tea, there's a good girl."

The tea was delivered lukewarm with the bag still floating in it. Aimee went to say something, then stopped. Took in the hunched curve of Shelley's back, the pressure with which she was pressing down on the page. She remembered thirteen.

Boobs and thighs and bad skin, and the tendency to cry without warning. "You weren't really human again until eleventh grade," her mother had said. Aimee and her mum had spent their last year together trying to share as many memories as possible, virtually pouring information into each other from the moment they got the diagnosis. She regretted those lost years, even if it was the same for every mum of a teenage girl. She shuffled her chair closer to Shelley instead.

"Why don't you and I make up a bit of a picnic, go have it down by the river," she said. She could see blue sky above dusty green hills out the window—another cracking day. "We could bike down, maybe get an ice cream or something."

Shelley shrugged. "Whatever."

"Do you want to ask Byron if he wants to come? Or it could be just the two of us?"

Shelley looked at her as if she was stupid. "He's not back yet," she said, angry.

"Back from where?" School holidays, her son usually slept till noon. He could sleep fifteen hours without waking. Aimee envied him.

"*Camping*. With *Cameron*." It wasn't anger, it was jealousy.

Aimee gripped her tea so hard a small tidal wave sloshed onto the table. "Shelley Verratti, what are you talking about? Are you saying Byron's gone off on some kind of camping trip? Without telling me? That Cameron Kasprowicz has been back in this house this morning?"

"Not this morning. Last night. They said it was a *boy thing*, that I couldn't come." Her face was red with the injustice. "It's not fair."

"But I checked on you both last night," Aimee whispered. Although she hadn't, she'd only looked in on Shelley. Too tired to take the extra steps down the hall. "What does he think he's doing?" She grabbed Shelley's arm. "Why didn't you tell me?"

"Ow!" Shelley pulled away. "That hurts." She rubbed her arm, aggrieved. "And I didn't need to, because they told you. Cameron phoned you, left a message. I watched him stand outside on the porch there and do it."

There had been no message on Aimee's phone; she'd checked it guiltily all night.

"Where are they? Where'd they go?"

"I don't know. They didn't tell me." Shelley grabbed her pencils. "Phone Byron and ask him. *He's* the one Cameron likes." And she stormed out of the kitchen, slamming the door so hard that Oscar made a little puddle on the floor.

Lou HAD ALWAYS prided herself on never having to go to Sharna for anything.

If Hensley had been a medieval village, then Sharna would have been the wizened old crone people approached when they needed to woo back a straying spouse or stop their chickens from dying. Not that Sharna was particularly wizened; she looked pretty good for a woman who'd spent a lifetime in the Australian sun. Fillers, Melinda used to say, and she would know. But she said it quietly. Even Melinda was a bit afraid of Sharna.

Lou wasn't so much afraid as wary. Sharna knew everything; it was the reason the townspeople climbed faithfully up her stairs with envelopes and passport applications and desperate expressions. Not because they needed *postal services*— there was a mailbox on the main street; passport applications were quicker online. They went because they wanted the one thing that gave Sharna power over the town. Not spells or magic potions, but information.

Lou avoided Sharna for that reason. Because Lou had a lot of secrets, and she assumed the postmistress knew them all. Oh, Sharna was friendly enough, always happy to stop in the street for a quick gossip. But her eyes said, "I'm on to you." Those eyes made Lou feel guilty, which made her defensive, and when Lou got defensive she got angry. Better to stay out of the way.

Except now she had no choice. Lou trudged up the post office steps, once again at the mercy of the Hensley hierarchy. Empty-handed; she was buggered if she was going to concoct some kind of ridiculous stamp-buying cover story. She braced herself as she pushed open the post office door, with its cheerful tinkle. There was no point in pretending she was there for anything other than what Sharna could tell her.

"Sharna," said Lou, "I've just found out Mum and Dad had a baby, before me. I need to know what happened to him. Or her."

"Well, good morning to you too."

Lou sighed. "Sorry. But this is important." She pushed the picture across the counter. "What can you tell me?"

Sharna didn't even look at it. "Hmmm," she said, squinting at her cross-stitch. "That's a conundrum."

"Well, do you know anything?"

"Maybe," said Sharna. "Depends."

Lou was riding on about three hours of sleep; she had no patience for games. "Just tell me."

Sharna set her cross-stitch down on the counter. "Why should I help you?"

"Because I've got a right to know," said Lou. "And you're the obvious person. You know everything."

"Yes, but why should *I* help *you*?" Sharna narrowed those all-knowing eyes. "Why should any of us help you, actually?"

"Because . . ." Lou had expected a bit of prickliness, but not all-out hostility. She felt her own blood begin to rise. "Well, I deserve to know."

"No you don't," said Sharna, calmly threading her needle. Maroon; she was cross-stitching the Hensley logo. "And no one in this town owes you anything."

Why was she surprised? Sharna was local, three generations. Exactly the sort of Hensley traditionalist Lou had battled with all her life.

"Forget it," Lou said, stepping backward into a display of greeting cards. "I don't know why I even bothered. None of you have ever helped me before."

"Now that's not true at all. I can think of one or two people who've done quite a lot for you over the years."

She probably meant Rex, giving her a lousy boring job that barely paid a living wage. And what were the chances Sharna already knew she'd lost it? Most likely agreed with the decision to fire her.

"All you lot have ever done is judge me," said Lou. "And talk about me. Ever since I got pregnant. None of you have ever liked me."

"We don't really," agreed Sharna. "But that's got nothing to do with you getting pregnant."

"Don't lie," said Lou. "You all sided with my parents when they kicked me out. And none of you have had time for me since."

"Again," said Sharna, "that's got nothing to do with you having Tansy. What, you think you're the only pregnant teenager this town has ever seen?" She bit off a piece of thread with her teeth. "We don't like you because you don't like us. You think we're beneath you."

"Oh please." Lou nearly laughed.

"Yes, you do," said Sharna, suddenly aggressive. "All you talk about is how much you hate this place. I hear you down the pub every weekend, we all do, slagging Hensley off. Talking about how backward and small-minded we are, how you can't wait to leave. While expecting the very people you're insulting to serve you wine and chips."

"I—"

Sharna flipped up her counter. "You want to know why people sided with your parents?" she asked, walking toward Lou. "Because Ken and Bev were good people, who did a lot for this town. And yes, maybe they didn't react to your news as well as they could have, but how well did you ever treat them?"

Lou shrank into the Valentine's card display. There was nowhere she could go.

"You act like they turned their back on a loving daughter, but the contempt you had for them? You judged them the way you judge the rest of us, as though they didn't quite meet your high standards." Sharna looked Lou up and down, taking in her too-small jeans, the T-shirt she'd thrown on even though it had a stain on it. "I'm not surprised they had enough. I'm not surprised Rex has either. I'd have sacked you long ago."

Lou tried to cover the stain by crossing her arms. "I don't have to listen to this."

But Sharna wasn't finished. "Yes, people were curious about your baby, and yes, they gossiped, but the real reason Hensley doesn't have much time for you is because you act as though we're losers." Sharna gave a little shake of her head, like a disgruntled horse. "You live here, you're one of us, but the way you talk about this town? You ending up at Hensley Council is just proof that God has a sense of humor." She stepped closer; Lou could smell the tea on her breath. "You know why you even got that job in the first place, don't you? Your dad got it for you. Couldn't bear to see you struggling."

"Couldn't bear to see his daughter collecting the dole," Lou muttered, but without her usual fire.

"Maybe there was a bit of that," Sharna conceded. "I'm not saying they're blameless. Beverly Henderson was one of the most stubborn women you ever met. 'Just apologize,' I used to say. 'Tell her you're sorry and she'll come home and bring your granddaughter with her.' But no. That woman wouldn't piss on a kitten on fire if she thought it had wronged her."

"Thank you," said Lou, uncertainly.

"But that doesn't excuse you. Walking around here like you're too good for us, turning up to every community event just so you can sneer at it. Writing snide little things on Face-book." Sharna turned suddenly, as though she was sick of the very sight of Lou. "And then you come in here, demanding answers, like I owe you something." Sharna picked up her cross-stitch again. "You know what's funny? Your friend Melinda, who genuinely is too good for this place, is at all our fund-raisers, trying to prove she's still one of us. While you, who's never done anything, keep desperately trying to prove you're not."

BYRON WASN'T ANSWERING his phone.

"Calm down," said Nick. He leaned against the kitchen door-way, strong forearm keeping him steady as he shook himself free of one workboot, then the other. "They won't be far away."

"You don't understand." Aimee made her hands into fists in the safety of her pockets. "He's bad news. Even Pete says so."

"So we'll tell Byron not to hang out with him anymore." Nick rubbed his hands under the tap, briefly turning the water a dull brown. "He shouldn't have taken off like that, without telling one of us. But it's nothing to freak out about. He's a fifteen-year-old boy. He can look after himself."

"Exactly! A fifteen-year-old boy, out all night with a

nineteen-year-old *man* who he has a crush on. A man whose own stepfather says is messed up. And who hates me for some reason, who looks at me like he wants to punish me."

Nick paused, one hand on the refrigerator. "What are you trying to say?"

"I think he might . . ." Aimee closed her eyes, saw the way Byron had gazed up at Cameron over dinner. Laughing too loudly at his jokes, rushing to get him another glass of water. "I'm scared he's . . ." Shelley and Byron had both been fighting for his attention. But Cameron had been much more interested in Byron, hadn't he?

"Do you think he'd interfere with Byron? Try something? Is that it?" Nick's face had gone white.

Aimee squeezed her eyes tighter, trying not to picture two boys in a sleeping bag. Her innocent, insecure son. Cameron, so good-looking, so blatantly untrustworthy. She nodded miserably. "He lied to Shelley. Told her he'd called me, asked permission."

"And Pete reckons he's a bit fucked up. Got issues."

Aimee nodded.

"I don't get it. Why would he want to punish you? He doesn't even know you."

Aimee stopped trying to keep her voice level. "Because he knows I had something to do with the plane crash! He thinks I killed his brother, and now he's disappeared with my son!"

"Oh for Christ's sake." Nick paced around the kitchen, hands pushed against his head as though he was literally trying to keep his hair on. "Not this again."

"I don't care if you believe me or not. But there's something going on with him. Pete's scared of him, almost."

"Really?"

"Honest to God. And Byron just *idolized* him."

Nick gripped the bench. "Why the fuck did you leave them alone with him then?"

"Because I didn't *know*." Aimee was shouting now. "And you weren't here either, so you can't bloody talk." She strode into the hallway. "I'm going to call the police."

"Don't be stupid, Aimee. Let's try and figure out where they've gone."

"You could locate his iPhone." Shelley stood in the living room doorway, staring at them both like they were crazy. "You made us give you our passwords, remember? If we were going to have phones? You can track him with that."

Aimee nearly dragged her daughter into the room. "Do it," she instructed.

"It'll only work if his location settings are on," Shelley warned, as she opened the menu on Aimee's phone. They all watched as a small blue dot appeared, pulsing, on the outskirts of Hensley.

"He's next to the river," said Nick.

"Near the old swimming hole," said Aimee, zooming in. A deserted spot, largely used by teenagers getting high or getting it on. She and Nick had driven out there a few times when they were dating and his parents wouldn't go conveniently to bed.

"Well then," said Aimee, scooping up her keys. "Let's go."

"Are you sure this is what you think it is?" Nick gave her a meaningful look over Shelley's head.

Shelley glared at her mother. "I don't know why you're so pissed off. You're the one who was worried he'd never get a boyfriend."

Nick plucked the keys out of Aimee's hand. "I'll drive."

Aimee grabbed her phone off Shelley. "One minute. I need to call Pete." And the police. She was going to call the police. If only so there would be someone there to hold her back.

Lou GOT AS far as the second post office step before she sagged into an exhausted heap. Her brain was woolly with sleep deprivation; she couldn't tell if Sharna's words were true or not. Had she really started the cold war with her parents? Had Lou rejected Hensley before it rejected her?

Ridiculous, she told herself. Lou didn't have to try hard to remember walking down the main street, ripe with Tansy, and seeing her parents' friends avert their eyes. Sure, some had spoken, but Lou always assumed people were being nosy when they asked how she was doing. Spying for her parents. Offering to babysit or lend her their old cot so she'd owe them something. She wasn't falling for that. The same way she wasn't falling for her mother's worried tone when she rang up to check on her. To gloat, she'd tell herself as she slammed the phone down. They just want to be able to say "I told you so." Lou put her head in her hands.

But look at the secret they'd kept from her. Lou pulled

out the photo again. She didn't even know if her sibling was a boy or a girl. *Isn't it funny*, Tansy had said, when she'd found Lou at the breakfast table staring at the picture, like she had been pretty much all night, *how babies always look like little old men?* The baby in the photo was essentially genderless, with its white knitted hat and standard-issue hospital blanket. Lou leaned back against a veranda post. The photo was annoyingly devoid of clues. There was no useful calendar in the back of the shot, no tiny name tag around the baby's wrist that Lou could blow up with computer wizardry she didn't possess. Lou stared harder, willing it to tell her what Sharna wouldn't. The hospital didn't even look like St. Margaret's, although it was possible they'd redecorated in the last thirty-something years. The only thing she knew for sure was that this was her mother, and this photo was taken by her father, and therefore her parents had had a baby before Lou.

But other pieces were beginning to fall into place. Her childhood made a lot more sense, seen through the lens of this photo. If there'd been a child who'd died, then that went a long way to explaining why her parents had been so strict. All the rules about not being out after dark, always leaving a note. And maybe why they'd been so paranoid about her future, so devastated when she "threw it away." Their words, not hers. Although here she was, thirty-five and unemployed, chain-smoking on the post office steps at 11 A.M. on a Friday, so maybe they'd had a point.

What happened to you? Lou silently asked the child in the photo. The baby couldn't have been born more than two or three years before Lou. Her mother had had Lou at twenty-three; she'd been a young mum then too. All yellow-and-brown paisley miniskirts, matching pigtails with her daughter. Which meant this child couldn't have lived long. Did it die in the hospital? Did her mother already know something was wrong; was that why she looked so sad? Or was there an accident? Lou had never been allowed near the water without an adult, not even a paddling pool. She'd been spanked severely once for running her own bath. Had her sister or brother drowned? Been hit by a car? And why never, ever tell her?

Although theirs was a family that hadn't discussed much. Lou's mother never told her the facts of life, just gave her a book and said stiltedly to ask questions after she'd read it. (Lou hadn't.) There was another book when her granddad died, about rabbits going to heaven. When her dog had been run over, her parents swore he'd gone to live on a farm. Honesty and openness weren't really their way. It wasn't inconceivable that they could lose a child and never speak of it. Put it behind them and move on. Hadn't they essentially done that with her as well?

But how devastating it must have been for them. Lou felt a genuine ache, deep in her chest. Her heart was already breaking for Tansy, and they didn't even know what they were facing yet. For her parents to silently bear such a loss, to lock the grief away like some kind of shameful secret, was such a tragedy she wanted to cry.

When the policeman had arrived at Lou's house to tell her about the car accident, she'd felt nothing. It was like listening to an actor say his lines in a TV show. They'd been killed less than twenty miles outside Hensley: an overtaking truck, a blind corner. Nearly ten months ago now. The policeman had thought Lou was in shock, because she'd smiled and thanked him, and tried to shut the door. But they'd been dead to her for years.

Lou stared up at the post office noticeboard, the fliers advertising snake catchers and help-yourself horse poo, all the things she hated about country-town life. Taking over the house had felt like an act of revenge, knowing she wouldn't have been welcome. But what if Lou had been wanted more desperately than she realized? What if her teenage rebellion had felt like losing a second child? Lou ran her thumb over her mother's exhausted face. She'd always thought her parents were cold. But it could have been grief. Grief shoved so far down it had frozen.

And hadn't Lou done the same thing, in a way? She loved Aimee, but she'd shut her out because she didn't have the energy for her anymore. She loved Melinda, yet she'd turned on her because she didn't know what else to do. Lou pictured her parents in the window of their ugly living room, watching her run around in the rain trying to save her possessions, flicking her middle finger up at them as she yelled and swore. Maybe turning their hearts off was the only way they could cope. It didn't make it right. But it did make it the tiniest bit more understandable.

"You still here?" Sharna stood on the porch above Lou, a dark shadow. The postmistress sighed. "One thing I'll say for you, you always were stubborn." She reached down and caught

Lou's arm, pulled her onto her feet. "Come on back in then, let's set this right. You keep sitting here, people will talk."

SURE ENOUGH, THERE was a small blue tent down by the swimming hole. Aimee made Nick cut the engine as soon as it came into view. Even though it was killing her to let Cameron Kasprowicz have an extra minute alone with her son, she had to make sure she was right.

The area was scrubby, just as she'd remembered. Few people came down to this part of the river, unless they had a reason. It was the point where the eucalyptus gave way to proper bush, a small clearing littered with abandoned beer bottles and dirty supermarket bags. Even the river looked scummy.

As Aimee and Nick watched, a man poked his head round the side of the tent. Aimee recognized the arrogant profile instantly. He walked bare-chested and stretching into the middle of the clearing, glanced around as if trying to identify a noise. Aimee tried not to breathe. Cameron wore a pair of faded shorts, nothing else. He looked like he'd just gotten out of bed.

He climbed back into the tent, unidentifiable bumps appearing in its sides. Laughter floated out the door, but it was easy, intimate laughter, not rowdy boy yahooing. And that was more than Aimee could take. She ran careering down toward the river, arms and legs pumping, chest heaving, but still with enough air in her lungs to yell.

"Byron," she shouted. "Byron, I'm here. Cameron, you leave my son alone. Don't you touch him."

Nick was a few steps behind her, walking but quickly.

"I've rung the police," Aimee yelled, as she got closer. "Get your hands off him, the police are coming." She overshot and had to pull up so she didn't slide into the river. Pivoting, she grabbed hold of the tent for balance, and braced herself for whatever faced her inside.

Beneath the awning, Cameron was desperately trying to shove a bong under a sleeping bag. Byron sat opposite, eyes large, chest bare, a plastic bag of weed at his feet.

"Mum," he said, horrified. "What the fuck are you doing?" He ducked and twisted. "Get the fuck off me!"

"You shouldn't be out here," said Aimee, tugging. "You shouldn't be alone with him."

"Mum. Oh my God. STOP!"

Someone had her other arm, was trying to keep her away from her son. "Sorry, Byron," said Nick. "Your mum was worried. She didn't know where you'd gone."

Byron looked as though he wanted the earth to open up and swallow him. He stared open-mouthed at his parents. "I can't believe you're doing this. We're *camping*."

The smell of weed hung heavy on the summer air. Aimee turned to Nick, waiting for him to say something, to do something, but he just kept holding her arm. "Sorry, mate," he said to Byron. "Our bad."

"But . . ." Drugs! He was giving her son drugs! Which surely was intent of some sort!

Cameron smirked at her, and Aimee yanked herself free. "I know what you're up to," she said, staggering toward him. "I know what you're doing." She turned toward Byron. "He's just playing with you, love. He's not really interested, you can see that, can't you?"

Byron sat mute with horror, one hand over his face.

"Don't worry, mate, we're leaving." Nick grabbed Aimee's shoulder. "You hang out here as long as you want. Just give it a bit of time before either of you drives anywhere, eh?" He gave Aimee a little push, back toward the dirt track. "Come on. We're off."

But there was a siren in the road behind them, then a squeal of tires.

"Please tell me you didn't," muttered Nick.

"I was *scared*," said Aimee. She reached a hand toward her son's acne-scarred shoulder, but he turned away from her.

"Aimee? Is he there?" There was crashing and puffing as Arthur lumbered down the track. "Cameron, your father's in the car. He wants to talk to you."

Cameron looked up at Aimee, shaking his head. "Nice one," he said.

"You're still going to be in trouble," she hissed. "Giving drugs to minors."

"It was mine," said Byron furiously. "Thanks, Mum."

"You don't need to cover for him."

"I'm not." Byron held out the weed; it was in one of Aimee's yellow Ziploc freezer bags.

"Shit, how much is in there?" said Nick. It was a lot. "Oh well done, Aimee. What a bloody mess."

LOU SAT OUT back in the little post office garden. She'd never been out there before, but it was lovely. The low fence lined with tufty grass and agapanthus, cockatoos flying between the trees. She sat at a faded picnic table, listening to Sharna shoo her customers from the shop, and feeling weirdly okay about whatever came next.

She'd visit the baby's grave, she decided, as she leaned back and tipped her face up to the sun. Wherever it was. Take Tansy. Show her that tragedy happened, but it was how you dealt with it that mattered. That they needed to keep loving each other, no matter what.

The back door creaked open and the postmistress pulled a chair out next to Lou. She held two Popsicles and a piece of paper. "Now, I'm not sure I should be doing this," Sharna said, as she ripped the paper off her own ice pop. "Your mother would be turning in her grave, but with your own daughter in trouble, maybe you do have a right to know after all. It might make you understand Bev a bit better, forgive her just a little."

How the hell did she know about Tansy? "We're not using that term," Lou said stiffly.

"Oh get off your bloody high horse," said Sharna. "I'm almost sixty-five, I'm not going to change the way I speak just because your generation doesn't like it." She placed the piece of paper on the table. "Now, I don't know everything, but this is the hospital she gave birth in, and this is the date. She called him David."

"I knew it." Lou scanned the piece of paper as she crunched into her Popsicle. *David Phillip.* He was an October baby, two and a half years older than Lou. "When did he die?"

"He's not dead, love. At least, not that I know of."

"I don't understand."

"Your mother had a baby before she was married. When she was twenty. And if you think they were tough on you, you have no idea what it was like for her."

Lou's grandfather had been a minister. She could feel her hand getting sticky where the ice was melting. "What happened?"

"She got pregnant before she met your father. I don't know who from, never asked and she never told. She went away to have it where no one knew her. Came back with a secretarial certificate five months later."

"Did my dad know?"

"I have no idea. Probably not. They made her feel so ashamed." Sharna sucked loudly on her cherry Popsicle.

"Then why wasn't she nicer to me?" Sharna wasn't helping her understand her mother—the opposite. If she were here, Lou would have shaken her. The hypocrisy. Like with Aimee. Lou had broken down in angry tears at Aimee and Nick's wedding, the unfairness of it all. Aimee had gotten pregnant less than eighteen months after Lou, but she was getting *married*, so that was all okay then.

"She left you the house, didn't she? I think she was probably horrified to see history repeat itself. Her parents did a real number on her. I daresay she piled some of her own guilt on to you, but then you're probably passing some of your own issues on to Tansy, aren't you, love. We all do."

"I'm not." Except she was, wasn't she. The crazy spending to keep her daughter close, the insistence that Tansy would make this work, would finish school, would have all the opportunities she hadn't. "Do you know anything else? Where he might be?"

"I know they took him to New Zealand. That was all she said, when she got back. Came in here, showed me that same photo and said, 'I'll never see him again, the family is moving to New Zealand.' We sat and had a little cry, and then she straightened herself up and never spoke of it again. Six months later, she was engaged to your dad."

"And no one knew?" It seemed impossible in Hensley, to keep a secret so big for so long.

"Oh I daresay a few people did. But no one would ever have said anything. Bev was one of us. Like you could be, if you wanted. Think what you like about this town, but it looks after its own. Everyone just wanted her to be happy."

Lou stared at her melting Popsicle. "This town has never liked me," she insisted, "not like that."

"No, Louise, you chose not to be liked. There's a big difference."

AIMEE SAT IN the back of the car, like a naughty child, while Nick—the adult—stood outside sorting things with Arthur. Byron sat in the passenger seat, face like stone.

"I thought he was taking advantage of you," Aimee burbled hopelessly. "You can see why I'd think that, can't you? Why I'd worry? He's so much older. So good-looking. I thought he was playing a game."

"What, because someone like that would never fancy me?" Byron wouldn't look at her. "God. It wasn't even like that. We were just hanging out." Aimee put a hand on his shoulder; he shrugged it off. "Don't touch me."

Nick opened the car door. "You're only making it worse," he said, looking at her as though she was one of the kids. "I'm sorry, mate," he said to Byron as he turned the ignition. "We didn't mean to embarrass you. At least you only got a caution, eh?" As though Byron having his own supply of cannabis wasn't even an issue.

None of them spoke the whole drive home.

The moment the car came to a stop Byron was off, running into the house like Oscar let out of his cage after a visit to the vet. Aimee took a few steps to follow him.

"I wouldn't."

"We need to speak to him about the marijuana," said Aimee. "God, did you see how much was in there?"

"I'll speak to him later. Right now, I need to speak to you." Nick looked over at the house. Byron's blinds were closed, but Shelley's forehead was pressed against her window. "Come with me, will you?" He started walking down into the vines.

All Aimee wanted was a cup of tea. "Can't we just go inside?" she asked, trying to keep up as he strode between the rows, grasshoppers bouncing furiously in his wake.

"Nope," said Nick, not turning round. "I don't want the kids to hear me yell at you."

He stopped in the middle of the shiraz and let loose. She had no judgment. Had lost control of her senses. Humiliated their son. Was putting her family at risk by refusing to take her medication. He wasn't sure how much more he could take. Out all day and night pursuing conspiracy theories. No more. There'd be no bloody more. Nick waved his arms as he shouted, his watch getting caught in the black nets, which only made him angrier.

"Did you even think about how Byron would feel?" he demanded. "Poor kid's got crap self-esteem as it is. And then for you to barge in on him like that?"

"You came barging in too!" Aimee yelled back. "You were frightened as well!"

"Because you told me to be!" Nick rubbed at his hair wildly. "My only mistake was believing you. And I won't bloody do it again."

"That's not your only mistake," said Aimee. She wasn't going to mention it, but she wasn't taking the blame for all this either.

"What's that supposed to mean?"

"I saw you," said Aimee. "I *saw* you. Coming out of Melinda's last night."

"So?" But his eyes darted left and right, a captured animal.

"I know you're sleeping with her. I knew you were while I was in the hospital, although I never said anything. Because I didn't want to rock the boat. But I fucking *know*, okay."

"You don't know anything."

"It's fucking obvious," said Aimee. No wonder people swore so much. Sometimes they were the only words that would do. "You echo each other, like bloody parrots. I say something to her, you say it to me. I say something to you, she magically knows about it. And you were out, nearly every time I phoned from the hospital. Do you think I'm fucking stupid?"

"We're. Not. Sleeping. Together," said Nick, through gritted teeth.

Aimee paused. He wasn't lying, because he was staring her full in the face, and Nick could only lie looking slightly away.

"Well, you're doing something," said Aimee. "Why else would you be over there, late at night, and telling me you were at the pub?"

"Nothing happened," said Nick, with a small glance at his grapes.

"Something doesn't have to happen for something to happen," snapped Aimee. "It's bad enough that you're there, when I need you here. It's bad enough that you take her seriously, but not me."

"Because she's not coming up with all sorts of crazy theories! Maybe I need to have a sane conversation sometimes."

"You can have a sane conversation with me."

"I bloody can't." Nick grabbed a handful of netting; the vine sagged underneath. "Melinda's worried about you," he said. "Thinks you've got your head all messed up over this plane accident."

"See! You believe her and not me. I'm the one you're supposed to listen to. I'm your wife."

"But I can't," said Nick. "I can't listen to this anymore."

"But Melinda was wrong! I was right! We did cause the accident, just with lanterns not fireworks. I should have told you straightaway, but now I've got proof." Her bag was in the car. "Come with me and I'll show you."

Nick shook his head. "Drop it, Aimee."

"But they found—"

"I said drop it."

He'd chosen *her* again. Like he always did.

Nick pulled the netting down, straightened it so no birds could sneak underneath. "I'm going to tidy up the cellar," he said. "You're going to start taking those bloody pills again if I have to shove them down your throat myself. You need to sort yourself out. If you want to have any kind of family, if you don't want all of us to end up bloody hating you, you have to sort yourself out."

"Mum? You home?" Tansy was sitting on the floor in front of their giant television, watching a Netflix documentary about natural birth. "Mum, you need to come and see this. It's *horrific*."

Lou stood in the doorway. "You don't need to worry about that," she said, but she didn't put her bag down. "They've got really good drugs these days."

"I can't believe you went through all this to have me. And I've never even said thank you." Tansy looked over her shoulder. "Did you have to have stitches?"

"Mmmm," said Lou, fiddling with her keys. "Seven."

"No wonder you get so upset when I forget Mother's Day."

"Don't worry about it."

"I'm never going to take you for granted again," Tansy promised. "I'm just going to think of your perineum whenever I get annoyed with you."

Lou would normally have found that funny, but right now . . . "Tans, are you okay on your own for a bit longer?" she said, slipping her shoes back on. "There's something I forgot to do in town."

THE BELL DOWNSTAIRS kept ringing, even though Melinda had buzzed whoever it was in. "All right, all right," she muttered, twisting out of her yoga pose and thumping un-Zen-like down the stairs. "Calm yourself."

She couldn't see a head through the narrow strip of glass above the door—not Nick or Clint then. Melinda's tread grew heavier as she reached the bottom steps. It had better damn well not be Lou. Melinda hadn't made a decision about the money, was still spinning from the sheer bloody *cheek* of it. After all she'd done for her. And it hadn't even been twenty-four hours. Lou could keep her bloody shirt on. Melinda stalked across the hall and flung the door open.

"Oh!"

Aimee stood on the footpath, pale-faced and red-eyed and looking a bit lost. Melinda took a step toward her, heart soaring. Lou and Melinda would probably never speak a civil word again, but Aimee was her *cousin*.

"Come in, come in," said Melinda. "Why didn't you let yourself up? God, I'm so pleased to see you. Are you okay?"

Aimee stayed where she was in the street. "I'm not coming in."

"Why not?" Melinda asked, her stomach slowly turning over.

"I'm only here to tell you to stay away from my husband."

Melinda's building was smack in the middle of Hensley's main street; you had to pass it to go anywhere. Teenagers and shopkeepers and nosy mums shuffled around Aimee, heads craned as they tried to figure out what was going on.

"I saw him leave here. Last night."

"Aimee." Melinda dropped her voice. "*Nothing happened*."

"You have to move on now," Aimee said, voice a monotone, as though she was reading from a bad soap script. "Because you never did. You came back here for him, but he isn't yours anymore. He's mine. And you're ruining things for us."

"Funny," Melinda muttered. "Lou thinks I came back for my dad." Why was everyone suddenly trying to psychoanalyze her?

Aimee cocked her head to one side. "When did you speak to Lou?"

"Doesn't matter." Melinda went to grab Aimee's arm, then thought better of it. "Look, if you won't come upstairs, at least come *inside*."

Aimee allowed herself to be guided into the downstairs hall. She stood stiffly at the foot of the stairs, right next to the umbrella Melinda had hit her husband with.

"Everything okay down there?" Melinda's PA poked her head over the banister. "Do you want me to make coffee?"

"We're all good, Kelly." Melinda considered her options as she waited for the office door to close. The only thing she could really do was agree. Agree and disarm. "You're right," she said. "I probably have been leaning on him a bit lately." Because she couldn't tell Aimee that Nick kept turning up *here*, to her; it would kill her. What was it her dad always said? Be honest, not stupid. "But that's all it was. A bit of support. Me wanting a bloke to do things around the place, listen to me have a moan."

"But he's supporting you instead of me," said Aimee. "Listening to you instead of me. And that's fucking up things for my family. You're fucking up my family."

"O-kay."

"I know you think you gave him to me, but you didn't. He didn't choose you, he chose me. He didn't want you. So stop trying to steal him back."

Was Melinda just supposed to stand around taking everything that anyone felt like throwing at her? "Now hang on——"

"What kind of woman makes a move on her friend's husband while they're in the hospital? Who does that?"

"I didn't——"

"What kind of woman tries to turn a friend's husband against her? Discredits her? He won't listen to a word I say about Pete's accident, thanks to you. Won't even let me mention it."

"But, Aimee, I haven't done that." Melinda tried to keep her voice gentle. "You've done that yourself, with your history——"

"Just because I was crazy once doesn't mean I'm still crazy." Aimee grabbed Melinda's umbrella and jabbed it in the air.

She was doing a pretty good impression. Melinda twisted out of the way. It would be complete karma if Aimee were to poke her eye out with it. This was more action than her umbrella had seen in *years*.

"You can't keep judging me on something that happened years ago. It's not fair. But you keep reminding him. Making him doubt me. I can't even show him I'm right." She prodded the umbrella angrily at the mat, making little holes in it. Melinda grabbed the handle and tried to wrench it from her.

"Okay, that's enough now. I'm sorry you and Nick are having issues, but you can't pin them all on me. You're not exactly blameless." Honest but not stupid, but not everyone's bloody punching bag either.

"Ha!" Aimee's laugh bordered on the hysterical. Her hands slipped as she clutched the umbrella fabric. "What would you know? Actually, don't tell me. You probably know *everything*."

"I know you're not supporting him enough. You're not doing anything to help him fix your financial situation." Melinda tugged.

"I know how to support my husband, thank you very much." Aimee tugged back.

"Really? Then why does he need to keep coming here to talk to me?"

Aimee's mouth fell open, a perfect O. *Whoops.* But Melinda was on a roll now. She gave a final yank, stumbling backward as Aimee let the umbrella slip out of her hands. "You don't want to help him because you're deliberately keeping your life small. *Safe.* You always have. Shutting down anything that might mean change, so you don't get scared. But you can't keep living like that. It's not fair on Nick. It's not fair on your kids."

"Don't you talk to me about my family. Yours is completely dysfunctional. Look at your dad. Look at your *brother*."

They were Aimee's family too, technically; it made no sense. Melinda stared down at the misshapen spokes of her poor umbrella. "Why does everyone keep banging on about my bloody family?" She tossed the umbrella into a corner of the hall; it knocked a little chip of paint off the wall as it landed.

"Because you bloody idolize——" Aimee stopped. "Lou mention them as well, did she? Ha."

"*What?*"

Aimee looked strangely triumphant. "What, you never guessed?" Almost smug. "I nearly said something, when you were standing in your kitchen, being all righteous about whoever got Tansy pregnant. About going after the father. Because you know who got Lou pregnant, don't you? Oh come on. It's written all over Tansy's face. *Matthew.* Your precious, useless baby brother."

"She's never said."

"She probably thinks you know, though. I bet she thinks you've known for years, and haven't bothered to do anything to make him step up. Just kept sending him money. I bet she hates you as much as I do."

LOU WALKED CAREFULLY through the tiny cemetery, navigating the clusters of weathered stones, trying not to step on

anyone. The late afternoon was thick with squawking cockatoos, judging her from on high. Somewhere a lawn mower
rattled and choked.

They were right up against the low stone wall, her mum
and dad. Lying side by side, not touching, a respectful distance
apart, as they had been in life. No show of affection just because we're dead. Lou sat cross-legged in the stubbly grass
beside the marble headstones.

She had no idea who'd come up with the inscriptions. Lou
had wanted nothing to do with it. Bland words about being a
loving husband and father, a devoted mother and wife. She ran
her hands across the stone, noting shamefully that theirs were
the only graves without offerings. Even the knocked-over jam
jars and dirty stuffed animals showed that someone cared.

"I'm sorry," said Lou, checking first that there was no one
around to hear her shamefaced apology. "I still don't really
understand why you did what you did, and I still don't actually
think you were right, but I'm sorry for my part in things. I'm
sorry if I didn't give you much of a chance. And I'm sorry I
didn't try to make things up with you, for Tansy's sake."

This was the bit where she was supposed to tell them how
much they'd have loved their granddaughter, how proud they'd
be, but Lou didn't say it because she didn't think it was true.

"I'm trying to do everything differently from you. And that
might sound rude, but I don't want Tansy to turn out like me.
I don't want her to break me, like I think I might have you.
And I'm sorry if that's how it felt."

She had surprisingly little to say. It was more a gesture, turning up here. An acknowledgment that she'd behaved badly as well. Her mother had had fifteen stitches, Lou knew. Not that she'd ever spared a thought for her perineum.

"Anyway, I'm declaring a truce. I'm not going to say bad things about you anymore. I'm going to make more of an effort here in Hensley, for Tansy's sake. I'll even bring her up here, with her baby, if we're able to. Explain that you were better people than I realized."

"I wish you'd have told me, Mum," Lou said suddenly. "I'd have seen things differently. It would have helped. I would have felt less alone." She laid one hand on the warm stone. "I wish you'd felt that you *could* tell me."

There was a family she vaguely knew entering the churchyard, the little girl clutching a bunch of bright purple pansies. Lou pushed herself back up on her feet, dusted the loose grass off. She didn't need the town thinking she was going soft. "I'll be off then. But I'll come back. And . . . thank you. For the stuff that you did do. It was probably more than I realized; I can see that now."

She stepped carefully around the ground that housed her parents as she headed back toward the path. There was a fresh hole next to the gate, raw and waiting. Lou paused, made it look like she was fiddling with her bag. "I owe you an apology as well," she quietly told the air, the body still to come. "We couldn't have known, but I'm sorry anyway."

Then she quickly walked on, before anyone could see.

MELINDA ENTERED HER password on the bank's website and watched the little colored disc spin.

Why am I even doing this? she asked herself, as she waited for the computer to decide whether to let her in. Aimee was clearly still a loose cannon; she probably wouldn't make it through the weekend without confessing to someone. Probably her bloody investigator friend. Why should she pay Lou to keep quiet when the whole town was going to find out anyway?

And Melinda might need this money, if everything did come to light. She opened her savings account. There was bound to be a fine, at least. Legal fees, maybe. Really, she should be keeping a war chest, she rationalized as she typed in the numbers: all those zeros. This was an irresponsible act. She owned a company. She had staff. She might be adopting a baby. She had *commitments*.

Lou's bank details were still on file from when she'd briefly sold for LoveLocked. In more than a decade, she'd never upgraded her bank account, never shopped around for a better deal. Never needed to. But that wasn't Melinda's fault. She wasn't responsible for what her brother had or hadn't done, if he'd screwed Lou over. Or if her father had. More likely her father. Melinda could hear her dad laughing as he told her about the money he'd given Matt to bugger off. Start again somewhere new with a clean slate. Because he'd caused too much trouble here. She'd thought he just meant the gambling; clearly not.

The bank needed secondary authorization, "for a transaction of this size." Melinda rested her head in her hands and

waited for the phone to ring. She'd heard her father bully people before, had sat silent as he recounted his victories over
their weekly Sunday lunch. Roast lamb with a side helping of
amused contempt; laughing stories of how he'd worn the other
party down with threats and legalese as he passed the pota-
toes. Had Lou been subjected to something like that? She'd
have tried to fight her corner, Melinda was sure of it. And she
would have lost. She pictured the two of them skirting each
other at social gatherings. Recalled her father's low opinion
of Lou. *Trouble.* Saw Lou's annoyance, as Melinda sent off yet
another check to Matthew.

So much, under her nose, for so long. And she'd had no idea.

Melinda looked around her perfect, sterile flat. Why had
she really come back? Because she was trying to impress her
dad? *You idolize him.* Did she think if she was living here, waving certificates under his nose like a skinny twelve-year-old,
he'd be forced to acknowledge her success? To pat her on the
head? Or did she come back because it was comfortable? *Big
fish in a small pond.* Easier to stand out here than compete with
a thousand other beautiful, successful women in London or
New York or Melbourne.

Or had she returned to Hensley for Nick? *Stop trying to steal
him back.* No. She hadn't. But it had been nice, knowing he
was watching. Seeing him compare. That had been comfortable too.

The woman on the end of the line was cheerful. Was this a
genuine transaction? Could Melinda please answer a couple of
security questions? She reeled off the name of her childhood

482   Brandy Scott

pet, her mother's maiden name. This was madness, all of it. But it somehow also seemed right. She might not be directly responsible for anyone else's mess, but she felt culpable, all the same. For causing Aimee so much distress. For not recognizing Lou's. But more than anything, she felt tired.

"We're going to send a four-digit number to your phone. If you could please enter it when prompted."

The inquiry started on Monday. Melinda no longer had the energy to try to shut Aimee down, to battle Lou, to control who knew what or said what to whom. Her phone pinged. At least it would be over, soon enough.

Chapter 36

"I'll leave you to sort this one out," Arthur said to Pete. "But, Cameron, I'm warning you. I don't want to hear your name so much as come up in conversation." The policeman paused to catch his breath. "Understand me?"

"I was only—"

"Understand me?"

"Sir."

Arthur's heavy footsteps retreated down the dirt path, leaving Pete alone with Cameron in the clearing. *He could kill me*, Pete thought, listening to his son move around the river-bank, little branches snapping under his feet. *Push my face in the water, hold me down. Say I slipped.* He thought of yelling out to Arthur, asking him to wait, to drive him safely home. But he didn't want Cameron to know he was afraid.

The river gurgled gently next to them, the mud making small kissing sounds where the water touched the sides. The current could be strong down here, but it wasn't particularly deep. Pete kicked off his shoes and walked blindly forward.

"What the hell?"

The bank was farther away than he'd realized. Pete stumbled slightly as he miscalculated the slope, gripping the mud with his toes so he wouldn't fall flat on his face. But then he was in. He kept walking, the water rising greedily up past his ankles, his calves. It was cooler than he'd expected, but it still had the soft, silty feeling he remembered from when they used to bring the boys down here.

"Pete!"

Pete's trousers grew heavy, slowing him down. The water reached his thighs before there was a panicked splash behind him.

"What are you doing?" A hand circled his good arm.

"You want me gone, I'm making myself gone." Pete took another step forward.

The grip tightened. "Don't be bloody stupid."

"What's left to live for? My wife's dead, my youngest is dead, and my eldest is turning into a sociopath."

"Hey!"

"You try to intimidate people. Mess with their heads. You've been doing it for years. Me. Suzanne. Now Aimee."

"We were only going camping."

"I know exactly what you were doing. You've done it before. Suzanne was too scared to drive to work."

"Well, maybe she should have thought twice about—"

"Enough!" Pete twisted and slipped free, strode deeper. The water rose to his waist, but he wasn't frightened. Well, not much. He knew this river. Something brushed past his leg, then returned; Pete carefully nudged it away. "You don't know the full story."

"I know we weren't there that night, because of her. Because you were with her. I know you cheated on Mum, when she was dying."

Cameron's voice was a couple of yards away; he'd never been very comfortable in the river. Always been frightened of what might lie beneath. Pete paused, the water cold around his chest. He must be a fair way out now—the current was stronger, the mud slippery. He turned, careful not to lose his footing. He didn't want to die. He just wanted to make a point.

"You're right, I wasn't there," he said. "And I can't change that. It's my biggest regret. But I didn't cheat on your mother. She knew where I was and who I was with. She knew what was going on."

"Bullshit," called Cameron. "I don't believe you."

"It was her idea." Julia had turned to him, when it became clear the chemo wasn't working. *I want you to get married again,* she'd said. *You need to find someone else, for the boys. So they have someone when I'm gone.* "She wanted you to have a mother."

"She would have wanted you to wait."

"She was sick for *three years.* She knew Suzanne. She liked her. It made her happy, to think we wouldn't be alone."

"I don't want to hear this."

"But you have to. You have to get over it now. It's turning you into something you don't want to be." Pete took another small step into the busier water, remembering that afternoon. He'd left his phone in the car. The smallest thing. Their daily visit with Julia had been depressing; he'd taken the boys to McDonald's for a treat, then left them alone for a few hours. Cameron was old enough to hold the fort. Pete and Suzanne had gone to see a movie. Something light, to take his mind off things. The irony. Pete stood in the swirl of the river, his mind faithfully replaying the scenes. They'd sat chastely next to each other, not even holding hands. Julia had chosen Suzanne: a *nice Christian woman.* Pete didn't even particularly fancy her, but it made his wife happy to think they were spending time together. And Pete wanted Julia to be happy.

"You're just trying to justify what you did. You're telling yourself stories, to make yourself feel better."

They'd gone for Chinese after; not much fine dining in Meadowcroft. Talked about work. He hadn't even noticed he'd forgotten the phone. It was a nice night; Pete decided to walk rather than drive Suzanne home. All in all, he'd probably been gone four hours. Maybe five. It wasn't till he was back in his own driveway that he saw all the messages. He'd walked into the house and found the children hysterical.

"You abandoned her."

"I couldn't be there twenty-four hours a day. No one could."

"You left her alone to die!"

"Well, then so did you!" Words Pete had vowed never to say flew across the water, like perfectly shaped skipping stones. "You were fifteen. You could have called your grandparents. You could have gone to the neighbors, explained the situation."

"You can't expect—I was a child!"

"I didn't expect it! Just like you couldn't expect me to live at the hospital." Pete was shaking now. "You know why you're so angry? Why you need to hate me? Because deep down, you know there were things you could have done as well."

"Fuck you."

There was a shallow splash, then another. Cameron's anger clearly winning out over his fear. Pete turned and tried to stride away, to get a bit closer to the safety of the bank. But his foot caught on a log resting on the bottom, and with barely a sound he slipped under.

For a moment, he was tempted to let the man drown.

Cameron watched Pete's hands dance above the thick green-brown of the river and thought of his mother, her thin wrists attached to so many machines. Saw his head bob briefly above the paint-shiny surface, and imagined her struggling for breath, fighting to hold on until one of them got there. But none of them had gotten there.

Cameron pushed his way through the water to where his stepfather had gone down.

He'd always hated the river, the way you couldn't see the bottom. The way it felt like drowning, even if you weren't. He felt wildly around in the dense water, grasping and failing. There wasn't so much as a bubble. Cameron took a deep breath and forced his head under. He worked his arms around. Nothing. Cameron pushed his eyes open; there was about a foot of grainy visibility. He couldn't even see his own hands searching in front of him.

He popped to the surface. Swore. Took another breath, and

pushed himself down. Ignored the slimy rub of fish against his feet. Rose again. Down again. On the fourth dive, he connected with something solid. Cameron maneuvered himself underneath Pete and willed them both to the top.

And now there were two of them, stuck out here in the middle of the river. Pete was breathing—coughing and spluttering, spitting up brackish fluid, but his lungs were definitely working.

Cameron felt for a bottom that wasn't there anymore. "Can you swim?" he asked, but Pete couldn't stop hacking long enough to speak. Cameron waited, then wrapped one arm round the top of his stepfather's chest, trying to avoid his busted ribs. "Lie back," he ordered. "I'll tow you in." He set off in a clumsy backstroke, using his free arm to pull them slowly toward the shore.

"No rush," Pete wheezed. "Take your time."

Like you did. Cameron tried to drown the thought as he frogged his legs, letting the river help, carrying them downstream but closer to the bank. He'd been fifteen. The same age as Byron. He could have phoned his grandparents; both sets lived less than an hour away. He could have gone to the neighbors, begged a lift. But none of that had occurred to him until afterward. He'd been too petrified to do anything except sit at the little table in their stifling kitchen, trying to distract Lincoln and waiting for the man he still called Dad.

They were heading too far down the river; if they went much farther, they'd hit the river traffic. Speedboats. Jet Skis. Cameron kicked harder, hitting his stepfather's leg. Pete's head was sinking. Cameron used his spare hand to prop his chin up and concentrated on using just his legs. Tried to stay calm. Again.

They'd sat all afternoon at the yellow Formica table, playing endless crappy card games. The phone ringing and ringing. When the sun went down they'd sat in the dark, too unsure to even turn the lights on. The hospital must have called half a dozen times. *We need to speak to your father. He needs to call us back, as soon as he can. Do you have another number for him?* It's just some rubbish about insurance, Cameron kept telling his brother, while watching frantically for headlights. His heart thumped in relief with every car that turned down their road. But it was never Pete's. Eventually the phone stopped ringing, and Cameron had known.

There was a distant engine whine and Cameron panicked. He wasn't a strong enough swimmer to do battle with river traffic. He flailed and both their heads went under. Pete almost slipped out of his arms as Cameron tried to right them both. And then a sickening crunch, on the back of his head. A branch. But a branch from a tree, a tree growing on the bank. Cameron grabbed it gratefully.

"Don't worry," he said, as he carefully inched his way along, pulling them to safety. The water was shallow enough now, he could stand and drag his stepdad the last few yards. Cameron pulled Pete up onto the bank and collapsed beside him. They lay, chests heaving, deep and grateful breath the only sound.

"Thank God," Pete said finally.

Cameron didn't want to ask, but . . . "You okay?"

"Just. You?"

Cameron let the anger come, now they were both safe. "What the fuck were you playing at?"

Pete laughed, and more water came up. "Had to get you to listen to me somehow," he said, when the spluttering stopped.

"It's not okay," said Cameron, furious. "You could have bloody drowned us both."

"Neither is what you're doing with Aimee," said Pete. "Knock it on the head."

"I wasn't——" But he'd thought about it. Not interfering with the boy, obviously, but disappearing with him for a bit. Just to warn her off. Driving over into New South Wales, convincing Byron they were having an adventure. But then the kid had said, when they were smoking, "My mum's not well." And Cameron had been right back there, at the glossy yellow table in the darkening kitchen.

Cameron peeled off his wet shirt. Byron would be a year younger than Lincoln, roughly. Except Byron was alive and well, while Cameron had missed his brother growing up. Had never had the chance to take him camping. Cameron stared down at Pete's balding head, tried to hate his stepfather for depriving him of those final years, but the familiar flame of anger wasn't there.

"Where's the car?" asked Pete. He'd propped himself up, was looking uselessly in the wrong direction.

Cameron stood. The river had taken them a fair way from the campsite. "A couple of miles, I reckon." Pete was shivering. "There are sleeping bags in the tent. I'll go and grab them."

Pete crawled over onto his knees, then stumbled awkwardly to his feet. "I'll come with you. Don't trust you to come back for me."

"Your call." But his stepfather was still unsteady. Cameron looped an arm under his good shoulder. "Don't worry, we'll go slow."

Chapter 37

The morning of the inquiry broke hot and still. Aimee pulled dress after dress over her head, rejecting them all. The black was too funereal. The coral floral too cheerful. And she was still far too fat for the red and white; it made her look like a peppermint, the way the stripes widened around her middle. Not that anyone would care what she was wearing. By the time she'd spoken, Aimee's waistline would be the last thing anybody was thinking about, including Aimee.

WE SHOULDN'T EVEN *be having an inquiry*, Melinda thought, as she pulled on one of her "approachable" wrap dresses. If there was a chance she was going to be outed as a murderer, then she wanted to look like a nice one. Melinda had spent all weekend on the ATSB website, and there was no precedent for this. The bureau released most of its reports online, with maybe a small press briefing in high-profile cases. But the Hensley Council had gotten involved, insisted on a public flogging in the town hall. Evidence would be raked over, witnesses called. The community needed answers, apparently. That was the problem with living in a country town—everyone cared a bit too much.

Lou's first thought was to wear a pair of jeans. The inquiry was all Rex's idea—a chance for the mayor to show his caring side, while demonstrating that he had the power to boss a federal agency around. She wasn't dressing up for that fucker. But her hands went instead to the expensive crepe she'd bought for her birthday. She pulled it out; there was only a small grass stain, and most of the creases were at the back. It looked respectful, that was the main thing. Lou didn't have to go to the inquiry, now she was no longer staff. She was choosing to, out of respect, for Pete, for Lincoln—the father of her daughter's baby, after all—and for Tansy herself. Lou tugged at the front of her dress, tried to pull it higher over her boobs. And Melinda; she was going to remind Melinda that she needed to pay up.

"You feeling okay?" Nick glanced sideways at Aimee as he drove, the first vaguely caring words he'd spoken to her in three days. She allowed a small balloon of hope to rise in her chest, then remembered he'd be a lot less caring by the afternoon.

"I'm fine," she said, aware of the kids in the back. She hadn't wanted them to come, but Nick insisted. A learning experience, he'd argued last night. Good for them to see local government in action. This morning, he'd decided they needed to attend for emotional reasons. "They've been affected by this as well, Aimee." But really, he was worried about leaving them alone. The scene by the river with Cameron had rattled him too. He just wouldn't admit it.

Aimee looked back at Byron, glued to his iPad, at Shelley already texting. Would she be able to go through with it, in front of them? It might have to be part of their learning experience. Aimee pushed down visions of her children in therapy, suffering PTSD as a result of watching their mother torn apart by a baying mob. Only vocally, she hoped. Although emotions were running high; anything was possible.

THE TOWN HALL was almost full by the time Melinda arrived, with seats set out to the wall on both sides.

"We're expecting nearly five hundred," Sharna reported as she walked Melinda down the narrow central aisle, as though she was an usher, as though this was a Broadway show. "Television cameras too."

Melinda's dad was already there, seated near the back. "Somewhere in the middle please, Sharna," Melinda said, eyes firmly forward. People were looking at her funny, or was that her imagination? God, she was going to end up as paranoid as—

"Oh, but you'll want to be near your friends." The postmistress kept walking and Melinda had no choice but to follow. Aimee was three rows from the front, where a small desk and microphone had been set up. "I saved you girls a row."

"There's no need—"

But Sharna had her arm, was making people move as she

guided Melinda toward her angry cousin. "Here you go, Aimee. Look who I've got for you."

"I'M NOT SITTING next to her," Aimee said flatly. Because she wasn't.

"Well, you can swap with Nick then," said Sharna, who didn't seem overly surprised.

"No." Aimee and Melinda and Nick spoke as one.

"Well then, you two can move over, and Lou can sit in the middle." Sharna was already waving at Lou, walking in with a tired-looking Tansy. Aimee did a double take; was she wearing a *cocktail* dress?

"Sorry," said Melinda. "But I'm not sitting next to Lou."

The seven of them stood there, waiting for Sharna to sort their mess out. "Right," she said. "Who doesn't care who they sit next to?" The children raised their hands. As Sharna moved them around like human chess pieces, Aimee could see her hiding a smile. "Everyone happy? Good." Although no one was happy, a blind man could see that.

PETE SAT RIGID in his front-row seat, Cameron an angry sentry next to him. He could feel the anticipation of the crowd behind them, as though they were waiting for a football game to kick off. There'd been a few campaigns, Cameron had told him. Justice for Lincoln, a collection for some kind of memorial. All for a boy who hadn't lived among them since he was seven. But the people of Hensley prided themselves on being a tight community. It was one of the reasons Pete had moved; life had begun to feel claustrophobic. Reprimanding pupils in the morning, then having to answer to their parents in the supermarket or the pub or even the street later on. There was also a sense of entitlement in Hensley that he hadn't wanted his own kids growing up with. This idea that they were *luckier* than other people. Although look how Pete's own luck had changed, almost as soon as they'd left town.

"Should we make a break for it?" Cameron murmured in his ear. "I'll distract them, you start the car."

Pete gave a quiet laugh, despite himself. But Cameron was right. Hensley wanted blood.

Lou tugged at her dress as she took her assigned seat at the end of the row. Next to Tansy, who was chatting away happily to Melinda, who sat beside a scowling Byron, who was pointedly ignoring a grim-faced Nick—wow, that was quite a lump on his forehead—who had surprisingly elected not to sit next to Aimee, who just looked knackered. In between them, Shelley was texting. Lou's closest friends, and none of them had even said hello. She pulled out her phone, fiddled around with the banking app she'd downloaded. *Your money in real time.* But her money still wasn't there. She looked over at Melinda, who was pretending not to watch her. There were maybe two hours, Lou reckoned, before her threats lost their power. She moved her bag onto her lap and opened it so Melinda would know she meant business.

Lou HAD BROUGHT the report with her. Melinda swallowed down a little ball of sick and tried to listen to what Tansy was saying about the pram she wanted to buy. Now that she knew, her brother's involvement was obvious. Tansy had her mother's lips, Matthew's slouch. Melinda's attitude. *I've always liked her,* she thought, trying to ignore the stack of papers in Lou's lap. They'd had fun during Tansy's driving lessons; Melinda would have enjoyed being an aunty. Which was never going to happen now. Tansy paused for breath and Melinda quickly leaned across her.

"I've sent it," she said quietly.

"Then where is it?" asked Lou. She held up her phone, and Melinda winced. God, was that what they were living on? No wonder Lou was angry. But she kept her face impassive.

"It's coming," she said. "Hang on."

AIMEE TRIED TO ignore the faint electrical pulsing in her head as a council worker fumbled with the microphone. She'd started taking her pills again, had swallowed the first only a few hours after they'd rescued Byron. Which *was* a rescue, thank you very much. She could see Cameron two rows in front, feet sprawled wide with no regard for anyone else. Aimee glared at him, feeling the slight zap of her brain chemicals recalibrating. Life in her lovely house had become something to be endured. Byron still wasn't really speaking to her; Shelley seemed wary. While Nick had spent the weekend acting as though she didn't exist. Taking the kids off on errands, leaving her at home to talk to the cat. At least Oscar had stopped crapping everywhere—the only thing that was going right. That and the fact that the pills seemed to be working already. Aimee usually hated being medicated, worried the drugs would make her numb, but at the moment, numb sounded ideal.

MELINDA SAT UPRIGHT as the mayor approached the microphone. There were an awful lot of journalists, but then the story had attracted national attention. She could understand why: a dead child, a father in the frame, a small community devastated by tragedy. Melinda risked a glance over her shoulder to where the press had been corralled behind the kitchen serving hatch. The photographers started clicking the moment she turned around.

"Welcome, everyone," said the mayor. "Thank you for taking the time to join us this morning."

Melinda's phone went off, and people turned to stare.

"If you could please silence your mobile phones."

The ringtone grew louder as Melinda fumbled in her bag. Louder still as she finally felt the smooth edges, flicked the little button to make it stop. She slipped the phone into her lap, not taking her eyes off the podium. The whole room was watching her now.

"We're here today to witness a public inquiry into the New Year's Eve crash of a private plane into the ranges alongside the Hensley-Meadowcroft Road, an area known to most of us as Maddocks Clearing. A crash that claimed the life of sixteen-year-old Lincoln Kasprowicz."

The phone in Melinda's lap was vibrating, trying to attract her attention, but it couldn't have it. Melinda kept staring at Rex, nodding to show how seriously she was taking everything.

"I'd like to hand over to the ATSB officer who has been leading the investigation, Steven Birch."

The two men shook hands; there was an explosion of camera flashes from the kitchen hatch. Melinda felt her stomach lurch. *Here we go*, she thought, as she laced her fingers together to stop herself from checking her phone. *Here we go*.

Chapter 38

"On the thirty-first of December, at approximately nine thirty P.M., a Cessna 182, registration VH-QDK, took off from runway two at Meadowcroft Airport. There were two people in that plane: the pilot, Peter Kasprowicz, and his son Lincoln Kasprowicz."

Aimee leaned back in her seat as the details of the flight were read out. The weather conditions, the visibility. The language was familiar; this was essentially the report Damien had read to her in his musty hotel room. It sounded, as it had then, like a story, maybe a feature from a weekend newspaper supplement. The type of thing Aimee had hoped to end up writing. It sounded like something that had happened a long way from here.

Aimee tilted her head to one side as she listened. She felt oddly relaxed for such a tense environment. There wasn't a sound in the room as the investigator ran through the plans for the Hensley fireworks display, an event Aimee herself had helped organize. But there was nothing to be nervous about. It

wasn't only medication that had Aimee sitting calmly in her uncomfortable plastic chair, waiting patiently for her moment. It
was also the fact that her decision had been made. Another thing
the doctors should have told her: panic came with indecision.
The moment she'd chosen, that particular drumbeat had ceased.

LOU SAT RIGID as the first witnesses were called. Ordinary
mums and dads, blinking at their unexpected role in this chapter of town history. She gripped her phone as, one by one,
they spoke of seeing the plane above the river. The right turn it
had taken toward the hills. Silly to be nervous, given she knew
everything that was coming. Lou had read the report twice
more over the weekend, had sat on the back porch with a pack
of Benson & Hedges and virtually memorized the damn thing.

"Did the aircraft seem to be in any distress?" the ATSB officer asked Sam the newsagent.

"Dunno," said Sam. "Don't think so. It was all in one piece,
and there wasn't any smoke or anything. It was flying in a
straight line."

But there was nothing to stop any of these people from remembering a glowing lantern bobbing across the river, straight
into the Cessna's flight path. At any moment, someone could
say, "Of course, there was the little flame I saw just before the
plane went down." And then the report in Lou's lap would
be worthless. She checked her phone again.

BY THE EIGHTH witness, Aimee's head was beginning to jerk.
She forced herself to pay attention as an older man in faded

overalls—"the aero club's mechanic at the time, now retired, Martin Smith"—described the workings of the plane in intricate detail. She could hear the signs of people getting restless: the rattle of chewing gum containers, the faint tap of fingers on phones. Restless and hot. There was no air in the hall; Aimee's hair was damp on the back of her neck. She discreetly tried to check if she had sweat marks.

"Can I go outside?" Shelley whispered, as the mechanic began to explain the plane's fuel system.

Aimee nodded. "But stay close."

"Me too," muttered Byron, as he slid from his chair.

Aimee smiled faintly as she watched her children weave past knees and handbags toward the fire exit. It would be easier without them.

Nick caught the smile and leaned toward her. "How you doing?" he asked.

"Good," she replied, and meant it.

He reached over and took her hand, a move as unexpected as when he'd held it in the Meadowcroft Chinese on their first date. Sixteen years, two children, and one nervous breakdown ago. Aimee felt her eyes prickle.

"Hang in there," Nick whispered. "I'm proud of how you're holding up."

MELINDA FINALLY TURNED her phone over as an aviation expert from Sydney began to explain the intricacies of engine testing. Hardly anyone was listening now; the fire door kept banging as kids escaped to the relative cool of the street. But her phone was alive with messages, its little screen full. Clint, wanting to talk to her. Lou, wanting to know where her money was. Melinda raised an eyebrow: *her* money? *Oz transfers take one day,* Lou had messaged. *Not over weekend,* Melinda wrote back. Because she'd sent the money on a bloody Friday night, hadn't she. *Check again,* she told Lou. There was barely fifteen inches between them, yet she was negotiating as though Lou were a jewelry manufacturer in Taiwan, trying to hammer her on price. *Trust me.* She could hear Lou snort as she read that one. But what was Melinda supposed to do?

PETE LISTENED TO the details of his accident as though it had happened to someone else. What amazed him was the lack of hard facts, rather than the information they'd collected. No flight plan had been logged; they hadn't had to. The aircraft hadn't been fitted with a data or cockpit voice recorder— neither was legally required. No one had actually seen the plane go down. There was talk of video and a television was wheeled in, but it didn't sound like it showed much. Pete listened to the tinny recorded bangs of the fireworks and remembered Lincoln's delighted laughter. The last happy sounds his son had made.

But still, there didn't seem to be any actual *evidence*. Just a long list of possibilities being slowly ruled out. If Pete had been a different sort of man, he could have stuck to his story about engine failure, and it would have been hard to discount. Which would have spared both him and Aimee Verratti a lot of grief. Pete rubbed a tired hand across his face. He'd tried to convince her the scrap of paper didn't mean anything, but he wasn't sure she believed him.

Lou stared at the back of Pete's head as Frank, the community ambulance officer, began speaking about lacerations and compound fractures. You had to give the man credit; he didn't even flinch as his son's injuries were read out. Beside her, Tansy took a shaky breath. Lou bit her lip. She should be feeling more guilt, or at least more grief. Lincoln was the father of Tansy's child, of Lou's grandchild. It should be her obsessing about the accident, not Aimee. Maybe she just didn't put very much stock in fathers. What's to say Lincoln would have been any more responsible than Matthew? Or the rest of the Baker family. Lou checked her phone again. Still nothing.

"I'd like to call upon ATSB investigator Damien Marshall to discuss the findings at the crash site."

Lou's heart sped up. They were getting there—to the discovery of the notecard, the only card Lou held. If she was going to say something, it would have to be soon. Could she do it? Lou looked wildly around the hall, full of Hensley old guard. She accidentally made eye contact with Melinda's father; he smirked at her. Lou scowled back. Yes. She totally could.

"I'm going to the loo," whispered Tansy. "I don't feel great."

She slipped out of the row, removing the buffer between Lou and Melinda. Lou placed her report-filled handbag on the empty seat. Just to remind her.

MELINDA WATCHED THE wordless exchange between Lou and her father. "Nick," she murmured. "Tell me something. Have you guys ever liked my dad?"

"Not really," he whispered. As though he didn't even have to think.

"Why not?"

"Pulls you down. Always has." Nick spoke without moving his lips.

You only stay here because you're trying to impress your father. Melinda thought sadly of the life in Melbourne she'd given up, the compromises she'd made to base herself out here. Just to listen to him bang on about whatever Matthew was up to. When she was the one who'd moved back to Hensley, the one who was bringing revenue into the town. She was the one making something of herself in her local community.

"He's jealous of you, you know that."

"Hardly."

"Course he is." Nick shot an anxious look at Aimee, then kept quietly talking. "Here you are, this business big shot, raising millions, and he's still a small-town lawyer helping people contest their parking fines. He's okay with Matthew because he's not a threat."

"But—"

Aimee shuffled closer and leaned across her husband. Melinda braced herself. But, "totally true," Aimee hissed.

"Right." Melinda sat slightly stunned, as though the world had realigned itself. "Thanks."

It DIDN'T MEAN she forgave her. Aimee sat back in her seat as Damien walked up to the microphone. But Melinda had been trying to impress her dad for far too long. Aimee had never figured out whether he refused to acknowledge his daughter's amazingness because it threatened his own sense of self, or because he liked her fighting for his attention. It didn't matter. It was cruel.

And Melinda *was* amazing. Aimee snuck a peek at her former friend as Damien leaned over to state his name and address. Even in the dim light of the town hall she glowed, not with perspiration like everyone else, but with intelligence and energy and expensive serums. Melinda had started out with the same opportunities and education as Aimee, as Lou even, and through sheer force of will and imported skin care, she'd managed to transform herself. But now, Melinda had to go and be amazing somewhere else. Aimee nodded to herself as Damien recited his credentials. It was obvious: Melinda was only running around in stupid circles after her father, after Nick even, because this town wasn't enough for her. Nature abhors a vacuum, Melinda always said. Yet she'd created one.

Aimee fiddled with her modest engagement ring. Maybe the same was true for her. Maybe her brain would benefit from more to do, rather than less. *If we get through this, I'll go along with whatever he wants to do with this cellar door*, Aimee promised the universe. Because look at how lucky she was. Her husband really didn't like her right now, but he was holding her hand anyway, to make her feel secure. Or to make sure she didn't do anything stupid. Regardless, it was nice.

Did she really want to risk this? Aimee asked herself, as Damien began to give his overview of the crash site. To hold a torch to the already flammable remains of her marriage? Damien caught her eye and nodded, reassuringly. She remembered the way he'd initially resisted her kiss. Stood back as she tugged off her shirt. She'd had to be the aggressor, pulling him clumsily onto the groaning hotel bed. He was concerned about her still, she could tell, monitoring her reaction as he carefully described the state of the plane they'd found at Maddocks Clearing.

Nick squeezed her hand as they heard about the fire that had consumed the little plane's fuselage. Two good men, making sure she made it through this inquiry, neither of them knowing why it mattered so much. Aimee looked sadly at Melinda, with nothing to hold except her phone, and stretched out a hand. Melinda looked suspicious, but took it. Aimee jerked her head toward Lou.

"No way," muttered Melinda.

"Do it," said Aimee.

And Melinda did.

WHAT THE FUCK? Melinda sat with her arms outstretched, linked to Aimee on one side and bloody Lou on the other. Because that didn't look suspicious at all. Lou clearly didn't like the idea any more than Melinda did; her sweaty hand lay limply in Melinda's with minimal contact, just enough to keep Aimee happy. And she was happy, smiling wetly at them as the graying investigator described the angle the plane would have been flying at when it crashed. The trees that had slowed its descent, saving Pete's life. The site findings must be coming up soon. Those bloody notecards. For the hundredth time, Melinda cursed herself for not using a sheet of A4, like everyone else.

In her lap, her phone began vibrating. Claudia Lang. It rang silently as the investigator explained about nose altitude. Cut out and rang again as he spoke about compression forces. Finally a message flashed up: *Sending email.*

Melinda waited what seemed like years as the investigator told them sadly how fire and impact damage meant there was no way of knowing what position the plane's controls were in before the crash. Well, that was good, right? The less they knew the better. Melinda's email icon finally lit up; she lifted her hand from Lou's loose grip and opened the email as technical details droned around the hall.

"The position of the flap-actuating rods suggests they were extended at the point of impact."

Sorry to inform you that I can no longer support your application for adoption.

"Unable to take fuel samples due to the postimpact fire."

Did say that this application could not afford any controversy or scandal.

"Damage indicates the propeller was still rotating at the time the plane connected with the terrain."

In light of your current situation, I would not advise you to proceed. Your chances of a successful adoption are extremely slim.

"While fire had consumed most of the cabin fittings, we

were able to ascertain that both seat belts had been manually undone."

Trust you understand.

Melinda gaped at her phone. Scandal? They were only halfway through the inquiry. How would Claudia Lang even know? She leaned toward Lou, still staring at that bloody banking page. "Who did you tell?" she hissed.

"No one," whispered Lou. "Yet."

Two hands rested heavy on Melinda's shoulders.

"I really need to talk to you," Clint said quietly. "Come outside. Now."

AIMEE WATCHED MELINDA stumble from the hall. Putting business first, as usual. She turned back to the stage, to Damien, as he began to describe the debris they'd found around the plane. This was probably the moment, she thought, as pictures flashed up on the television next to him. One of Pete's shoes. A pair of blackened headphones. Aimee felt the weight of her husband's hand around hers. A set of navigational charts, curiously intact, likely blown from the windows on impact. And a small piece of pink-and-gold cardboard, around an inch and a half long, possibly from a birthday card. Lincoln had recently turned sixteen.

PETE LISTENED CLOSELY. No one would have given his son a pink birthday card. And Lincoln hadn't taken any of his presents up with them, except for the new Bose headphones he'd begged for. He'd been so proud of those headphones, exactly like Pete's own. They were a bit big, but he'd grow into them, Pete had thought. Years of use in those. He took a deep breath, but said nothing.

AIMEE ALSO SAID nothing. She listened to Damien describe the mystery piece of card and didn't act. Just pressed her lips together and let the moment pass. Because she wanted to keep what she had, fragile as it was. *You don't really want to do this, do you?* Damien had whispered as she'd fumbled with his belt, eyes closed. *Aimee. Stop it. You're kidding yourself.* She was worried he'd be angry but he just smiled sadly as he handed her back her shirt. *I don't know what's going on with you, Aimee, but this is not the solution.*

She met his eye and gave him a small nod. Damien had understood. Had made them both dreadful coffee, granules from an ancient sachet that hit Aimee like a train. They'd climbed back on top of that lumpy bed, him reading the report out loud as she lay staring at the dingy molding on the ceiling, realizing she might still lose everything anyway. Aimee laced her fingers through Nick's. But she'd keep it as long as she could.

MELINDA COULD HOLD her hand all she liked; it wasn't going to stop Lou from doing what was necessary. And now Melinda wasn't even bloody there. The moment of truth, their evidence, and she'd walked out, as though the inquiry didn't concern her. As though any repercussions would simply slide right off her, splattering Lou and Aimee instead. Worse, she was probably right. Lou gripped her phone. Melinda could afford to pay whatever fine they were served. Melinda could simply leave any scandal behind, move somewhere else. Melinda's father would bully or coerce or sue anyone who tried to hold her accountable. Melinda . . . Melinda had paid her the money. Lou blinked at her phone in disbelief. There it was, a column full of zeros. She refreshed the page, but the money didn't disappear. It was hers.

THIS WAS BAD. Very bad. Melinda stood blinking at the article in the harsh January sun while Clint raged at her.

"The investors are freaking out, Melinda. I don't know what to tell them. You took your eye off the ball."

"I took my—you turned my company into something it was never supposed to be! These are your reforms. This is all you."

"This woman's been calling you for the last week, trying to get comment. You could have shut this down, if you were paying attention."

"I pay you to pay attention!"

"No, you pay me to do the things you don't want to do, except when you decide you want to do them." Clint's face was twisted. "You signed off on all these changes, so don't try and pass the buck. You wanted profits and you wanted investor interest and you didn't care how I got it." He shoved the newspaper at her. "You were interested when it suited you. Like with me."

Melinda's mind spun. Had he sabotaged her company because she'd stopped *sleeping* with him? But no, she thought sadly, gazing down at the orderly columns of tiny words tearing her business apart. The rot had set in before that.

"Just go," she said. "I'll take care of this. Just leave."

"Look, we can fix this." Clint walked around in a circle on the concrete, hands on his head. "Give me a couple of hours. I'll make some calls, rustle up some testimonials. Women who dispute these claims. You've got hundreds of happy curators, it won't be hard. You'll have to make a statement, denying it all. Maybe backtrack a bit on some of the reforms—"

But Melinda was through with his fancy ideas. "Please go," she said again, hugging the newspaper to her chest. "I need to make this right myself."

SHE SHOULD THANK her. It seemed only right. Although what was the proper etiquette for blackmail? But she should acknowledge the money at least. Reassure Melinda that she'd bought her silence. Just like her father. Lou pushed that thought out of her mind as she got to her feet. Half their row had buggered off, there was no need for Lou to even sit here. She'd grab Tansy, take her home, get on with their lives. Put all this behind them. Lou paused as she picked up her bag. Tansy had been gone an awfully long time for somebody who just needed a quiet spew.

SOMEONE HAD OPENED the fire doors to try to let some air in. Pete could hear a couple yelling, the buzz of a helicopter as he leaned forward, trying to catch a breeze. Not much traffic noise though; everyone old enough to drive in Hensley was inside this hall. Arthur was in the hot seat now, talking about Pete. It was slightly surreal, hearing his own habits and routine described in the third person. And sad. Arthur spoke of a man who drove to work every morning at quarter past seven, returned home like clockwork at half past five. Rarely went out in the evenings except to pick up his son from sports practice. Pete tried to focus on what the policeman was saying about phone records, but it didn't sound like they had any concerns. His only call the day of the crash was to the dentist. His phone was switched off the night before at eight thirty. *Dull*, thought Pete. *Boring, predictable.* It was good for the inquiry, but really, what they were hearing was the description of a man who'd already given up.

"Tansy?" called Lou, as she pushed open the door of the ladies' room. But quietly—sound carried in this building. She could hear old Arthur droning on from the main hall. "Tansy?" she said again.

There was a rustle in the far stall. Lou stood listening for the flush, the smell of industrial disinfectant giving her flashbacks to all the times she'd popped Tansy on one of these toilets, urged her to go before forcing her to watch whatever public event her parents were patronizing. There was a click as the lock turned. Lou looked up smiling, but it was an older woman. One of her mother's friends. Lou nodded in recognition, then fled.

Melinda sat in the old tire swing and read the newspaper article again. It was well written, she'd give Stacey that.

LoveLocked's early days. Melinda's drive to make it more than just another direct-sales business. Lou's story—Melinda winced—without her name, but it would be obvious to anyone local who they were talking about. *I credit her with my company,* Melinda had apparently said. *Without her, there would be no LoveLocked.* The article described the company's caring ethos, its determination to put people before profit. Yes. She'd done that. Melinda swung listlessly. But then the story turned darker. Curators complaining their terms and conditions had changed, and not for the better. Fees for everything, unreasonable targets. Worse, they said, there was a growing emphasis on recruiting new members, taking a cut from their sales rather than selling yourself. It had become a kind of pyramid.

Lou stood on the town hall steps, scanning. The main street was deserted, and why wouldn't it be? All the action was taking place inside. She wandered down the road, not quite sure what she was looking for. Tansy emerging from the supermarket with a bar of chocolate? Tansy, bored, flicking through magazines in the newsagents? But her daughter was nowhere to be seen. Neither, she realized, as she turned back toward the hall, was her car.

The newspaper had gone into considerable detail about what constituted a pyramid scheme in Australia. Technically, LoveLocked was not—Melinda could hear the warnings of the paper's lawyers in Stacey's careful sentences—because there was still a genuine product changing hands. But it had veered well into the murky territory of multilevel marketing schemes, the paper declared. It quoted women whose families were avoiding them after they'd tried to sign up relatives for extra revenue. Women who'd taken out multiple credit cards to buy stock. Women who'd been promised other people would earn the money for them; all they needed to do was sit back and collect. Consumer groups were calling for tougher laws on selling practices. Potential investors were thinking twice about getting involved. The paper's business editor questioned LoveLocked's IPO valuation, whether the offering would go ahead at all. Melinda buried her face in her hands.

LOU RAN BACK toward the town hall. She could see Melinda slumped in a swing in the children's play area. A young bloke smoking out in front, fag held inward toward his palm like a guilty secret. And Byron, propped up against a side wall, his too-long legs sprawled across the concrete as he watched a video on his iPad.

"Byron," said Lou, trying not to sound frantic. "Have you seen Tansy? I can't find her anywhere."

EVERYTHING SHE'D BUILT, everything she'd worked for. Melinda crumpled the newspaper in her hands, trying to process what had just happened to her. The adoption at least had been a long shot, although now it had been ruled out, she realized that she wanted it very, very much. But her *company*—Melinda began to tear the paper into furious shreds, angry, not at Stacey or Clint, but at herself. She hadn't been watching. "Melinda Baker did not respond to repeated requests for comment." Worse, she'd been greedy. Wanting to set records, to force her father to take notice, to have a nicer apartment and car and wardrobe than everyone else. To be the best. And in doing so, she'd turned LoveLocked into the very thing she hated. A company that profited from women, rather than one that helped them. Just another multilevel marketing scheme, a logo you scrolled quickly past when you saw it on a friend's Facebook feed. Jewelry this week, aloe vera and coconut oil the next.

Melinda wiped uselessly at her face as voices floated out from the town hall. It almost didn't matter what they were saying in there. Everything she cared about was already going up in smoke.

IF THERE WAS anyone else, anyone at all, Lou would have asked them. But the parking lot was empty, even the smoking bloke had wandered back inside for the next installment. Lou walked slowly over to the playground.

"I really wish I didn't have to do this," she said to Melinda, deliberately not meeting her red eyes. "But can I borrow your car? I think—" Lou paused, trying to keep the panic out of her voice. "I think Tansy might be about to do something really stupid."

Chapter 39

"I'd like to call upon the pilot of the plane, Peter Kasprowicz."

You could feel the mood in the hall change. Mothers shushed children, rustling ceased. This was what they'd come to see: justice, or some small-town equivalent. Cameron jumped up to help his stepfather find the red vinyl seat at the front of the hall, even though he knew the layout, had insisted on arriving early to count the steps.

"I'm fine," said Pete, waving him away.

"I know," said Cameron. But he was pleased when Pete stumbled slightly, misjudging the distance between the chair and the table in front of it. A bit of sympathy never hurt.

THE SILENCE IN the car was beyond awkward—it was excruciating. Lou squirmed in the passenger seat. "Say something," she begged, as they waited to pull out onto the highway. "Anything. Please."

Melinda sighed. "I don't understand," she said. "Why would

Tansy want to get rid of the baby? I thought you said she wanted it. I thought *you* were the one who didn't want it."

"She does want it," said Lou, mentally willing the truck in front of them to pull the fuck out already. "And so do I. But there are complications." She and Tansy were still waiting for the test results. The end of the week, probably. But Lou was already prepared for the worst-case scenario. In her mind, the test was only a formality.

Melinda turned to her in disbelief. "How have you not told me all this?"

Lou snorted. "Well, we're not exactly mates."

"But this is huge. This is far more important than——" Melinda broke off as the truck finally lumbered onto the dual carriageway. "*Thank* you."

Lou understood what she meant. But it was hard to know what the rules for their friendship were anymore. Did a problem with the baby supersede all the bad blood of the last week? Did it cancel out attempted blackmail? Actual blackmail. Lou felt slightly sick.

"Can you just drive?" she pleaded, wishing that the money hadn't gone through after all. "As fast as you can."

THE ATSB OFFICER—STEVE, Pete remembered him from the hospital—went to great lengths to remind everyone that this inquiry was all about prevention. The ATSB's job wasn't to assign blame, but to make recommendations and prevent further accidents. Any criminal charges were the domain of the police.

But everyone in the hall, Pete included, knew those words were just window dressing. Whatever happened today would influence Arthur's decision on whether to press charges. And it would be remembered in Hensley for the rest of time. Pete tried to look unflustered. He reached for the glass of water Cameron had carried up for him and promptly knocked it over.

EVERY QUESTION MELINDA wanted to ask was full of judgment and best not said. Or it came back to the money. She wouldn't mention the money, not right now.

"How do you know this is what she's doing?" she said finally. "Or that we're even going to the right place?"

Lou gripped her handbag. "Because she's with Shelley," she said. "And Shelley looked up the clinic on Google Maps. Byron found it. That whole family is tracking each other, small blue dots all over the place. It's really weird."

Melinda congratulated herself on not pointing out that a bit more tracking of Tansy might have been a good thing. "Is that the clinic that was in the news? With the protesters?"

Lou gave a curt little nod.

"Don't worry," said Melinda. "It's not that far. And I think they make you have counseling first, check you're sure about your decision." She had no idea what she was talking about, but it sounded good. "Why do you think she changed her mind?" she asked. "If she'd made her peace with the possibility something might be wrong." The way Lou spoke, Tansy—a teenager—had cheerfully accepted the very thing Melinda couldn't. She remembered her interview with Claudia Lang, her insistence that she was too busy and important for a child with additional needs, and flushed.

"Because she thinks we don't have the money," Lou said flatly. "She's worried we can't afford the baby."

Melinda couldn't help herself. "Well, you can now."

Lou didn't answer, just stared out the window at the fields and vineyards flashing past them.

"Oh no," said Melinda. "Don't try and make out that she would have chosen differently if that had come through earlier. Don't you dare. You didn't even know what she was planning."

Two council workers rushed to the stage to rescue the microphone, another ran over to Pete and mopped him down, as though he were a baby. Stop it, Aimee wanted to shout. Just stop this whole circus. Pete sat completely still as the girl dabbed at his trousers with a paper towel. Humiliating, that's what it was, from start to finish. Pete shouldn't have to answer to the town, as though he was some nineteenth-century horse thief. This should be dealt with discreetly and respectfully, behind closed doors. Aimee shot Pete a supportive look, one she hoped was full of understanding. Then she remembered he couldn't see it.

"What do you think's happening back there?" Lou asked as they sped down the highway. Faster than any other car on the road, but not fast enough.

"Nothing, hopefully." Melinda still wasn't really looking at her, just clutching the steering wheel as though she could push the car forward.

"I think maybe Aimee read the report," admitted Lou. Because it didn't matter anymore. She might as well be honest. "I saw a page in her bag."

"I think she probably has. She said something the other night about trying to show Nick proof."

"Then why . . ." That made no sense. If Melinda knew Aimee had the report, there was no reason to pay her. None at all. Lou shook her head. "Do you think she'll say anything?"

Melinda overtook a semitrailer, causing both the Range Rover and Lou to shudder. "I'm *hoping* she's read how much alcohol Pete Kasprowicz had in his system. I'm *hoping* she realizes that it cancels out any stupid scrap of paper, which, let's be fair, could have floated in from anywhere." Melinda passed another truck. "I'm really, really hoping she doesn't get it into her head to stand up and say something."

"We're not there to stop her, though," said Lou.

"No," said Melinda grimly. "We're not."

THE QUESTIONS STARTED innocuously enough. Pete ran through the timings, the checks they'd done before taking off. Answers he'd given so many times he knew them by heart. There was a sense of anticipation in the room; Hensley was waiting for the good stuff. It didn't have to wait long.

"There were traces of alcohol in your blood," said Steve. "Had you been drinking?"

Pete resisted reaching for his refilled water glass. "I had two beers that afternoon." Which didn't explain a positive reading at ten o'clock at night, he knew. "Late afternoon." He tried desperately to calculate. "And then another, just before dinner."

"What time was that?"

"Around six o'clock. We ate early."

"And what time did you fly?"

"We went up at nine thirty. The fireworks were scheduled for ten."

"You know the regulations about flying under the influence? About drinking at all before a flight."

Eight hours bottle to throttle. "I do, yes. But I wasn't drunk."

"But you *had* consumed alcohol. Even though you knew you were flying."

"Yes."

"And not just flying yourself, but also a passenger. Your son."

Pete bowed his head. "Yes."

SHE HAD TO say something. She couldn't keep sitting here, feeling like this. "I'm sorry," Lou said, twisting around in the passenger seat.

"Really," said Melinda, that wasp-swallowing expression still on her face. "For what, exactly?"

She was going to make her say it. "For threatening you. For taking your money." Lou forced herself to keep looking at Melinda instead of safely out the window. "It was the shittiest thing I've ever done, and I've done some really shitty things."

Melinda just kept driving.

"You can have it back. I'll transfer it, tell the bank there was a mistake." Lou wanted to suggest pretending the whole thing had never happened, but that was hardly her call.

"You *blackmailed* me." Melinda didn't look at her, just stared at the road ahead of them. "It's the worst behavior I've ever heard of."

Well, I don't know about that, thought Lou, thinking of Matthew and his responsibility-free life on the Gold Coast, but this probably wasn't the time. "Yes," she said. "It is."

"It's beyond bad, Lou. It's really, really low. I don't even know what to say." Melinda leaned on her horn. "MOVE IT," she yelled at a little hatchback puttering along in the fast lane. "I'm not driving you because it's all okay. I'm driving you because Tansy's my niece, and this baby is my second-great-cousin or something, and I'm not a total bitch."

Lou's head whirred. "How do you know?" She twisted around again. "Have you always known?"

"Aimee told me. For Christ's sake, Lou, why didn't you say something? What's been the point of the past thirty years? Do you not trust me at all?"

Lou TRIED TO explain about the contract, without dropping Melinda's dad in it. Because Melinda still hero-worshipped her father, and Lou wasn't really in a position to be slagging anyone else off.

"I'm not trying to make excuses," she said pathetically. "It doesn't—"

But Melinda cut her off, shoving an arm across her stomach as she braked violently. "Bugger, that was the turnoff, wasn't it," she demanded. "It was. Damn." She started reversing, to an ear-splitting chorus of horns. "Next time, Lou, bring Byron and his bloody tracking app. This is ridiculous."

AIMEE KNEW HE'D had a drink, but not that much. Listening now, it sounded irresponsible. But Pete still didn't deserve the buzz of shocked whispers. *We've all made mistakes*, she wanted to hiss at the murmuring crowd. *Can everyone here honestly say they've never driven back from the pub after a few too many? Dropped the kids off at school after a heavy night, knowing you could still be over the limit?*

"He's screwed," Nick whispered sadly in her ear.

Maybe, thought Aimee. Or maybe not. A couple of beers wasn't exactly a bender. And drunk or sober, there was little you could do if a flaming lantern flew into your plane.

LOU DIDN'T EVEN wait for Melinda to turn the engine off before she shot out the door. There was no sign of any protesters, which was probably safer for everyone. The last thing she needed was to be arrested for punching someone. She wasn't sure Melinda would bail her out.

Please don't let her be too late. Lou raced toward the stucco villa. The door was locked. She pressed on the buzzer. Inside, she could hear footsteps, too slow and too far away. "Come on," chanted Lou. "Come on." She would be caring. Caring and understanding and love Tansy regardless, but for fuck's sake, could someone just open the door?

"Shhhh." Melinda put a hand on her shoulder. "They're coming. Keep calm."

"Do you often drink before you fly?"

"No."

"Have you ever flown under the influence before?"

"I wasn't—"

"Have you flown under the influence with a passenger before? With your son?"

"No!"

"Was Lincoln worried? About the fact you'd been drinking? Did he mention it?"

Pete shook his head.

"So it was normal then."

"No! God! It was a one-off!"

There was a pause. "How often do you drink and fly as a one-off, Mr. Kasprowicz?"

The nurse didn't want to let them in. Not without an appointment. Melinda could see the decision process in her face, a judgment call she no doubt had to make several times a day. Were they troublemakers, protesters? Or women who needed help? Melinda wildly considered claiming she was pregnant, that she needed to see a doctor, but Lou was already explaining.

"I'm sorry," the nurse said gently, and sounded it. "But I can't let you in to see a patient. No, I can't tell you if she's here either. You're going to have to wait."

Lou stuck her foot in the clinic door. "Tansy," she called. "Tansy, are you in there?"

"I'm going to have to ask you to leave." The nurse was losing her sympathy, and her patience.

"Tansy!"

"If you don't remove your foot, I'll have to call the police."

Lou didn't care. "Please," she begged. "I just need to speak to her."

"Umm, Lou." Melinda tugged on her arm. "You might want to look behind you."

And there, walking up the road with a can of Coke, was her daughter.

CAMERON HADN'T COMPLETELY forgiven his stepfather, but that didn't stop him wanting to punch the man who was interrogating him.

"Let's look at your medical history," Steve Whatshisface said, finally moving on from Pete's alcohol intake. "You received a diagnosis of depression a little over three years ago, am I right?"

Cameron sat forward, shocked, as Pete nodded.

Steve seemed to soften slightly. "Can you tell us what was going on?"

It was a story Cameron had never heard before. One of desperate grief and insomnia and a lack of interest in anything, including his children.

"It started when Julia passed away," said Pete, speaking quietly. "The world just went dark without her. Inside me too. There didn't seem to be any point to anything anymore."

Cameron flushed. He'd been there, and he hadn't seen any

of this. Hadn't taken any notice of Pete's emotional state at all. He felt his throat tighten as his stepfather spoke about trying to hold it together for his sons, plural. How determined he was that life would continue as normally as possible for them. Even though he was dying inside.

"But you didn't speak to your doctor until several years after your wife's death. Why did you wait so long to ask for help?"

Pete turned his still-bruised face toward Cameron. "Because I didn't think I deserved it."

"MUM! WHAT ARE you doing here?"

"Tansy." Lou forgot all about being caring and understanding. She grabbed her arm, pulled her daughter away from the clinic. "What the hell is going on?"

"Sorry," said Tansy. "It was the only time we knew we could get away." She bit her lip. "I didn't think you'd mind too much."

"Didn't think I'd mind?" Lou tried not to rip her daughter's arm off. "How can you even say that?" After everything she'd done.

"Lou," said Melinda. "I think we might have the wrong end of the stick here."

"What, did you think I was going to—" Tansy looked insulted. "Mum!"

"Tansy," said Melinda. "Where's Shelley?"

Tansy rolled her eyes. "Yeah, we're not here for me, Mum." As though it was crazy to even think that. "She's inside. She thought she'd caught something."

"Shelley?" Lou's eyebrows nearly hit her hairline.

Tansy sighed. "Yeah, it turns out I'm not the only one doing stuff at parties. She didn't actually have sex-sex, but still."

Aimee's perfect daughter. Lou forced herself not to smile.

"Grab her," Melinda said. "Grab her, and throw her in the car." She started running across the road. "We've got to get back."

This was unbearable. Aimee squirmed as Pete continued to answer questions about his wife's death, tears leaking from his blank eyes. No one with a shred of decency could let the man continue to go through this. She looked to her right, where Nick sat grimacing in sympathy. At the empty seat along from him that Melinda had left. And then realized the rest of the row was empty as well. Aimee sat very still. There was no one to stop her. She carefully took her hand back from her husband and placed it in her lap.

Melinda ignored the flickering of her speedometer as she raced down the highway, the wide-eyed silence of the girls in the back.

"I think you're setting a new land-speed record," said Lou, laughing nervously.

"As long as I don't set one for traffic fines," murmured Melinda. "Keep an eye out for cops, will you?" They didn't have time for a "yes sir, no sir" conversation.

"Why are we rushing?" asked Shelley. "Are you worried about Mum?"

Melinda met Lou's eyes in the rearview mirror.

"I'm worried about her," said Shelley. "So's Dad. That's why he made us all go today. Says we need to keep an eye on her."

Melinda put her foot down so hard the accelerator nearly touched the floor.

"But you'd stopped taking the antidepressants, hadn't you, by August of last year."

This was the bit Pete had been dreading. *Promise me,* he'd begged Arthur, when he'd confessed to screwing up the navigation, *that they'll keep this out of it.* He'd thought the policeman understood.

"I felt better," Pete said.

"Did you seek advice from your doctor before stopping the medication?"

"No."

"Did you inform him you were going to do so?"

"No."

"Did you declare your depression at your last flight review? When you did your medical?"

"No."

"Even though the medical *specifically asks* about any mental health problems?"

"I didn't think . . . It was under control. There wasn't an issue."

Steve paused. Pete could hear papers shuffling.

"Is it true you'd discussed having suicidal thoughts with your psychologist?"

MELINDA AND LOU tumbled through the main doors just in time to hear the last line. Melinda had wanted to use the side entrance, not draw attention to themselves. But there was nothing to worry about. No one in the hall even turned around to look.

PETE COULD HEAR his heart beating in the sudden hush.

"Mr. Kasprowicz, I'll ask you again. Did you discuss having suicidal thoughts with your psychologist?"

"Yes, but that was before I even went on——"

"Is it true that you'd considered taking a plane up and, I quote, 'not bringing it down again'?"

"That wasn't . . . Look, that was a very long time ago. I hadn't——"

"Mr. Kasprowicz, what *was* your state of mind when you took that Cessna up on New Year's Eve?"

THE WHOLE TOWN hall tilted forward, a collective forty-five-degree angle. Even Cameron found himself holding his breath, even though he knew it wasn't true. Didn't he?

At the front, sweating in the heat and accusation, his stepfather was silent.

"Mr. Kasprowicz, I need you to answer my question. Were you suicidal when you took the plane up on New Year's Eve? Were you intending to kill yourself?"

"No!" But the denial didn't come from Pete. Cameron whirled around in his chair. Two rows behind him an unkempt but determined-looking woman was clambering to her feet. Aimee Verratti.

"THAT'S NOT WHAT happened." There was a rushing in Aimee's ears, a kind of roller-coaster feeling, as the room seemed to tunnel around her. But she had to do this. Pete was being crucified for exactly the same thing she was. These people thought he was capable of killing his son because once upon a time he'd been depressed. Melinda and Lou and Nick thought she wasn't to be trusted because once upon a time her head had told her stories. No wonder people didn't bloody seek help.

"Excuse me." The ATSB officer was on his feet as well. "I'm going to have to ask you to sit back down."

"Aimee?" Damien, from the side of the hall, confused.

"Aimee!" Nick, next to her, tugging on her arm.

"I'm sorry," said Aimee. "But you have to listen to me. Pete didn't try to kill himself, or his son. He didn't cause the accident."

LOU WAS HALFWAY to the chairs before Melinda grabbed her arm.

"But—"

"No," Melinda said quietly. "Let her."

"Mum?" Shelley whispered, behind them. The girls. Oh God, they'd forgotten about the girls. Lou wrapped her arm around Aimee's daughter, pulled her close. Melinda reached for her niece. And then she grabbed Lou's hand as well and held it, tight.

THANK GOD THE children weren't there. Aimee watched the room explode around her, the press almost climbing out of their serving hatch as they scrambled over each other to take her picture.

"He didn't cause the accident," she repeated. "I did. I let off lanterns, illegal lanterns, and they caused Pete to miscalculate."

Next to her, Nick sat with his eyes closed. But Aimee had to keep going now. "You don't need to look at Pete's medical history," she said. "You need to look at the debris that was found at the site."

"She's wrong." There was a scrape and a thud as Pete stumbled to his feet, knocking his chair over. "She doesn't know what happened."

"I do," Aimee said, louder, so she could be heard over the confused crowd. "And it wasn't his fault."

"It was," insisted Pete. He took a step forward, into the table.

"Aimee!" Nick was standing now. "Aimee, whatever this is, just stop."

"But he can't take the blame for this."

"I have to," shouted Pete.

"Just let me tell them," she shouted back.

"There's nothing for you to tell," Pete yelled, above the hubbub. "I'm the only one at fault, because I let Lincoln fly the plane. I wasn't the pilot. Lincoln was."

THE HALL FELL silent. Pete stayed standing, leaning on the table for support. "Lincoln was flying the plane," he repeated.

Words he'd never intended to say. But he couldn't let Aimee sacrifice herself either.

"It was his birthday present. From me. A night flight. He'd never done one." Lincoln had spent weeks putting a flight plan together, emailing Pete coordinates of the best viewing spots for the fireworks. "He was so excited."

"Peter." Steve's voice was gentle. "Your son didn't have a license, did he?"

No. "He'd been taking lessons, had a good grasp of things. And I was licensed. So I thought it would be all right, you see?" He gripped the edge of the table. "We'd gone up together before, I'd let him take control. Everyone does. It's not that big a deal." Convincing himself, or convincing his jury? "Night's a bit more risky, but I thought I could take over if I needed to."

Except the usual dual-control plane hadn't been available. Just the older Cessna, with the copilot control removed for skydivers. And Pete hadn't had the heart to call their adventure off.

"Can you tell us what happened?"

Pete shook his head. "I'm not exactly sure," he admitted. "One moment we were fine, the next Lincoln had pulled us into a dive." He looked out to where Aimee's voice had come from. "He panicked, Aimee, but it had nothing to do with your lanterns. We'd already seen them float over the river, watched them take off from your house. We were well aware." Pete bowed his head. "He lost his bearings and panicked," he repeated. "Simple as that. I leaned over, tried to take control, but it was too late. All I could do was shield him with my body and hope for the best."

Pete wiped his nose on the back of his hand. "I didn't want you to think badly of him. Because it wasn't his fault. He should never have been flying, but I was the one who let him. Because I wanted to make him happy. The only person at fault is me."

Chapter 40

Pandemonium. That was the only word for it. People elbowed their way across the town hall as though trying to find a life-boat on the Titanic, blocking the main doors, the emergency exits, gossiping and grabbing and gesticulating as the press swarmed around them like flies. The ATSB officer had called for order, as though they were in an American courtroom drama, but the noise only rose, so Rex had declared the inquiry adjourned and ordered everyone to go home.

Lou and Melinda stood at the back, wide-eyed.

"Does this mean we're in the clear?" whispered Lou, truly confused.

"Well, no one seems to be coming after us with pitchforks," murmured Melinda. "Yet."

"Don't joke," said Lou. But it seemed Melinda was right. She could see Aimee having a subdued conversation with old Arthur, a confused Nick hovering behind. But even from the other end of the hall, she could tell that Arthur's eyes were on Pete, not Aimee, and certainly not looking for them.

"Why didn't you want to stop her?" Lou said quietly, mindful of the girls behind them. "I thought that was the whole point."

Melinda shrugged. "It would have come out anyway," she said. "I don't think me trying to control things is working very well."

"Can you please CLEAR the HALL." The microphone squawked, sending a clutch of Hensleyites fluttering for the doors, their words and feet tripping over one another.

"So what do we do?" asked Lou. "Just go home and get on with our lives?"

But Melinda was miles away. "You go," she said. "There's something I have to do first."

MELINDA STRODE TO the front of the hall where the cameras were thickest. "Excuse me," she said in her boardroom voice, guaranteed to cut through hysteria and small-town furor. "I have an announcement to make."

The press followed her as she walked briskly outside toward the playground, and the nosier residents of Hensley followed them. When she reached a nice oak she turned and stopped. The sun was dappled on her face as Melinda began to speak. The photos would be flattering, if nothing else.

ARTHUR WAS DISAPPOINTINGLY uninterested in Aimee's lanterns. "I don't think they add very much to the situation, Mrs. Verratti," he said. "Come in tomorrow morning if you want, make a statement. But I think it's fairly clear what happened up there."

Nick, though, was suddenly very interested. "How could you not tell me?" he demanded, quietly angry. "That you were going to do something like that?" They stood in the middle of the emptying hall, volunteers stacking plastic chairs around them. Aimee moved to help but Nick stopped her. "Don't," he said. "You need to talk to me."

"I've been trying to talk to you for weeks," said Aimee. "You wouldn't listen."

"Because I thought—"

"You thought I was unreliable. You thought I wasn't worth listening to." A few chair stackers turned to stare, but Aimee didn't lower her voice. "But I was right."

"Well, not really," said Nick, trying to pull her to one side. "You heard Arthur. It's unlikely you had anything to do with it."

He was still discounting her. Aimee turned away. "Forget it."

"Wait." Nick moved in front of her. "You're right," he said, voice low. "I didn't take you seriously. I should have."

Aimee nodded. "Yes."

"Do you want to talk about it now?"

Aimee wasn't sure what she wanted. She knew she should be relieved, grateful even, that her life was still intact, but instead she just felt flat. "I don't think I have very much to say." Nick had held her hand, but only because he was pleased she was keeping quiet. It wasn't the same as believing in her.

Nick sighed. "Don't get all righteous, Aims. You haven't exactly been the easiest to deal with lately. You've freaked all of us out, kids included."

"I—" But Lou was picking her way through the stacks of chairs toward them, her face unreadable.

"I think you should come outside," Lou said. "You and Shelley probably need to have a bit of a chat."

"I've DECIDED TO turn LoveLocked into an employee-owned company."

There was a confused murmur from the crowd, most of whom were news or local reporters, not business journalists.

"It means there won't be a public offering," explained Melinda. "I'm going to give ownership of the company to LoveLocked's curators instead. They'll hold all the shares, and the company's leadership will work for them. Including me. They'll be able to fire me, if they want." She smiled, wryly. "I'm hoping they won't, of course." Melinda lifted her chin for the cameras at the back. "There are still a few details to be ironed out. This is very much an idea in progress, and I still have to inform the board." She'd only come up with it as she'd watched Pete fall on his own sword. "But this is what's happening. No listing. No international investors. No big expansion, unless our new owners want us to. Just empowering the women who've actually built the company. From now on, we do what they want."

People began to wander away, not sure of the significance of what Melinda had just said.

"Did I lose you at empowering?" she joked. But it would be huge; thousands of women would become business owners, have a stake in the company's finances. "We'll be releasing a statement," she called after them.

One journalist moved forward into the gap, recording device outstretched. "Why are you doing this?" Stacey asked.

"Because I made a mistake," said Melinda. "I lost sight of what was important. And this is the only way I can think of to rectify that."

AIMEE'S HEART SANK as she listened to Shelley's sad little whispered tale. There was barely anything to it. Fumbling, kissing. New Year's, down by the river, a group of kids. Aimee didn't love the thought of her thirteen-year-old daughter messing around with anyone, but the real heartbreak was in how Shelley had tortured herself.

"Oh, sweetheart, you're not going to catch something just from that," she said, guiding her away from the stragglers on the hall steps.

Shelley tugged on a little tuft of hair at the nape of her neck. "But I might have," she said. "It happens. I googled it."

"Google isn't always the best place for advice," said Aimee. "You know that. Why didn't you talk to me?"

"Because I'm supposed to be the good child. The one you don't need to worry about."

Aimee bit her lip. "Shelley, you know I don't mean that."

"And I didn't want you to have another nervous breakdown, because of me."

Aimee swallowed. "How do you know about that?"

A Shelley look she recognized, as though Aimee was too

stupid for words. "You can unpick that filing cabinet with a bobby pin, Mum." Her daughter kicked at the concrete. "You were scaring me. I didn't want to make things worse."

Aimee stroked Shelley's thin little braid. Thank God they'd banished Nick to the car.

CLINT STOOD WITH his arms crossed at the edge of the playground, leaning against the chipped paintwork of a jungle gym. As the last of the small crowd slipped away, he began to clap.

"Very nice," he said. "Very savvy. You've totally turned the narrative around."

"That's not why I did it," said Melinda, as she started toward her car. She had a whole new ownership structure to figure out; she needed to get cracking.

"They'll be holding you up as the new face of corporate social responsibility. I can see the headlines now— Is this the future of Australian business?" Clint puffed slightly as he tried to keep up with her. "No flies on you, are there?"

Melinda turned in the middle of the road. "It's the right thing to do."

"But you didn't do anything wrong. We were just trying to grow the company."

"Oh, I did," she said. "Just not how you think."

IT WAS DECIDED. Pete would appear in the station first thing for questioning with both the police and the ATSB. There would be consequences. Pete felt strangely relieved.

"Nine o'clock," said Arthur, "and nothing but the truth this time. Or I'll charge you with obstruction, for starters."

"I'll bring him," Cameron promised.

They walked slowly out into the midday sun, Cameron leading his dad, even though he didn't need to. But it was nice to have someone to lean on.

"You know, it's easier to hate you," Cameron said as they negotiated the front steps.

"Of course," said Pete. "It's always easier to be angry. Keeps you looking outside yourself." He paused, leaning against a warm stone wall to rest. "You were right, though. I was irresponsible. If I'd stuck to the rules, he'd still be here."

"I heard you," said Cameron. "Apologizing to Lincoln. Saying it was all your fault. And then I found your phone, after you said it burned up."

"I lied," Pete said. And lied, and lied. "Lincoln and I had messaged each other about the flight. And I didn't want people to blame him, you see? For him to have to cope with that when he woke up. And then when he died, I couldn't bear the thought of everyone thinking badly of him."

"I do see," said Cameron. He guided Pete down onto the pavement. "Do you think you'll end up in prison?" he asked quietly.

Pete shrugged.

"I'll have a word, if you want. Explain how hard it's been since Mum died. How difficult I was."

Pete gave a half smile. "I think Arthur probably knows."

They walked slowly down the quiet street, deserted now,

by the sounds of it. Show's over, nothing to see here. Everyone gone home.

"Will you stay?" Pete asked, as they headed toward the car. The thought of being alone in that silent house, rattling around the place that had once housed his family . . . "There's loads of room."

"I can't," said Cameron. "I'll stay till this is over, but I don't belong here. It's too sad for me, you know?"

Pete nodded. Fair enough. His real punishment wouldn't come from Arthur, or the aviation body. Pete had already created his own purgatory, a life sentence of empty rooms and microwave-ready meals. Maybe he'd get a dog. If his sight didn't come back, he'd have to. One man and his service companion, for the next forty-something years.

"Hey, I think that woman's waiting for you," said Cameron, as they approached the car.

Pete's heart sank. He wasn't sure he had the energy for Aimee right now. But—

"Hello, Pete," said Lou. "Can I have a word?"

MELINDA'S FATHER WAS waiting by the side of the Range Rover. "Tried to call you," he said.

"I know." Melinda pipped the key ring, and the car's side mirrors unfolded in response.

"I suppose Louise has been talking to you. She always was trouble, that one. You remember when—"

"I don't want to hear it." Melinda placed her handbag on the backseat. "A contract with a seventeen-year-old is illegal; you know that, I presume."

Her dad fiddled with his own key ring, out of his depth for the first time she could remember. "I was just trying to look out for you all."

"You were trying to look out for Matthew," Melinda corrected. She climbed up into the driver's seat. "But don't worry. I took care of it."

Her father didn't move. "I caught your little press briefing."

Always with the subtle put-down. "I suppose you think that was sentimental."

"No, it was exactly right. But then you always get it right."

Melinda turned the ignition off. "You don't act as if I do." She'd wanted to avoid him, not to have this childish argument, but— "You never act as though anything I do is any good. You just talk about how great Matthew is." Melinda could hear her voice getting higher. Brilliant. Everything she'd been through today, and this was going to be the thing that tipped her over the edge?

Her father looked genuinely surprised. "But I've never had to worry about you the way I do Matthew. You're fine on your own."

"I don't want to be—" Melinda shut her mouth. There was a compliment in there somewhere, and she was going to take it.

THEY WALKED AROUND the back of the hall, the first time they'd been alone together in more than a decade. It wasn't that Lou had been avoiding him. More that she'd never known what to say. That chapter of her life was well and truly over; there'd seemed no point in reminiscing with one-night stands. But there were a few things she needed to say now. Lou led Pete over to a battered park bench, helped him prop his stick against the side.

"What did you want?" he asked softly.

Lou checked there was no one else within earshot. "Why'd you lie?"

"I didn't want people to blame Lincoln," he said. "I didn't want them to think he'd brought it on himself."

Lou stretched her legs out in the sun. "Why'd you lie about seeing the lanterns over the vineyard?"

"But I did see them."

Lou shook her head. "The lanterns didn't come from Aimee's, they came from Melinda's balcony. Totally different direction. And right into your flight path."

Pete froze.

"It's okay, there's no one here but us." She took advantage of the fact that Pete couldn't see her to scrutinize his face. "Were you trying to protect Aimee?"

He nodded. "And you."

"Why would you need to protect me?"

"Because I knew you must have been involved. You three haven't done anything independently since you were playing jump rope."

Lou allowed herself a smile. "But why were you looking to protect me?"

She knew what he was going to say before he said it. "Because I've always wondered if Tansy was mine."

Lou sighed. "Pete, she's not. You know that. I told you at the time." He'd been the only one who'd checked, who'd asked if she needed help. "I wish she was."

"I worried about you. Coping on your own. It didn't look as though your parents were much help."

Once upon a time that would have been a glorious invitation to bitch. "Not their job," she said simply. "Although you know, I think they might have cared more than I realized."

"Oh really?"

"They never came out and said anything. Never made peace. But thinking about it now, there were groceries on my doorstep, the odd hundred-dollar bill. A buggy in the hallway. That kind of thing."

"Good."

Lou leaned back against the cracked wood of the bench and examined Pete's face. Skin starting to leather beneath the purple and yellow bruising, ears a bit thick from contact sports. A Hensley face, cradle to grave. "So what happens with you now?"

Pete drew himself up. "Well, I have to find out how bad what I've done actually is. In the eyes of the law. Arthur's pretty pissed off at me, and the ATSB aren't too pleased either." He shifted, and the wood beneath them complained. "I won't be able to teach if I'm being investigated, but I don't think I'm up to it anyway. It's a shame, I'll miss the kids. But it's only fair."

It wasn't her place to say anything. But she could set the

stage. "Would you like to spend some time with us?" asked Lou. "Me and Tansy? Hang out? It'd be good for her to have a bloke around, and she's about to go into her junior year. She could use some homework help."

She could see him brighten. "If she didn't think that was weird."

"You know what, I think she'd really enjoy it."

SHE'D BEEN HIS one indiscretion. Pete listened to Lou's footsteps disappear down the concrete path, quick and light, as though she'd gotten something off her chest. His only infidelity.

Cameron had been right: not about Aimee, or Suzanne, but Pete had cheated. He'd justified it to himself at the time. Cameron was a difficult toddler; he and Julia were snapping and fighting. Pete hadn't been sure his new marriage was going to make it, or even if he wanted it to. And Lou had been there, cheerful and carefree, hanging out at the rugby club that had become his refuge. The drunken walk down by the river was a one-off, he'd told himself. As he did the second time, and the third. She'd sent him back to his wife in the end. Surprisingly sensible, even at that age.

"Did you tell her?"

Pete's head swiveled, trying to figure out where the voice was coming from.

"Behind you." Sharna sounded like she was standing in the kitchen doorway. "I saw you talking to Lou," she said. "Did you tell her about the money? The stroller you bought her?"

Pete shook his head. "Not yet."

Chapter 41

She could hardly not have gone. Melinda had stared at the invitation on her desk for the past week, deciding and redeciding as she signed off on the paperwork divesting the shares in her company. But in the end, there was no decent reason she could think of not to be there, other than fear. Melinda didn't do fear. She parked up under a tree and joined the stream of people picking their way carefully across Aimee's lawn. *I'll sit at the back,* she told herself. *And if it gets too uncomfortable, I can always leave.*

SHE COULD HARDLY not have invited them. Although Aimee had thought of a dozen reasons why, and a dozen reasons more not to have the party in the first place. But Nick had intervened.

"It's all about extending hospitality," he'd said. "Even when you don't feel like it. And it's not like we're going to be able to discriminate."

A vineyard in the Clare Valley was in the news for refusing to host a pagan wedding. Aimee's new psychologist gave

her exactly five minutes each session to discuss any irrational fears, no more, no less. Being set upon by angry Wiccans
hadn't even made this week's cut.

SHE COULD EASILY have stayed at home. Lou stood on the
edge of the crowd, feeling conspicuous in her best crepe
dress. Tansy had proper morning sickness now. "All-day sickness, Mum." No one would have judged Lou for choosing to
take care of her instead. But she'd had Sharna on the phone
that morning, checking she was coming, reminding her that
you didn't get to pick and choose when you wanted to be part
of a community, and hadn't they all benefited from a generous community spirit and open minds recently? Lou had gotten the message, and so here she was, heels sinking into the
earth.

"YES, I'M CHIEF commercial officer now," Melinda told a gag-
gle of curious curators, all bedecked in LoveLocked jewelry.
"No, not the CEO anymore. Yes, it was my choice. I'm going
to set up LoveLocked's operations in America."

She'd proposed it to the new board herself: organic growth,
boots on the ground. And a fresh start for Melinda. The old
hotel was on the market; someone was coming to pick up the
car on Tuesday.

"I'll be based in Iowa. I know, not exactly New York. But
we wanted to start with real women, rural communities, like
we did here. Stay true to our roots."

LOU WATCHED MELINDA speak to her admirers. Letting go of the reins obviously suited her—she looked softer almost, as though she had fewer edges. Lou had seen the outrageous asking price for her building, had read about the new LoveLocked structure, including the CCO package. Melinda might have given up control, but she hadn't sacrificed much in terms of salary. Still, that didn't stop Lou from going into the bank and requesting that one hundred thousand dollars be transferred to Melinda Baker's personal account. Or doing it again, one week later, when Melinda transferred the money back.

"TESTING, TESTING."

The microphone squawked, and Aimee recoiled. *Growth opportunity,* she reminded herself.

"Hello," she said, heart thumping. "Thank you all for being here on such a big day for Verratti Wines." Beside her, Nick gave a small nod: go on. "Today we're opening our cellar door, a passion project of my husband's that he's finally managed to talk me into." Soft laughter, from those in the know. "Eleven till three, six days a week, we'll be open for tastings, coffee, and light lunches. And don't be scared, but I will be the one in the kitchen."

Counter food, not a la carte. Only a dozen tables. For tour groups, they'd get in a chef. There'd been a number of compromises, on both sides.

"YOU'VE REALLY GOT to stop sending the money back," Melinda said quietly. "The bank thinks I'm involved in something dodgy."

Lou gave a small snort. "I can't keep it," she said. "You're not the one who owes me. It's not fair."

"I thought you'd say that." Melinda kept her voice low as Aimee began to talk them through the war exhibits that the cellar door would display. "Which is why the Baker family would like to set up a trust for Tansy and her baby. With you and me as the trustees. The *whole* Baker family will contribute, by the way. Which I think is entirely fair."

"WE'D ALSO LIKE to give you a sneak peek at our new labels." Aimee's voice shook slightly as she took the bottle Nick handed her. "This is the Verratti prosecco, which this year will be sold for charity, with a hundred percent of the profits going to the Lincoln Kasprowicz memorial fund for training new pilots."

All the profits? Nick had asked. What about just a percentage?

All, Aimee had insisted. Compromises, on both sides.

"DO YOU THINK we got off too lightly?" Lou asked quietly, as they admired the renovations. "I feel like we slipped through the net a bit. I feel like we didn't really pay."

Lou had spent the week following the inquiry waiting for a phone call or a knock on the door. But there was only silence, broken occasionally by Tansy bolting for the loo. A sign of a healthy pregnancy, according to their nice new doctor at St. Margaret's.

"Oh, everyone's paid," said Melinda. "One way or another."

PETE TIPPED HIS face toward the sun, waiting for everyone to finish looking round the new cellar door. There were more people here than there'd been at the funeral, but they'd kept that deliberately small in the end. Just close friends and family. "Been enough of a circus already," Arthur suggested, and Pete agreed. The ceremony had been cathartic but it was still hard, listening to people enjoying themselves, making plans. Moving on. Aimee's kids, excited about going back to school. Lou off to New Zealand with Tansy and her wrongful-dismissal payout to meet this long-lost brother.

"Finally getting out of Hensley," Lou had joked. But she'd be back in two weeks, and Pete was having them round to dinner before they left. Tansy wanted to make an announcement. Not another memorial, hopefully. Pete wasn't sure his emotions could take it.

MELINDA WATCHED AS Aimee popped the cork on a bottle of prosecco and let it fizz over the entrance to the cellar door. Everything had changed, and yet nothing had changed. Aimee and her family clustering together as the local newspaper took photos—a little warier than before, maybe not standing quite as close, but a unit nonetheless. Lou and Pete gossiping with Sharna, an unexpected threesome. And Melinda, alone as always. Well, not exactly alone.

"Drink?" a waiter asked, brandishing a glass.

Melinda wrapped a protective arm around her stomach. "Not for us," she said.

Acknowledgments

As Lou would say, this isn't the Oscars—but there are a number of people I need to thank.

Firstly, my agent, Vicki Marsdon, without whose encouragement, belief, and occasional hand-holding there wouldn't be a book at all.

Thank you to everyone at HarperCollins Australia and William Morrow in the U.S. who took a chance on *Not Bad People* when it was only a few chapters old. A special thank-you to Catherine Milne for all her insightful advice and support while I was writing, and to Carrie Feron for her enthusiasm. I'm also extremely grateful to the many talented people inside those publishing houses—copy editors, designers, publicists, sales—who've done so much to get this book on the shelf, especially Scott Forbes.

Outside the publishing world, so many people have been amazingly generous with their time and knowledge.

Thanks to Nick Humphrey for his legal expertise, and to my pilots Andrew MacKenzie, Nathan Muller, Russell Jenkins,

Robert Ball, Charlie McQuillen, and Lynne and Paul Napier. While I have at points willfully ignored their advice for the sake of plot and characterization, it's all hugely appreciated. It goes without saying that any mistakes are mine alone. More on that below!

Thank you to Dr. Stephanie Kerr for patiently answering a million medical questions; Dr. Jacques Kobersy; Nurse Emma Hedges; the Victorian Law Reform Commission; Josh Collard at the ASX; the helpful folk at CASA for giving me my own plane registration number; Morgan Lonergan for steering me right on superyachts; the talented Ebony Lamb of Eb & Sparrow for allowing me to borrow a line from one of her songs; and Dr. David Lee for advising me on what might be going on in Aimee's head. Again, all errors are mine.

As part of the research for this novel, I spent a thoroughly enjoyable month driving around country Victoria hanging out at wineries. (Top tip: always set a book somewhere with great food and drink.) Thank you to all the winemakers who so patiently answered my questions: Julian and Adam Castagna of Castagna Vineyard; Barry and Jan Morey at Sorrenberg; Ben Clifton at Amulet Wines; Daniel Balzer at Willem Kurt Wines; the team at Morrison's Winery (Moama); and the lovely Deborah at Munari Wines, who didn't know it but gave me Aimee's sheep. Also Praew Jitjuajun and the team at Ford who kindly provided the wheels for my road trip.

Thank you to my first readers and sounding boards—Fionna Cumming, Jennifer Boddicker, Bron Colgan, Sonia Kerrigan, and Craig Gamble—who must all be completely sick of this book by now. Special mention must go to the real Sharna, Sharna Benton, who spent a year answering ridiculous questions about speed-camera positions in country Victoria.

Despite all this fantastic expertise, there are things in this book that are not true to life. I've taken a number of liberties, especially with the roles and procedures of the police and the ATSB, in order to keep the timeline and number of characters tight. I've also made them quite unprofessional in places— sharing confidential reports! Interviewing traumatized people in the hospital!—which I hope casts no shade on their organizations. It's certainly not intended to. This is fiction, and a book about people behaving themselves—Very Good People—would be dull indeed.

On a personal note, I have to also thank my employers and cohosts for being so tolerant over the past year while my head has been in this book; the International Institute of Modern Letters for such a good grounding on the how-to-write-a-novel front; and my whole family—mum, dad, sister, brother-in-law, stepmother—for the pep talks and unflagging support. I can't overstate how much I appreciate my parents making books such a big part of my life. I can't order a pizza without opening the front door to check what number I live at, but I still remember my childhood library card number. On that note, a big shout-out to all the amazing library spaces, from Echuca to Bendigo, that this book was written in. Libraries rock.

About the author
....
2 Meet Brandy Scott

About the book
....
3 A Conversation with the Author

9 Reading Group Guide

Insights,
Interviews
& More . . .

Meet Brandy Scott

Vera Schoppe Photography

BRANDY SCOTT is a New Zealand–born, Dubai-based journalist. Over her twenty-year career she's worked as a magazine writer, newspaper editor, and radio presenter. Brandy has an MA in creative writing from Victoria University of Wellington's International Institute of Modern Letters. *Not Bad People* is her first novel. ⌒

A Conversation with the Author

Q: Where did the idea for Not Bad People come from?

A: *Not Bad People* was inspired by a real-life letting go ceremony I was invited to years ago. A group of women stood on the balcony of quite a posh house, letting off lanterns full of secret wishes. As the lanterns disappeared, I found myself wondering what would happen if they hit something. I wrote the first chapter almost exactly as it appears here shortly afterwards but put it to one side because I wasn't sure what happened next. When I took it out nearly a year later, I knew.

Q: How much of the book is fact, and how much is fiction?

A: *Not Bad People* is firmly fiction— but it has been colored in places by real life. I've had three-way friendships with interesting dynamics, and ex-boyfriends I've hung onto for far too long. Friends and I have spent many hours discussing the vagaries of dating in our late thirties and wondering why we were still single when we were, quite frankly, bloody awesome. Lou's house contains décor I have known.

Where I've most drawn on my own experiences is in writing about Aimee's ▶

3

mental health. I began having what I now know were bouts of anxiety and OCD in my twenties, when—like Aimee—I started working as a journalist. I worried about upsetting people with what I wrote and would strip anything contentious—and interesting—from my copy. (Fabulously, I once spent a year writing an opinion column that contained no actual opinions.) I was also petrified about getting anything wrong and would fact-check excessively, taking newspaper proofs home with me to reread even after the paper had gone to bed. I wrote restaurant reviews for a while, and my lovely boyfriend at the time (who earned more than I did) would pay for us to eat at the same restaurant over and over, so I could make sure my comments were accurate. Like Aimee, I've spent a long dark night paralyzed with the realization that I'd gotten the accents wrong over the words *crème brûlée*.

Q: You're using the past tense. Do you no longer suffer from anxiety?

A: I felt like I'd largely beaten my "head stuff" when I moved into radio. I host a talk show, and there's no time for continuous checking or ruminating in live radio—if you make a mistake, you've got no option but to keep going. The anxiety retreated as I thrived in this job, reappearing occasionally in times of major decision-making but nowhere near the issue it had been.

However, it came galloping back when it came time to edit this book. The writing of *Not Bad People* was tremendous fun; the story just flowed. Creating Aimee was actually incredibly cathartic. But the moment we shifted to reviewing the copy—checking!—something in my head shifted as well. I began worrying about things I'd written that might be offensive or insensitive or just plain wrong. Before long I was overthinking, overchecking, and had lost my sense of perspective.

Q: So what did you do?

A: I got help. Anxiety is a thief, and I could see that it was stealing my happiness, my health, my time—and also the time of those I was working with. I began working with a professional and also prioritized taking better care of myself: exercise, nutrition, meditation.

The "head stuff" hasn't completely disappeared, but I can recognize the patterns and triggers, which is hugely helpful. I'm not sure I'll ever be totally free of it—I can see now that the times in my life when I thought the anxiety had gone it was still ticking away in the background, subtly dictating my life choices, as Aimee's has hers. But I'm also making my peace with that. I've come to the conclusion that the part of my head that makes up stories like this novel might also be the part of my head that, well, makes up stories. ▶

A Conversation with the Author *(continued)*

Q: Why did you write about Australia when you're not an Australian?

A: I did worry—ha!—that Australians wouldn't take kindly to me setting a book in their country. But I've been an expatriate for most of my adult life— I've spent less than two years in my native New Zealand in the past two decades, so I'm a foreigner there too in many ways. And I borrow Australia with genuine affection. As a child, it was the holiday destination of choice; our bigger, more exciting neighbor with its proper cities and brand-name shops and better weather. These days, it's home to several of my godchildren and some of my closest friends, so I have plenty of reasons to visit and beds to stay in. Ultimately, though, it was a matter of plot—the illegality of the lanterns— that made the decision of where to base the book for me.

Setting the book in Australia was a wonderful excuse for a road trip, though. I took a month off work and drove around country Victoria, "helping" on vineyards and taking copious notes and photos. I had no real plan except to be in a town called Echuca for New Year's Eve, because they were having a fireworks display over the river, like the one I'd already planned for my book. It seemed like a fantastic coincidence, so I booked an Airbnb in the town's old post office (hello, Sharna!) and slowly made my way across the state toward it, driving from small town to small town, noting what time the sun set and what kind of birds were making all that racket, and finding inspiration at every stop.

There was one horrible coincidence I could never have foreseen: during my trip, a seaplane crashed into a river near Sydney on New Year's Eve. Talk about goose bumps. I've deliberately taken out the year this book was originally set in, because I didn't want anyone to think I was basing Pete's accident on the real crash, which tragically claimed a number of lives.

Q: Where did the town of Hensley come from?

A: Hensley is a mix of my favorite small towns from my road trip. When I think of Hensley's main street, I picture Beechworth, which is surely one of the most beautiful towns in Australia. The river in my mind is the section of the Murray that passes through Echuca, while the ranges outside Hensley are those that overlook Heathcote. Sharna's post office is a mix of a number of wonderful buildings on the Mornington Peninsula.

I've spent a lot of time in Australia over the years, but I didn't realize until this trip that nearly all of it had been in the bigger cities. This visit made me fall in love with country Victoria and its people. I come from a small rural town myself, and we're pretty friendly, but I was taken aback by how welcoming ▶

everyone was. Winemakers sat with me for hours, patiently talking through the stresses and joys of Aimee and Nick's livelihood. I saw a small plane in the sky in Echuca and sat at the local airfield waiting for it to land; the pilot has not only answered countless questions over the months, but also kindly taken me flying so I could experience the pleasure of floating above such an amazing landscape. More than once, I found myself in front of a real estate office window looking at houses for sale and thinking—why not? I'm currently plotting a new novel, the seeds of which were planted during this trip and which will be based in a similar setting— so who knows? ➶

Reading Group Guide

1. Lou, Melinda, and Aimee have formed some strong opinions of each other over the years. Aimee and Lou don't think Melinda would make a good mother; Lou and Melinda believe Aimee is partly responsible for her own instability; Aimee and Melinda feel Lou should try harder to "fix" her life. Are they right in their assessments of each other?

2. Which of the women did you have the most—and the least—empathy with?

3. Which of the three women holds the most responsibility for their friendship and the events in general going downhill? Are any of the characters actually bad people?

4. Aimee's friends and family don't take her concerns about the accident seriously because of her mental health history. How much of an issue is discrediting people—especially women—on this basis? Where have you seen it in public life or the media?

5. How do you think Melinda's relationship with her father has shaped her? ▶

6. Sharna tells Lou that it's her fault Hensley doesn't have much time for her, that she's brought their indifference on herself with her bad attitude. How much is Lou responsible not just for her relationship with the town, but also for the relationship she had with her parents? How much of Lou's situation is of her own making?

7. Was Melinda's present-day friendship with Nick wrong? Did they overstep the line?

8. Cameron spends most of the novel blaming Pete for the circumstances of his mother's death. Does he have a right to be so angry?

9. How responsible do you think the women were for the accident?

10. Lou suggests that the women didn't really pay for their mistake in letting off the illegal lanterns. Do you think they did? Who paid the most?

11. Did you see Pete's confession in the inquiry coming? Was he right to hide this information?

12. *Not Bad People* ends with a few hints about what Lou, Aimee, and Melinda are planning to do next. What do you think—or hope—happens to them? ❧

Discover great authors, exclusive offers, and more at hc.com.